Praise for th[...]
of Jennie Sh[...]

Eating Heaven

"*Eating Heaven* is about the meaning of family, about the great richness of small moments, about the tender struggle and complicated joy of the truest relationships of our lives. Jennie Shortridge's lovingly drawn characters will inherit your soul and win your heart."
    —Lisa Tucker, author of *The Song Reader* and *Shout Down the Moon*

"*Eating Heaven* is exactly the kind of book I most love to read—rich, funny, sad, sensual, and hopeful. I devoured every single word and wanted to lick the bowl at the end. Jennie Shortridge is a wise woman and her books are a tonic to the heart."
    —Barbara Samuel, author of *Lady Luck's Map of Vegas*

"Powerful and provocative, Jennie Shortridge's *Eating Heaven* is a novel you don't soon forget—and it'll give you a craving for pineapple upside-down cake too."   —Valerie Frankel, author of *The Girlfriend Curse*

"Shortridge serves up a tasty meal with a perfect balance of sweet, sour, salty, and savory. A delightful offering, *Eating Heaven* will leave you feeling deliciously full."
    —Jackie Moyer Fischer, author of *An Egg on Three Sticks*

"In *Eating Heaven*, Jennie Shortridge has created a delightful, charming heroine plagued with an appetite smaller only than her good and gracious heart. I loved the book!"
    —Ayelet Waldman, author of *Daughter's Keeper*

continued . . .

Written by today's freshest new talents and selected by New American Library, NAL Accent novels touch on subjects close to a woman's heart, from friendship to family to finding our place in the world. The Conversation Guides included in each book are intended to enrich the individual reading experience, as well as encourage us to explore these topics together—because books, and life, are meant for sharing.

Riding with the Queen

"Shortridge does a fine job of molding her heroine into a sympathetic, even admirable character. . . . Shortridge hits all the right notes."
—*The Miami Herald*

"An absorbing novel of a family with hard edges but an unbreakable bond. . . . Shortridge's finely crafted sentences often use a single telling detail to suggest the larger picture. It's a notable debut."
—*Rocky Mountain News*

"Imagine a blend of Margaret Atwood and Dolly Parton—Shortridge sneaks up on you. . . . Funny, sexy, smart . . . Jennie Shortridge has done something few writers accomplish. Her first novel is a delight, a tightly woven tale of a nearly on her last legs country singer who finds that while you can go home again, there may be reasons not to like it—that is, until life makes you look at yourself and your relationships more honestly."
—*Statesman Journal* (Oregon)

"A promising debut."   —*Seattle Post-Intelligencer*

Other NAL Accent Novels
by Jennie Shortridge

Riding with the Queen

eating
heaven

JENNIE SHORTRIDGE

FICTION FOR THE WAY WE LIVE

NAL Accent
Published by New American Library, a division of
Penguin Group (USA) Inc., 375 Hudson Street,
New York, New York 10014, USA
Penguin Group (Canada), 90 Eglinton Avenue East, Suite 700, Toronto,
Ontario M4P 2Y3, Canada (a division of Pearson Penguin Canada Inc.)
Penguin Books Ltd., 80 Strand, London WC2R 0RL, England
Penguin Ireland, 25 St. Stephen's Green, Dublin 2,
Ireland (a division of Penguin Books Ltd.)
Penguin Group (Australia), 250 Camberwell Road, Camberwell, Victoria 3124,
Australia (a division of Pearson Australia Group Pty. Ltd.)
Penguin Books India Pvt. Ltd., 11 Community Centre, Panchsheel Park,
New Delhi - 110 017, India
Penguin Group (NZ), cnr Airborne and Rosedale Roads, Albany,
Auckland 1310, New Zealand (a division of Pearson New Zealand Ltd.)
Penguin Books (South Africa) (Pty.) Ltd., 24 Sturdee Avenue,
Rosebank, Johannesburg 2196, South Africa

Penguin Books Ltd., Registered Offices:
80 Strand, London WC2R 0RL, England

First published by NAL Accent, an imprint of New American Library,
a division of Penguin Group (USA) Inc.

First Printing, September 2005
10 9 8 7 6 5

Copyright © Jennie Shortridge, 2005
Conversation Guide copyright © Penguin Group (USA) Inc., 2005
All rights reserved

 Fiction for the Way We Live
REGISTERED TRADEMARK — MARCA REGISTRADA

LIBRARY OF CONGRESS CATALOGING-IN-PUBLICATION DATA:

Shortridge, Jennie.
Eating heaven / by Jennie Shortridge.
p. cm.
ISBN 0-451-21643-1 (pbk.)
1. Women journalists—Fiction.   2. Overweight women—Fiction.   3. Food writers—Fiction.
4. Women cooks—Fiction.   5. Uncles—Fiction.   I. Title.
PS3619.H676E18 2005
813'.6—dc22   2005008533

Set in Goudy
Designed by Ginger Legato

Printed in the United States of America

For my dad
And in memory of those who left too soon

acknowledgments

This book is a labor of love made possible by many kind people:

My dear husband, Matt Gani, whose love, conviction, and support never waver. My agent, Jody Rein—her guidance and friendship always rings true. My editor, Leona Nevler, who provides wisdom and clarity, and her assistant, Susan McCarty, the answer woman.

Early readers whose enthusiasm invigorated me as I plowed on: Sherry Brown, Pam Vallone, Marianne Fry, Carol Frischmann, Carol Hickman, Jeri Pushkin, Ellen Johnson, Laurie Stoneham, Anne Cook, Lynne Kinghorn, Mary Bartek, Kristen Ashley, and Cindi Packard.

Portland's many authors, who have been nothing but wonderful and welcoming to me and generous in sharing their knowledge, especially April Henry.

Bette Sinclair, Kathryn Kurtz, and Lorinda Moholt, who introduced me to Portland's wonderful world of food and food writers. Food and wine expert Heidi Yorkshire, whose impeccable taste and eye for detail served this book well. Julie Pysklo, who provided her medical expertise for this book many years ago. Oncologist and editorial ace Nancy Boutin, and eating disorder experts Rick Ginsberg and Ruth Anderson, whose knowledge and insight were invaluable. Hospice nurse Carol Miller, who took care of my stepmother, Jeanne, and introduced my family to the loving kindness of hospice.

My family and friends, whose love sustains me. My readers, whose eagerness for more inspires me. And the many women who shared their stories with me—their honesty and generosity make them heroes in my eyes, and in the world.

To love is to receive a glimpse of heaven.

—Karen Sunde

Part 1

Tonight, Why Not Eat Light?
7 Super-Easy Suppers
That Won't Weigh You Down!

BY ELEANOR SAMUELS

You've picked up little Susie from soccer practice, and Tommy's on his way home from the swim meet. Your husband dashes in, clutching his briefcase and gym bag after his postwork spinning class. The last thing you want to do is load up your active family with unwanted fat and calories. How can you make a quick, easy dinner that's also healthy?

Yes, that is the burning question, isn't it? Not "How can we end world hunger?" or "What exactly is in fat-free cheese?" Not "What on earth is this woman doing cooking for everyone else while they're out doing something for themselves?"

More to the point, what am I doing writing crap like this?

chapter one

Cheese. Bread. Butter. Noodles. You can almost hear America screaming, "Fat! Carbs! Fat! Carbs!" and it's my job to calm the masses, to lead them down the "lite" path. Sure, writing for the kinds of magazines I do won't fetch me any journalism prizes, but if nothing else, it's easy. I start with a perfectly wonderful recipe and subtract and substitute everything good until it tastes like a rough imitation of its former self. Then I think of the most insipid, alliterative title I can, incorporating the tried-and-true "magic number"—that tantalizing digit that promises the impossible:

5 Fantastic Low-Fat French Fry Recipes!
6 Sexy New Desserts That Will Help You Stay in Shape!
7 Stupendous Suppers to Make Everyone Love You and Achieve World Peace!

If I could write anything I wanted to, I'd write about the splendor of butter and sugar hitting your taste buds at the same time, or smooth pasta and sharp Romano, or a fat strawberry dipped in bittersweet chocolate. That kind of nirvana can only be achieved through fat and calories, and, yes, carbohydrates. Eat, for God's sake, I'd tell the food phobes, the Atkins addicts, the warily weight watching. They've made consuming food far too complicated.

Here's the article I should write:

How to Eat: 6 Surefire Techniques to Get Food into Your Mouth

1. Place food on fork
2. Insert fork in mouth
3. Slide fork out, leaving food on tongue
4. Chew (food, not tongue)
5. Enjoy!
6. Repeat

I wish getting food into Uncle Benny's mouth was that easy.

"What'd you say this stuff was?" he asks, sitting at his kitchen table in the same chair he's always sat in, as long as I've known him. He stabs a piece of tofu with his fork, brings it close to his face to inspect it. "Mongoose and peanuts?"

"Very funny," I say.

He's fighting a flu bug, so he's wearing the green robe that's seen better days and tube socks, drugstore reading glasses parked on top of his not-quite-convincing comb-over. Thai tofu with Broccolini and peanuts is probably a stretch for a meat-and-potatoes kind of guy, but I had a batch left over from my last article: "Why Order In? 8 Asian Dishes with Half the Fat."

He sniffs the tofu, wrinkles his nose for effect.

I sigh, feigning irritation. It's a dance we do, Uncle Benny and I, an old soft-shoe. He almost always likes what I bring him.

"For God's sake. Just taste it, you old fart."

A hint of a smile sneaks across his grizzled mug and he winks, then slides the fork into his mouth. He closes his eyes and smiles for real, face crumpling in that papery way I've loved since I was six years old.

"See? You gotta trust me, Ben. Cooking is the one thing I know how to do."

Uncle Benny, on the other hand, knows how to do almost everything: He can unstick a door, quiet the squeaking of car brakes, and banish the burning rubber smell that wafts from my KitchenAid mixer when I use it too much. He means more to me than my own father did, but the truth is, he's not my uncle. I only wish he were.

"Why do we call him Uncle?" Christine asked once when we were eating our allotted two Oreos in the kitchen after school.

"Because we can't call him Dad," I said, and our older sister, Anne, looked up from her math book and widened her eyes, stifling a snicker. She'd started junior high and was rapidly developing a superior attitude along with breasts.

Mom turned from the sink, face stricken, and walked two steps toward me. She raised her delicate hand, dripping with dishwater, and slapped me. She'd never hit anyone, as far as I knew, but I wasn't surprised. At the age of eleven, I'd recently changed my formerly reverential opinion of her, and it was almost as though I wanted her to slap me.

"Mom!" Christine cried. "Why'd you do that?"

She didn't answer, just glared at me. I returned her stare until her eyes began to soften and fill and she turned back to the dishes. Anne slunk down behind her book. Christine looked at me, nine-year-old eyes welling. "Why'd she do that?" she asked again.

I shrugged. I wanted to touch the hot, wet swath of skin on my face, to cool it against my glass of milk. To feel where she'd laid her hand on me, if only in anger, but I wouldn't in front of her. I grabbed the Oreo package and headed for my room, knowing my mother would be horrified at my brazenness. When I'd finished eating every cookie, I tilted the package and slid the crumbs into my mouth, then licked the blobs of white filling from the cellophane. Feeling sick to my stomach, I reclined on the bed, holding the side of my face, annoyed that it no longer hurt.

After I've cleared the dinner dishes, Uncle Benny breaks out the cards for a game of gin rummy. I watch his hands as he deals the cards: yellowed nails, fingers bent, skin spotted and sallow. Hands aged beyond their years by twisting greasy bolts, scraping knuckles on engine blocks. He never complains about the arthritis, but it's painful to look at. I pick up my cards and say, "Nice hand, Ben. Maybe for once I'll beat you."

The kitchen's sunshine yellow was Aunt Yolanda's idea shortly after they married, an antidote to the gloom of Portland's long, rainy winters. The metal stool I sit on now was here before she was, paint spattered and worn, and like me, it's now outlasted her. Even though they had a long and, we thought, happy marriage, Yolanda left Benny last year with no explanation. A page of secrets ripped from a diary.

My sisters and I speculate: midlife crisis? She's still in her fifties, even though Benny's on the downhill slide to seventy. A younger man, maybe, closer to her own age? "A woman?" I say for effect, knowing it will get a rise out of stodgy Anne, a gasp from Christine. What we don't mention, of course, is Mom, but it seems impossible after all these years. I certainly can't ask Benny why Yolanda left. He mists over at the slightest reminder of her: her name on a piece of junk mail, a pink emery board discovered between couch cushions.

When Benny's beaten me soundly three games in a row, he pulls the cards into a pile and rests his hands upon them.

"You look tired," I say, and he nods. It's not quite eight o'clock.

At the door, he helps me with my raincoat. "Thanks for the dinner, honey. You should be feeding some young fella, not your old fart uncle."

I snort. Young fella. Benny will forever think of me as a kid. "Yeah, well, when he shows up, I'll let you know." I swing my purse onto my shoulder, patting my pockets for keys.

He squeezes my arm. "Believe I'll just watch TV until bed," he says, then shuffles toward the couch, settling slowly into the cushions, clutching his abdomen. His face is too serious, his movements too careful.

"What's wrong? I didn't poison you, did I?" Maybe tofu wasn't such a good idea.

He waves a hand at me as he rolls onto his side. "Nah, I'm fine, Ellie. Just can't seem to shake this goddamn flu. It up and hits me every so often."

I walk over and pull the throw from the back of the sofa, place it on his scrawny legs. I'm tempted to tuck him in, but I just stand and look at him, wondering now if I should leave.

"What're you gawking at? Go home, Miss Roosevelt. I'm fine."

"You're sure?"

He raises his eyebrows, an empty threat.

"Have you been going to the tanning parlor?" I tilt my head, look closely at his face. It's been bugging me all night, and I just figured it out. The color of his skin looks artificial and tawny. Who knows—maybe he's thinking about dating again.

He guffaws, inspecting his arms in the dim lamplight. "What the hell are you talking about?" he says, shaking his head, and he looks like himself again, just sleepy and getting older. He grabs the remote from the coffee table and clicks on the TV. "Now if you don't mind, *Matlock* comes on at eight."

He's fine, I decide. I resist the urge to lean down and kiss his cheek, something we reserve for only the best or worst of occasions.

"Okay, okay," I say, walking back toward the door, digging through the lists and receipts and wayward mints in the bottom of my purse until I hear the jangle of keys. "I'll be back Thursday, and I promise I'll bring you something with meat in it this time. But you have to promise me you'll call the doctor tomorrow, okay?"

There's no answer, and I turn to look at him. He's already asleep, jaw drooping, hand hanging idly off the couch, remote dropped to the floor. I hold my breath and count—*one, two, three, four, five*—until he begins to snore. Then I turn out the lights, click the lock into place, and step out into the cool March night.

chapter two

The first time I met Benny, I was six years old. I'd never have guessed, based on that night, that in time he'd become a member of our family.

Mom had invited her fellow students from the beginning photography class at the Lake Grove Community Center over for a Sunday night barbecue. Entertaining was her hobby, as was taking whatever class she considered avant-garde, a term that made my father roll his eyes. Once it had been artificial-flower arranging; another time it was Renaissance art appreciation. She'd majored in art history at Northwestern University, where she met Dad, who was finishing up a geology degree. She quit school to marry him, and I've often wondered if she regrets it.

Rock solid, she used to call him, and it was a good bet she didn't mean it as a compliment. Dad's interests consisted of work and disappearing into his basement den, an ugly utilitarian room filled with core samples and lumps of quartz, obsidian, pumice, hardened lava, and creepy-looking stalactites or stalagmites, whichever is which.

I don't know why Mom married him, especially since she knew moving to Portland—more specifically Lake Grove, the wrong side of the preferable Lake Oswego suburb—came with the package, but I know why he married her. In the black-and-white photographs of Mom as a young woman in Chicago, she looks like a movie star: perfect Cupid's bow lips, dark curls framing her heart-shaped face. In just the tilt of her head, the sure carriage of her slender shoulders, you see that she knows she is beautiful, she knows she is special. It's intoxicating.

That night may only have been a backyard barbecue, but she looked just as alluring, maybe more so with the confidence of maturity. She'd dressed in a new red-and-white floral sundress, red lipstick to match, delicate white sandals upon her pretty feet. She smelled like lilies and hairspray, as sexy as a smell can be, as far as I was concerned, and I tried to stand near her whenever she stood still for a moment.

At six o'clock sharp, three couples arrived, one with a sullen teenage boy who looked at my young sisters and me as if we were piles of dog doo on the sidewalk. Moments later, a man came by himself. Earlier in the day, Mom had informed us that he'd lost his wife and that we should make an effort to be nice to him.

"He's a kind man," she said, "but he's very sad."

Later, I overheard her talking on the phone in her bedroom with the familiar tone that meant it was her sister in Chicago. "Why shouldn't I invite him? We're just friends—you know that." She paused. "Besides, why shouldn't I be able to have this one thing—" Her voice broke then, and the bed, where she'd been sitting, creaked as she stood. "This one person who is so simpatico."

The sound of her voice drew nearer to the door, so I beat it down the hall to my room. I sat on my bed, running my hands over rows of yellow chenille, and shivered at this development—this would be no ordinary dinner guest. I pondered the word "simpatico." Finally, I decided it must mean they were both sad.

That night was a scorcher. The men's shirts stuck to their backs in dark patches, and the women fanned themselves with cocktail napkins. They milled about on the patio, forced cheerfulness in their voices, first beers in hand. The teenage boy had found the television set in the living room.

My sisters and I loitered around the swing set, wearing the dresses Mom had laid out, so we couldn't hang by our knees from the monkey bar. We'd never had to dress so formally for a barbecue before. We moped on the swings, kicking at the worn dirt underneath.

"Don't get those shoes dirty," Dad warned from the concrete patio, for not only were we wearing dresses, but we'd been made to wear our patent leathers. Mine bit at the heels, and I slid them off and on for relief. "Kids today don't realize how much shoes cost," Dad commented to the adults on the patio, with the tight, uncomfortable smile he wore whenever my mother entertained. His tall frame stood rigid over the other guests, all awkward right angles as he tried to place his hands casually on his chino-ed hips.

"Well, thank God for that," the lone man replied, tapping ashes off his cigarette. "They're just kids."

I perked up my ears, looking at my sisters to see if they'd heard. Anne had stiffened, a deer awaiting the next sign of danger, but Christine was too young to notice anything. She babbled as she lay on her stomach across the yellow seat of a swing. Anne and I looked at each other, then back at the patio. The man winked in our direction, then lifted his beer to Dad. "No disrespect intended."

The flush on Dad's face was visible across the yard. He said he'd see what was taking Mom so long in the kitchen and yanked the patio screen door from its tracks, then righted it and closed it carefully behind him.

The man stubbed out his cigarette and sauntered across the yard.

"Need a push?" he asked, squinting into the late-day sun.

Anne and I looked at each other, then nodded our complicity and settled onto hard plastic seats, clamping sweaty fingers onto steel chains. He pushed each of us in turn, up and down the row, Anne, me, Christine, over and over. The rush of wind was invigorating after the hot day, and my insides lurched into my throat as I crested high in the sky, feeling like I could see my whole neighborhood, maybe even the world. I wondered if I could see heaven if he just pushed hard enough, or the deep, dark indigo of space with its twinkling stars and multicolored planets. I wondered if the two were the same.

"You girls get off that swing set. You're wearing Mr. Sloan out," Dad finally called. "Besides, it's chow time." He'd now had a couple of beers; his voice was friendlier as he relaxed into his role as host, the murmur of adult conversation punctuated by his offerings of beer refills, lights for cigarettes, more chips and dip.

The man slowed and stopped our swings, then held his hand out to each of us to shake: "Benny Sloan. Good to meet you." He was smaller than our dad, thinning hair slicked back and eyes the color of a swimming pool.

We tittered and snickered, embarrassed by the attention, but we each shook hands with him, our hands swallowed in his work-worn grasp. His interest in us was captivating.

"Are you the sad man?" four-year-old Christine asked, staring up at him. I could tell by the look in his eyes that he saw it: She was going to be the beauty of the family.

"Christine!" Anne shoved her with an elbow. At eight, Anne was already lanky, forever trying to accommodate the length of arms and legs she'd inherited from Dad, along with his long, hatchet-nosed face.

The man just chuckled and said, "It's okay. I get that a lot."

As we headed toward the patio, Anne and Christine ran ahead to ensure they got the best spots at the kids' table, slowing when they saw the teenage boy already sitting there. Benny ruffled my hair and said, "You, kiddo, look like your mother." I'd heard it plenty of times but never believed it. I was nothing like my mother. I was too tall already, too bulky. She was dainty and ladylike; she was perfect.

As my sisters and I endured the pimples and greasy hair of our dinner guest, I sneaked glances at Benny with the other adults. He smiled a lot, I noticed, especially at my mother, and a gold-framed tooth flashed from the outer edge of his grin. He seemed to watch her every move as she cleared the table, replenished beers, swinging her summer dress through the sliding door and laughing in that melodic way of hers.

At the end of the evening, after the couples and the teenager had departed, my sisters and I sat, tired and worn out from the day, picking at our second servings of marionberry pie. Benny had long ago stood to leave with the others, but he and Mom kept smoking and talking in the deepening twilight, their words foreign to the rest of us: focal length, aperture, f-stop, shutter speed. The embers of their cigarettes danced through the air like fireflies.

Dad hovered near them, but Benny and Mom didn't notice until Dad finally stood right next to her and wrapped his arm around her waist. "Don't you think it's time these girls were in bed, Barbara?" he said. He was the only one who wouldn't call her Bebe.

"Oh, hey. Yeah." Benny backed up a step. "I didn't mean to monopolize your wife here." He placed his beer on the table and reached into his pants pocket, withdrawing keys. "You have one heck of a family, Richard," Benny said. "But who am I telling? You know that."

"You bet I do," Dad said, only his voice didn't sound so friendly. The air on the patio had grown still; even the crickets had quieted. My stomach knotted and I reached for Anne's plate, where half a piece of pie sat untouched. She narrowed her eyes at me but didn't object.

After a protracted silence, Benny shook Dad's hand. "Well, thanks for your hospitality, and for inviting a fifth wheel like me."

Mom intervened then, taking Benny by the arm and walking him into the house, saying, "Of course you're not a fifth wheel. We're delighted to have you." I followed, licking berry juice and crumbs from my fingers.

"I really enjoyed meeting you girls," Benny said at the front door, then turned and disappeared down the front walk into the darkness.

"He seems awfully nice for a sad man," I said.

My mom smiled and nodded, and we both stood gazing after him for a long while.

It was the closest I've ever felt to my mother.

The next morning, before I even brush my teeth, I call Benny.

"Myello?" he says. After all these years, I still smile at his odd pronunciation.

"You feeling any better today?"

"A little tired is all."

"You need to go to the doctor," I tell him. "Even if it is the flu. They have stuff now that can make you feel better."

"You know I hate those sons of bitches," he says. I can hear him slapping down playing cards on the kitchen table, reds on blacks, jacks on queens.

"Yeah, well, who doesn't?" I say.

Slap, I hear, *slap*, *slap*. Then silence.

"Uncle Benny."

"Yeah, yeah." He sighs, takes a slurp of something—day-old coffee would be my guess. "I know."

"So you'll call today?"

"Since when did you get so bossy?"

"Someone's got to take care of you."

He's quiet. After a too-long moment, he clears his throat. I'm relieved at the sound of cards snapping against the table.

"You winning?" I ask, trying to turn the moment back to light.

"Only when I cheat," he says.

Later in the morning, I hike eight blocks through the drizzle gray from my apartment to one of my favorite guilty pleasures: the expensive and exceptional Nob Hill Grocers on Northwest Twenty-third Avenue—Trendy-third, as it's called for the upscale shops and restaurants along its sidewalks. A true-blue Portlander, I don't carry an umbrella, but I do have hooded rain gear and an eco-friendly canvas shopping bag, along with my detailed list. This could well be the best part of my job.

I push through the door of the market into the fragrance of Stargazer lilies and roses, then coffee brewing and briny oysters fresh from the coast. I stroll the aisles as if in a museum, looking at every item, loading work recipe ingredients into the wire handbasket along with the odd little goodie: Cozy Shack flan, Scharffenberger chocolate. What I'd really like is ice cream: Tillamook Brown Cow or a Dove dark chocolate on chocolate ice cream bar—heaven on a stick—but it would melt long before I could get it home. I grab another Scharffenberger bar to compensate.

Inside the gourmet deli case, white plastic tags poke out of luscious mounds of cheese, each with handwritten names bordering on the orgasmic: Burrata with Truffles, Evora, Brescianella, Bleu d'Auvergne. I can almost feel the creamy sensation against my tongue, smell the musk of perfect aging, taste its tang, when an unmistakable laugh coming from the wine aisle jerks me to attention: a charming bell-tinkle sound almost certainly accompanied by a coy tilt of the head. I've alternately loved, blushed under, yearned for, and despised that laugh my entire life.

Immediate remorse at my choice of rumpled sweat clothes makes me clammy and frantic. One hand flies to the frizz of hair left untamed after my shower; the other swings the handbasket in front of my midsection.

Should I sneak through the condiment aisle to the cash register? Throw money at the beanie-clad young checker with lower lip fuzz, and make a run for it?

"For crying out loud, Eleanor," I mumble. "It's not like you're eleven years old." I'm thirty-eight, in fact, flying straight into the face of forty. I doubt most people this age quake at the thought of their mothers catching them with chocolate bars in their groceries.

She rounds the corner, spots me, and says, "Ellie, dear! What a nice surprise."

As petite as a teenager, she is stunning in a tailored raincoat, a pretty sylph of a scarf bringing out the hidden jade of her eyes. Even in the damp Portland mist, her dark curls are neat and coiffed, her ever present rose lipstick in place. It's no wonder every man on the planet loves her.

I pull the basket tighter against me, wishing I'd filled it with big, bulky things like boxes of bran cereal or five-pound bags of flour.

"Mom. Hi. I'm just, um, getting ingredients for an article." Implying, not for me. I pull a bag of carrots on top of the pudding. "What are you doing in town? I mean, you didn't call or, or anything."

"Oh, we just thought we'd be impulsive and drive in to celebrate the first day of spring—have some lunch, do a little window-shopping." She reaches to smooth her hair, eyeing mine, and continues. "Country life is wonderful, but the shopping is less than spectacular, as you can imagine."

A from-the-can cook my entire childhood, my mother has become a born-again gourmet, which, like reformed cigarette smokers, is the worst kind.

She turns to her new husband, who has now walked up to join her, and takes his arm. "John, what time's our reservation, dear?" Without waiting for his answer, she turns back to me. "We've found this wonderful little restaurant up the street called Chanterelle. You'd love it, Ellie. It's our new favorite."

"I think I told you about it, actually." And apparently, this isn't the first time they've driven an hour into Portland, into my neighborhood, without telling me.

"And the wine list! Well, you know, living in wine country now, we've gotten pickier. Haven't we, John?" She turns and shines her benediction upon him, and he smiles back in that grateful-puppy way most people do in her presence.

"Would you care to join us, Ellie?" John asks, his easy solicitude a testament to years in the real estate business. "I'm sure we could get a table for three."

Mom's eyes do that little sweep thing up and down the length of me, almost quickly enough that I shouldn't have noticed. My face simmers and I'm suddenly too warm. *Please let a fire alarm go off, a tornado blow through the door, anything.* I wish this basket were bigger, my body smaller, my hair smoother, my inclination more toward fashionable clothes than comfortable ones.

A fraction of a second too late, Mom says, "Of course, dear, where are my manners? We'd love to have you."

"No, that's okay," I say. "I can't, actually, I'm on deadline. I'm working on a piece about French food for *Cooking for*—"

"Oh, now, we couldn't possibly take you away from your work, honey."

The relief is palpable all around.

Even though I know I shouldn't, especially in front of the new husband, I ask, "Have you talked to Benny lately? He's been really sick."

"Well, you know that horrible flu is going around. Everyone seems to have it. I just keep knocking wood that we haven't gotten it yet." She reaches up to tug at the scarf at her throat, loosening it slightly.

"I don't think it's the flu," I say, trying not to sound testy. "Maybe you could call him and convince him to go to the doctor. You know how he is, but he might listen to you."

"Mm," she says, her noncommittal answer to everything, then changes the subject. "And how are you, dear? Everything okay?"

"I'm fine," I say through clenched teeth. "Everything's fine."

She looks at her watch, and John says they'd better hurry. We exchange empty pleasantries as if we're former neighbors, and then she's gone, a cool breeze leaving trash and my own silent screaming in its wake.

I turn back to the cheese case, try to refocus. I have to find a way to take most of the calories and all of the fat out of *Brie en croute* for a piece called "Lighten Up Your French Favorites." Cheese in pastry, for God's sake. I love my life as a freelance writer, the way lifestyles editors count on me for my food expertise and dependability, but I want to write for someone other than 110-pound soccer moms between carpools and dental appointments, women who feel guilty if they use half-and-half in their coffee. I want to be a real food writer and work for the good food magazines, the *Gourmets* and *Bon Appétits*, where anything less than five hundred calories is just an hors d'oeuvre.

"That had to have been your mother." The younger and nicer of the sisters who run the market is standing behind the case, wiping her hands on a white apron. "You look so much alike."

"No, we don't," I say.

She smiles. "I know, people have told me that my whole life, too. Pisses me off. What can I get you?"

"I don't suppose you have anything like low-fat Brie, do you?"

"No, but I do have a new triple-cream with toasted walnuts that's amazing. Want a sample?"

Does a pig want truffles? "Well, just a little," I say, disappointed at the sliver she shaves from the wheel to hand me.

Walking home through the drizzle and bustling lunchtime crowds, I pass bento stands and soup-and-salad bistros, suddenly and desperately in need of something to eat. Nothing sounds good, nothing sounds right until I'm almost upon Frozen Moo. I push through the doorway into waffle-cone sweetness, past the only other people in the place, a thin couple sharing a hot fudge sundae, and toward the young alterna-girl behind the counter. Half of her hair is platinum, the rest shocking pink, and she's dancing with abandon to loud 1970s funk music. Despite the weather and her own zaftig size, she wears the skimpiest of tank tops, like most eyebrow-pierced young women do these days. I wish my generation had that confidence. I feel funny showing even my thick upper arms in the full heat of summer.

"What's shaking?" she asks, when it seems obvious to anyone watching that she is. Her hips are gyrating in little circles now, her hands above her head; she looks like a flamenco dancer, shaking the ice cream scoop like a maraca. Somehow she manages to make her size look exotic and sexy, and I wonder how she got this way, this free and uninhibited.

"Hi," I say, settling my bulging shopping bag between my feet. "Can I have a dish of Mocha Fudge Chunk, please?"

"Single? Double?" Her lips are as plump and enticing as the rest of her, and I feel older and plainer by the second.

"Hmm. How about a double? I'm sharing it." I motion my head toward the door, like my hunky husband is waiting outside. Like she cares. The girl obviously eats plenty of ice cream herself.

She dance steps to the right, leans into the case, and begins to dig.

The bell on the door tinkles, and I turn to fake smile at the svelte and stylish woman who's just entered the shop. She fake smiles back and sweeps her eyes over me the same way my mother just did.

My ears go hot, my scalp, my chest. I turn back around but I can feel the woman behind me, her eyes struggling to take in the girth of me, the expanse of cotton jersey across my butt.

"You looked like you could use a triple," the girl behind the counter says, and I wish I could just disappear. She hands me what looks like a snowman built by Lilliputians; it's gargantuan even by my standards. "The extra scoop's on me."

I shove bills and coins across the counter, take the dish, and say, "Thanks! My husband will love you," jovially and loudly enough for the woman behind me to hear, then sprint for the exit.

In the vestibule, I stop to juggle my wallet back into my purse without dropping the groceries or the ice cream. On the bulletin board, amid peace rally and Yoga-robics flyers, a pretty business card with swirling watercolor hues catches my attention: SUZANNE LONG, MSW, FOOD THERAPIST. I'm scoffing at the title—what, she counsels bananas?—until I read the rest: SPECIALIZING IN CONTROL ISSUES, ESPECIALLY THE LACK THEREOF.

The heat returns to my face, and I pull open the glass door to escape into the cool, moist outdoors, then stop and look back. The shop girl is handing the stylish customer a child-size dish of something peach colored, and the thin young couple are engrossed in feeding each other spoonfuls of hot fudge. The music has changed; a husky-voiced young man sings about his girlfriend's wonderland of a body.

On the bulletin board, the business card glows in the silver afternoon light, and I read it over and over. A food therapist? I've never heard of such a thing. *Control.* I swallow, not looking at my hulking dish of ice cream. *The lack thereof.*

After making sure no one's watching, I put my bag down and step over to yank the card from its thumbtack, and slide it into my purse.

Outside, I'm still lightheaded, shaky. The cute little shops and rehabbed Victorians look different, more colorful and detailed than I've ever noticed, and the trees look taller, the light stranger. Trendy-third is bustling, bumper-to-bumper with luxury SUVs and eco-hybrids, hippie Volkswagen campers and kamikaze bicyclists. People sit beneath the awnings at Coffee People, linger in doorways, amble up and down the street with leashed dogs, strollered babies. Sun-starved Portlanders can smell spring a mile away, and even though it looks like any other misty winter day, they've all come out to herald its arrival. Usually, I'd join right in, but all I want is to disappear.

The top scoop of ice cream starts a precipitous slide, and I look for a place where I can eat in private. I follow a narrow sidewalk between two buildings and back out of sight from the street. The permanently shaded walk is wet and mossy; my right foot skids across a bright olive patch, sending the ice cream dish and grocery bag into the air. I flail wildly not to fall, and end up with a scoop of ice cream in my left hand.

"Oh, for God's sake," I say, looking behind me toward the street, then at the scatter of groceries on the ground, the other two scoops of ice cream splatted on concrete. For a moment I consider dropping the remaining scoop and going back into the shop for a napkin.

That's what a sane person would do.

Instead, I hide behind a Dumpster, lean against the cool concrete wall, and slide down so that I'm sitting on my haunches. Then I bring the sweet comfort of Mocha Fudge Chunk to my lips.

The next afternoon, I'm seated on a chintz-covered couch inside the elegant old mansion I've always admired at Twenty-fourth and Lovejoy. Suzanne Long, MSW, Food Therapist, asks me if I think I have an eating disorder.

"Eating isn't the problem," I tell the trim, pretty, perfectly kempt and perfectly nice woman in front of me. "Stopping is."

Meant to sound lighthearted, but yesterday's little episode scared me more than any of the others. I don't know what happens. There are just times when I lose complete control and all that matters is filling the black hole of my stomach. It's as if I'm sleepwalking, even though I'm wide awake, eating and eating whatever it is that feels like it could possibly sate me—Thai noodles, French toast, chocolate chip cookies—but it never helps. I just end up feeling disgusted and disgusting, sick to my stomach and sick of my nauseating secret. One thing is for sure: I hope never to eat Mocha Fudge Chunk ice cream again, especially not from my bare hands, licking between my fingers, crouched in a near-fetal position with the smell of Dumpster all around.

"Besides, there's no way I could be bulimic," I say, wondering how on earth someone this thin could understand. "I haven't thrown up since fifth grade."

"Not everybody purges," she says, leaning back into a chintz armchair and crossing one slender leg over the other.

Kids at grade school called me Ellie the Jolly Green Jelly. I was tall for my age. I still am. I've always been big-boned, bigger than my sisters and classmates, and just big enough that people see my bigness before they see me.

In fifth grade I switched to my full first name. I figured no fat jokes could rhyme with Eleanor. I was wrong. Jeffrey Hanover immediately began to sing, "Ellie, Ellie, Eleanor, can't get out the kitchen door."

"How did you react?" Suzanne asks.

"I don't know." I try to think back. "I probably ate." *Heh, heh*, I laugh. Another little joke, but Suzanne Long's not having any of it.

"And now?"

"Well, now I try not to think about it. Isn't that better than getting caught up in what everyone else wants me to be?"

"Who wants you to be something else?"

"Who doesn't?" Nobody likes a big girl, Mom always told me.

"And what do you want?" Suzanne asks, a reasonable question. She squints through her stylish rectangular glasses.

I start to speak, and stop. I open my mouth again and nothing happens. My face is growing warm, and I'm afraid I'm about to cry.

"Let's start with something else," she says, shifting in her seat. "Let's start with food. Tell me about your relationship with food."

How can I tell her anything she'd understand? Has she ever eaten a pan of brownies in one sitting? A half dozen salad-bar baked potatoes? A baker's dozen?

What is it about slippery-sweet ice cream, about half-melted chocolate chips or moist homemade birthday cake, juicy steak seared on the grill, creamy potato salad, watermelon freshly cut and dripping with juice? It's too easy to say that if I close my eyes while eating any of these things, I can almost feel the summer sun warming my skin, smell charcoal smoke and freshly cut grass, hear swings creaking across the yard and my sisters' singsong chatter, the adults' steady murmur of conversation, matches striking matchbooks, ring tabs escaping beer cans and the effervescent sigh that follows. I can almost feel people around me, my mother and Uncle Benny smoking cigarettes in green webbed lawn chairs, my father poking at the coals on the grill, the curve of Aunt Yolanda's waist, into which I am tucked, her warm arm embracing me, and the pleasant rhythm of her laughing.

It doesn't take a shrink to figure it out and yet here I am, asking her to without telling her any of these things. If I talk about them, then even these memories will desert me.

chapter three

On Thursday, it's as dark as twilight instead of the soupy dove gray it should be by ten a.m. Outside my apartment window, drizzle gives way to rain. Large drops fall randomly at first, then in waves, pelting the bushy azaleas and parked cars, bending the spring-green grass, the daffodils. Portland's springs are always wet, but this year it's frightening how much moisture we're getting. The earth is saturated, the rivers rising, and the sky perpetually low and heavy.

From my second-floor vantage point I can see Irina Ivanova across the street. She's balancing baby Tatiana on her hip while she struggles to right a broken umbrella before dashing to her rusty Impala at the end of the block. I've seen her at Fred Meyer, picking over day-old bread, rummaging through the free dog bones in the meat section for a good soup bone. She probably can't afford a luxury like a new umbrella, even if it is from Freddy's.

I tried once to take her a pot of clam chowder I'd made for an article, but the embarrassed indignation in her eyes coupled with the language barrier made it impossible to explain that I always have extra food, and I always give it away. Next door in my building, the Nguyens both work and have three kids, so I take them a casserole or dessert whenever I can. Old Mrs. Wittsler on the ground floor loves anything made with potatoes, so I make her potato-sausage soup or potatoes au gratin or plain old mashed potatoes, and pretend I'm working on yet another potato recipe article.

Turning back to my stainless steel Viking range, I stir wine-and-garlic-marinated sirloin cubes, feeling ostentatious and lucky. The stove is my only indulgence in this hopelessly outdated apartment, but I never have to worry about being hungry or out of work, as I know Irina is. How do you work, anyway, with a small child to take care of and no husband in the picture? I sigh, absently poking the lean meat, which pops and sizzles like the bacon I can't use.

Cooking for Life shuns all things caloric and fatty, so this version of *boeuf bourguignon* will not include bacon or pancetta as it should, nor will I use even half as much olive oil as I'd like to. I will increase the wine, and it'll be pretty good beef stew without the potatoes, essentially, which will delight Uncle Benny when I take him his casserole dish tonight. *It certainly won't hurt me to eat gourmet lite for dinner,* I think, then shake my head to clear it. It's amazing how one five-minute conversation with my mother can undo every affirmation I've ever taped to my bathroom mirror.

After giving the beef another poke or two, I scrub the cutting board in the dish-crowded sink, then chop and stir in carrots, celery, and onions. I mince fresh thyme and Italian parsley for flavor and color, pour in defatted beef stock, then leave it to simmer for a while, the individual aromas already commingling and filling the apartment.

I look to the window again, but condensation has glazed it over. On the notepad I keep by the stove I write:

> Double herbs.
> Find out how much olive oil is okay.
> Brie???

I chew the pen a moment, then write:

> Atkins book?
> Weight Watchers?
> Calories or carbs?

Disgusted, I cross out the last three items and write, *Buy umbrella.*

• • •

Sometimes when I'm trying to fall asleep at night, listening to my neighbors laugh, fight, watch TV, have sex, when I'm smelling their curry and garlic and Spam, their cigarette and marijuana smoke, I wonder, *Whose life is this?* It can't be mine.

I should be married with kids in junior high by now, arranging flowers from the back garden of our old Portland foursquare with a remodeled kitchen, not living alone in a one-bedroom apartment that masquerades as a condo. I was supposed to be writing sumptuous cookbooks, throwing lavish dinner parties for intellectual friends, not churning out lighten-up-your-favorite-dish-until-it-tastes-like-cardboard recipes and eating family-size chocolate bars while watching *Cooking with Caprial* on OPB.

Our family has disintegrated. My sisters never came home after college. Mom sold our house in Lake Grove when she remarried last year. She and John moved to the bucolic wine country of the Dundee Hills, an hour southwest of the city, full of empty nesters in McMansions, telling themselves that this is living, all right. No kids, no neighbors, no messes to contend with—just the rolling vineyard hills, echoing rooms, and Mount Hood framed perfectly in the picture window.

Lying in the dark, more alone than I know how to cope with, I feel a shrinking sensation I remember from childhood fevers. I have to open my eyes and draw a deep breath to keep from disappearing, touch my skin to make sure I experience sensation.

Then I conjure a man in my bed, one who can comfort me with kind eyes and a body large enough to cover mine, and creep my hand into my flannel boxers to make sure I won't forget pleasure.

Early in the afternoon, my eyes blur with fatigue from staring at the computer screen for three hours straight. I stand to stretch and look out the window, gasping to see the steady rain has turned to snow, covering the grass and bending the daffodils. It figures. We've made it all the way through winter without one flake, but now nature has decided that spring is just out of the question.

I sigh and gather my frizz of hair in two handfuls to tie a knot on top of my head. Then I take a deep breath and pick up the phone to call my editor at *Cooking for Life* to explain there is no such thing as fat-free Brie. I dial, but nothing happens. "Hello?" I say.

"Beep, de-goddamn beep. I thought you'd never quit punching those buttons," Benny says cheerfully.

"But I didn't call you, I—"

"I called you."

"Ah. That would explain it." I settle back. "What are you doing?"

"Watching it snow. It's something, isn't it? I don't believe it's ever even sleeted here after the first week of March."

"Yeah, it's pretty strange. Maybe it's the new Ice Age. Maybe they have that whole global warming thing backwards."

"Say, Miss Roosevelt, do you know where I put my reading glasses? I've been looking all over for them."

Like I'm in the same room instead of a good twenty-minute drive up I-5. "How would I know? Did you look on top of your head?"

He chuckles. I shake my head. It's become another of our routines, these phone calls to discuss the minutiae of life. The weather. His neighbors. Local gossip. The weather. These days, my closest relationship is with him, and as much as he means to me, this thought does little to make me feel better about my life. The lack thereof.

"Heard from your mother?" He slips it into the conversation so neatly that I almost miss the shift in his voice. He hasn't asked about her in months.

"Um, no, not in a while," I lie. It would hurt him even more than me that she's been sneaking into town. "She's busy decorating their place. You know how she is—always up to something."

I never say the new husband's name to Benny. The vague "they" and "their" seem kinder somehow. "She's into that whole French-country thing now, florals and chickens everywhere. God, remember when she made our house all yellow and green?"

"It was cheerful," he says, defending her as he always does.

"Dad hated it."

"Yeah, well . . ." Benny says. "May he rest in peace."

Or not, I don't say. I'm not nearly as generous as Benny is.

"Sure you want to come over today?" he asks. "The roads could get pretty slick."

"Of course I'm coming. It's just a little snow." He sounds lonely, and I resolve to spend more time with him, make Mom call him. It wouldn't kill her.

When I first saw my father at the funeral home two years ago, I was amazed that the clichés about death were true. Without his energy, his body was no longer him. His face had gone flaccid, losing the tension between his eyes, along his jaw. His sandy gray hair had apparently been washed as he lay on his back, drying perpendicular to the floor. Days later, at the funeral, someone had styled it like a newscaster's.

Coworkers found him at his desk at the Clackamas County offices on a Monday morning, slumped over his Day-Timer, coffee pooling under his elbow. The autopsy showed cardiac damage and scars from previous incidents that had gone unnoticed. We had a simple service on a gray but dry winter afternoon, and it puzzled me how genuinely saddened the people from his office seemed to be.

"He was such a good man," said a bird-faced woman, a geologist like Dad. I fought the urge to say, "Really?" and nodded instead. To me he was the Invisible Man, nothing but a ghost in the basement, a dent on the couch, a disembodied memory when he'd take one of his long business trips. Mom told us he loved us, but I didn't buy it. How could he love us if he never talked to us about anything other than grades and chores, and later, when we were adults, jobs and money?

The last thing I remembered him saying to me, a month before he died, was, "Are you making any money yet? Why you ever quit that cushy PR job is beyond me." I wanted to say, "And why you ever had children is beyond me," but even as an adult I could never bring myself to talk back to him.

The funeral was over in half an hour. It was more like a perfunctory church visit, like the ones we'd made each Christmas Eve and Easter, than mourning the passing of a human life. Mom was quiet most of the day, and Christine had blubbered like a baby at the service, but Anne and I remained steadfastly dry-eyed.

Mom had a reception after the service, putting out clam dip and tiny cheese-filled sausages, carrot and celery sticks, Ritz crackers and canned olives. Her former idea of gourmet. The only clue that she wasn't truly enjoying the opportunity to entertain was the grip she kept on her glass of vodka and tonic, and the frequency with which she refilled it. My mother rarely drank more than half a beer.

Late in the day, as people began to filter out and Aunt Yolanda helped my sisters and me clean up, Mom headed for the basement. We looked at each other, shaking our heads, figuring she was going to sit in Dad's den, commune with the spirit of the man who'd sat alone there so often, unencumbered by human interaction.

Moments later, Mom appeared at the top of the stairs, face bright, eyes shining. "It's perfect," she said. Even at sixty-four, she had the exuberance of a schoolgirl.

Not quite knowing how to respond, we all just stared at her. Benny, deep in a discussion with one of the neighbors, looked over at the sound of my mother's voice, and then excused himself to walk to her side.

"Bebe?" he said, and we all waited.

"The den will make a perfect darkroom," she said.

Benny tipped his head and frowned at her. "You sure you should be making those kinds of decisions right now? I mean, it's only been—"

"Of course I'm sure." She laughed, looking around the room. "My God. Richard would have wanted me to have a darkroom, wouldn't he? And Benny," she said, hooking a conspiratorial arm through his, "I'll even let you use it. It will be like old times."

The platter Yolanda was drying dropped to the floor, smashed against the tile, scattering pink and blue flowers across the room and bringing all conversation to a halt.

"Oh, my, and your good china, too," Yolanda murmured, and my sisters and I kneeled down with her on the floor to gather the pieces.

At four o'clock, I've spooned beef over buttered noodles in a lidded casserole dish, pulled on my rubber boots and parka, and made it down the narrow hall and stairs without slipping on puddles of melting snow. When I push backward through the front door into the cold, I realize this is no ordinary storm. Where not shoveled, the snow buries my feet, and the wind is whipping pellets of ice into my face. I try to shove my hair under my hood while juggling the casserole and my purse, then walk as quickly as I can to my car parked at the curb.

Plenty of traffic sloshes by out on Everett, so if I can make it the half-block there, I should have no problem with the cross-town drive south to Benny's. Once on the main roads, I take it slow, ignore the maniacal pickups and SUVs whizzing by and sending up dirty spray on I-405, I-5, then Boones Ferry Road. The usual afternoon rush hour seems to have been canceled, though; what does everyone else know that I don't? Did they tune to StormCenter 5 or KNUZ instead of burying themselves in drivel about low-carb croissants and *pommes frites* without the *frites*?

Portland is known for shutting down at just the hint of snow, but I'm almost to Benny's. I'll drop off the dish quickly, run by the grocery store for tomorrow's supplies, and then settle back in at home with a bowl of beef, no noodles, and fruit for dessert. I'll call my mother. Somehow I have to make her remember that for most of her life, Benny was her best friend.

Uncle Benny's house always felt like a home should, even when we first started making quick stops on our way to the shopping center with Mom, to see if he needed anything. They'd have a cup of coffee and smoke while my sisters and I explored the house, room by room, until it became familiar territory. I'd run my fingers over the spines of his books in the living room, hide from my sisters underneath his bed, eat butter-and-sugar sandwiches while perched on the stool in the kitchen, listening to Mom and Benny talk about nothing I could understand. I always felt a sense of calm there—a respite from the choppy waters we navigated at our house. No one got mad at Benny's. He let us have the run of the house, and never made us feel that kids were an annoyance to be put up with. And Mom always smiled more, let us get away with more, when she was around Benny.

It felt possible, at those times, that she might have enough love for all of us: for Benny and for Dad. For Anne, who was the smartest, and Christine, who was the prettiest. And for me, who had no special talents other than eating, a proclivity my mother tried to discourage. "You don't want to be fat like your grandmother, now, do you?" she'd ask when I'd beg for one of Benny's famous sugar sandwiches. I'd shake my head, feeling no connection whatever to the photos of her mother in a tent-shaped housedress at the age of fifty, just wanting that sweet, crunchy texture and flavor inside my mouth and knowing I shouldn't.

One day at Benny's, Anne and I were hiding from Christine under the bed. When we heard footsteps coming down the hall, we tucked ourselves together into a tight ball, trying not to giggle. We heard Benny's voice and immediately fell silent.

"I don't know why you worry so much, Bebe," he said, coming closer. "She'll grow into it. It's just puppy fat." We saw his grease-stained boots beneath the overhang of blanket, then my mother's tan flats. They came toe to toe, then parted.

"Not in my family," she said. "I have to starve myself to stay thin. And besides, Ellie's the spitting image of my mother. It just makes me sick—"

I didn't hear the rest because Anne clamped her hands over my ears and didn't let go until Mom and Benny had gone back into the kitchen. I tried not to cry—Anne always accused me of being a crybaby as it was—but she pretended she didn't notice when my jaw quivered.

"Don't listen to her," she whispered, kicking the underside of the box spring. "She's the one who's bad, you know, cheating with Benny."

I didn't know what she meant. To me, cheating had more to do with board games and tests at school. I didn't think Mom was doing anything wrong by being friends with Benny, even though he was a man and it was a bit odd, but I liked the whole arrangement. I told Mom so on the car ride home, adding, "It's not really cheating if you're not breaking any rules, is it?"

Her face in the rearview told me I'd said the wrong thing when all I'd been trying to do was get on her good side. "Who told you we're cheating?" she asked. I shook my head, mumbled that I didn't know, and felt Anne relax beside me.

"You're to go to your room when we get home, Eleanor," Mom said. "You need to understand that it's malicious to spread lies and rumors, and I don't want you ever repeating that one, do you hear me? Not to anyone. It's shameful to talk like that."

I nodded, felt the tears threaten again, and clenched my teeth to keep from making any sound. For a moment I thought Anne might confess, but silence filled the car for the rest of the ride home.

I turn in to Benny's neighborhood and slide sideways in the untracked snow. "Come on," I coax the car, downshifting into second, and fishtail the last two blocks to Benny's house. The huge firs and hemlocks that line the street are laden with snow, and the magnolia limbs are bent, the buds destroyed. The small frame ranches look shuttered against the storm; there's no sign of human life in sight. I pull up in front of Benny's house, not daring to turn into his driveway, and leave my hazard lights blinking.

The door's locked, so I ring the bell. After shivering there for a minute, I knock once, then twice. Something's not right. Finally, Benny cracks the door an inch and peers out, looking bewildered and older, somehow, than he did just three days ago. He's wearing his tattered bathrobe again, and I wonder if he's gotten dressed at all this week.

"Are you okay?" I ask, stepping inside and stamping my boots in the entryway. "You remembered I was coming over, right?"

He nods and clutches his robe in front of his gut. A game-show host blathers from the TV in the living room. Benny's blanket lies rumpled on the couch.

"Go back and lie down, Ben. I'll put this stuff away and bring you some supper, okay?"

He follows me into the kitchen instead. "Supper," he says.

"Patience, patience," I say, settling the dish on the counter and opening the fridge door. "What, are you starving to death? You should have plenty to snack on in here." The leftovers from Monday are untouched, and the casserole from the previous week has grown moldy.

"Ben?" I turn to look at him. "What exactly have you been eating?"

He looks like hell, now that I can see him in the light. The skin around his eyes looks tender and dark, and the fake tan I accused him of is now the yellow of mustard. My heart starts to beat rapidly in my chest.

"Uncle Benny?"

His eyes look confused. "Sup, sup, sup," he says, brow furrowing.

"Oh, Jesus, Benny. Oh, God." A surge of something—panic, fear—is pushing into my throat. I swallow hard against it and say, "Okay. First thing we're going to do is get you back on the couch, okay, Uncle Benny?" I take his arm, walk him slowly back into the living room. Like a docile child, he settles back into his spot, and I pull the blanket over him. "Okay, I'll be right back," I say, but he doesn't respond.

I race back to the phone in the kitchen, dial 911.

A young female voice asks, "Is this an emergency?"

"I-I think so. My uncle has been really sick and he looks jaundiced. And, God, he's kind of, I don't know. Babbling." I try to talk quietly so he won't hear me.

"You'll have to speak up. I can barely hear you. Is he there with you now?"

"Yes," I say loudly.

"The address?"

I give it to her and ask, "Are you going to send someone, or . . . I don't know, should I try to bring him in?" All I can think of is the snow piling higher around my car, covering the windows, the tire tracks.

"An ambulance has been dispatched, but it might take a few extra minutes with the weather, okay? Stay with me on the line, though, until they get there. What's your name?"

"Ellie," I say, then correct myself. "Eleanor. Eleanor Samuels."

"Okay, Ellie," she says, "and how about your uncle's name?"

She's nice. She asks me question after question, things I can answer, things I can't, until finally blue and red lights flash through the front window.

Through it all, Benny has fallen asleep.

It takes forever to get my car unstuck, rocking back and forth with tires spinning and screaming, but one of Benny's neighbors finally comes out with a bag of kitty litter. She throws some under my tires and enlists her stout son to help push me free.

The ambulance is long gone, Benny warmly bundled in the back, and a female paramedic at his side, which makes me feel better about not riding with him. If I leave my car here, it will be days before I can get it out.

The drive to the hospital is eerie, the twilight deepened by low cloud cover and the omnipresent snow. It's falling in triplicate, gangs of flakes clinging together, covering the windshield as my skinny wipers struggle to keep up. I stretch my eyes wide, wondering if I'm stuck in a nightmare. There's no way this is all really happening. The snow, the ambulance. Benny's yellow skin and hollow eyes.

A battered pickup truck slides sideways through the intersection in front of me, my car skidding slightly before the tires grab at the crunchy slush. An inch-thick layer of accumulated snow slides from my roof and veils the windshield. For a moment I'm afraid I'll suffocate. I can't see, I don't know what's out there, what's coming at me. I jump from the car to brush off the snow with my coat sleeve, looking out behind for approaching traffic. There's no one out on the road but me and the truck's driver, a swarthy-looking man who is cursing and gunning his engine, spinning his tires as he careens sideways down Boones Ferry into the darkness.

It feels like hours until I get to the ER. I hurry in and look around, then head for the only sign of life: a beehived woman reading a newspaper at the reception desk.

"They just brought in Benny Sloan," I say. "I'm his niece. Where can I find him?"

She checks a log, then makes an indecipherable page; it sounds like she's calling for Dr. Scary. The lobby is empty except for me, a surprise given the road conditions. I stand at the desk, trying not to tap my foot, my fingers, trying to relax to the strains of unidentifiable Muzak from somewhere overhead.

After a few moments, a kid who looks like a college student in a lab coat walks up and introduces himself as Dr. Terry. His breath smells of Altoids. I shake his hand, although it seems idiotic in an emergency. "I'm Benny Sloan's niece," I say. "How is he? What's going on?"

"He was complaining of severe stomach pain, so we've sent him for a scan that should give us a better look at what's happening in his belly."

"He was coherent?" I ask. "He was completely out of it at home."

He nods. "Yeah, I noticed some confusion. Could be any number of things either associated with the other symptoms or not."

He's entirely too young, with ski-jump hair and chewed-to-the-quick fingernails, but he seems to be in charge, even though he's holding a clipboard that has a SHRED TO LIVE, MaxRush SNOWBOARDS sticker on the back.

"How long has your uncle been jaundiced?"

"I think I first noticed it a couple of days ago, but I didn't know what it was. Do you think he has hepatitis?"

"And the time you saw him before that?" He looks up at me.

"I, um, I don't know. It was last week. I think he looked okay."

"And how long has he been sick?"

I shrug, helpless. "I don't know. A long time. He doesn't admit to feeling bad unless he's dying." I clamp my mouth shut to take back that word.

"A guess?"

I think back and back, without the filters of Benny's excuses, his cheery assertions that he's feeling much better. "Four weeks, maybe? Five?"

He writes something down and I feel better, having supplied this tidbit.

"Does he have any immediate family?"

"Not really," I say, biting my lip. I've flunked the good-niece test.

"No wife? Kids?"

"Well, yes, a wife, but they're separated."

"But she'll know his medical history?" he prompts.

"I don't know her new number, but her name's Yolanda Sloan. Unless she's gone back to Duran, her maiden name." I pause. "Just how sick do you think he is?"

He looks up from his clipboard. "You're close to your uncle?"

Whatever's wrong with Benny, I have to know, so I confess. "He's not technically my uncle. But, he's . . . you know." I shrug, chew my lip. "My family."

It works. He says, "We're looking at a few possibilities here. The best outcome would be something like pancreatitis, which we could treat with antibiotics. It could also be hepatitis, as you mentioned, which, depending on the type, might not be too bad to deal with."

"And the not-so-good outcome?"

"Probably what you're thinking. Liver failure. Cancer. His liver didn't feel enlarged when I palpated it, but it's still a possibility."

"Would he be able to get a transplant or something?"

"Let's take it one step at a time," he says. "We'll get the results of the tests and then we'll have a better idea of what's going on, okay?"

"Oh. Right." He's just a kid, but he's clearly used to these kinds of things, people with serious illnesses, family members with stupid questions. Somehow, I'm almost forty and I don't have a clue how to do this.

"I'll go track down his wife," he says, tucking his pen inside his shirt pocket. "When I know more, I'll let you know."

He walks away, high-top sneakers squeaking as they hit the linoleum of the hallway. I take a seat in the middle of a row of hard gray plastic chairs and say, "Tell her Ellie says hi," although he doesn't hear me. Suddenly, I miss her more fiercely than if she'd died.

chapter four

When I was a child, I didn't know it was unusual for a mechanic to take photography classes and read books and listen to classical music and jazz singers, to cry at school plays even though he had no children of his own. He seemed normal to me; he was just Uncle Benny.

I borrowed his books all the time—I discovered brand-new copies of Mark Twain, Ernest Hemingway, Harper Lee, John Steinbeck, Louisa May Alcott lurking on Benny's shelves between the potboilers and old Zane Grays, the Ford and Chrysler specifications manuals, and kitschy joke books. Sometimes in school I'd find that I'd already read the required book for a class and I'd be surprised that other people knew about Benny's and my secret.

I decided to be a writer in sixth grade; someday I'd write beautiful, heartfelt stories about important things, like the starving children in Biafra or maybe poems like Rod McKuen's. Sometimes now, as I shift in my chair at the computer, searching for a new way to say "sauté onions until translucent," I try to conjure the old fantasies, but it gets harder every year. I am a writer, I tell myself, *I get paid to do it,* but somehow I can never recapture my childhood enthusiasm.

It seems now that we always knew her, but Yolanda didn't come into our lives until the summer before I entered junior high and developed my own breasts. One muggy July day when a Pacific storm was brewing, Mom came home from the grocery store, looking dazed. She unloaded just two bags from the car instead of the usual eight or ten, setting them on the counter before hurrying to her room, leaving the perishables to spoil.

Alarmed, I went to her door. She lay flat across her bed, hand over her eyes.

"Are you all right?"

"I just have a headache," she said quietly, but I saw the spasmodic movement of her chest. She was crying.

"Mom? What's wrong?"

She took a deep breath, then smiled at the ceiling. "Guess what. I just saw Uncle Benny at the store, and he's getting married." Her breath caught and she made an embarrassing snorting sound, then laughed. "To a Mexican girl, from that restaurant he likes, El Something-or-other. Isn't that wonderful?"

I hated the strange tone in her voice. "But why are you crying?" I asked.

"Because I'm just so happy for him, honey," she said. "He's my dearest friend."

I knew nothing then of adult friendships, nothing of adult love or heartbreak, but I knew enough to leave her lying there and pull the door closed. I felt protective of her somehow, and I didn't say a word to Anne or Christine, who were in the family room watching cartoons and doing homework. I went out to the kitchen, unpacked the groceries, and put on water to boil spaghetti for dinner.

The hospital waiting room has a CELL PHONE ZONE sign on the wall. I pull out my phone, search the directory for Anne's number, then hit CALL, even though it's nearly eleven o'clock in Boston. "You've reached Anne Samuels-Richardson," her professional voice message tells me, wisely omitting husband number one's name. "Please leave a message."

"It's me," I say. "Benny's in the hospital, and I think it's bad. Call me as soon as you can." Next I dial Christine in California and leave a message on her machine.

It feels as though there should be someone else I could call, as though someone's missing from our family. It's not that Dad's gone.

I dial once again.

"John Weinert," a smooth male voice answers.

I don't know what to say to him; he's a species I've never had to deal with before, outside of buying a used car or encyclopedia set. "Could I speak with my mother, please?"

"And this is?" he says pleasantly.

"Eleanor. It's kind of an emergency."

"One moment," he says, and puts me on hold. Mantovani oozes from the earpiece for a moment, and then my mother comes on the line.

"Hello? Ellie? Are you all right?"

"I'm fine, Mom, but—"

"Oh, thank God. I thought maybe something had happened, with the snowstorm and all. I'd say we have a good five, six inches out there, wouldn't you, John? At least, he says, and the news says we could get another couple of inches by morning."

Breathe, I think, not sure who I'm talking to, her or myself.

"Mom?" I interrupt. "Benny's in the hospital. Something's really wrong. He's jaundiced, so they're doing tests on his liver."

"Oh. Oh, no." She sighs. "Dear God."

"I'm the only one here," I say, sounding like a kid. What do I want, for her to drive through this blizzard to sit with me? To be here when Benny is through with his tests? For her to come to her senses and move back to our old house, our old life?

"I just thought I'd let you know," I finally say.

"Well, you'll give him my best, won't you, dear?" she says, but there's something else there, something old and aching and deep, and it comforts me.

I shared my love of books with Benny, but Aunt Yolanda opened my eyes to the world of food as art, cooking without cans. She introduced me to the magic of spices, the exotic perfume of fresh herbs crushed between fingers. Younger than my mother, she was rounded in just the right spots from her love of good food, and when we talked she looked right at me and listened, nodding and laughing loudly when I'd tell jokes, holding my hand when we'd walk, as if we were best friends or sisters.

She liked Anne and Christine, too, but I could tell I was her favorite. She took me with her on shopping trips, to the fish market near the waterfront and the farm stands out west. Sometimes she'd journey to the Asian grocers in Northeast Portland or the hippie vegetarian markets on Hawthorne to find something special. We'd come home laden with ingredients that I knew my mother had never heard of, and the resulting feasts would fill me with a yearning to go different places, to try new things.

After Dad died, Anne predicted everything would change between Yolanda and Benny. She was right about everything but the particulars.

"You just wait. Benny'll dump Aunt Yolanda now to be with Mom," she said the night after the funeral, when she and I had finally left Christine at Mom's house and gone for dinner at Chanterelle, my favorite Trendy-third Avenue restaurant until Mom discovered it.

Anne and I were imbibing our second dirty martinis, and she'd ordered hazelnut-encrusted salmon and goat cheese salad while I'd asked for the macaroni with three cheeses and Dungeness crab, comfort food for the well heeled, or those with a paying sister.

"Oh, Anne," I moaned, annoyed at the subject matter after the grueling day. Anne always had a way of picking at sore spots, scratching off scabs. It must be what made her a good lawyer. Besides, she'd already gone through two husbands herself; she was no expert on love. I said, "Mom and Benny have been friends for so long now, they're like brother and sister."

She shook her close-cropped head, let her long jaw drop in exaggerated incredulity. "You are the most amazing person," she said, though I knew she did not mean it kindly. "You will defend them until the day you die."

"I'm not defending anyone," I said, taking a long, hard drink to feel the burn in my throat. "I'm just saying." I looked around for our waiter, but it seemed he'd deserted us in favor of a long midshift break. "I'm starving. Aren't you?"

"Why do you always change the subject? God, Eleanor."

She'd always seemed cynical and mean-spirited when it came to this topic, but seeing her at that moment, the way her eyes looked into mine for a moment, then away, the way she traced the rim of her glass over and over, made me realize I'd missed something.

"What?" I asked. "What do you want to talk about?"

She widened her eyes and I said, "I know, I know. But you can't think they're still at it, after all these years. I mean, why wouldn't they just have run off together years ago if they were that in love?"

She tipped her glass into her mouth, closing her eyes at the sear of the vodka, then set her glass down and looked at me. "Maybe they were protecting us."

"Why not after we'd all left home, then?" I asked, trying to find the chink in her logic.

She shrugged and smoothed a hand down the arm of her suit jacket. "I don't know."

"Then why didn't Dad leave?"

Anne looked at me. "Eleanor. Come on."

"What?"

"He did."

"He took business trips."

"He lived in a motel out on the Sunset Highway."

"You don't know that."

"Jesus, Eleanor. I give up."

We sat silently for a moment, the murmur of conversation and clink of silverware suddenly loud around us. "Damn, where's that waiter?" I said, half rising to go look for him.

"He's right behind you with our plates, Eleanor," Anne said. "Don't worry, you get to eat now."

It stung like she knew it would. She rarely used my weight against me, only when she was out of other options. To the waiter she said, "Could we have another round, please? And you might as well bring out the dessert menu now so my sister can start studying it."

Had my macaroni and cheese not been exquisite, I might have only picked at it, just to show her—and the waiter—that I had some self-control. Failing that, I tried to leave a few bites on the plate, and when that failed, I said no to dessert, only to eat half of Anne's poached pear in caramel sauce.

As it turned out, Benny didn't leave Yolanda; she left him. Last summer, six months after Dad died. Even then, though, Benny and my mother did not become a couple. Instead, she surprised us last September by coming home from a trip we'd thought she'd taken alone to San Francisco with a new husband at her side. Before we had time to digest that, they'd sold our old house and everything in it my sisters and I didn't want. They moved into the five-thousand-square-foot house John was almost finished building on a prime view lot in the Dundee Hills. My mother cut all ties with Benny, and it pisses me off that she'd do that for this man she barely knew. She never did it for our father.

I'm still sitting in the hard plastic chair two hours later, my posterior as numb as my brain, when my cell phone rings. It's Christine. "I just got in and picked up your message," she says. "Are you okay?"

It is so like my younger sister to ask after my well-being, even when I'm not the one who's sick, that I have to take a deep breath before replying.

I tell her about the results of the CT scan, that it shows something going on with Benny's pancreas, which to me sounds better than the liver. Dr. Terry didn't share my optimism. They've scheduled Benny for a procedure where they stick a tube down his throat, look around with a little camera, take a biopsy of the pancreas, and insert a stent to stop the jaundice. He's staying in the hospital until he's stabilized and the results are in, which could be a few days.

"How's he doing?" she asks.

"I don't know. He's been asleep every time I've looked in on him."

"Why are you still sitting there? It's late. Go home."

"I will," I say. "In a while."

"Take care of yourself, okay? Are you still taking your B vitamins and essential fatty acids?"

I mumble something about trying to and she says, "They don't do any good in the cupboard, Eleanor. Now go home. I'll call Benny in the morning."

"He'll love that," I tell her. I may have been Yolanda's favorite, but Christine was Benny's. He treated us all as if we were his own, but he always smiled at Christine's impassioned lisp, not quite drilled out of her in second grade, and her dainty girl ways. She was the one like Mom, not me.

"How are you, anyway?" I ask.

"Oh, you know," she says, sounding tired. "The same. Too busy."

For the past five years, Christine has worked evenings at the local library while teaching eighth grade so that her husband can pursue his dream of filmmaking. They've moved to a smaller house in a worse neighborhood, and they never go anywhere except on "scouting" missions in his 1972 Honda, camping amid the towering redwoods of northern California.

Reid's documentaries tend toward subject matter like the plight of three-toed tree frogs and people who live in sequoias and call themselves Rainbow. Christine fell for him when she took his environmental sciences class at UC Berkeley, and has stuck by him ever since, even though he's fifteen years older than she is and refuses to use Kleenex when he has a cold, opting instead to blow his nose on towels. *Love is strange*, I tell myself, as I always do when I think about Christine and Reid.

"Has Reid decided whether or not he's going to go back to teaching?" I ask. Apparently, environmental documentaries don't quite pay the rent.

She sighs. "No, but I'm not going to teach summer school this year, so I'll get a break."

"No way," I kid her. "You? Get a break?"

"Well, actually, I probably won't go back to teaching or work for a while," Christine says, then stops. "I messed up, El. I'm pregnant."

"What do you mean, messed up? That's fantastic, Christine. You've always wanted a baby."

"I know," she says.

"Reid will get used to it. He'll discover his paternal instinct as soon as he sees Reid Junior's tiny little squished-up face."

She's quiet.

"God, I'm sorry. I mean, I just assumed you were having it or—"

"Oh, I'm having it," she says. "I am definitely having it."

"That's wonderful. Congratulate me. I'm going to be an aunt."

"I'm glad somebody's happy about it."

"Have you told Mom?"

"Not yet," she says. "You're the first to know besides Reid. I was waiting for the second trimester to tell people."

"I cannot wait to hear how she'll react to being a grandmother."

"Don't you think she'll be happy?" She sounds so worried that I tell her of course she will, I'm just kidding about Mom's extreme case of vanity.

After we've hung up, I stand and gather my coat and purse. Pins and needles wage war on my butt as I walk to Benny's room.

At the doorway to Room 623, I stop. It's dark except for a small light over an empty bed at the opposite side of the room. Benny is still asleep in the bed closest to the door, an IV tube taped to the crook of his arm. He breathes in two three, out two three, without faltering. I watch for a moment longer, then turn to go home.

Back in my apartment, I turn up the heat and put my wet boots, jeans, and coat in the bathtub to dry. My car is stuck two blocks away, even after a couple of sweatshirt-hooded guys tried to help me push it free. I pull on my robe and thick socks and wrap my hair in a towel, then settle in front of the TV with the clicker and a bowl of *boeuf bourguignon,* topping just a small portion of noodles, no butter. It tastes better than I'd hoped, and I know Stefan, my editor at *Cooking for Life,* will be pleased. As much as I complain about my job, I live to please Stefan.

When I first felt the pangs of lust for him, I cut his handsome, laughing photo from the letter from the editor page and signed it *XOXO, Stefan,* then slipped it inside a red-jeweled frame. It sits on the top shelf of the bookcase, which also includes a red pomegranate-scented candle, a tri-folded piece of cardboard covered with heart stickers and magazine cutouts of sexy photos and the words "love," "boyfriend," "sex," and now "Stefan."

Christine introduced me to the idea of creating an altar of love to attract the object of my desire, and I thought, *why not?* Who besides me will ever see it? No one comes to visit, so I won't have to explain that, yes, middle-age women can act like thirteen-year-olds, given enough time without a man. If nothing else, he makes great fantasy material when I take my pathetic sex life into my own hands.

Thinking about him now makes me wander over to the computer by the window to check my e-mail. Nothing but the usual forward from Christine, this one titled "More Happy Thoughts to Live By," which I automatically delete out of habit. Even though I succumbed to the vitamins and the love altar, she's become more Californian than I can deal with, living in a New Age haze that seems to be a cross between Zen Buddhism and Wayne Dyer platitudes.

I still haven't heard from Anne, which isn't unusual. I rarely do. Last year she made partner at her law firm in Boston and bought a new condo on the waterfront. She's permanently too busy to do anything like make phone calls or visit Portland, except when someone dies, and I'm too broke to do anything like go back East.

I return to the TV, click through a few channels. I pick up the empty bowl and swirl my finger around the edge, lick it off. I'm starving.

"No, you're not," I say aloud, trying to believe it.

What I should be doing is working on ideas for my new *American Family* article: "Back to School: Packing Smart Lunches Your Little Einsteins Will Eat." Magazine writers have to think six months ahead of everyone else. My whole life is like Christmas in July. Without the presents.

I pick up my notebook, start a list:

> Peanut butter pita pockets
> Funny-face quesadillas

I really am hungry.

> Strawberries with chocolate-frosting dip

I try to ignore the insistent messages being sent to my brain by Pauncho, my stomach and lifelong companion. Suzanne Long called it "inner hunger," hunger that has nothing to do with food. "Ha!" I snort. Tell that to Pauncho.

Chocolate. I want chocolate. And now that I've let that thought enter my head, it won't go away until Pauncho is satisfied.

In the bathroom I pull on my soggy coat and pants and carry my boots to the front door. Mini-Mart is just a few blocks away. Maybe the exercise will counteract the calories.

chapter five

The day after what the media is now calling the Spring Snow Surprise, Portland is effectively shut down under seven inches of the stuff. It's never snowed this much this late in March in recorded history, according to StormCenter 5 and every other local channel. You'd think the world had spun out of its orbit. It's weather twenty-four hours a day, reporters standing in snowdrifts, wearing silly hats, throwing snowballs at the camera. Reporting every millimeter of accumulation from every remote spot in town.

I can't drive to the hospital; my car is still stuck out on Everett, marooned like hundreds of other cars around town. Every time I call Benny's room, I'm told he's sleeping or otherwise unavailable. "But is he okay?" I ask the nurse on his floor, and she assures me he's stable. The doctor will call when he knows anything further.

I am fidgety and sick to death of TV news. The snow stopped sometime in the middle of the night and the temperature is well above freezing now that it's afternoon, so I decide to walk to Fred Meyer for groceries, only a half mile or so away and surely open, even with the weather. The *Cooking for Life* article is due tomorrow. I've talked my way out of the *Brie en croute*, but I wasted all my eggs this morning trying to make a decent low-fat crème caramel.

Out in the hallway, Mr. Nguyen says, "Act of God," shaking his head when I ask how he and his family are holding up. It's probably the most snow they've ever seen; they only arrived in the United States last sum-mer. His kids cower behind their red front door, looking at me in my parka like I'm a Martian.

"Snow is good," I tell them. "It's fun! Snowballs! Snow angels!" I mimic these things, but they run away when I swoop my arms up and down to make an angel. "I'm going to the store. Do you need anything?" I ask Mr. Nguyen.

He shrugs, looking worried. "Work," he says. "I need bus to run."

I knock on Mrs. Wittsler's door. "It's Eleanor, from upstairs," I say loudly. She won't open the door unless she knows it's not a criminal. "I'm going to the grocery store. Do you need anything?"

The myriad security devices on her door *click* and *tock* open. She looks at me through smudged eyeglasses, pink scalp tender-looking be-hind wisps of white hair. "I could use more potato flakes," she says, reaching into her housedress and extracting two rumpled dollar bills. "Store brand, like always."

I have no idea how she can choke down that stuff, especially when real potatoes are so cheap. "Of course," I say, taking the money, and she closes the door and clangs the locks back into place.

Outside, a few intrepid souls have shoveled their walks, but most haven't. I'm glad for my knee-high rubber rain boots and the distraction of an adventure as I plow slowly up Everett through the slushy snow.

Past our building, tall Victorian homes sit quietly beneath the weight of all this white: gingerbread houses with fondant frosting. Some of the old homes are in disrepair, gray and sagging from years of weather and gravity, but others have been beautifully restored, ornate detail painted in plums, golds, trendy new shades of green. I like to imagine who lives in them: urban families, artsy and alternative types. Our Fred Meyer is known for its colorful clientele. Where else in Portland will you find drag queens doing their weekly shopping at three in the morning after a show, thumping cantaloupes and squeezing lemons alongside the shift workers and people like me who get cravings for frozen chocolate éclairs in the middle of the night?

The store is buzzing with shoppers from the neighborhood, all frenzied and harried, and too many of them toting manic kids with cabin fever. An inch of slippery muck has been tracked across the industrial gray-spotted floor. One look toward the back and I can tell the shelves are stripped. I stand there shaking my head, and one of my favorite baggers, an older man with Down's syndrome, tells me there's no milk, no meat, no bread.

"Eggs?" I ask, and he shrugs, then takes his station at checkout stand number 3, where a huge order is piling up at the end of the conveyor.

I weave through the desperate crowd, consulting my list, making substitutions, picking up nonfat cream cheese, evaporated skim milk, egg substitute. Things no one else wants. I've never succumbed to fake eggs before, and I have no idea if they will set up like real eggs, but I don't have much choice now.

Back outside, it's warm in my parka, and my bags are unexpectedly heavy. I trudge steadily along for a while, occasionally trading the heavy bag of dairy products in one hand for the other equally heavy bag, which contains a large box of potato flakes and a half dozen Yukon gold potatoes for Mrs. Wittsler, a bag of Oreos for the Nguyens' kids if I don't eat them first, and a fold-up umbrella for Irina Ivanova.

My mother may not have been a great cook, but what she lacked in quality she made up for in quantity. We loved to help her unpack the grocery sacks each week, finding Little Debbie boxes beneath the dinner rolls, six-packs of Pepsi and Fanta ripping the brown paper bags under their steely weight. Our friends were envious of our well-stocked refrigerator, our junk food–laden pantry. We always had ice cream in the freezer and chocolate syrup and whipped cream in the fridge door. Oreos in the cookie jar. M&M's in the candy dish. Count Chocula cereal one week, Cap'n Crunch the next.

Mom said a full refrigerator made a house a home, even though she cast disparaging looks my way whenever I'd try to enjoy the bounty. Dad said we should just be happy we had a home, for Christ's sake. Why on God's green earth did we need chocolate cereal? Cheerios were good enough for him—they were good enough for his brother Lewis's children. They should be good enough for us.

I hated it when they fought, and my sisters and I never spoke during their arguments. We ate our canned peas if it was dinnertime, stuck our noses in books if we were driving to the coast for a picnic. Turned up the television if we were lucky enough to be in the family room and they were in the kitchen, Dad running the long strip of receipt through his fingers, complaining about each item that was not one of the four basic food groups.

Then, when no one was looking, I'd sneak handfuls of candy into my pockets, or line the waistband of my pants with cookies to enjoy in the privacy of the bathroom. When it was all gone, I'd want more, licking my finger to dab the crumbs from my skin, searching for bits of M&M shell in the lint of my pockets.

That evening, with six ramekins of faux crème caramel in the oven, I dial Benny's room at the hospital again. It's black and frigid outside, moonless and no cloud cover to reflect the city lights. There's no answer, not even a nurse. A sliver of fear zaps through me. I call again, in case I misdialed, but nothing.

The timer dings on the oven. I peek inside, jiggle the rack. The custard hasn't set up, so I set the timer for another five minutes, dial Benny's room. Nothing.

I wait a few minutes, then call Benny's room one more time, let it ring seven, eight times. Finally, there's a click, and a sleepy-sounding Benny.

"Mm . . . myello?"

"Geez, Ben. You had me scared half to death," I say, sounding angrier than I mean to. It's the first time I've talked to him since last night at his house, so I soften my tone. "I'm sorry, I've just been worried. Are you okay?"

"Bebe?"

My heart rips inside my chest. "No, Ben, it's me, Ellie."

"Yolie?"

Jesus. That's what he used to call Aunt Yolanda.

"It's Eleanor, Benny. El-uh-nor. What's going on? Are you all right? Is there a nurse anywhere?"

The phone clicks dead, so I dial the nurses' station on his floor. There's no answer.

He's been alone in there for nearly twenty-four hours.

I pull on my wet boots and coat, find my keys and purse. I'm halfway down the stairs when I remember the crème caramel and run back up to turn off the oven. There goes my article, and Stefan's appreciation of me as his best freelancer right along with it.

I walk as quickly as I can to my car; it's been buried in dirty slush and ice by a snowplow. "Oh, for God's sake," I mutter, digging my cell phone out of my purse to call a cab. At least the major streets are passable. The taxi takes forever to show up, during which time I realize I could have given them my address and been waiting in the comfort of my living room. Instead I pace and shiver on the corner and try not to imagine the worst.

After a painfully slow ride with a chatty Somalian driver, I rush through the hospital to Benny's room, only to find him sleeping as peacefully as a child, curled on his side, hands splayed expressively in front of him as if he fell asleep while telling a story.

I settle into a chair near his bed and close my eyes.

I was not quite twelve in the late-summer days just before Benny married Yolanda. Mom regained her composure and decided to throw them a party. "They have no family here," she said by way of explanation to Dad, who always looked grim when she announced party plans, especially if her plans included Benny. If only he would have said no to her, but he'd grimace and make some comment like, "So Freddy the Freeloader's invited?" She always got her way, though, as she did this time. "We're their family now," she stated in a way that sounded like she had just arrived at this decision for all of us, and that was that.

It wasn't true, of course. Yolanda had family by the carload in Northeast Portland, but we knew Mom was talking about Benny. He'd moved here years before from somewhere in the Midwest to be with his first wife, leaving behind a family he never talked about and never returned to after his wife died.

We weren't invited to the wedding—it was just to be a simple ceremony at the courthouse downtown, with Yolanda's unhappy Catholic parents as secular witnesses—and Mom didn't trust that they'd throw themselves a decent party afterward. We'd heard rumors of cake and coffee at two in the afternoon.

"What, no booze?" Dad said, getting on board with the idea. It must have hit him that Benny would soon no longer be single.

In the week or so between her decision to have the party and the Friday night of the event, Mom threw together the swankiest backyard affair we'd ever seen. Twenty people were coming, she said, and I couldn't imagine what our backyard would look like with so many people in it. She'd called the guys at the auto shop where Benny worked, told them to bring their wives, invited the photography-class couples and a neighbor of Benny's she knew he liked. She told Benny to have Yolanda invite her parents.

We helped Mom sew lace to the edges of white squares of cotton for tablecloths, arranged white roses in bud vases, set up the buffet tables and chairs she'd rented. "Why can't they all just bring lawn chairs?" Dad asked, but Mom shut him down with one of her favorite lines: "That may be the way things are done out here, but where I come from we've got a little more class than that."

She set out to prove it by buying a case of champagne along with the Blitz beer and RC Cola. She looked up recipes in her Betty Crocker Cookbook, and after studying for a while with a cigarette at the kitchen table, she looked up and announced, "Finger foods."

My sisters and I helped make miniature quiches in muffin pans. Mom stirred grape jelly and tomato sauce into a Dutch oven full of meatballs, wrapped crescent roll dough around chunks of hot dog, and shoved a cookie sheet full of bacon-wrapped pineapple into the oven. She set out blocks of Swiss and Tillamook cheddar cheese surrounded by Ritz crackers, and chips and two large bowls of dip, one onion and one clam, Benny's favorite.

Yolanda had called and offered to bring something, but Mom told her in a saccharine voice, "Oh, no, not at your own party. No, dear, you just leave it to us." After she'd hung up the phone, she said, "The poor girl doesn't realize not everyone likes such spicy food." I noticed the lines forming around her mouth then, the way she held her lips tight sometimes, making her look more stern than pretty.

The guests all arrived promptly and began devouring food in lieu of making conversation with people they didn't know. Mom fretted and replenished platters, wanting everything to look perfect for Benny and Yolanda's arrival, which took another twenty minutes. I knew what Mom was thinking: Benny had never been late before.

When he finally slid the screen door across its tracks, all eyes turned to watch as Yolanda stepped out in front of him, laughing at something he'd just whispered into her ear, her orange peasant dress bright against her brown skin, her dark hair escaping its barrette. Benny looked different. His face was fuller, his clothes newer, but it was more that the sadness had left his smile.

I turned to look at my mother, and as I suspected, her face had changed, too, her fixed-on smile barely able to restrain the ache behind it.

As the evening turned to twilight, Mom disappeared inside the house, reemerging with a large sheet cake decorated with flowers and fancy script congratulating the happy couple. She held a flat, rectangular present between her elbow and side.

"I thought you said no gifts," a mechanic's nervous wife said. "We didn't bring anything."

"Oh, this is just a little something," Mom said, settling the cake on the table and presenting the gift to Benny. "It's not really a wedding gift." The expectation in her face was childlike as he unwrapped it, and she urged him to rip the paper when he tried to neatly remove the tape.

From the white-and-silver wrapping he pulled a framed black-and-white photograph. He stared at it for a long moment without smiling, then looked at my mother with an odd expression. If her smile faltered, I did not see it. "Hold it up for everyone to see, Ben," she said. Then to everyone, she added, "It's one of the best photos I've ever taken. I printed it myself."

He turned it around to show us a portrait of himself, taken outdoors somewhere. There were trees in the distance, and he leaned into the picture, wearing an expression not unlike the one he wore now, haunted and vulnerable in a way I wasn't used to seeing him.

"It was for my depth-of-field assignment," Mom explained to the party guests, who murmured politely with confused looks on their faces.

It was an odd image for a wedding gift, after all. "Benny and I took a photography class together. That's how we met, actually."

Benny nodded and cleared this throat. "Yes, well, thank you, Bebe. Not sure I want to look at this ugly mug all the time, but I'm sure we'll find a place for it." He looked at Yolanda and gave her an apologetic smile. "Won't we, honey?"

She looked back at him for a moment, then turned to Mom. "It's a lovely photograph. I'll keep it by my side of the bed."

"Perfect," Mom said, eyes filling. Then she picked up the cake knife. "Now, who wants cake?"

In the countless hours I spent at Benny and Yolanda's house over the years, I never saw that photo again.

The first thing I see when I get home from the hospital after midnight is the glint of the stainless steel oven in the semidarkness of the kitchen. The air smells sweet and eggy. I walk to the oven and pull open the door. Six white ramekins hold six perfect-looking crème caramels, and I wonder if they're safe to eat. It's been more than three hours since I turned off the oven. I remember a Swedish chef telling me years ago when I worked as a prep cook that unrefrigerated food will keep for four hours, but he also cleaned his fingernails with the tip of his chef's knife, so who knows.

I pick up one of the dishes and sniff it. It smells fine. Without taking off my coat, I dig into a drawer for a spoon and eat the crème caramel in five seconds flat. The texture is silky and it tastes sweet and custardy, if not perfect. I pull the rest of the dishes from the oven to put in the fridge, telling myself one was enough. An extra treat at the end of a hard day. I've put three ramekins into the refrigerator when I can't stand it and dig into the second, eating more slowly this time, slipping out of my coat, savoring the custard on my tongue. *Two is definitely enough,* I'm thinking as I lick the inside of the cup, *two is perfect.* I'm picking up the remaining cup to put in the fridge but I turn instead, head for the bedroom with ramekin in hand. *At least wait until you've gotten undressed and in bed,* I tell myself, *surely you can wait.* I make it as far as the doorway and I'm digging my spoon into a third crème caramel. *Don't beat yourself up*, I think when I'm done, *it's just fake eggs and skim milk, a little sugar. It's for Cooking for Life, for God's sake, it can't be bad for you,* but I feel bad somehow as I finish off the third ramekin. *Okay, I'm satisfied now,* I tell myself, *and I can go to sleep.* I get undressed, pull on my T-shirt and flannel boxers, head for the bathroom to brush my teeth, but suddenly I'm taking a detour to the kitchen, opening the fridge, staring at the three remaining custards. If I eat just one more, there'll be two left and I can take them to share with Benny tomorrow. That won't be so bad. I pick up the fourth ramekin, close the fridge, and eat as slowly as I can to truly appreciate the flavor. Restaurant desserts are easily as big as four of these little things. I finish the fourth crème caramel, set the dish in the sink with the others, and go into the bathroom to brush my teeth, wash my face, moisturize my almost-forty-year-old skin.

I look into the mirror and see the droop in my jawline, the skin looser than I remember, there and over my eyes. And then it hits me that Benny might have cancer, Benny might die. My eyes brighten with moisture in the reflection, my cheeks flush pink with heat. What would I do if he disappeared, too?

I could vomit at my selfishness, at the thought of eating four crème caramels in a row, at the thought of him lying in that hospital all alone, but I don't throw up anymore, not since fifth grade, so I give in and go to the kitchen and eat the remaining two desserts.

"So what's the big deal about fifth grade?" Suzanne Long asked at our session.

"What do you mean?" I knew already that I was never going to tell her anything important. I don't know what made me call her in the first place. I was feeling particularly panicked that day, and out of control, and weakened by the sight of thin people eating ice cream at Frozen Moo. I guess I wondered if I could be like them—an ice cream eater and a smaller body size—even though I didn't want to admit it. Not skinny, just a size less conspicuous and more conducive to dating.

"You keep talking about fifth grade. That was when you decided not to care about your eating or your weight. That was also the last time you threw up. Why was that?"

"I got the flu and puked for four days straight. It was so awful I decided that I'd never throw up again, and I haven't."

"What happens when you get the flu now?"

"I feel like I'm going to die, but I don't throw up," I told her. "That's it."

"That's amazing self-control," she said, not looking all that impressed.

"I'm an amazing person," I said, happy to see that our time was nearly up. I haven't gone back.

It's true that I had the flu in fifth grade and threw up for four days. Somewhere around day two or three, I remember languishing in agony in the living room, goose-bumped and sweaty, feeling myself shrink whenever I'd close my eyes, a frightening feeling like I might disappear. I was struggling to lie in a position on our green floral couch that wouldn't make my head whirl, my stomach lurch. I was trying to watch the images on the television set, the soap opera actors extraordinarily animated about something, but I'd float in and out of their conversations, losing the thread and mixing it up with dream thoughts, with other voices. My mother's voice from the kitchen, saying, "Of course I'm worried about her, silly." Wondering if we were on TV, if I was lying on the fancy leather couch in the living room on the show. "Come on, just for a minute." Mom's voice, laughing softly. "I can sneak out when she's sleeping. She won't die on me, it's just a stomach bug." Trying to shout, from down inside my dream, "No, don't leave me here alone!" The soap opera actors laughing, too, with my mother, telling her that Richmond would be beautiful this time of year, that she should definitely go to the reunion, but she'd better take her husband with her. After all, Genevieve had always wanted to get her clutches on him, and while the cat's away . . .

"Just five minutes, okay? Meet me in front," my mother said, and I snapped to life.

"Where?" I called out, a crying sound in my voice. "Where are you going?"

Her cool hand was on my forehead then, her voice soothing. "Only to get you some ginger ale, Ellie, to help you feel better."

"I don't want ginger ale. It makes me throw up," I moaned. "I don't want you to go to Richmond."

She laughed, and I hated her for sounding so happy when I felt so miserable, for looking so lovely when I knew I looked half dead. "Honey, you're having bad dreams because of the fever. I'm only running down to the market, just for a minute. I'll be right back. Close your eyes and you'll never even know I'm gone."

I closed my eyes as she said and the world spun around me. I began to cry because I knew I would have to run to the bathroom soon. "Mom, I'm going to get sick," I whispered, but I opened my eyes and she was gone. I sat up on the couch, shaky and unsteady, then realized it was far too late to run anywhere. I threw up on the green floral couch, my pajama bottoms, the white shag carpet, my feet. I'd vomited so much by then that it was only yellow bile and the water my mother had forced me to drink, hot and foul all over me, but I knew the smell and the stains would last forever. My mother would hate me.

Even more, I thought, staring at the television set, where a man wearing a wedding ring was locked in a tortured embrace with a beautiful red-haired woman in a gold lamé dress. He whispered, "Genevieve, my darling," and I knew something had changed forever.

I wake in my dark room, sweaty and confused, and look at the red digits on the clock: 3:47. Nausea overwhelms me, and I moan, "Those stupid fake eggs." I lie still, trying to make it go away.

"Most people feel better when they throw up," I can hear Suzanne Long saying.

"Not me," I told her. "It just makes everything worse."

I stand now, grope my way through the dark to the bathroom, leave the light off, sit on the cool tile floor next to the toilet. I hang my head over the rim, the smell of commode water still familiar after all these years. Saliva collects in my mouth and my stomach roils, then stops. After ten minutes I give up, stand at the sink, and splash cold water on my face. It doesn't matter anymore whether I want to vomit or not. My body has been conditioned.

I'm now wide awake and nauseated, so I walk to my computer on the table by the window, hit the button, wait for it to boot up while looking out at the snow-covered trees. When the computer whir has stopped, I check my e-mail. Sure enough, there it is, a message from Stefan. The subject line reads: *Article???*

Should I open it or go back to bed? Would I be able to sleep now, anyway? I double-click the message and read:

> Eleanor,
> As of today, I still have not received the French favorites piece from you.
>   I hope someone has died or the dog ate your computer, because this is unacceptable and puts me in a bind.
> S.

I hit REPLY and type:

> Stefan,
> I'm not sure if he'll die, but my uncle is in the hospital undergoing tests to determine if he has cancer. Good enough?
> E.

Then I hit DELETE and open the article, type in the crème caramel recipe. Just reading "egg substitute" makes me shudder, but I'm feeling mostly better. I go back through the piece, tweaking it here and there. Maybe I'll say I sent it and it bounced back; it wasn't my fault he didn't get it. He's never used such a snippy tone with me, although I know he's capable of it from hearing his stories. He once brought another freelancer to tears, he claims, over the simple issue of paragraphing.

"Professionals shouldn't need to be told to give me lots of white space," he said. "I mean, insert an indent every once in a while, for Christ's sake. I shouldn't have to hold anyone's hand. There are plenty of good freelancers out there, like you, Ms. Samuels."

In the hierarchy of freelancers' transgressions, I'm pretty certain that missed deadlines are far worse than long paragraphs.

chapter six

Near daylight, I've just hit SEND when the heart-thudding sound of metal slamming into metal shatters the morning quiet. I jump to look out the window. Down at the corner, the front end of a mammoth SUV is wrapped around the back of a Hyundai on icy Everett Street. A business-suited woman jumps out of the SUV, waving her arms and screaming at the Hyundai driver, who has her hands to her mouth, shoulders quaking with sobs as she looks not at the accordioned back end of her car, but in front of it. She's hit something or somebody, so I dial 911 on the cordless for the second time in less than twenty-four hours and run down the stairs.

"Nine-one-one, is this an emergency?" a male operator asks as I yank open the glass door and step into the cold. The signal begins to cut out, so I stand, shivering, halfway in and halfway out of the open door.

"There's been an accident on Northwest Everett and Eighteenth."

"Are there any injuries?"

Without injuries, a car wreck doesn't qualify as an emergency? "Anybody hurt?" I yell to the two women.

The crying woman looks over at me and wails, "I think I killed a cat!"

"She thinks she killed a cat," I report to the operator, then add, "but she looks pretty shaken up herself."

"We're following storm-emergency guidelines," he says. "If there aren't any injuries, the drivers can just exchange information and report the accident within twenty-four hours."

"He's alive!" the distraught woman yells, and suddenly a gray blur shoots straight down Eighteenth, bounding through snow and slush, past the neighboring apartment building and up the sidewalk. I start to close the door, but it's all happening too quickly, and he tears past me into my building. "He's alive," I tell the operator, who starts to explain that he's hanging up to handle real emergencies as I click the OFF button.

The Hyundai driver chases the cat, plunging headlong through the snow in a knee-length dress and moon boots. When she reaches the building, she pushes me inside and pulls the door closed. The SUV driver is still standing in the street, arms held to the sky, a stunned look on her face.

"We have to catch him," the Hyundai woman says. "I think he's hurt." She is quick and nervous in her flowered corduroy jumper and puffy red coat, and something tells me she's enjoying the drama. "Did he go up the stairs?"

"I don't know. I don't think so," I say. "But I'll go look." *And sneak into my apartment*, I'm thinking. This is her problem, not mine.

She busies herself looking under the stairwell as I head up the stairs. I'm opening my door when she yells, "Here he comes!" The same blur I saw before comes barreling straight for me, then veers left through my door.

"Oh, for God's sake," I mutter, then to her as she crests the stairs, "He's in here somewhere. And he doesn't appear to be too terribly hurt. He runs like the Tasmanian Devil."

"We have to find him," she says, pushing past me into the apartment.

Downstairs the SUV driver has now come inside and is shouting, "Excuse me? We're blocking traffic out there, you know! We can't just leave these cars in the middle of the freaking road!"

"Listen," I say to the woman. "She's right. You need to go deal with the accident. I'll find the cat, and you can take him with you, okay? You'll come back for him?"

She looks annoyed to leave the searching to me, but she nods and heads back outside.

"Kitty?" I call, looking under the table, around the corner into the kitchen. "Where are you? Don't be scared." Right. A car's just hit you, you have a wild woman on your tail, and you're not supposed to be afraid. "It's okay, kitty. You can come out. She's gone." I get down on my hands and knees to peer under the couch, the chair, the bookshelves. Nothing. In the bedroom I look under the bed, the dresser, inside the closet. The bathroom is tiny; a quick glance and I know he's not there, either. I dig through a pile of dirty clothes on the floor, look behind and under everything again.

Minutes later, a worried voice calls through the open front door: "Did you find him?"

"He must have run back out," I say, walking to the living room. "He's not in here." The Hyundai woman now has a man with her. He's wearing brown coveralls and a baseball cap with ED'S TOWING in Old English block letters on the front. His boots are leaving gray puddles on my floor.

"What am I going to do? They're towing my car and I have to go with them," the woman says.

The man affirms this with a nod. "Use your facilities?" he says, and I don't know how to say no, so I point toward the bathroom and watch as he leaves a trail of dirty slush across the floor.

To the woman I say, "The cat seems to be fine. He probably lives around here somewhere, and he'll find his way back home, right? I wouldn't worry about it."

"You'll keep an eye out for him? He might still be in the building somewhere. Can I give you my phone number? Will you let me know if you find him?"

Anything to make her go away, so I take the business card she offers me, which reads: ALICE DESMAY, CARING HOME CARE. She cares a little too much, I'd say, but I assure her I'll call if the cat turns up. The toilet flushes, and the tow truck driver walks out, zipping up his coveralls.

"Let's boogie," he says to Alice, and I imagine the two of them disco-dancing all the way down the steps.

• • •

At eight a.m. I call the hospital and ask how Benny's doing. The nurse on his floor says, "He's been up for hours. I'll transfer you." Then it's Benny, and he sounds so much like himself that I relax, let myself believe that everything might be okay after all. He says he's just about to go down for the procedure, and why don't I come for a visit sometime this afternoon?

"Great," I say. "I was there last night, but—"

"I know you were, honey," he says. "My eyesight's fine. It's just my guts that are playing tricks on me."

"You saw me?"

"We sat here and talked about that party your mother's throwing. Don't you remember?"

"Of course I do," I say. The saliva thickens in the back of my throat. "I just wanted to see if you did."

"Hey, and if you got any more of those oatmeal cookies around, they wouldn't go astray."

"You got it. Nuts, no raisins, right?" I say, trying not to sound as panicked as I feel.

When we hang up, I call the nurse back. "He's not just disoriented," I tell her. "He's hallucinating." She promises to tell the doctor as soon as he makes his rounds.

The nausea comes back full force. Again, I head for the bathroom to sit on the tile floor, but the tow truck driver has left the seat up, and the slush from his boots has melted into a gray puddle. I clean the floor, scrub the toilet. By then I don't feel queasy anymore, just clammy and exhausted, so I head back to bed and crawl beneath the covers. Something moves beneath my pillow, and I jump up.

Nestled between my headboard and pillow is a comfortable-looking gray-striped cat. Lazily, he opens his pea green eyes to give me a meaningful look, then puts his chin against his paws and goes back to sleep.

"Oh, please," I say. "What next?" I sigh and think for a moment about what to do. He does look peaceful, and I can't work up the energy to carry him all the way downstairs to throw him outside. "Okay, just until I get up," I say, shoving him to the other side of the bed. "And then you're going back outside so you can find your way home."

I wake later to find him snuggling up to Pauncho, kneading me like dough with his paws and purring with the gusto of a tiny engine.

The cat rubs against my bare legs as I stand at the bathroom mirror, putting on super-duper antiaging miracle moisturizer that costs thirty-nine dollars per jar, wondering if they price it that way to remind their demographic that forty is just around the corner. "You do realize that as soon as I'm dressed you're out of here, right?" I say. The cat looks up at me with those mesmerizing green eyes. I swear he winks, and I'm wondering what would be so bad about having a cat around the place.

"It's supposed to warm up today," I say to fortify myself. "I'm going to dig my car out to go to the hospital, and you're going back to your real people. They're probably worried to death about you." He jumps from the floor to the toilet, then steps nimbly into the sink and sniffs the faucet. He settles into the smooth round of the porcelain as if it were his special bed and lifts his front leg to lick his decidedly pronounced ribs. I look closer and see he's not just preening as I am. He's nursing a three-inch gash that looks fresh and is surrounded by puffy skin. "I killed a cat," I hear the Hyundai woman say, thinking I should call her. This is her problem, after all. But first this cat needs something to eat, he's so skinny, so I walk toward the kitchen, saying, "Come on, buddy. Let's get you some fake cream." He jumps down and trots behind me as if we've been doing this together every day for years.

After rescuing my car and parking it in front of my building, I dial the number on the Hyundai woman's card and get her machine. "Hellooo," her syrupy recording says, "you've reached Caring Home Care, and this is Alice, your personal home-care provider. I must be out caring for another client. If you'd care to leave a message . . ."

What I'd care to do is give her message a good edit, but I leave a terse reply telling her I've found the cat, he's hurt after all, and I guess I'll have to take him to the vet since she's not around.

In the phone book I find a vet just a few blocks away, on the way to the hospital. I pick up the cat, careful not to get too close to his wound, and he lies placidly in my arms, purring. "Okay, buddy, you better not get used to this," I tell him as I carry him outside through the melting snow and settle him on the passenger's seat. After his wild romp this morning, he seems to be the mellowest cat I've ever seen, completely comfortable and a perfect gentleman in the car.

At the vet's office, the neohippie girl behind the counter says, "Poor baby, hit by a car. You wouldn't believe how many car-accident patients we've had since the storm." She scratches his ears, revving his purr engine to maximum horsepower. "What's her name?" she asks. The smell of wet dog, antiseptic, and patchouli surrounds us.

"I don't know. He's a stray," I tell her. "I've been calling him buddy. I just assumed he was male."

"Well, let's take a peek," she says, and rolls up a hind leg. "I'd say you have a little girl on your hands, but I think Buddy is a sweet name for her." She writes "Buddy" under "Name of pet," then looks at me when she gets to "Name of owner." Her pen hovers over the paper. "And your name?"

"Um, Alice Desmay," I say. "Listen, I can't stay for the examination. I'm on my way to the hospital to see someone."

"Is there a number we can reach you at? A cell?" She's written "Dismay" on the form, and I start to panic.

Even though I've memorized Alice's number, I give her my cell number. "You may have to leave a message, though, because I have to turn my phone off everywhere but in the waiting room," I say.

"No problem, Ms. Dismay," she says, smiling, reaching for the cat. "We'll take good care of little Buddy for you."

It makes no sense at all, but I am torn at leaving the cat behind, even though he—she—seems to be happy to be here. She looks at me for a long moment, then winks one of her pea green eyes.

"Sorry to be a pain," I say, "but could you change the name on the form?"

"Did you think of a better one?" She snuggles the cat to her cheek.

"No, I mean my name. It's Eleanor Samuels."

"No problem," she says like it happens all the time, and sets Buddy on the counter so she can make the correction.

• • •

I am amazed at how quickly snow can melt. It's barely an inch or two deep where not cleared, and the streets are shiny black with runoff. The only evidence of how much damage the storm wrought still lies beneath the snow: frozen spring flowers that will never recover. Whether or not they'll be back next year is anyone's guess.

On the drive south to the hospital, I dig my cell phone out of my purse, scroll through the directory, looking down every few seconds until I get to Anne's home number. I hit CALL and prepare to leave a message. It's still midafternoon in Boston; she'll be at the office writing torts or whatever it is she does all day.

"Hello?" Anne says, sounding wary and uncharacteristically unprofessional.

"I was going to leave you a message. I'm on my way to see Benny now, and we should know more from a test he had this morning. A really creepy one, actually. They stick this thing all the way down his throat and take some of his pancreas. God." I shudder thinking about it. "What are you doing home?"

"I take it you don't watch CNN," she says.

"What? What happened?" I picture bombs, falling buildings, looting in the streets of Boston.

She sighs long and hard. "Shit," she says, sounding angry. "My firm's in trouble, meaning I'm in trouble. Haven't you heard about the Dynoco case?"

"The gas station?"

"The oil company. Our biggest client. They're suing us."

"But why are *you* in trouble?"

"I'm their chief counsel, and I'm a partner. The media wants to eat me alive." She sighs again. "You always hear about these things, but you never think. . . . Anyway, I'll be hanging around home for a while, laying low. I'm trying to get some paperwork in order."

"You mean you're doctoring it?" I ask.

"God, Eleanor, you watch too much TV. Of course not. Whose side are you on?"

I don't really know, without knowing the facts, but I decide to keep my mouth shut.

I've always vacillated between feeling that I know Anne utterly and wondering if I know her at all. She is the female version of Dad: serious as pencil lead, tall and straight and all business. She has his gray eyes, his not-really-a-color sandy hair. She lived to please him as a kid, showing him her aced math tests and asking him to help her build a weather station in the backyard when she was twelve. I'd watch them out there together, bent over the picnic table, and wonder how she did it, how she got him to come up out of the basement on a Saturday and talk to her about gauges and turbines, rainfall and barometric pressure. It seemed so intimate.

She even liked the old music he listened to. Christine and I would make gagging noises behind Dad's back when he'd put one of his records on the stereo in the living room, but Anne would ignore us, close her eyes, and nod along to Tony Bennett or Ella Fitzgerald.

When our parents argued, she'd turn stony. She didn't care, she'd say, and flop down on her bed with a *Reader's Digest* condensed book or one of Dad's *Popular Science* magazines. She read everything and she read all the time, except when she was tossing some sarcastic comment my way about my obsession with our Mystery Date game or my tendency to cry whenever Mom and Dad started yelling.

She is impenetrable if predictable, in perfect control of every aspect of her life.

Until now, it seems.

At the hospital, I step into an elevator that smells like a freshly opened box of Band-Aids. Before the doors can close, a young couple with a child in a stroller shoves through, apologizing, and then an older woman in a white lab coat and prim pumps. Passengers keep loading on until finally the alarm sounds and a trio of a sheepish teenagers steps off, and we are on our way. At my stop I say, "Excuse me," and squeeze past a large, dark-skinned family heading for the oncology floor. I shudder and make my way past the nurses' station to Benny's room. The other bed that was empty last night is occupied by an elderly man who is staring out the window, and Benny's bed is vacant.

Back out at the nurses' station I ask a ponytailed woman where

Benny Sloan might be. "Just a sec," she says, then calls over a divider, "Benny's yours, isn't he, Jess?"

A bright female face pops out from the divider, smiles at me. "You looking for Benny?" She has one of those perky blond bobs that swings when she tilts her head, which I can already see she does a lot.

I nod and she says, "What a guy! We just love having him on our floor."

"Mm hmm," I say, trying not to tap my fingers on the counter.

"He just went for his stent procedure about fifteen minutes ago," she says. "It'll probably be at least an hour."

"Really?" I look at my watch even though I know what time it is. "I thought that was supposed to be this morning. I would have come and visited earlier if I'd known he was just going to be sitting in his room." I want to deflect this guilt outward, to make this happy nurse feel as awful as I do.

"Oh, he was okay," she says. "We kept him company, and he had another visitor."

"Who?"

She shrugs. "I think she might still be in the waiting room."

I turn without replying and walk quickly back the way I came, thinking the miraculous has happened and my mother has broken her vow of silence. I stop suddenly in the doorway to the small waiting room, gazing instead upon the miracle I should have expected.

"Hi, honey," Yolanda says, looking up from a magazine. The long hair she always kept wound in a braid on the back of her head has been cut short, but otherwise she is the same, from her soft mocha-colored eyes to her silver-ringed fingers and wrists. She pats the seat beside her, bangles chiming the way they always have, and says, "I was wondering when you'd get here."

After Benny married Yolanda, we didn't see them for a long time. When I asked Mom why, she gave me a look that made me never ask again.

Dad quit taking his business trips. Mom still threw her parties, inviting neighbors, people from her new life-drawing class, but not Benny. She still seemed the perfect hostess at these occasions, but it was as if she were forcing it, a not-very-good actress playing the role. Her makeup would be too thick around her eyes, the beer would be warm, she'd lose track of conversations.

One winter evening she served dessert to a group of Dad's coworkers and their wives, using our new microwave oven to warm the brownies she'd baked from a mix earlier in the day. They smelled delicious beneath melting vanilla ice cream as she passed plates around the dining room table.

Never shy about digging in, I stuck my fork down through the soft ice cream, hoping to create the perfect bite with just the right balance of warm, chewy chocolate and creamy vanilla. The fork stopped dead at the top of the brownie, though, no matter how hard I pushed. I looked around and saw my sisters and our dinner guests all doing the same thing, a mixture of confusion and determination on their faces.

Oblivious, my mother sipped her coffee, talking with the woman next to her about drawing the female form in all its glory. The woman looked appalled, but it wasn't apparent if it was the word "nude" or the rock-hard status of her dessert that caused it.

I wasn't going to say anything. I scooped ice cream into my mouth before it could all melt into a puddle on the plate. Dad looked nonplussed and set down his fork. Christine managed to get her fork partway into her brownie and picked it up, turning it over like a lollipop.

Aghast, Mom barked, "Christine!"

"But it's too hard to cut," she said, setting it back down and crossing her arms over her chest to pout. She was allowed to get away with such behavior, even though Anne or I would have been sent from the table for it.

Mom picked up her fork, tried to cut her brownie with the edge of it, then tucked her lips together and set her fork down. "They were just fine when I cut them five minutes ago," she said.

The woman next to her said, "How long did you heat them in the microwave, dear?"

"Just the five minutes," Mom said, annoyed to be proven imperfect in front of company. In front of anyone.

The women tittered around the table, and Mom set her lips tight.

"Oh, don't worry, Bebe," the woman said. "We've all made the same mistake. I'll never get used to those darned contraptions. They're just so powerful. You probably only needed a minute or so." The other women nodded, giving Mom sympathetic smiles, but she would not meet their eyes. She was silent the rest of the night.

One evening not long after, Mom announced that she was inviting Benny and Yolanda over the following weekend. Dad gave her a look. I could almost feel his body slump against his chair.

"There just aren't that many people I can relate to in this town, Richard," she said before he could utter a word. "You know that. No one here cares about art, music, poetry."

Dad shook his head, rolled his eyes, but remained silent. That night after we'd gone to bed, though, I heard their loud voices in the kitchen.

I sneaked out of my room and sat on the stairs, the carpet cool and scratchy beneath my bare calves and feet.

"I can't believe you're throwing it in my face," Dad said, voice angry but anguished in a way I didn't recognize.

"There's nothing to throw, Richard. I've told you that."

"For Christ's sake. You can't expect me to live in this fantasy world of yours."

It was quiet then except for a long sigh, my mother blowing her nose.

"Fine," Dad finally said, "we'll do this your way. But only for the sake of the girls."

A chair scraped, my father's oxfords hit the linoleum. I crept quickly back to bed, heart beating as if I'd witnessed a murder and couldn't tell anyone about it. I wanted to talk to Anne, to ask her what she thought it meant—what was Mom's fantasy world, what was Dad doing for our sakes—but I knew I shouldn't. Instead, I added it to the scrap heap of secrets I'd probably never figure out.

When Benny arrived with Yolanda the next Saturday night, Anne and I held back, but Christine ran and jumped into his arms. He loudly smooched her cheek, and we realized it was the same old Benny. Yolanda stood behind him, smiling nervously. I was struck by how much she looked like my mother—a fuller, younger, darker version—but I'd never dare mention it. She'd brought my sisters and me hand-crocheted vests in vibrant colors, yellow and turquoise and fiery red. Mom declared them very hip, and took Yolanda by the arm into the kitchen.

I was torn between wanting to follow them and going into the front room with Dad and Benny. My heart beat with trepidation at the thought of either of those two strange couplings alone. I toed the carpet for a while in the hallway between the two rooms, trying to keep up with both conversations at the same time. Finally, laughter drifted from the kitchen along with the sound of pots and pans banging. I decided the women were fine and drifted toward the front room.

The two men sat stiffly opposite each other, Benny on the couch and Dad in his chair with his hands planted firmly on his thighs, as if at any moment he might launch from his seat. Benny looked more casual, with his arm across the back of the couch, but the muscles in his jaw jerked once or twice. Neither of them noticed me to the side of the doorway.

"I just hope we can put the past behind us, is all," Benny was saying, stroking the couch back, his wedding ring shiny on his finger.

"How do you propose I do that?" Dad asked, his knuckles almost white from his clenched grip on his legs. I looked at his hands to see if he wore a wedding ring; I'd never noticed before that he didn't.

"Well, I don't rightly know, Richard." Benny's voice changed, taking on a steely edge. "But I'm prepared to try, for everyone's sake." He must have seen me then, because his friendly voice came back. "Like Ellie here." He patted the couch beside him, his slow, easy grin coming back. I shuffled past my dad, feeling like a traitor, but pleased to have been noticed and summoned.

Dad stood then and said, "Believe I'll catch the Blazers game in the family room. Anyone else?" I knew this signaled that everything was okay, at least for the moment, and I exhaled; I hadn't realized I'd been holding my breath.

"Nah, I'll just catch up awhile with little Miss Eleanor Roosevelt." Benny winked at me, and when I looked back toward Dad's chair, he was gone.

From that time on, Uncle Benny and Aunt Yolanda were just part of the infrastructure. They never had children of their own, though they were desperate to, and eventually we sewed them into the seams of our family. Any holiday party or family celebration was incomplete without them. Mom and Yolanda would perform an almost syncopated dance around the kitchen, checking steaming casseroles, stirring pots, and smoothing back errant strands of hair with the crooks of their arms. They seemed like sisters, the way they chatted and rolled their eyes at private jokes, and Aunt Yolanda became an even closer confidante than our mother as we grew older, especially when it came to advice about pimples, friends. Boys. We could tell her anything and never suffer the repercussions we would have had we told Mom.

Benny usually played cards and board games with my sisters and me while Dad read the paper or watched television. Anne, Christine, Benny, and I made a perfect foursome until Anne decided she was too grown-up and sophisticated to play with us.

I asked Dad to join in a game of Monopoly one night when Anne refused to participate. He lowered his newspaper and raised his eyes to a point above my head. "Oh, I don't think you need me, do you?" he said, but it didn't seem he was talking to me. I turned to see Uncle Benny behind me, returning Dad's stare just as coldly. I felt clammy with hurt and embarrassment as Dad left the room, newspaper tightly tucked underneath his arm.

Uncle Benny sighed and patted my shoulder. "It's okay, kiddo," he said, then hugged me to his side. He smelled like cloves and soap. "We'll be all right without him."

The pieces clicked neatly into place, though they'd been that way in my heart since I first met Benny that long-ago summer night. I knew never to talk of it, of my shifting alliances, but I felt better loved under Benny's and Yolanda's affectionate gazes than I ever had before.

chapter seven

So much can change in just three days, although they are long, gray days spent waiting. I'd give anything for sunshine—even just a sun break, Portland-speak for those rare glimpses of sun between clouds. The poststorm reprieve didn't last long, and now it's back to the usual spring routine: mist, drizzle, sprinkles, showers, rain, and flat-out downpours. Oregonians have nearly as many names for rain as Inuits do for snow.

I keep busy when I'm visiting Benny, which is most of the time, rearranging his cards and flowers, filling his water pitcher, clicking through the channels on the television mounted high on the wall in front of his bed, trying to find him something decent to watch. We don't talk about what the future may hold, just the safe topics of his current pain level, the drugs keeping it at bay, and our usual everyday natterings. He's worried about his house, although I check on it every day. "The stove is off," I try to convince him, "and I've set the timer on the light in the living room," but sometimes he forgets and asks again. His confusion comes and goes, and they've scheduled another scan, this time for his head.

Aunt Yolanda is my aunt again, although she still plays it cool with Benny, visiting him only briefly each day. She avoids his eyes, which tear up when he sees her. Yesterday, I watched as she smoothed his blanket where he'd rumpled it, then withdrew her hand quickly, as if she suddenly realized what she was doing and found even that small intimacy too painful.

We no longer watch CNN in Benny's room. Anne has been reduced to a media villain, five seconds of videotape shown over and over, a late-night talk show joke. She's laying so low she doesn't even answer the phone.

Christine, who calls Benny every day, is considering the option of single parenthood. Reid apparently threw a tantrum over the fact that she would not choose him over their baby, coloring his arguments with his whiny and extreme eco-liberalism. "How can we bring a child into this world?" he said. "This self-destructing, polluted, out-of-control world?"

"How can you not?" I ask her this morning on the phone. I'm at home reading the Sunday *Oregonian* and watching Buddy play on the rug, batting a pencil around like it's a dead snake with serious rigor mortis, the shaved patch on her chest pink and tender beneath the stitches. I'm trying not to think about what still looms ahead. At one o'clock today, Benny, Yolanda, and I will meet with the doctors about the results of his biopsy.

"They'd have told us immediately if it was good news, don't you think?" I ask Christine. Quietly, I eat another chocolate chip cookie, holding the mouthpiece away from my face while I chew.

"Maybe you should just not think about it until the meeting."

I snort so hard I inhale crumbs into my windpipe, and cough for a full minute before I can speak again. "I'm sorry," I tell her finally, "but isn't that like saying maybe you shouldn't think about the baby until it's born?"

"No," she says, "I don't think it is."

We're quiet for a moment, then I say, "Did I tell you I have a cat?"

"Really?" Christine says, sounding skeptical.

We aren't exactly pet people in our family. We once had a gerbil that died after less than twenty-four hours under our care. Looking back, I doubt it was our fault. Shopping mall pet stores are breeding grounds for disease, but it shook our confidence and bolstered Dad's arguments against our desire for something warm and cuddly in our lives. We never asked for another pet.

It was Christine, in fact, who insisted upon a proper burial for our still-unnamed gerbil, which meant squatting in late-winter rain, digging mud with soupspoons we'd pilfered from the utensils drawer in the kitchen while Mom chatted on the phone in her bedroom. After school, Christine had rescued the dead animal from the trash, where Dad had deposited it the night before, and placed it in her school pencil box, surrounded by pink toilet paper.

When the hole kept puddling with rain, Anne and I gave up. "Come on, Christine," we begged. "It's just a gerbil."

She couldn't have been more than seven or eight, but she was fiercely determined to do the right thing by this creature, and long after Anne and I had retreated to our bedroom, where we kept an eye on her through the window, she worked the ground until the hole was big enough to hold the box; it bobbed and floated as she spooned wet earth back over it. Then we saw her stand and clasp her hands in front of her, speaking solemn words that only she could hear, periodically stomping at the pile of mud that kept rising against her good school shoes.

It's still early after Christine hangs up, only nine thirty, so I refocus and try to get a jump on what surely will be a tough workweek. I'm avoiding an e-mail from Stefan titled *RE: Re: Article???* Instead, I turn my attention to a new assignment from *American Family*: "Home Cooking: The Comforts of Old Family Favorites."

Easy. Baked macaroni and cheese with crunchy bread crumbs on top; simple mashed potatoes with no garlic and lots of cream and butter; meatloaf with sage and a sweet tomato sauce topping. Not that I experienced these things in my house growing up, but these are the foods everyone thinks of as old family favorites, only improved. If nothing else, my job is to create a dreamlike state for readers in which they feel that everything will be all right if only they find just the right recipe to bring their kids back to the table, seduce their husbands into loving them again, make their friends and neighbors envious.

I'm tapping my keyboard, thinking, *what else?*, when it hits me like a soft thud in the chest. I want to write about my family's favorites, the strange foods that comforted us in tense moments around the dinner table. Mom's Midwestern "hot dish": layers of browned hamburger, canned vegetable soup, canned sliced potatoes, topped with canned cream of mushroom soup. I haven't tasted it in years. Her lime Jell-O salad with cottage cheese, walnuts, and canned pineapple; her potato salad with French dressing instead of mayo.

I have a craving, too, for Dad's grilling marinade. "Shecret Shauce" he called it in those rare moments of levity when he'd perform the one culinary task he was willing to do. I'd lean shyly against the counter and watch as he poured ingredients into a rectangular cake pan. Vegetable oil, soy sauce, garlic powder, salt and pepper, and then he'd finish it off with the secret ingredient: a can of fruit cocktail. Somehow the sweetness of the syrup was perfect against the salty soy and the biting garlic. Everything he cooked on the grill, save hamburgers and hot dogs, first bathed in this marinade overnight in the refrigerator. Rump roasts, pork chops, chicken legs all seemed more exotic this way, and dinner guests raved at Dad's genius on the grill. They were never the wiser to the secret of his sauce because the fruit bits had been safely washed into the garbage disposal.

Surely most people have these odd family foods. I could do some research, make the article something interesting instead of rehashing what everyone expects. Show a true slice of Americana instead of the safe one.

I click to my e-mail program to write the editor about it, and Stefan's e-mail blinks back at me.

"Oh, for God's sake," I mutter, then click it open.

> Eleanor,
> If your article were not perfect I might be tempted to berate you for your tardiness, firstly, and secondly, your brazen attempt to cover it up. What is the world coming to when a sweet young thing such as Eleanor Samuels of Portland, Oregon, heretofore my best freelancer, resorts to such tomfoolery? Straighten up and fly right, bucko. I have the biggest assignment of your career sitting on my desk. It will take you to the next level. Are you up for the challenge?
> S.

"No," I say automatically, but my curiosity gets the better of me and I hit REPLY.

> Stefan,
> Firstly, I find it pretentious when people enumerate items of discussion. Secondly, you would have been even snottier had I not at least tried to pretend that I sent the article on time. Thirdly (this is why I hate enumeration), of course my article is perfect. And lastly, don't tease me, for God's sake. Just tell me what the stupid assignment is.
> E.

I sigh and hit DELETE, then begin a new reply:

> Stefan,
> Glad you liked the article. Please send information about the new assignment.
> E.

My affection for him is dimming rapidly.

At ten till one, I'm walking down the hospital corridor toward Room 632, carrying a pan of cream cheese–frosted spice cake, one of Benny's favorites. A few steps from the door I hear voices, and stop, edge closer. A monotone male voice is saying, "I've been working on a protocol for cases such as Mr. Sloan's, and we're interested in starting him on it right away. With his approval, of course."

Benny coughs. Yolanda—I can tell it is Yolanda somehow—sniffles, blows her nose.

I lean against the wall, try to breathe, the cake pan trembling in my hands. Why did I think this would be an occasion for a cake? I straighten up and walk into the room, depositing the pan as quickly as I can on a shelf near the door.

"Well, hello," I say, acting surprised. "You're all here early."

The doctor, lumpy shaped and stringy haired, avoids my eyes, and I avoid Benny's. Yolanda looks at me and tries to smile. "Hi, honey. Dr. Krall was just telling us about the test results." She motions for me to come stand by her, and takes my arm in hers. "This is our niece Eleanor. Would you mind starting over?"

He wheezes a sigh and looks up from beneath heavily lidded eyes. I miss Dr. Scary.

"What I was explaining to Mr. and Mrs. Sloan was that we believe the initial mass to be inoperable. In most cases we prescribe—"

"Wait a minute," I say, hating him. "What are you even talking about? Initial mass? Do you mean his pancreas? Was it . . ."

I falter, swallowing hard, and Yolanda squeezes my arm. "Yes, honey," she says, "it was. And they think it spread to . . . to his . . ." Now she wavers and trembles, crying silently beside me.

Benny stares at the floor, touching his head gingerly, as if feeling for the tumors I already know are there. He looks like he's pondering something from the ordinary world—what socks to wear, what to eat for breakfast.

"But how can it be inoperable?" I say, arguing so I don't cry, too, so I don't break down in front of Benny. "Why can't you just cut it out?"

Dr. Krall clears his throat. "It would seem Mr. Sloan's cancer is quite advanced," he begins, but I cut him off again.

"It would seem? Do you not know? Do we need more tests?"

"Honey," Yolanda says, and I know I am being terrible, I know I'm making it worse, but this is ridiculous, unfathomable. How can someone have the flu one day, and less than a week later have inoperable cancer?

The doctor seems unfazed by my behavior. "I was just starting to tell your aunt and uncle about a new trial—"

"Experimental?" I say. "You want him to be a guinea pig?"

Benny clears his throat, and I finally look at him. "That's all they got, honey," he says. His eyes are red-rimmed, his skin still sallow. His combover is now waving warily on top of his head and I want to smooth it back down. I want to lather his face and shave off the stubble he'd never wear in public in any other situation. I want to cover him with the blanket, tuck him in like a child, shut off the lights and shoo everyone from the room so he can get some rest, so his body can heal. Uncle Benny is steel; there's no way something as obscure and formerly inconsequential as a pancreas can take him down. This doctor knows nothing.

"So, how long, Doc?" Benny's asking, and the doctor's sighing, shaking his head.

"I hate that question," he says, and attempts a smile meant to look sympathetic. "We've had one patient on this protocol beat the one-year mark."

Yolanda gasps, and Benny closes his eyes, and I turn and grab the stupid cake pan so no one will see how idiotic I was. I stride quickly down the hall past a gowned elderly woman walking an IV stand, past the ponytailed nurse, the waiting room, the nurses' station, to the elevator. It is just opening and I force my way onto it, past a group of exiting doctors. At the lobby I run toward the front doors, push out into cool gray mist and birds chirping. In my car I throw the cake pan onto the passenger's seat, squeal from the garage out onto the busy street choked with the remains of lunchtime traffic. I am hungry, so hungry, and I yank the cake pan closer to me on the seat, toss off the aluminum foil, dig a chunk out with my fingers. I stuff it into my mouth and lick frosting and crumbs from my fingers. I've barely swallowed it when I am digging again, maneuvering with one hand through the bunched-up traffic, looking for an opening to break free and race ahead. The drizzle turns to hard rain and I hit the wipers, then dig harder at the cake, feel the icing jam under my fingernails. I pull a larger piece free. I don't look into the windows of the cars surrounding me. I know they are staring at me— thinking, *What a pig. How can she do that to herself? Does she have no self-control?*—but it doesn't matter what they think. I've nearly cleared the contents of the 13 inch × 9 inch pan when suddenly I choke on a glob of frosting, the sugar burning like acid in my esophagus. My eyes water, my chest and throat contract. I cannot breathe. I'm making this horrifying sound—part gasp, part scream—and I can hardly see to drive, barely keep a grip on the wheel. I force myself to cough, hard, painfully, trying to expel the stupid frosting and draw enough air into my lungs so that I don't black out and crash. So that I don't die alone with an empty cake pan at my side, fingers sticky with the evidence.

• • •

At home, I strip off my clothes, scrub myself pink in the shower. Then I look into the mirror, although I have to force myself to. My eyes are raw and glassy, my hair hangs in long, wet strings around my face, but I don't look any different. I don't look like I just ate an entire cake. I don't look like someone who would run out on someone dying of cancer.

A sob erupts from my gut and I sink to my knees on hard hexagonal tiles, feel their corners dig into my flesh at the bones, the grit of dirt on the floor under my hands. I crawl to the toilet, push up the seat, and steel myself. Then I open my mouth, put my index finger inside, tentatively at first. When nothing happens, I shove it farther back until I am gagging, choking for air, but not throwing up.

"Come on," I sob, trying again with my middle finger, maybe it's long enough, but I just choke and sputter, cough nothing but air and spit and snot into the toilet.

Benny is lying in his darkened room when I return, watching an *Andy Griffith* rerun. His roommate appears to have gone home.

I take off my raincoat, shake the mist from it. He doesn't see me in the doorway or notice as I approach his bed. His eyes are fixed to the screen, his face illuminated in the gray-blue glow of the television. He is clean-shaven, his hair combed, and his hands rest lightly on top of the blankets. His wedding ring still shines from the third finger of his left hand.

"Benny," I whisper so I don't startle him, but he doesn't turn his head. "Uncle Benny," I say a little louder.

He turns and looks at me, eyes vacant. He stares for a moment, then turns back to the television.

"Please don't be mad at me," I say, pulling a chair to his bed. "I'm sorry." If I were a hand holder, I'd take his hand in mine, squeeze the hard, dry palm, the crinkled skin on top, to feel the warmth of him. Instead, I lay my arm next to his, the sheet soft and cool.

We sit this way for a long time, watching Barney's apoplectic gyrations, Andy's calm demeanor as they do the relationship dance with their respective girlfriends.

"Always had a soft spot for Thelma Lou," Benny says, and reaches over to squeeze my hand. "Even though she's not nearly as pretty as you."

I laugh, so relieved I actually feel blood course through my body, as thought it's been waiting until this moment to nourish me.

"Ah, Bebe," he says, "why did we never do this together? Just sit and watch the damn TV?" His face buckles and he begins to cry.

I swallow, then move to sit beside him on the bed, wrap my arm around his shoulders. "I don't know, Ben, but we can now."

At home, there's a note taped to the door:

You didn't leave your phone number. I'd be happy to take care of the cat from here on out, including the vet bills. Please call me and let me know when I can come and get it.

Alice Desmay

I ball up the note and stick it in my pocket.

The kitty lets me pick her up and hug her when I come through the door. After a few moments, though, she struggles, so I put her down and walk to my computer. There's no e-mail about the assignment yet from Stefan. I sit and choose "compose new e-mail" from the menu, then type:

Dear Stefan,
I know it's no excuse, but my uncle, my favorite uncle, is in the hospital. He is dying of cancer and I am a complete mess. I probably shouldn't take on a big assignment right now, although you know I'd love to. I am sorry my article was late, and that I lied to you about it. Please don't hate me.
Yours,
E.

I hit SEND, then stare at the screen. I have no energy to undress, to get ready for bed, to turn on the television, to eat. I am a big, empty hole that nothing can fill. I can't even cry.

Buddy jumps into my lap, purring. "Do you need some food?" I ask her, scratching her ears. "Am I a neglectful mommy?"

I pick her up and carry her into the kitchen. "How about some cream?" I say, setting her on the floor, getting out a bowl, opening the fridge. I pour it for her and she prances like a pony, as happy as a living being can be, it seems. "Good for you," I say, then walk back to the computer to shut it down for the night.

A new message has popped into my in-box. It's from Stefan. He's reading my e-mail on a Sunday night. I click it and read:

> Oh, Ellie.

I gasp that he's used my nickname.

> Can I be any more of a cad? Please don't worry about miss-ing the deadline, or the new article. I will hold it for you un-til you're ready. I had you especially in mind for it, and no one else will do. I lost my mother to breast cancer six years ago, and I know what you must be going through.
> Love,

Love!

> Stefan

I read and reread his e-mail until I have it memorized. Then I shut down the computer, turn out all the lights, and crawl into bed fully clothed, listening to the steady rain tap the windows as I wait for sleep.

Part 2

Home Cooking: The Comforts of Old Family Favorites
9 Nostalgic Recipes You'll Cherish

BY ELEANOR SAMUELS

What do the words "meat loaf and mashed potatoes" or "chicken soup" have to do with love? Everything, according to psychologist and family therapist Nancy P. Levy.

"Our earliest experiences of love include food, starting with mother's milk," she says, adding, "but it depends on your own family and traditions. Those words could be 'soba noodles and pork balls,' or 'potato latkes.' Every family has its own comfort foods."

After a quick poll around the *American Family* office, the list of family-inspired comfort foods is varied and surprising: everything from apple strudel to zabaglione, and a few wacky Jell-O salads in between.

Clichéd. Trite. Drivel. If only someone had actually said "zabaglione." While my editor thought it might be interesting to explore some unusual family favorites, she didn't exactly give me license to write the article I wanted to, which now just sounds like a bad idea, anyway. What the hell does food have to do with anything? It isn't love or life or a solution to anything. Why have I spent my professional life so devoted to it? And who am I kidding when I say "professional life"?

To hell with food and its false love, its deception. It lures you in, says, "I'll make you feel better, I'll be there for you." And then it drives everyone else away.

chapter eight

I am developing a strange and ugly new vocabulary.

Endoscopic retrograde cholangio-pancreatography: the procedure they did on Benny to relieve the jaundice and secure his diagnosis. Acinar cell carcinoma: the name of his rare pancreatic cancer, which is always terminal. Always. And so these words become necessary: "palliative," "quality of life," "hospice."

The tumor on Benny's pancreas is the size of a grapefruit (why must they measure in food?) and he has "involvement" in the liver. This cancer seldom metastasizes to the brain, but Benny has always been a rare bird. His brain is riddled with small masses, all less than a centimeter in diameter. Raspberries, maybe? Blueberries? Dr. Krall didn't say when I finally got the nerve to call him yesterday afternoon. In his wheezy, plodding voice he recited what sounded like an AMA report on the state of Benny's disease, sparing me nothing, but after a while I loosened up, encouraged him to tell me more. Each new medical term, each new quantifiable factoid (stage IVB is the end of the line for how advanced a cancer can be) filled the space in my head that had previously been littered with panic, terror, and an unspeakable sadness somewhere at the outer edges, lying in wait. Scientific words and facts feel far more purposeful and concrete, weighty and bulky in a way that is comforting.

Today, just five days after his diagnosis, Benny started Dr. Krall's experimental course of chemotherapy, which, of course, is strictly to relieve his symptoms. For a while. He's also taking a steroid to shrink the brain metastases. Temporarily.

This morning, when I ask the perky-bobbed nurse *how* temporarily, whispering so Benny doesn't hear, she waits to answer until she is hovered over his bed, checking his vitals. "I'll be honest—it won't feel nearly long enough, but at least you'll have your uncle back for a while. Enjoy it. Make good use of the time."

I look to see how he's taking such frankness. He seems unfazed, watching *The View* and scratching the back of his neck, but then his hand runs up along his skull, over the top and back, fingers probing gently.

"How long until he can get out of here?" I ask.

"A day or so. We just want to make sure he does okay with the chemo." She taps the hose of one of the three fluid-filled bags on his IV stand. "Then he's free to blow this pop stand."

"Wow, Ben, hear that?" I say, fake cheerfulness to rival hers. "You get to go home soon."

"Yup," he says, eyes never leaving the television. His hand drops from his head and settles into his lap with the other one, folding together like a child's hands in prayer.

Last night, Christine called to give me Anne's new unlisted number.

"Do you think she . . . ?" I couldn't finish the question.

"I don't understand exactly what happened, but I do know Anne. You know it, too, Eleanor; she's ethical to a fault."

"But maybe she didn't realize what she was doing was wrong."

Christine sighed. "She sounded pretty sure to me, but how would I know? I'm just a knocked-up schoolteacher."

"Are you okay?"

She ignores the question. "And I talked to Mom a couple of days ago. I told her about Benny."

"And?"

"She must have been in shock. She just thanked me for calling and said she had to go fix dinner. I had to throw up, anyway. Morning sickness doesn't always happen in the morning, apparently."

This afternoon, when I get home from the hospital, I dial Mom's number and break out in a sweat. When the machine answers, I don't know whether to be relieved or disappointed.

"Hello, Mother. Just calling to update you on Benny's condition, which I'm assuming at some level you care about. Basically, he's dying and there's nothing they can do but make him feel better for a while. They're shrinking his brain tumors so he can hold a normal conversation, just in case you ever decide to talk to him again. He's going home in a couple of days. If you're not too busy over the next few months, which is probably all he has, you may want to at least tell him good-bye."

I punch the OFF button with relish, then immediately feel scummy, knowing I've crossed a line. The phone shrills in my hand, but I let the machine answer. Two can play this game.

"My God, Eleanor," Mom's voice spits from the speaker. "How can you talk to me that way?"

"This isn't about you," I say to the machine.

"I'm sorry that your uncle Benny is so ill," she continues, "and I know you're going through a hard time, but really, Ellie. We all are." There is a sharp click, then silence.

Buddy mews insistently for her evening bowl of cream. Usually by this time of day I'm starving, but I haven't been able to work up an appetite for anything other than crackers, and then only to stop the burning gnaw in my stomach. I pour half-and-half into Buddy's bowl. She crouches over it protectively, lapping furiously like a drug addict getting a fix.

I lean over to stroke her spine, tease her tail, and she twitches it away from me, scooting around to place herself between her precious cream and me.

"Boy, you're quite the little piggy," I say. Her sides have already filled in; she's no longer the skinny ragamuffin that ran into my apartment just a week or so ago. "Maybe I should cut you back to milk."

When she is finished drinking, she is all purr and affection again, letting me scratch her ears, rub her belly as she rolls side to side on the floor.

"Look at that little tummy," I say, cupping the silky rise of it in my hand, remembering something about pets growing to look like their owners. "It's definitely milk for you from here on out. I don't want to get any lectures from the vet next week when she takes out your stitches."

I've become a cat lady. What if someone heard me talking to her this way? And why shouldn't she be fat and happy? What would that hurt?

"I need a life," I tell Buddy, but she has become engrossed in the intricately choreographed process of licking her paw and swirling it around her cream-spotted muzzle, whether to clean her face or consume every last drop, I'm not sure.

The next morning, a familiar ding announces the arrival of the hospital elevator, and I step through the swishing doors, knowing without looking exactly where the number 6 button is, knowing how long my ride will take, barring any stops at other floors. I walk the corridor toward Benny's room, nodding at the staff at the nurses' station; I know three out of four by name. I recognize the patients in each room as I pass; the old man with the bony legs and distended belly in 642, the youngish woman who stares out her window in 634, the unidentifiable figure in 627, always buried in bedding, never moving.

I stop just before Benny's door and take a breath. It's become a ritual: stop, breathe, relax. Then I step inside. He is sitting in the chair beside his bed, eyeglasses perched at the end of his nose, engrossed in the morning paper. He doesn't notice I'm there until I'm standing right in front of him. He looks up, smiles his old, easy smile, lays his paper in his lap.

"Benny!" I say. "You look so . . . good." They said the drugs would kick in quickly, but I didn't believe it.

"Don't sound so surprised. You know I don't give up without a damn good fight."

Tears spring to my eyes, but I make myself laugh, relief flushing through me. "Me, either," I say, and he takes my hands in his.

"Well, all right, then," he says, giving them a little shake. "They're springing me the day after tomorrow. I've got a hankering for some pineapple upside-down cake, and ham with brown-sugar glaze. Reckon you're up to it?"

I push my lips into a smile. "Of course I am," I say, although I'm not. I so am not. "I just happen to have a recipe for pineapple upside-down cake that will make you think you've—"

I stop abruptly.

"Died and gone to heaven?" he says, winking. "Sounds like just the thing."

Somehow, the rest of the world doesn't get that life as we previously knew it no longer exists. Assignments are piling up faster than I can check my e-mail, which I do much less frequently since becoming a hospital regular—just first thing in the morning and then again when I get home, like now. "10 Surefire Ways to Get Your Family to Eat More Fish." Easy enough. "Are Root Vegetables the New Potatoes?" What is so wrong with potatoes? "Chicken Soup Recipes to Cure Just About Anything!" At this one I gasp, but two weeks ago I wouldn't have noticed what was wrong with that sentence. I have to get a grip. Regardless of what Benny's going through, I still have to make a living.

I've never said no to an editor, but how am I going to keep up? How can I write total bullshit now, of all times? If I start turning down assignments, will my editors give me any more work? Or will they move on to the next freelancer who always says yes?

"Yes," I e-mail back to the fish article. Yes to the root vegetables. After a few deep breaths, I say yes to the chicken soup piece, then go in search of Stefan's e-mail from the other night.

I'm reading it (why I don't know, since it's forever committed to memory) when my computer bleeps that I have a new message. My pulse quickens. Stefan?

It's from the food editor at the *Oregonian*. I wrote for her when I first started out, but soon discovered that newspapers couldn't pay freelancers nearly what magazines could. Still, I liked writing for Sandra, and seeing my name in the local paper. I open her message.

> Hi, Eleanor,
> Long time, huh? Loved your latest piece in *Healthy Fit*. Who knew you could make ice cream with nondairy creamer?

There's a fantastic new chef in town who has been living in Tibet and studying its cuisine. He's taking over as head chef at PanAsia in the Pearl District, and I'd love an in-depth piece about him, Tibetan food, how he's going to influence PanAsia's menu, whatever personal details he'll share. I know you don't do restaurant reviews—this is strictly a profile. I can double what I used to pay you. What do you say?
Sandra

Ugh. Exactly why I hate writing profiles. I write about food, not people and their personal details. Still, I could use the money.

I hit REPLY:

Sandra,
Yes, it's been a long time! Glad you liked the faux–ice cream piece, but for the record, I wouldn't actually eat it or serve it to anyone I care about. It tastes like artificially sweetened school paste.

And yes, I'd love to do the profile. Who is this guy and how do I get ahold of him?
Best,
Eleanor

As if I don't have enough on my plate. I sigh and close my eyes, fighting the eddy that threatens to pull me down.

Later, after staring at Stefan's e-mail for far too long, I hit REPLY.

Dear Stefan,
Thank you so much for your generous and caring note. I am heartsick to learn about your mother. I'm just beginning to learn how the world, how everything changes when someone you love has cancer. How did you work? How did you function? How did you eat, sleep, talk to anyone without crying?

I stop here to shuffle to the bathroom for Kleenex, wipe my face, blow my nose, then continue.

> Anyway, it was incredibly kind of you to respond so person-
> ally. I know you're a busy person with a magazine to run. As
> soon as I'm feeling up to the task, I will be in touch about the
> new assignment. A week or so? I don't really know. Sorry to
> be so vague.

I type "Love," then delete it and type "Yours, Eleanor."

The rain outside slashes through the purple-black night, pelting the windows in thuds and plinks. It's not even ten, but all I want to do is go to bed. At one a.m., though, I'm still awake, rolling from side to side to try to get comfortable, throwing blankets off, then pulling them on, disgruntling Buddy at every turn. Finally, she jumps off the bed and trots into the living room. I get up, too, and follow her, wander over to the computer. I have mail. I click it open and read:

> Up late on deadline. I'll call tomorrow.
> S.

I'll never get any sleep now. It's already four a.m. in New York.

I have never been lucky in love.

My last attempt was seven years ago when I got that "cushy" job my dad was so fond of, working for the Oregon Nut Growers Board. The PR director, Daniel, and I were quick friends from the moment he briefed me on the state of nuts in Oregon (the most salient points being that Oregon is the largest hazelnut producer in the United States and the word "filbert" does not play well with the demographically desirable).

We shared a cynical sense of humor and grew closer over the next few months, dreaming up silly nut slogans and campaigns that bordered on subversive. One night, working late over a "101 Ways to Savor Your Nuts" brochure concept, the inevitable happened. We became lovers in his office, on the floor, in a breathless rush of deadline tension and hormonal proximity. It was our secret.

Technically my boss, Daniel didn't feel comfortable letting anyone know, so we rendezvoused undercover for the next three years, usually in my apartment late at night. The secrecy was exciting at first, fueling our risky groping sessions at work, our kisses stolen in the hallways, the too-long eye contact in meetings. When I started to complain that we didn't really have a relationship, he agreed to movie dates if we arrived at the theater separately, and we occasionally escaped to his family's Cannon Beach cottage on long weekends.

One day in our third year together, he hired Alicia as his assistant, for no apparent reason other than her proclivity for high heels and artificially induced cleavage, somehow always revealed in tight, barely buttoned blouses. To be fair, she did have a slavish quality that must have been part of the equation. I knew something was up. Daniel's late-night work sessions no longer involved me; he'd given me a research project that required hours alone with statistical data. He was too tired to come over to my apartment after work. When I reached for his hand in the hallway, he stiffened and swiveled his head angrily to make sure no one had seen.

Within two months, Daniel and Alicia came out of the doing-it-on-the-floor closet and announced they were an item. To everyone except me. I found out sitting in a stall of the third-floor restroom, the too-tight waistband of my pantyhose binding my knees together.

"Don't they look great together?" our receptionist said to the controller's assistant as they sneaked cigarettes in the stall on the end.

"Yeah," sighed the other woman. "But she has to transfer to another department now. Company rules. I hear marketing has an opening."

When I finally worked up the nerve to leave the bathroom, I walked with superhuman tunnel vision to my cubicle, gathered my personal things, and left without a word to anyone. I called the board president the next day to announce my resignation, effective immediately.

I couldn't imagine going on a job search with my permanently puffy eyes, my propensity to cry at radio songs I previously considered sappy, and those damn black-and-white diamond commercials on TV. I began to freelance, hidden from the world in my little cave on Eighteenth Avenue. I realized what a dead-end nut PR had been, in so many more ways than one. I ate everything I could find but hazelnuts.

That was four years ago. Mostly, I've gotten over it. But since then, I haven't been touched by human hands other than my own.

There are torturous moments of unrequited horniness. There are times when I miss the feeling of a warm body on top of me, breathing into my neck, making primal utterances no one else is allowed to hear. I can take care of the physical-satisfaction part myself, but I miss the company.

My Stefan fantasies are supercharged now, his cocksure voice growing needy and urgent as we writhe together in the tangle of my sheets, his neatly clipped hair mussed by the rake of my fingers. There's no way I'd ever let him see anything of me other than my doctored head shot, but I figure he's safe as a mental partner. Love is easier that way. No risk of rejection, no messy breakup. No three months spent burrowed under the blankets, still air growing stale and rank, unanswered phone calls and e-mails piling up along with bills and empty Chinese food and pizza boxes. If only Ben & Jerry delivered.

Of course, I could have it all wrong. In his e-mail, Stefan was kind and sensitive. He clearly likes me, or he wouldn't have sent it. And just because he speaks with the cadence and vocabulary of someone straight out of a 1940s musical doesn't necessarily mean he's gay.

When it is officially morning, I roll out of bed, foggy and grumpy from sketchy sleep. My mission today is to finish as much work as possible so I can devote my day tomorrow to Benny.

Dear Mr. Bouche, I type to one hbouche@panasia.com. A Frenchman, to boot. I already see him in my mind: He is spruce and wiry and quick with his hands, in his late fifties and impeccably dressed beneath his chef's jacket. Single, obviously, or he wouldn't have just spent two years in Tibet. Not gay, but happily divorced from his beautiful French wife of twenty years, dating women half her age and dress size now. I grit my teeth and type:

I'm delighted at the opportunity to interview you for the *Oregonian*. Please advise when a good time to meet at the restaurant might be. Our photographer will contact you separately.

All best, blah blah blah.

I hit SEND, then try to work on the chicken soup piece, but all I can think of are those sappy books about medicating your soul with the stuff. Suddenly, they sound appealing. Comforting. Maybe there's one for the cancer-patient soul or the niece of the cancer-patient soul. I could order it online, so no one would see me with that distinctive cover, like a billboard shouting SENTIMENTAL NITWIT LOOKING FOR AN-SWERS IN PAP!

A new e-mail pops into my mailbox: *RE: Oregonian Interview*.

Dear Eleanor, it reads. After I addressed mine to Mr. Bouche!

I am delihgted too! today is good, for you too? 3:00 OK?

I wince at the typos and the exclamation point and the English-as-a-second-language syntax. At least he doesn't sound too snobbish. I hit REPLY and answer simply: *I'll be there at three p.m.*

Despite my reluctance, profiles are truly the simplest form of journal-ism. Make the subject a chef, and it's even simpler. Once you get one talk-ing, you don't even have to ask questions. Though they may feign humility at first, they love to talk about themselves, their personal mani-festos, mission statements, and what they consider utterly unique outlooks on the art of food preparation and its (and their) importance in the world. Most could spend hours talking about their influences alone, all the way back to nursery school, when they made that first mud pie using a delicate blend of sand, soil, and dried grass for just the right consistency.

Bearing this in mind, I don't bother to prepare questions for the in-terview. I just hope I'm home in time for *Cooking with Caprial*.

At two o'clock, I pull myself away from explaining the intricacies of homemade chicken stock to get ready. I haven't had to dress for business in so long I don't know what to wear to the interview. Why must he be French? Any regular Portlander, and I could wear khakis and a T-shirt and look dressed up. I rummage through my old PR suits, hopelessly outdated and stuffy-looking. And no doubt too small. Why have I never thrown them out?

At the back of my closet, I find a dusty pair of black slacks from a fat period. The dust shakes out and they zip almost all the way up. Luckily, I'm not a big tucker-inner, so the gaping waistband is easily concealed. I pull on a eucalyptus-colored top—I did listen when Mom taught me about setting off my eyes—and heels, and feel almost sophisticated. Hair twisted and clipped, a pair of earrings. Lipstick. I look in the mirror. Fake smile. Stick out my tongue.

I let down my hair and pull on a bulky cardigan: camouflage, armor, I know. But familiar, anyway, and at last I can go out into the world.

PanAsia is a Portland institution, the first restaurant here to fuse Asian influences back in the 1980s—although certainly not the last—and they're still packed every night. They were innovators when they opened and they continue to be, although the fact that they've hired a new head chef is worrisome. Will the arrival of Henry Bouche be the beginning of something wonderful, or will he break the hearts of Pan-Asia's devoted clientele, as hot new chefs so often do in established restaurants?

It wasn't raining when I left home, but in the four minutes it takes me to drive east to the Pearl District, the clouds have decided to wring themselves dry with a light but decisive pelting rain. An April shower, in Northwest vernacular. Sure, it may not last all day, but it will definitely drench me before I even get near PanAsia, so I circle endlessly, looking for a parking spot close to the restaurant's front door on Northwest Twelfth and Glisan.

One block past the restaurant, I turn right on Hoyt, home of my favorite bakery and its sumptuous chocolate chip cookies. Any other time in my life and I wouldn't be able to drive past without stopping, but somehow even cookies don't excite me at the moment. All I can stomach besides crackers is cereal and milk, the occasional bite of banana.

Around the block, and then I'm cruising by PanAsia again. Ahead about a half-block, a woman with a newspaper over her head inserts a key into her car door, so I gun the engine, determined to cut off the rusty Jeep in the next lane that's also making a beeline for the spot. I look over at the chubby young guy driving, like, *What, are you nuts?*

He's not paying attention. He's talking or singing, gesticulating with his hands, and he's gaining on me. There's no way he's getting there first. I'm already five minutes late, so I floor it until I am nearly at the spot, then throw on the brakes as the woman pulls into the street. The Jeep flies by, chubby guy waving his hands; the woman's face appears in her rearview, eyes and mouth wide in horror.

"Sorry!" I yell, then slip into the spot and walk quickly back to the restaurant, feeling my hair frizz at each drop of moisture.

Inside, the restaurant is dark and lacquered with gold highlights, sparsely furnished, elegant. PanAsia serves only dinner, so there's no one on the floor yet. I walk back toward the kitchen, my heels loud on the glossy black-washed floor. "Hello?" I call out, pushing open the swinging door. "Mr. Bouché?"

A small Asian man looks up from the prep table, where he is mincing herbs into six-inch-high piles. "He not here yet, lady," he says. "You have appointment?"

I nod, breathing in the smell of lemongrass and cilantro, anise, garlic. The kitchen is larger than I would have thought, orderly and gleaming. "Will he be here soon?"

"Yes, just late," he says, and goes back to his work, skillfully chiffonading a pile of basil at lightning speed. "Always late."

Figures. Frenchmen. I smile, lingering in the doorway so I can check out the amazing knife collection hanging on a magnetic strip above the prep table, the sheen of stainless steel cookware arranged in neat rows on wire shelving units along the wall. "Nice kitchen," I offer. I'd give anything to cook in a kitchen like this.

"Yes," he says, expressionless. "You wait in bar, okay, lady?"

I don't know if he wants me out of his kitchen or if he saying it's okay to wait in the bar, but I smile and let the door fall closed. I've never enjoyed being called lady, but today, in some perverse way, I like it.

I wander back toward the front, through the minimalist tables and chairs, toward the sleek black bar. In every room, there's one of those curious offerings you always see in Asian restaurants: a tray with oranges, almond cookies, tea. Incense burning, thin wisps of smoke dancing toward the sky. My knowledge of religion is weaker even than my desire to practice it, but I always find these monuments charming, earnest. Hopeful.

Outside, a figure speeds past the closed bamboo shades, and I steel myself for Henry Bouche's entrance. Should I call him *On-ree? Monsieur Boo-shay?*

His voice precedes him through the door, singing "Just give me some kind of sign, girl, oh, my baby," in a loud falsetto. It's not Henry Bouche. It's the chubby guy from the Jeep, and he's not that chubby, just tall and built like a grizzly. Smiling, shaking rain out of his unruly ginger-colored hair.

"Oh, it's you," I say, not sure if he's tracked me down to yell at me, but I don't think so since he's smiling, so I stammer something about being late for my appointment.

"Hell, I'm the one who's late," he says, reaching out a bear paw to shake my hand. "You must be the reporter. Geez, I had you figured for some little old gray-head, Eleanor Samuels. Name like that. You are most certainly not what I expected, Mrs. Leadfoot. Or should I say *Miss* Leadfoot?"

I shake his hand, which is damp and strong and almost covers mine, and stammer some more. Surely, he isn't. Maybe he's his assistant. "And you are?" I ask.

He laughs. Loudly. Throwing back his head. "Good thing I'm not one of those snooty chefs, or I'd be insulted," he says. "I'm Henry. Henry Boosh. You have exactly forty-two minutes of my time, and then I've got to get to work. I hope you've got some good questions, Eleanor Samuels. I hate this interview bullshit."

chapter nine

On Columbus Day 1963, my parents were expecting their first baby, Anne, to be born within hours. The autumn winds had kicked up that brisk morning, rustling the mammoth fir boughs that canopied Mom and Dad's first little house in Lake Grove. As the storm worsened, so did the intensity of Mom's contractions, and Dad worried that the trees would break and crash down upon them. By the time they got on the highway, high-profile vehicles were having trouble staying upright and on the road, and Dad held tight to the wheel, a writhing thing beneath his grip, struggling against him, jerking uncontrollably, pulling him and Mom and their unborn baby toward the unthinkable. The winds howled and screeched to well over one hundred miles per hour before measuring instruments all over Portland broke apart from the pounding.

At the hospital, four orderlies ran out to help Mom inside, to keep her from being swept away, as so many things, living and inanimate, would be that day. By the time Anne entered the world, the sky had calmed and night had descended, but thousands of acres of timber, countless houses and buildings, unimaginable wildlife and livestock, and forty-eight people had been lost.

I have loved windstorms since I first heard this story, probably before I could talk. I was always jealous that my own birth was so ordinary and modest, an uneventful delivery on a mild February day two years later. I wanted to be part of a great force of nature, unearthed from some cata-

clysmic event that had nothing to do with anything that could be con-
trolled.

Which would probably explain my fascination with Henry Bouche,
né Boosh. Head bobbing, jaw working, eyes wide one moment, crinkled
down the next—watching him talk is like flying around in up-and-down
circles on the Spyder at Oaks Amusement Park. My neck cranes, my
torso leans, my face stretches wide open to keep up with him.

The page of my notepad is as blank as when I pulled it from my purse.
Beneath it the stainless steel work top is cool and smooth. Henry sug-
gested we talk in the kitchen, and I am sitting here like a happy village
idiot, grinning, nodding, not writing.

His skin glows pink in the bright light, his cheeks stubbled with
strawberry growth. Dark brown eyes where there should be blue, considering his coloring. He doesn't look like he's reached thirty yet, or if he
has he's decided not to, dressed in hiking shorts and a T-shirt. His hands
have not stopped moving since he first passed me in his Jeep.

"It's not like I thought, hey, how about this for a big career move: I'll
go to Tibet," Henry's saying, throwing his arms open. I've yet to ask a
single question and already I know more about him than I do about, say,
Stefan, even Daniel.

I try to take notes, but I'm distracted by the fact that I love Henry
Bouche. I will miss him if I never see him again. I don't want to rub bodies. I don't want to live with him. I just want to do this, sit here talking
in this storybook kitchen with its fantasy appliances and fully stocked
walk-in, mesmerized by the rhythm of the prep cook's knife and hands,
the aroma of some succulent sauce Henry is stirring. I want to live here,
somehow, be a part of all this energy and creativity.

"It was more that I was on a personal journey, you know?" he continues. "I wanted to escape this culture as much as I wanted to study theirs.
I mean, come on. Tibetan cuisine is not exactly the buzz, right? It's not
even that exciting, truth be told. If it was my career I'd been thinking
about, I should've gone to Latin America, Africa."

This is the closest we've gotten to the topics I'm supposed to be covering, so I clutch my pen, purse my lips in concentration, trying to think
of a question.

"What?" he says, laughing. "Something I said?" He fishes a teaspoon from a drawer, dips it into the sauce he's stirring, and sips. "Oh yeah, baby, that's good. You want a taste?" He tosses the used spoon in the dish sink and grabs another from the drawer, dips it in the sauce. "Here."

I slide around the prep table to the cooktop. My eyes come to his chin, which is square and dimpled. His forearm is nearly twice the width of mine. I have never felt smaller.

Henry hands me the spoon, thick fingers nimble and callused, holding it tight for a few seconds after I take it, teasing me. The sauce is a rich brown color flecked with green. "Peanut?" I guess, bringing it to my nose. "No," I say, shaking my head in unison with his. "Tamarind? No, that's not it, either."

"Taste, Eleanor Samuels," he says, folding his arms across his T-shirt, and I wonder if I am being tested.

I bring the spoon to my mouth and close my eyes. The immediate pungency of chile pricks my sinuses but doesn't burn. It's followed by a smoother taste, earthy and sweet, and the finish is delicately tinged with cilantro. I open my eyes. "Oh, my God, it's delicious!"

He smiles. "So?"

"There's some kind of chile—"

"Emmo," he says, a variety I've never heard of.

"—and cilantro—"

He nods, face expectant.

"—but that's it. That's all I can identify." I shrug. "And me a food writer."

"Don't worry," he says. "Nobody gets it, and I don't tell."

I nod, lick the rest of the sauce off the spoon like a lollipop, then catch Henry watching me intently, still smiling.

"What?"

"Nothing. I just like watching you eat."

If I could melt into a puddle and slide out of the room through the floor drain, I would. My face is so warm I know I've turned tomato red, and I can't think of what to say. I have reevaluated my assessment of Henry Bouche, however, and decided I definitely do want to rub bodies.

"Wanna know a secret?" He grins like a mischievous child.

I try not to look too eager when I nod.

"Promise you won't tell."

"I'm a writer. You can't ask me that."

He stares at me until I say, "Okay. I won't tell."

"It's not Tibetan. I just made it up." He watches for my response.

"So is anything you cook Tibetan? I mean, it's a newspaper. I'm kind of supposed to tell the truth."

"Of course," he says. "The curries, the dumplings, the tsampa—"

"Sam who?"

"Tsampa. It's a barley paste that's mixed with traditional Tibetan tea." He raises his eyebrows. "It's buttered and salted."

"Ugh."

"Right. The Tibetan food of today isn't too appetizing to Westerners. When the Chinese invaded, they cut all the trade routes to India, so spices—with the exception of stuff like emmo that was locally grown—went right out the window, along with the Tibetan's lifestyle and religion. These days it's a lot of yak jerky and dried goat cheese and salty tea."

"So you make it up."

He laughs. "I reinterpret what was. I adjust for the reality that Americans probably won't eat yak meat. I'm trying to get at the spirit of Tibetan food."

"Which is?"

He pauses and looks dead into me. "Earthy, subtle. Kind of sweet and slightly spicy." His eye contact is so intense, so expectant, that gravity ceases to exist for a split second; my feet feel as if they might come up from under me. Then he winks at the prep cook, who smiles a nearly toothless smile at me, and the warmth of color returns to my face.

"Eleanor Samuels, you are welcome to stay, but I have to start prepping. We have a full house tonight."

"God, I haven't even . . ." I glance over at my notebook.

"My fault," Henry says. "I got off on a tangent or two. Stay. Shoot some questions at me. If I get too far behind, though, I'm throwing you an apron. Deal?"

"Great, no problem," I say, sliding back around to my notebook. I tap the pen on the pad. "Let's see. Why don't we start with your earliest influences?"

When I finally leave two hours later, I am buzzing with energy, over-caffeinated perhaps by strangely flavored tea, but it's something else, too. I haven't had an animated conversation with someone else who loves food in so long I'd forgotten what it feels like.

I walk down Twelfth Avenue toward my car. In the distance, the high arc of the Fremont Bridge disappears into low-hanging clouds, cars driving straight into heaven.

At home, my phone machine is blinking: five messages. Christine, sounding happy, saying she and Reid have patched things up. "He really is a wonderful man," she says. "He really wants what's best for everyone." She really doesn't convince me.

Anne, sounding angry. "If I have to sit in this damn apartment one more day without even opening the curtains, for Christ's sake, I am going to scream," she says. "They camp out there in the parking lot, Eleanor, with their cameras and sound crews and satellite-tower trucks. They sleep out there, they eat fast food some stupid little assistant brings them. They are never gone. It's un-fucking-believable."

Yolanda, saying, "Ellie? Are you there? Have you talked to the home hospice people yet?" She sounds shaky. "I hope you understand, honey, but I just can't be his caretaker. I know it's a lot to ask, but . . . God, he loves you so much." She stops, and while I don't hear her crying, I know she is. When she speaks again, her voice is raw. "I hope you understand, Ellie. I just . . . well, I think you know. Call me, if you want to."

Stefan (Stefan!), who sounds businesslike and distracted. "Oh, uh, Eleanor, I got your message about being ready for the assignment next week, and I think that's doable. Just e-mail me back to confirm. I'm on vacation for the next couple of weeks, but my assistant David can get you the info. When you're ready, of course. But next week, right?" Silence, except for the clicking of computer keys. "Oh, and"—the clicking stops—"I hope everything's going well there. Really." Another phone rings in the background. "Gotta go. Take care."

I turn off the machine, even though there's one message left. I close my eyes, will my heart to slow, my jaw and stomach to unclench. I am his employee. That's what all his care and concern is about. Managing me so that he gets his precious article done on time. I had been manipulated this way far too many times by Daniel. Why do I fall in love with the same prick over and over? I even did it with the high school yearbook editor.

"Oh, for God's sake," I say, standing up, marching to my bookcase, grabbing the red-jeweled picture frame. Stefan sits in a casual pose on a high chrome stool, one foot propped on a rung with a slim hand on the thigh of his neat slacks. The other hand gestures to some presence off camera, and he is laughing, but carefully so that his face is not distorted by his smile. He is handsome, I'll give him that—good bone structure, small nose, tight body—but he's faking the smile, the casual pose. I see that now, having just been in the presence of Henry Bouche. Stefan is a phony, a pretend person behind the warm and caring facade.

I flick the catch on the back of the frame, slide out the magazine clipping, and crumple it in my hand. Buddy looks up with interest from her perch on the windowsill. "Here, kitty," I say, and throw the paper wad to the floor. She leaps upon it, covering it with her front paws, then rips her teeth into a fold of paper and shakes the thing until it is surely dead. When she tires of it she stands, looks at me, winks an eye and mews.

"You definitely deserve real cream," I tell her, going to the kitchen to fill her bowl.

Then I go back to the bookcase, take down the trifold cardboard with heart stickers, move the candle to a lower shelf beside some others, put the empty picture frame flat on the floor, and crush it with my heel. How stupid was I, how childish to even think that way? It's not Stefan's fault. He's just doing his job. I'm the one acting like a thirteen-year-old. I survey the broken glass and bent frame, the scatter of red jewels on oak planks. Life is different now, I'm different, and I have more important things to attend to.

After sweeping up, I go back to the answering machine, knowing who will and will not be on it. My mother can hold a grudge forever. I tap the LISTEN button.

"Ellie? Hey, I guess I need someone to take me home tomorrow and help get me set up. They're sending round some home-care person, you know, to make sure I . . ." Benny clears his throat. "Well, that I got everything I need, but I'm supposed to have someone to help me out. Yolie's too busy with her new job and all that, and I was wondering . . ." He stops again, and I picture him swallowing, Adam's apple rising and falling. "I know you're busy, too, honey. I hope it's not too much to ask."

Why me? I wonder. How did I end up being Benny's only choice? He is not my blood. Some would argue he tore my family apart. And even though I have no life, it's not like I couldn't. I could travel, maybe, do something exciting, something different.

I dial the number at the hospital, looking at the clock. It's six fifteen. They'll have brought him his dinner tray, a collection of soft foods that wouldn't appeal to a schnauzer: Jell-O, broth, tea, vanilla ice milk. He'll eat the Jell-O, maybe the ice milk.

"So what color is your Jell-O today?" I ask when he answers.

"Well, they brought me a new color, Ellie, one I've never seen before. You ever hear of blue Jell-O?"

"You still feel like ham, and pineapple upside-down cake?"

"Maybe some mashed potatoes?"

I doubt Benny even knows how to eat meat without potatoes.

"You got it," I say. "When are they springing you? I'll get there half an hour early. And I'll bring you a fresh change of clothes."

"Ah, Ellie, you don't have to go to the trouble. I don't want to be a pain in the ass."

He sounds so happy I have to swallow, suck hard on my lip for a moment before replying.

"Well, it's too late on the pain-in-the-ass thing, Ben, but it's no trouble. It's not like you've never helped me out." *Light; try to keep it light.* "Anyway, I'll be there. Okay?"

It's quiet on his end.

"Ben?"

"Yeah," he says. "Okay, honey," and from the quake in his voice, I know I have done the right thing.

● ● ●

At seven the next morning, I am faced with the to-do list from hell:

> Grocery shopping for Benny and articles.
> Bake cake, glaze ham, cut potatoes.
> Time for fish recipes?
> Benny's house: Air out. Change linens,
>   straighten up, put food away.
> Hospital at noon.
> Back to Benny's. Ham in oven, potatoes on
>   to boil.
> Home hospice person?
> Call: Christine, Anne, Yolanda. Mom?

I chew the pen top, then write:

> Henry? To ask more questions? Thank for
>   interview?

I cross out "Mom" and circle "Henry," then jump into the shower.

Every good housewife used to know that pineapple upside-down cake could only be prepared in a deep cast-iron skillet, carbon black and well seasoned from years of frying. Modern recipes seem to forget this, calling for glass baking dishes; in a popular celebrity cookbook, the errant and ill-informed cook even suggests a tart pan.

My cast-iron skillet was my mother's, retrieved from her garage-sale pile after she'd purchased her matching set of All-Clad cookware. All-Clad! For a woman who never cooks. She probably liked the way the stainless steel matched her appliances. I will be attending her next garage sale, that's for sure, when she decides that Le Creuset red goes well with her curtains, or that Calphalon graphite is perfect with her floors.

Right now I should be making fish ten different ways or experimenting with rutabagas and turnips, but they'll just have to wait. I've melted butter—real honest-to-God butter—in the skillet, stirred in brown sugar to caramelize. Fresh, juicy pineapple rings—not from a can—encircle not maraschino cherries but lovely candied cherries from Nob Hill Grocers. When the fruit has browned slightly, I pour the sweet, dense batter over it, slide the pan into the oven, set the timer, and peel, dice, and brine the potatoes for tonight. I've glazed the precooked ham so it can just heat in Benny's oven. Everything will be easy for his homecoming. Everything will be just the way he wants it.

At Benny's house, I throw open the windows, glad for the partly sunny sky and light April breeze. I stand at the kitchen window after I've put the food away, gazing at the lovely garden he and Yolanda nurtured over the years. Somehow, with all that's going on, I've almost missed the fact that it's Portland's most beautiful season; the show has started without me. Plumes of white, pink, and purple blossoms offset the one hundred shades of green our little city is known for this time of year: lime, celery, and avocado, butter lettuce and kale, Granny Smith apple and broccoli and sage. The swirl of color is more chaotic than I've ever noticed before, and when I look closer, I realize the garden is unkempt and overgrown, not neat and ordered as it has always been. If I didn't know how much Benny loves to garden, I'd chalk it up to Yolanda's departure. Benny, in his right mind, would never let it get like this.

I make myself turn away, go to strip the sheets from Benny's bed. As I'm gathering them to take to the washer, a book falls to the floor. *The Old Man and the Sea.* I stoop down to pick it up, run my fingers over the dog-eared pages, as soft and worn as flannel. Benny must have suspected something was going wrong. I sit on the naked bed, close my eyes, take a few deep breaths before I jump back up. There's too much to do.

The blue jeans and plaid shirt I brought for Benny to wear home look clownish on his thinner frame. The jaundice has not quite faded. He sits hunched from the pain in his gut on the edge of the bed. A new nurse I've never seen before—Jean, according to her name tag—helps him on with socks and shoes.

"You know, I'd do that myself, but I just can't bend down that far," he says, gripping the mattress. "Damnedest thing."

"I don't mind," Jean says. "I'd rather be tying shoes than giving enemas any day." She looks like someone's mom, rounded tummy and gargantuan bosom, smooth black skin and strong hands, which pat Benny's knees when she's finished. "There you go, Mr. Sloan. Now, think you can stand up?"

He's been in bed so long his muscles have atrophied, his inner ear has forgotten what it's like to balance. The medications don't help. Like a geriatric skateboarder, he holds his hands out, palms to the floor, surfing gravity. "I think I got it," he says, taking a shaky step, then another.

"Well, you'll be getting a free wheelchair ride downstairs, but you're on your own at home," she says, watching him carefully. "You want me to order you a walker?"

"Hell, no," he says, grabbing a chair back. "I'll be fine. It's just walking."

She looks at me. "If he needs one, the home hospice folks will take care of it."

"What else does he need? I mean, I don't know anything about . . ." My top teeth dent my bottom lip, worrying a tender spot that's developed there.

"The hospice caseworker will meet you at the house at two. She'll get you all set up, tell you everything you need to know, okay?" Jean drops her chin and looks at me. "Okay? You don't have to figure everything out—that's their job, and they're very good at it."

I nod and watch Benny move from chair to sink to bed, his tentative steps growing slightly more sure. The nurse says she'll go check on that wheelchair, and I leaf through Benny's box of cards and stuffed animals and unopened candy boxes. "Sure you don't want the flowers?" I ask. His room looks like a floral shop.

"Nah. They're going to share them around the place."

"You got a lot of cards, huh?" None have Mom's handwriting.

"Yup." He grabs the footboard of the bed, out of breath.

"Ben, sit down. You've proven yourself, okay?" I go help him to the chair, try to ease him into it, but it's awkward and I lose my grip. He drops to the seat like a bareback rider at full trot.

"Sorry, sorry," I say, but he shakes me off.

"I'm not gonna break, okay?" He sounds angry, but I know it's just his pride.

"Okay," I say, and we wait together in silence.

"Home." Benny stands in the front doorway of his house, holding the doorjamb. His eyes move from object to object: the photos on the wall, the bookcase, the kitchen table, the coatrack in the corner, where his battered work coat hangs next to his old yellow slicker. He says it again, stronger, "Home at last, thank God." Then he moves slowly, unsteadily forward, toward the kitchen and his chair at the table. "They say a little walking every day and I should get back to normal," he says.

Normal.

"Feel like some lunch yet?" I ask, opening the fridge. He wouldn't eat at the hospital, and now it's nearly one thirty.

"Wouldn't mind some coffee."

I turn, say, "Should you—" and stop myself. Should he drink coffee? What's it going to do, cause cancer? "I mean, would you like a little something to eat with it?" I sound like a mother of a two-year-old, cajoling him into a more nutritious choice.

"Just coffee," he says. "Black." Like I don't know how he takes it.

I pull out the industrial-size red can, put three scoops in the filter, the way he likes it, trying not to cringe. Benny is a true-blue all-American guy. Weak coffee, and don't give him any of that fancy designer stuff.

As it brews, I take a seat at the table. "Feeling okay?" I ask, and he gives me a look.

"You gonna keep asking me that?"

"How about once an hour? Every two hours?" I try to tease.

"How about never?" He looks away, then back at me, eyes moist. "I know you're trying to help, but I don't know what good is does to sit around moaning about it."

"It helps to know if you're feeling okay or not," I say. "The nurse said you shouldn't have to be in too much pain." Exactly what he doesn't want to talk about.

"I will tell you if I'm in too much pain. How's that?" he says, looking tired.

The coffee gurgles and sighs as it finishes brewing, and I stand, pull cups from the cupboard, fill them, set them on the table. He sits, listless, miserable, but he is determined to sit here, damn it, and have a cup of coffee rather than go to bed, where he should be. I run through my mind for safe topics and can't find any. I'd like to tell him about Christine's baby, but she wants to tell everyone herself, in her own time. Anne's situation is too bleak.

"I met an interesting guy yesterday," I say. "I think you'd like him."

"Yeah?" His hands are shaky on the cup as he brings it to his mouth.

"Yeah. This guy's a chef. Went to culinary school in New York and everything, and one day a couple of years ago, he just up and moves to Tibet. Didn't know a soul there, didn't know what to expect. Just . . . decided to be adventurous." I sip my coffee and try not to make a face. Cream. I need cream. I stand and grab milk from the fridge.

"Divorce?" Benny asks.

"Oh. Well, I don't know," I say, dribbling a thin line of white into the murky brown. Why didn't I ask him that?

"Did he turn Buddhist?"

"I don't know that, either. Hell, Ben, you'd make a much better interviewer than me. I just asked him about Tibetan food."

"What's that, yak and snowberries?" He snickers, pleased at his little joke.

There's a knock at the door, and I jump before Benny can even try to stand. "I'll get it."

I don't know what I expected a home hospice worker to look like, but not the petite, freckled redhead in jeans at Benny's door. "Ruthann Clark, Riverview Hospice and Care Facility," she says, extending her hand. It is strong and square and mannish on such a small woman. "Sorry, I'm a little early. You're the niece? Ellie?"

"That's me," I say, leading her back to the kitchen.

"I'll be visiting your uncle every day, make sure he's doing okay. Once he's stabilized, that might drop to three or four times a week." Then to Benny, in a volume slightly louder, "Mr. Sloan, good to see you. Remember me? Ruthann? From the hospital yesterday?"

"Benny. Mr. Sloan was my father," he says, rising unsteadily off his chair to shake her hand. "And it was only yesterday. Of course I remember."

"Good. Sounds like the dexamethasone is working on those brain mets. Excellent." She takes a seat, looks at our cups. "Is there any coffee left?"

"I was just going to offer you a cup." I head to the cupboard. She's a pushy little thing.

"How about lunch?" she says, and I'm thinking she's going to make me feed her. But she says, "What did you have for lunch today, Benny?"

"Funny, Ellie and I were just discussing what to have," he says, folding his hands on the table like a straight-A student. "Did we decide on the yak or the snowberries?" he asks me, twisting in his seat to give me a wink.

I shake my head, smile. "I picked up sandwich stuff—roast beef, pastrami."

She grimaces. "Way too heavy to start with. Anything sweet?"

"How about that pineapple upside-down cake you've been promising me?" Benny says.

"Perfect," Ruthann says. "I'll have some, too."

"Perfect," I say, trying not to sound sarcastic. At least I did something right. I pull out plates, forks, napkins, and cut two hefty wedges of cake and one thin slice. Benny needs the calories, and I need something to do with my mouth so I don't blow my cool. The two of them chat amiably, and it's clear that she is exactly the kind of person who is perfect for this job: straight, honest, and a little bossy. Already Benny trusts her; I see it in the way he's leaning in to listen to her, the way his hands lay on the table, hard palms up, as he tells her how rotten his gut had been feeling, how low the headaches (*headaches? what headaches?*) had laid him.

"Ellie here saved my life," he says then, looking at me with his swimming pool blue eyes, and Ruthann looks at me, too, smiles, and pats his hand.

"No," I say, "I just—"

"During that big snowstorm, she drove all the way over here and got me an ambulance. I'd probably've died if not for her, stranded here like that, sick as I was. Doctor said so."

I don't know what to say, so I do what I'm best at. I carry the plates to the table.

As the two of them lift forkfuls of moist, sweet cake and slippery fruit to their mouths, I push it around on my plate, mashing crumbs between the tines of the fork, cutting pineapple into tiny slivers.

"Jesus, Mary, and Joseph," Ruthann says, "this is the most delicious thing I've ever tasted." I look to see if she's buttering me up, but the way she's inhaling the cake makes me think she's sincere.

We talk about things that should frighten me—medication schedules, doctors' appointments, home remedies for the chemotherapy's side effects. Where to put the hospital bed and portable potty-chair, later, when he needs them. I should be crying, at least, but the only thing I feel is numb. There's definitely a shift, but it's less *Oh, my God* and more *Oh, so this is how it's going to be.* This is how we "transition," to use Ruthann's vernacular, from here to there, from today to that day.

From now to never again.

chapter ten

In my twenties, I thought that the day I owned a dishwasher would be the day I could finally say I was an adult. The apartments I rented were usually studios with one strip of wall dedicated to a bare-essentials kitchen: four feet of counter, a stained sink, a doddering range, and a college-dorm fridge. I yearned for a real kitchen, a real house, that Portland foursquare with a chef's kitchen and vegetable garden out back.

When I decided to buy the Nob Hill apartment, just after taking the ill-fated PR job, it was based on not only the location but also the retro-fitted built-in dishwasher, taking up precious cabinet space in a kitchen so small, but fulfilling my wish. I'd arrived.

Now I'm back to hand washing dishes at Benny's. Yolanda said they had no need for a dishwasher, with just the two of them. As the sink fills with hot, sudsy water, slippery and satisfying on my hands, I realize how much I miss the ritual of scrubbing, rinsing, stacking, until everything is neat and tidy and as it should be. I wash the cake plates, the forks, set them in the dish rack, gaze out the window. I let my eyes blur and the myriad greens become one hue, dimensional like a bank of hills in wine country, or a green patchwork quilt thrown over a sleeping body.

Down the hall, Benny's giving Ruthann the lay of the land: where he sleeps, how many steps it is to the bathroom, the width of his doorways. Really, he is telling her his stories. I know he's pointing to the black-

and-white wedding photo of his mother and father in the hallway when he says, "They fought like cats and dogs, but they held hands everywhere they went, even if it was just out to the milking barn." Sloan Dairy was a family operation back in Joplin, Missour-uh, as Benny pronounces it. His older brother was supposed to take it over when he returned from the war, but he never made it. "I was next in line," Benny's saying, and I know what he'll say next: "but the thought of milking cows the rest of my life didn't really moo-ve me."

Ruthann chuckles, and I don't think it's just politely. She likes him, corny jokes and all, and she asks if the photo next to his parents is his brother. I know he's nodding, getting misty-eyed, when he says, "Hal."

I pull the drain plug, chase the soap bubbles down with the sprayer, then grab a clean dish towel from the drawer to wipe my hands. I'm folding it and tucking it around the fridge door handle when they return to the kitchen, Benny's arm supported in the crook of Ruthann's.

I pull out Benny's chair so that she can settle him into it. I watch how she does it, gently but assuredly. She is strong and deft, and she doesn't let go until he is completely seated. "So you got the full tour?" I ask.

"Everything but your room, Ellie," she says, straightening up, putting her hands on her hips. "Are you close enough that you could hear if he needed help in the night?"

A tingling washes over me from scalp to calves, and my brain locks down.

"I know it may seem weird," she's saying, "but some people use those baby monitors. You know, just in case. That way, Benny would know you could hear him."

"Oh, I don't live here. I didn't . . . I mean, I . . ."

"But you have to live here to be his primary caretaker," Ruthann says, face tightening. "In order to be at home, Benny needs live-in help. Nobody told you that? Who'd you talk to at the office, Bob or Marie?"

"I didn't talk to anyone. I didn't know," I say, looking at Benny now, but he's hung his head and his crooked fingers twist together tightly, like they are trying to make a knot.

"They're usually so good," Ruthann says, shaking her head. "I can't understand how this happened."

"They talked to my aunt," I say. "She told me to call them, and I forgot." Maybe she said that and I wasn't listening.

"No, it's my fault," Benny says. "I think I was supposed to tell you but I must've forgot. Yolie even said, 'Don't forget, you old buzzard,' because she knew I would." He rubs his hand angrily over his head.

Ruthann still has her hands on her hips, stymied. "I've never run into this before. What are we going to do?" She looks from me to Benny, shakes her head again. "We have to have a primary caretaker living here."

Benny's hands have curled into fists. "Or?"

I don't want to hear the "or."

"It's not a problem," I say. My head is like a helium balloon, rising, bobbing on a string. None of this seems real. "I've slept in the sewing room before, right Ben? Lots of times." I look at Ruthann, try to smile like everything's all right. "My sisters and I used to spend the night here. I'll just bring my stuff over." As I'm saying it, I realize "stuff" includes cat. Computer. Kitchen appliances. I'll need an extra phone line for the modem. And this isn't just a night or two.

"Breathe," I remember Suzanne Long, Food Counselor, saying to me in her chintz office. I try, but I can't get enough oxygen. My throat is too tight.

"No, honey." Benny looks up at me, face weary and beaten. He unfurls his hands. "You can't do that. I can't ask you to. You've got your own life."

I walk over to sit by him, take his hand in mine, because I'm pretty sure that's one component of being a primary caretaker—holding a dying man's hand.

"That would be where you're sadly mistaken," I say, winking to convince him it's okay. "The one thing I don't have is a life."

He bows his head, squeezes my hand. Ruthann looks relieved.

"So, Ben," I say. "How do you feel about cats?"

• • •

On a bright May day in 2001, when most of us were contemplating where we might spend our summer vacations, Henry Bouche quit his

venerated position as head chef at San Francisco's award-winning
Green Spot restaurant and embarked on a journey to one of the world's
most sacred places: Tibet. He went not for prestige or money, not for
love (check?), and certainly not for comfort. "I didn't know exactly
what I'd find there," the thirty-two-year-old chef says, "but I knew I had
to go."

My list of questions for Henry Boosh is growing. What exactly
prompted his decision to go halfway around the world? Was it a bad
breakup, a divorce? Did he seek enlightenment? This is a newspaper I'm
writing for; they want information, not fluff. Why didn't I ask any of
these questions when I had the chance in his kitchen, instead of letting
my hormones take over?

I have two and a half hours to get some work done and pack up a few
things to take to Benny's for the night. I'll leave Buddy here for now and
come back for everything in shifts over the next few days. Ruthann
agreed to stay with Benny until I returned later this afternoon, pulling
me aside as I headed in my dumbstruck daze for the door.

"Look, Ellie, I know this is a shock. I can't believe it fell through the
cracks like this. But it's not forever, and it's not always. Benny won't
have to have someone around twenty-four/seven after he's recuper-
ated a bit. Not until later. And there are people who can help, respite
care services, home health-care providers, aides who can supplement
what we do. And if it becomes too much"—she paused, looking at me
carefully—"we have a wonderful facility. Really."

"Facility?"

"Riverview Care Facility. It's a nursing home with hospice care. You
might want to bring Benny over sometime, when you're both up to it,
and take a look around. I think Benny would be very comfortable
there."

"No, I can handle it," I said. "He wants to be home."

"Well, just so you know. For later."

I nodded, but I've never wanted to get away from someone faster.
Why would she think talking about putting Benny in one of those
places would be a comfort to me?

I close my Henry Bouche file and open a new one for the fish article. I can wing the recipes; I've cooked enough fish to know the drill. Ten preparations—no problem. Teriyaki tuna, lemon-basil salmon, snapper Provençal . . . let's see. Teriyaki tuna . . . I bang the table in frustration. This should be so easy.

My computer dings that I have new e-mail. Relieved, I click, and it's from David, Stefan's assistant.

> Dear Eleanor,
> Attached please find an assignment sheet and contract for the "Regional Foods of the West Coast" piece Stefan assigned you as part of our annual "Foods of America" issue. He mentioned that you'd be able to start next week. Please e-mail me ASAP with travel arrangements—

Travel arrangements?

> —and interview choices for the following cities: Seattle, Portland, San Francisco, Los Angeles, and San Diego. I've also included an expense form and contact info for a photographer in each city. Congratulations on the assignment; this issue is usually one of our top sellers.
> Sincerely,
> David Rhys-Miller

Biggest assignment of my career, Stefan said, and he was right. Something like this could launch me into the big culinary magazines. I hit RE-PLY and type:

> Dear David,
> Thank you for forwarding the assignment sheet and contract. I'll begin making my travel plans right away and contacting top chefs in each city. My initial instincts are to go with Zen Garden in Seattle, Chanterelle here in Portland, Hopi Café in San Francisco, and maybe Fish-Fish in L.A. I'll

have to do some research on San Diego, but I'm thrilled to
do this piece for you and Stefan and *Cooking for Life*.

My fingertips are trembling on the keys, my breath is coming in
gulps, and then I am crying as I hit DELETE. I type:

Dear David,
Due to a family emergency, I am sorry that I won't be able to
take on this assignment after all. Please convey my apologies
to Stefan.
Best,
Eleanor

I hit SEND, then cradle my face in my palms. Ragged moans escape
my throat as I sob into my hands. Buddy, who has been sleeping on my
bed, trots into the room at the sound of my voice, looks at me with concern, then jumps into my lap, rubbing her head up and down the length
of my arm.

"Good kitty," I say, scratching her ears, and she settles in my lap like
a bird in a nest. "How do you feel about moving down to the suburbs for
a while?" Maybe I can get a wink out of her, a sign that everything will
be okay, but she just closes her eyes to continue her nap, purr engine
chugging to the rhythm of her breathing.

"So tell me more about your mom and dad," I say to Benny after
Ruthann has left. We're playing gin rummy at the kitchen table, and the
smell of ham wafts around the kitchen as the sky turns to twilight outside. Apparently, Ruthann got Benny to take a nap while I was gone,
and now he's as chipper as a spring robin.

"They were just simple folks," he says, playing the eight on my seven
of clubs. "Salt of the earth, country people." He's silent for a moment
and I assume that's the end of the story. Then he says, "Mother had Hal
when she was eighteen, one year after she and Dad got married, then it
took a while for her to have me."

"He looked so much like you," I say.

He winces, and I wish I hadn't brought it up.

"I'm sorry—"

"No, it's okay. That was all a long time ago. A lot of young men died. Hal didn't make it a week over there. I'm just grateful he didn't have to suffer through years of it, then die, anyway." He goes quiet again, either contemplating what he's just said or trying to figure out his next play.

"So, do you have any other brothers or sisters?" I ask. Maybe there are happier stories, better memories.

He shakes his head, fingers his cards. "Nope. Mother tried to have more but never could. Dad didn't like that much—kids were farmhands as far as he was concerned, and he wanted as many as he could get." His voice takes on the edge I remember hearing him use with my father. He snaps down the three, four, five of spades, then plays an ace on my king of hearts. "He got a whole lot more human after Mother passed. I guess he didn't believe she was really sick until it was too late."

"What did she die of?"

"Being sick. I don't know, honey. In those days things weren't so cut-and-dried. There weren't always names for what folks had, especially country folks. Doctors did the best they could, but . . ." He shakes his head again. "Your turn."

Suddenly, I want to know everything about Benny's life, not the scattered bits of his stories. I fold my cards and lay them on the table.

He looks at me. "What?"

"I don't know anything about you."

"'Course you do. You've known me your whole life."

"Exactly. And I know nothing about before . . . you know. Before we met you."

"What? You want my life story?"

"Sure."

Benny lays down his cards, his gnarled hands suddenly empty and searching for something to do. In the old days, this is when he would have lit a Winston. "Like what?"

"Something juicy. Who was your first love?"

He chuckles. "Well, that'd be a tie between our old hound King and my first car, a 1938 Century Sport Coupe I rebuilt from junk parts."

"Tell me the rest. Start at the beginning."

He nods, folds his hands together, index fingers pointing skyward: *This is the church. . . .*

Benny was born and raised in Joplin. Farm country at the time. Springfield was the closest city, and he remembers occasional excursions there with his parents. "There were still trolleys then, and Hal and me would get all excited about riding them. Dad would say, 'It's too damn expensive,' but Mother would sneak us nickels to ride while Dad was looking the other way."

"Think he knew?" I smile.

"I don't know. Bastard."

"What were their names?" I ask, trying to picture Benny and his family in the 1930s and '40s, farm folk in the big city. I can only envision them in black-and-white.

"Dad's name was Herman. Mother's was Elsa," he says. "Everyone called her Ellie."

I look at him in surprise. "Like me?"

He winks and takes a sip of coffee. "See those old photo albums on the shelf in the living room? Grab the big one."

Later, after I've served dinner, watched Benny eat his few bites, and pushed my own food around until he's finished, after I've washed the dishes and put the substantial leftovers away, Benny falls asleep on the couch in front of the television. It is seven forty-five. I wait until eight o'clock to gently shake his shoulder. "Benny? Wouldn't you be more comfortable in bed?"

He opens his eyes and closes them, and I shake again. "Ben?"

His eyes flutter open—rheumy, unfocused—and search the room for a reason for waking.

"Benny."

He looks at me, and recognition dawns.

"Want me to help you to bed?"

He nods, then shakes his head no, slowly pulls himself into a sitting position. "I got it." He places his hands on his bony knees, tries to push himself up from the couch.

"Here," I say, standing, leaning in to place my arm and shoulder under his the way Ruthann did.

"I don't need—"

"I know, I know. You don't need me, but humor me, okay?"

He twists away from me. "I don't want you to do this."

Like I do. "Fine," I say, backing off.

He struggles again, hands pushing on knees, face straining, body not cooperating. He goes limp, silent, and we engage in this standoff for a few moments more, then he looks at me and sighs.

My teeth find the sore spot on my lip, my nose and eyes water. I look away, then back at him. "I know, Uncle Benny. It sucks. The whole thing sucks."

He nods, looking at the floor.

"But this is what we're doing, okay? So, let's just see if we can figure out how to get you up."

He nods, lets me tuck my arm under his. He holds on to me, and something in my back twinges as I pull him upright. Ruthann told me to use my knees, and I will remember next time. Slowly, we walk arm in arm across the living room, close, companionable, as if we were strolling through the public market in Seattle, say, or along San Francisco's North Beach strip.

It's only nine o'clock. Benny's snoring sounds like a chain saw. He managed to get himself ready for bed, thank God, but I know there will be a time when he can't. I'll have to dress and undress him, help him in the bathroom. Will he be able to stand it? Will I?

I wander back to the musty, long-unused sewing room, the sofa bed pulled out and my overnight bag on top of it. This room was meant for the child Benny and Yolanda never had. When did they finally give up trying?

I shake my head and turn away, surveying with new eyes the small bathroom Benny and I will share; the darkened hallway, walls filled with framed photos, white squares where Yolanda's family used to be. This is where I will live for the next few . . . months. Year, maybe. It's no comfort that it won't be more than that. Do I sell my apartment? Not yet. If

I can keep up with work I'll be okay, but I'm not so sure I can count *Cooking for Life* as one of my clients anymore, and they've always been my bread and butter.

I'm not in the mood to read, and Benny doesn't get the Food Network. I want to talk with someone, tell them what's happening to Benny, to me. I've left messages with my sisters that I'm here for the duration. It strikes me that Benny would have been on my old call list; he's one of the few people I could talk to about something like this. He'd tell me I'm doing the right thing.

In the living room, Benny's battered old family album leans heavily against a few other photo albums on his bookshelves. These never used to be here; I know because I've worshipped at this wall of books from the time I could read. Each album cover depicts a distinct era. I wander over and pick up two that are obviously from the seventies—our time with Benny: one avocado green and one with orange geometric designs.

Settled back on the couch, I flip open the green book to somewhere in the middle, and there I am in our old backyard, seven or eight years old, tanned and pixie haired, in shorts and a sleeveless top. Barefoot. Grinning as I brace myself on the side bar of the swing set, ready, I can tell, to perform my prized skin-the-cat maneuver.

And not chubby. My arms are muscular in that jungle-gym fanatic way, and my torso is straight. Yet my mother already nagged me about my predilection for sweets.

There are other pictures of my family and me on our back patio. Clearly, it's one of our early barbecues with Benny, but I don't remember it. I've never seen these pictures before, but they are familiar, comforting. Yes, we did have this life; we did just hang out for hours in the backyard as the summer evening turned dusky, not doing anything, really, but being a family. My sisters and I smiled and laughed and played, and my parents toasted the camera with their cans of Blitz beer. My father smiled, and it doesn't look all that forced.

Some of the photos make me *tsk* or say, "Oh, my God." Dad kneeling behind Christine, arms around her as he helps replace a Barbie head on a naked doll. Anne giving me a piggyback ride across the yard, and I know it's to the cherry tree in the corner so that I can pick the ones higher than we can reach. Mom bending over the cooler to get herself another Blitz, her backside rounder than I ever realized, her arms thicker in her summer dress. She wasn't always so fashionably slim.

There's just one photo of Benny, and it could only have been taken by my mother. In it, he is sitting at the picnic table, chin in palm and cigarette smoldering between his fingers. He looks my age, hairline just starting to recede, handsome the way Anthony Hopkins was in his thirties, but not as pretty. A small twist of a smile plays at his mouth, and his bright eyes look so directly into mine that it seems impossible there was a camera between him and my mother.

chapter eleven

P anAsia," a young woman's voice says, almost muted by the clamor of the busy restaurant. Why did I think ten p.m. would be a good time to call? A breeze raises bumps on my arms, and the concrete of Benny's back porch step is cold beneath my jeans.

"Is Henry Bouche there? I mean, I know he's there. Is he busy?" *Is he busy? Jesus, Eleanor.* "I mean, I know he's—"

"Pardon? Can you speak up?"

Why don't I just hang up? I press the cell phone tighter against my face. "May I speak with Henry, please?" I say in the loudest voice possible without waking the neighbors.

"One moment," she says, and then I am listening to Chinese opera. I could still hang up. The guy is obviously swamped.

"Eleanor Samuels!" Henry's voice booms in my ear, and I smile.

"How did you know it was me?"

"Well, I'd like to say I have the divine power of intuition, but it's just technology. Caller ID."

"Ah," I say. "The divine power of AT&T."

"Indeed." He is waiting for me to tell him why I'm calling him at ten o'clock.

"Sorry to bother you when you're working. I just had a few more questions. Can we set up a phone appointment sometime in the next few days?"

"I'm almost finished for the night," he says. "Just helping the pastry chef get out a few more desserts, and then it's Miller time. Why don't you come down for a drink?"

Un-fucking-believable, as Anne would say. I am being asked out for a drink—granted, it's business, but still—by a man I find extremely attractive, for the first time in four years, four long years during which I had complete freedom to go anywhere, do anything I wanted, yet sat at home eating and moping. And now I can't go.

"As much as I would love to," I say, emphasis on "love" so he might ask me again someday, "I'm afraid I can't."

"Lunch tomorrow? Coffee?"

Doctor's appointment at eleven, and another visit from Ruthann in the afternoon to make sure we're doing okay. "Sorry. I guess it'll have to be a phoner." I'd explain, but I barely know the guy, and sympathy is not the first emotion I'd like to evoke in him. Besides, look what happened with Stefan.

"Hey, I understand," he says, spooling away from me faster than a fish on an untended line.

"Well, maybe I could sneak away for a just a little bit," I say before I let myself think about it. Benny's warm and safe and asleep in his bed, as he has been every night of his life when I wasn't here. Benny's fine. "I could be there in about half an hour."

"Excellent," he says, then: "Ah, Jesus, the busboy just dumped a tray of glasses out in the dining room. I'd better get out there."

"See you soon," I say, mind racing through the few pieces of clothing I brought with me, and discarding them just as quickly. A little lipstick, a little deodorant, and I'll be as good as I get.

Inside, I leave a note for Benny reminding him of my cell number, saying I just stepped out for some groceries. That's a reasonable thing to do, even at ten p.m.

At night, PanAsia has a dark sparkle, low light emanating from the wide front windows, reflecting off shiny surfaces. Candle flames daub the interior, where happy, beautiful people wear designer clothes and laugh around their tables, then stroll outside and wait for the valets to bring them their BMWs and Audis.

It's the Pearl District. What did I expect?

I sit inside my car, checking my watch. I thought the place would be empty by now. The restaurant's small bar sits off to the left, windows opened to the night air, spilling voices, laughter, and the pinging of ice cubes against glass.

"Oh, for God's sake," I mumble, tugging my T-shirt sleeves lower on my arms. I grab my purse and notepad, double-check that my cell phone's on, then walk toward the door.

As I get closer, I see Henry standing over a table of patrons, a mixed group of casually hip, thin people. His arms are crossed over his chest. He's laughing and handsome in his chef's jacket.

It's too late to turn back, so I continue through the open door toward the bar. The young bartender looks up at me, pink cocktail umbrellas tucked into her pigtails. "Good evening," she says, and I can't help but notice the deep plunge of her neckline, her young, unsupported breasts pointing straight at me through tight, flimsy fabric. "Can I get you something?" She offers a cocktail menu.

"No, um, no. I'm just here to see . . ." I nod toward Henry, who has yet to notice me.

"Oh," she says, withdrawing the menu, losing interest. She turns toward a pile of beverage tickets to tally. I stand there, hoping he'll notice me. She looks back up, pity filling her black-lined eyes, and calls, "Henry! This lady's here to see you."

I gulp as every eye turns toward me. Lady, for God's sake. My ass expands, my hair grows wilder, and my clothes glow neon where every drop of food, coffee, water has spilled on them today.

"You made it!" Henry says, dodging through the crowd toward me. "This place is a zoo." Then, in a low voice: "I wish everybody would just go home." He smiles and pulls out a chair at the bar for me to sit in. "Except you, of course."

"Right," I say, barely suppressing a snort. "You're very popular, Chef Boosh."

"Suck-ups," he whispers, squeezing the back of my neck. Under my hair. And suddenly I know I have a new imaginary partner.

• • •

"This time, I'm taking notes," I say, placing my pad of paper squarely in front of me and next to my sake-tini, a drink Henry ordered for me that contains nothing but vodka and sake. Well, and a slice of cucumber. It tastes fabulous.

Henry's having a local boutique stout, made, he says, with cocoa and espresso beans. "Want a taste?" he offers, and I nod, then flush when he watches me take a sip.

I set the glass down too quickly, tipsy already on the few swallows of my drink. I watch the beer glass wobble on its edge, then tip, and I can already feel the dark liquid in my lap, see it splashing Henry's white jacket. Henry, however, is quick and nimble, catching the glass and righting it before it spills.

"Oops-a-daisy," he says.

"Guess I should have eaten," I mumble, face flushing, and Henry jumps up from his seat.

"I'll go get you something. What sounds good? Here, let me get you a menu."

I grab his sleeve as he starts to run off.

"No, really. I'm fine."

"You sure?" He gives me a worried look.

"Yes. Look, I'll eat the cucumber." I pop it into my mouth, chew, swallow. Nutrition. "See? All better." I smile, and Henry takes his seat.

"Sorry. It's a reflex. I hear 'hungry,' I feed."

I laugh. "You, too? Wow. I thought only girls got that one."

"If you're questioning my manhood—"

"No!" I realize too late I've practically yelled it. The bar quiets for a beat, then resumes its noisy hum. "No," I say again, at normal volume. "I would never, you know. Question. That."

Henry smiles. "Good." He takes a long pull of beer, and we sit quietly for a moment. Companionably.

The loud group of hipsters stands and makes a slow, laughing exit single file past us, smelling of alcohol and cologne and personal-care products I'm sure I'm not even aware of. The men pat Henry on the back or shake his hand. The women kiss his cheek or the air next to it. The last to leave is a fawn of a girl, gangly limbed but gorgeous in that way of females just growing into their womanhood. Her smooth, straight hair is tucked behind a diamond-studded ear. Her glossy lips are the color of burnt sugar.

"I'm serious, Henry," she says, play pouting. "Think about it, and call me." She plants a dewy kiss on his cheek, leaving behind two fat crescents of lip gloss.

We're silent again when they've left, but not quite so comfortably.

Finally, I say, "You have, uh, some lipstick . . ."

"Where?" He reaches to wipe the wrong side, so I dab my cocktail napkin in my drink and wipe away the mark.

"Apparently," I say, "she's serious."

"About cooking lessons." He sighs, smiles at me apologetically. "If only being a chef meant just cooking. I'm beginning to remember why I left it behind the first time."

"Ah," I say, sounding much like him. "So, have you always been a cook? Or do you have some secret, exciting past?"

"Like what?" He laughs, picks up his beer.

I study him for a moment, chin in my hand. "I don't know. Gunrunner in Bogotá? Corporate executive on Wall Street?"

"Why, Eleanor Samuels! Why would you pick such evil occupations?"

"Because they seem the opposite of you." I turn back to my drink, take a small sip so that I don't get drunk and lose whatever control I still have. Henry clears his throat, and I look at him.

He looks back at me, studying my face the same way I've been poring over his—memorizing each mole, line, curve, and scar.

"I've always been a cook," he finally says.

"And so the interview begins." I sigh and pick up my pen.

Fifteen minutes later, this is what I've written on my paper:

Q. Catalyst for going to Tibet? Life change? Bad experience?
A. I don't know what I was looking for, but I didn't expect what I found.
Q. Which was . . . ?

A. The Tibetans are the underclass, the outcasts in their own country. I mean, I knew that, but the Chinese occupation destroyed everything, their lifestyles, their freedoms, their culture, their customs. Even their basic human rights. Did you know women are coerced to have abortions, to get sterilized? The Chinese are systematically reducing the Tibetan population. It's . . .

Here he trailed off, and I tried to bring it back to a lighter topic. Well, a topic that had me curious.

Q. Did you become close to any Tibetans?
A. Yes. I made some good friends.
Q. Any in particular you'd like to talk about?

He tilts his head. "You mean for the article, right?"

"Of course," I say, nodding too hard, downing the rest of my drink. "For the article."

At this point, he becomes the best interviewee ever and talks at length about his food experiences in Tibet: the local markets, the small family restaurants, cooking beside his landlady Sangmu in her outdoor kitchen with a woodstove, but what I really want is for him to tell me about his past, who he is, who he's loved. Or if I had the nerve to ask, if he loves anyone now.

Finally, he notices I've stopped writing. "God, I'm sorry. I'm rambling."

"No, no—you're great," I say, then flush. "I mean, it's all great stuff. I've just had a long day."

"Why didn't you stop me?" He smiles. "You look beat. It's nearly"—he looks at his watch—"Jesus, it's almost midnight."

"I'm fine," I say, but I could easily curl up in one of the booths by the window and pass out cold.

He stands. "Go home, Eleanor Samuels. It's time for bed."

God, why'd he have to go and say that? "Yeah, okay, you're right." I gather my things and move toward the door. The restaurant is empty. "I'll call you if I need anything," I say, and he smiles.

"Even if you don't," he says, watching me walk to my car.

It feels odd to drive south on the highway this late at night. PanAsia was five minutes from home, from my real home. I'd give anything to be able to go there and crawl into my bed.

I park in front of Benny's house, searching for signs that anything might have gone wrong. What if I've failed as primary caretaker on the first night? What if he needed me and couldn't find me? What if he's awake when I walk in, and I'm carrying no groceries? I'm clammy and nauseated from drinking vodka and sake on an empty stomach, and lonely in a way I haven't been in a long time.

Inside, everything is as I left it. There are no sounds, not even snoring. Tiptoeing to Benny's room, I stand outside the door, then push it open wider. Benny is lying with his back to the door, on his side, blankets tossed off. In the dim light, I focus on his pajama-clad torso, trying to determine if he's breathing. After a minute or two, I still can't be sure, so I move to his bedside, heart thudding so loudly I'm sure he'll hear, but he doesn't move. Not at all.

"Benny," I whisper, touch his shoulder. It's warm through the thin fabric.

He snorts, half wakes. "Mmph, mm hmm, okay," he mumbles, then rolls over and falls back to sleep.

Later, when I'm struggling to find a comfortable position on the old sofa bed, horizontal bars digging into my shoulder blades, my lower spine, and then my shins when I roll over, the reality of my situation is suddenly all too clear. This isn't the time to be thinking about myself, drooling over a guy six years younger than I am who could have his pick of any thin twenty-something in that beautiful-people crowd. He's a nice guy. Okay, a really nice guy. That doesn't mean anything other than he's a nice guy.

And I have more important things to attend to.

"What were you thinking?" Anne says in her judgmental-older-sibling tone. I press the cell phone closer to my ear so that her voice doesn't leak into the quiet kitchen where Benny and I are each having coffee and pretending to eat Special K. "I mean, it's not like you have an obli—"

"Don't." I cut her off, glance at Benny, but he's scanning the want ads, reading glasses perched precariously at the end of his nose. "It's fine."

"He's right there."

"Yes."

"God. Tell him hello."

I lower the mouthpiece. "Anne says hi, Uncle Benny."

He looks over his glasses at me for a too-long moment. "Tell Miss Annabelle hello." She doesn't ask to speak with him.

"Anyway," I say into the phone, "what's going on there? What's happening with the case?"

She sighs. "In two months I get to testify before the grand jury. Until then, who knows? I haven't been charged with anything, and I don't think they could make anything stick, but it doesn't seem to matter. The other partners don't want me to contact any of my clients." She's silent for some time, and I resist the urge to tell her everything will be fine. Clearly, it won't. Finally, she sighs again. "I'm hamstrung. I feel like I'm just rotting in a jail cell until the public execution."

"Why don't you come home for a while?"

Benny's eyebrows rise, then fall, although he never looks up.

"Home?" she says, as though it's a foreign word.

"My apartment's available."

"I don't know," she says. "It's so far away."

"Exactly. Maybe your fan club won't find you." God, what if they did? What would they do to my lovely little neighborhood? What would the Nguyens think?

"Thanks, but I don't think so. I can't imagine trying to run my life from Portland." She says "Portland" the way other people say "Podunk," or "Bumfuck," but I'm relieved.

"Anyway," she says, "there are fewer of them out there lately. I think I'm boring them to tears. If I stay in here long enough, maybe they'll just go away."

This sentence runs through my head as I clean up the breakfast dishes, as I dress and start making a list for the day. Such a pathetically passive statement—maybe if I just wait long enough, it will all work out—and such a familiar concept. Is this what I've been doing? Waiting for something good to happen? What if it never does? Do I want to be forty and still waiting? Fifty, sixty?

I think of Benny's life, Mom's. They're always doing something, even now, not waiting for it to happen. Throwing parties, redecorating houses in my mother's case. Having an affair. At least they pursued the thing they thought would make them happy. What am I doing besides waiting for life to work out? Hiding, waiting to die? Where is the strong young girl who can skin the cat twenty times in a row, pick berries until her fingers are purple, get excited about a book written a hundred years ago?

I call PanAsia and get a message: Do I want to make a reservation?

I don't know what I want, and that's the whole problem. I hang up without leaving a message.

In the car, on the way to Benny's appointment with Dr. Krall, I want to reopen the conversation from yesterday with Benny, glean a little more information about how exactly he came into our lives. He looks stronger, drumming his fingers on the console. His ring finger bears a naked white strip of skin for the first time since he married Yolanda in 1976.

"You took off your ring," I blurt before I can stop myself. Benny and Yolanda are only legally separated, and I'm pretty sure he's always thought they'd get back together.

He curls his hands into his lap, turns his head to the window. "Yup."

I turn the wheel hand over hand until we are out on Boones Ferry Road, heading west toward the highway. "You're okay? With that, I mean?"

"It's time."

"She take off hers?" I didn't even notice.

He nods. Surely, she won't divorce him. Not now.

"Uncle Benny?"

He turns to me. What am I about to ask?

"Would you ever want to . . . I don't know. Just talk about it all? All the stuff that we never talk about?" My heart is pounding. The ramp for I-5 is just ahead. I turn on my blinker. Benny is quiet.

"Or, or not, of course," I say, hugging the curve of white stripe on the highway entrance, noticing how the green of the tall grass just beyond it is the color of unripe bananas.

"You want a deathbed confession or something?" he says. He sounds angry, and it stuns me. He's never been mad at me before. Maybe annoyed, but this is different.

"Ben. Of course not. I just thought you might like to talk about . . . stuff."

He harrumphs, sits back, folds his arms. We're silent for a good ten minutes until the exit for Providence Medical Center comes into view. I flip the turn signal and it ticks like a clock. I try not to take it personally. Maybe the tumors affect more than his memory.

We veer down the exit ramp, toward the massive complex that is hospital and doctor's offices, parking lots and hundreds of cars, all carrying someone who must need to be here for whatever reason, but few of them good.

Benny clears his throat, rubs the raw white strip on his finger. "Honey, don't pay any attention to me. I'm just a crotchety old fart, like you always say."

"It's okay," I say, but I'm surprised at how hurt I feel.

"No," he says. "No, it's not, but there are just some things I figure it does no good to talk about. Like my son-of-a-bitch father always said, only pansy-ass whiners cry over spilt milk."

Even though I hate Dr. Krall, I have to admit his office is strangely pleasant. Low lighting, muted colors, and comfortable seating, including a few easy chairs. I guide Benny toward one by a massive fish tank and sit next to him on a leather couch. "Wow, some place, huh?" I say, and Benny nods, already mesmerized by the slow-motion purples and oranges of the tropical fish. I've read just one page of the latest New Yorker short story when a nurse-uniformed woman walks toward us. "Mr. Sloan? The doctor is ready for you. Do you need some help?"

He makes no move to stand on his own, just nods and mumbles, "Yes'm."

As she helps him from the chair, I concentrate instead on the smooth glide and quick dart of fish, the waving sea plants and bubbles rising. I wish he'd said no, tried again to get up on his own. If he loses that annoying independent streak of his, what will he have left to fight with?

The two of them disappear down the hallway and around a corner. I move over to the easy chair, feel the warmth of Benny's body beneath me, watch the fish until I can't control my eyelids any longer. I'm going to have to do something about Benny's sofa bed if I want to get any sleep from here on out.

Ruthann's minivan is at the curb when we pull into Benny's driveway. The air is misty but warming up, muggy and close. A light layer of moisture coats my forehead, my upper lip, the back of my neck. I slide out from behind the wheel, walk toward her car. She's shuffling paperwork in her lap and eating an orange as if it were an apple, biting right through the skin.

I lean in to talk to her through the open window. "Are we late? Have you been waiting long?"

"The first person you should worry about is your uncle," she says without looking up. Her short hair is the color of old pennies, her hands freckled and blue-veined on the white paper. "Doesn't he need help getting out of the car?"

Of course he does, but I didn't think about it. It's so hard to get used to all of this. "I was just—"

"Take care of him first. I'll be there in a minute."

I walk back to my car, perspiration now dampening my back and underarms, along my bra band. Why does she always make me feel like such an idiot?

Benny's opened the passenger's door and swung his legs around. He braces himself on the doorframe and scoots forward, feet finding the ground.

"You don't need me, do you?" I say, standing close in case he pitches too far forward. "You've got this nailed."

"I don't know about that," he says, breath heavy with exertion. He leans toward the door, grunts, and slides his full weight to his feet. He just about has it when Ruthann's car door slams.

"What are you doing?" she says, striding toward us.

"He's okay."

"Not if he falls and breaks something," she says, pushing past me.

"Don't yell at Ellie," Benny says. "And don't treat me like I can't do anything. I'm just about up."

Ruthann leans in and pulls him to his feet. "I'm sure you can do it, Benny, but my job is to make sure you don't end up lying in bed with a broken hip and bedsores and pneumonia, okay? Be patient—you'll be able to get around by yourself again soon enough." She gives him a stern look. "You big show-off."

He chuckles and lets her guide him up the sidewalk to the front door. I stand by the car, hot and clammy and feeling like I just got in trouble with my mother.

Ruthann's head pops out of the front door. "Aren't you coming in?"

I shake my head. "I'm going to go pick up my stuff."

"Back by two?"

I look at my watch. It's already twelve thirty. "That doesn't really give me—"

"Two thirty? Three? I can do three." Her face softens and she looks behind her, then steps outside and walks down the path. "Look, I know you were trying to do what's best for him. It's just that that might be different from what he wants."

"I don't understand that," I say, feeling stubborn, childish. "If he's . . . you know, if he doesn't have much time, anyway, what can it hurt? Shouldn't he just be happy?"

"Yes. Absolutely. And I happen to think happy includes being as physically well as possible. He breaks a hip, cracks a vertebra, he's not going to be happy for the time he has left. Trust me. Okay?"

I nod, knowing my face is bright pink. "I don't know how to do any of this."

"Nobody does," she says, "until they have to."

It's been seven years since I lugged my belongings up the stairs to my apartment, and now I'm not finding it any easier lugging them down. I must have thrown away the boxes for my computer, so I gather the keyboard, mouse, and monitor together in my arms, cables and wires springing out like Medusa's head. If I unplug them, I'll never figure out how to make it all work again. Next it's the KitchenAid, the food processor, my largest Dutch oven and favorite skillet, two saucepans. The gallon tin of good olive oil, vinegars and specialty condiments and sauces crammed into shopping bags. I can buy the more traditional staples to use at Benny's, but these things cost too much to replace.

Buddy strolls through my legs in a figure eight as I throw clothes into a suitcase. Sweats, khakis, T-shirts, sweaters. It's a tricky time of year to figure out what to wear. It could be a pleasant 65 degrees one day and bone-chilling the next, but it will certainly be wet for some time yet, so I throw my various raincoats on top: the light one, the warm one, the semidressy one, just in case. I leave the heavy parka in the closet for next winter. Native Portlanders like to say summer begins in July, and it's mostly true. I shouldn't have to worry about hot weather for at least a couple of months.

I've got everything in the car except Buddy when I realize I need her food and bowls and the faux-sheepskin bed I bought her. Toys, scratching post, her favorite blanket to keep her happy in the foreign environment.

What about me? What do I need to keep me happy? I wander through my apartment, Buddy in my arms, purring. Not long ago, the answer to that question would have been cookies, pasta—anything with enough substance to trick my neurotransmitters into telling me I was sated. Without my appetite, I don't know what I want. I don't know what I am. My mother would say I was a good girl, the way she used to when I'd actually pass on seconds at dinner, or leave half a bowl of ice cream uneaten.

Maybe that's what I want: to be good—good enough to take care of Benny. I know it's ridiculous, like something out of a TV movie, but maybe if I were just good enough . . .

"Jesus," I sputter, then throw back my head and yell: "This is too damn hard!" Buddy springs from my arms to the floor.

• • •

Outside, it's started to rain—not drizzle, not showers, but full-bore rain—and I quickly stuff the remaining items onto the backseat. Just one more trip back up the stairs for Buddy.

"Hallo!" Across the street, Irina Ivanova is waving from beneath the umbrella I bought for her, her little girl standing and holding on to one of her legs.

"Hi!" I call back over the traffic, ducking under the awning at the front door.

"You are moving?" She cups her free hand around her mouth like a megaphone.

"No, just going to help my uncle out for a while," I yell. "I'll be back."

"Yes! Good!" She smiles, leaning down to stroke Tatiana's glossy white-blond hair. "You will have to come visit. Tati is starting to walk!"

She looks so excited to be reporting this that I nod vigorously and yell, "Wow! That's great!" We smile and wave before each turning back to the business at hand.

Even though I promised myself I wouldn't, I drive past PanAsia on my way back to Benny's. My rear windows are blocked by the trappings of my life, piled high all around me. Buddy has found her bed on top of my suitcase in the front passenger's seat. If Henry saw me now he'd think I was a Clampett. What the hell am I doing? It's a quarter till three; I should be hightailing it down the highway. I turn right at the next street, wanting now only to get out of this neighborhood as quickly as I can. Another right and I'll be on my way toward Burnside and the highway.

Just ahead, it seems yet another trendy coffee shop has opened in one of the rehabbed brick warehouses that fill this neighborhood. It has a colorful sign that reads KAFÉ KIZMET, and, despite the rain, black-clad people sit under a metal-and-glass awning at outdoor tables. One person stands out from the hipsters, and I recognize Henry Bouche immediately: mustard yellow T-shirt, disobedient hair. He is sitting with a woman, and all I can tell at twenty-five miles per hour is that she has stick-straight dark hair and is incredibly petite. I'm almost safely past when Henry looks up, and a flash of recognition crosses his face before I turn my head the other way. Like if I don't look at him, he won't see me.

I don't breathe until I reach Burnside, and then I yell "Shit!" so loudly that Buddy jerks as if she's been electrocuted.

My cell phone rings.

"No," I say, fumbling for it in my purse. "It can't be." The plastic rectangle is tangled in debris at the bottom of my bag. I manage to free it and stay on the road, after the third ring. Why did I never upgrade to a new phone with Caller ID? It could be Ruthann. It's close to three and she's probably worried I won't make it on time.

"Hallo?" I say, affecting a throaty, low voice with a trace of a Russian accent, just in case.

"Geez, Eleanor Samuels, you sound horrible. You have a cold or something? Was that you that just drove past?"

I could keep up the charade, say, "I'm sorry, dahlink, you must have zee wrong number." I could make static noises, hang up. I could gun the car straight up the Burnside Bridge and over it, finding merciful release at the bottom of the Willamette River.

"Oh, was that you?" I say. "I thought it might be, but I wasn't sure. I'm just moving a few things."

"You're moving? Why didn't you say so? I can fit a lot of stuff in my Jeep."

"No, no," I laugh, and it sounds stilted. "I'm not moving. Just helping out a friend."

"Must be a pretty good friend."

"Yeah, yeah. He is."

"Oh," he says, lilt leaving his voice.

"He's my uncle," I say quickly. "Kind of."

"Oh." He pauses. "Just kind of."

"It's a long story. Can I call you later this afternoon? I really need to finish your profile, but I've got some other things to take care of first."

"Sure," he says. "You know where to find me."

Having coffee with someone far younger and thinner than I am, I don't say.

"You know, I was thinking about stopping," I lie, "but I saw you were busy." Two can play this fishing game.

"Ah, yes. Actually, you should have stopped. I could have introduced you to my wi—"

A noise erupts from my throat, a hissing, whooshing crackle that sounds just like static.

"Hello?" Henry says. "Can you hear me?"

I push the OFF button and toss the phone in back. It clangs against something metal and drops to the floor.

"Loud and clear," I say.

chapter twelve

A week passes, then two, three, and suddenly it's May. With my computer set up on the old sewing machine table (sewing machine conspicuously absent), I can gaze out the window at the lace whites and cotton-candy pinks of the dogwood and cherry trees, bursting with blossoms like there will never be another spring. The gray days are tempered by partly cloudy ones, sun threading in and out of streams of clouds from the coast, and the evenings grow longer, revealing hazy yellow-mauve sunsets when it's clear.

I've never felt so focused on my work. Somehow, I have fewer distractions at Benny's, an incongruity that's hard to fathom, considering why I'm here. Benny doesn't require that much from me at the moment other than cooking and keeping the place in order, rides to his appointments, making sure he takes his complicated routine of pills, and that he doesn't fall over and break something. And companionship. Sometimes I think that's the most important reason for me to be here; Benny won't have to face anything alone.

He's back to puttering around the yard, albeit slowly, and playing solitaire at the kitchen table, yakking on the phone with his cronies. Ruthann comes three times a week to check his vitals, listen to his gut with her stethoscope, grill him about what he's eating, how he's sleeping, how he's feeling. They almost always fit in a game of gin rummy and a snack, usually something I've made for an article and stuffed into the refrigerator after a quick taste. Benny's appetite is mostly back, but mine is just gone. It's a miracle. I've lost eleven pounds, and earlier this week I had to go back to the apartment for my formerly too-tight jeans.

The articles on fish, root vegetables, and chicken soup are finished, along with the family favorites piece, which covers meatloaf, mashed potatoes, mac and cheese, and my mother's lime Jell-O salad.

The profile of Henry Bouche took a bit more effort. I did not return his calls. I went online for more details on Tibetan food, and found biographical data from Mr. Bouche's time in San Francisco. (I did note that he was unmarried at the time but had a live-in "partner," which in San Francisco-ese could mean anything. The man is more complicated than a ten thousand–piece jigsaw puzzle, and I have never enjoyed wasting time trying to fit strange little bits of things together.) In the end, I wrote a perfunctorily nice article about a chef and the food he cooks, with none of the personal journey crap I thought would be so important. Sandra loved it.

Benny still falls asleep in front of the TV every night. I wake him, he gets that wild, frightened look, but he manages to get himself up and to bed without too much trouble. Sometimes I hear him roaming the house late at night, but when I ask him about it the next day, he says he was just up to use the john. He tells Ruthann he sleeps fine. Since the day in the car, we've talked about nothing more important than finding a neighbor kid to mow and trying to take his pills on a full stomach. He thinks I can't hear him throwing up because he turns the bathroom faucet on full blast.

We've agreed that I don't need to be here around the clock, but I don't know where I would go. My apartment feels stripped, devoid of its old coziness, although I miss my stove. Buddy loves it here at Benny's, sitting at the sliding glass door and mewing at every living thing that passes by: spider, bird, neighbor cat. I suppose I could let her out, but I won't. Who knows why her former owners lost her. Benny's warming up to her. He thinks I don't see him sneaking her table scraps.

Stefan e-mailed a week ago, saying how sorry he was that I hadn't been able to work on the regional foods piece. He hinted that he might have a few things to send my way in the future, but mentioned nothing specific. His warm, funny tone was mostly back, but I kept my reply brief and businesslike.

Seeing Henry with his wife opened my eyes to a lot of things. To my chronic naïveté when it comes to men. To my willingness to throw myself into absurdly inappropriate relationships. To the nature of the male species, the biological imperative to entice any female into mating position, then stand up, brush themselves off, and trot off to find more prey.

And what of me, my biological imperative? To foster, to nurture, to please. To stay put and raise the brood, which for me consists of one dying old man with a corny sense of humor and a chubby feline with wanderlust. This, for now, is my family. No doting, long-term mate, no hormone-addled junior high school kids.

I don't even ask myself anymore how all this happened.

I'm shutting down my computer for the day when Benny shuffles behind me in the hallway.

"You doing okay?" I turn. He's been making more trips to the bathroom.

"Yup," he says, and the bathroom door shuts, the lock turns, the faucet blasts. I can't stand to hear what comes next, so I walk through the living room, out the sliding glass door onto the back patio, and close my eyes, inhale the nostalgic, sweet scent of lilacs. I wrap my arms around my ribs, hold tight. Is this really how it happens? We act like everything's normal until it's not?

I open my eyes. The tulips are almost finished for the year, and in their stead come long green shoots of iris. It's warm this afternoon, mild and muggy. I kick off my clogs and walk through the long, moist grass, trying not to think about how badly it needs to be mowed. I helped Benny plant these tulips one fall when I was nine or ten, or their ancestors, anyway. Benny was reading a lot of poetry at the time. Anne and Christine and I would tease him when he'd insert a particularly florid phrase into his everyday patter, like "The leaves of autumn have no mercy," where before he might have said, "Those goddamn leaves keep piling up."

As I punched deep divots in the summer-hardened earth and carefully

inserted bulbs, sprout side up, I asked Benny what exactly we were doing. "Winter's coming. I thought you were supposed to plant flowers in
the spring."

"Spring bulbs need a long sleep," he said, grunting as he leaned heavily onto his trowel. "For now we're just sowing the anticipation of
beauty."

It struck me as so sad and lovely that I didn't snicker or reply. I just
kept digging holes until the burlap bag of bulbs was empty.

At the scratchy slide of the screen door behind me now, I turn to
look at Benny. He stands in the opening, arms spread wide as he hangs
on to each side.

"Can I pick these tulips to bring inside?" I ask. "They're almost done,
anyway."

He nods slowly, his face the color of spoiled turnips.

"Are you sure you're okay?" I take a step toward him.

"They said to expect a little nausea, Ellie. I'm fine." He draws a heavy
breath, then lets it out. "Why don't we just let those little stragglers be,
on second thought," he says. "They've made it this far." He turns back to
the living room and makes his way to lie on the couch.

Later, I'm scrubbing yellow Finn potatoes to boil and mash for dinner
when the phone rings.

"It's me," Ruthann says. "How is he?" She calls every evening on her
own time. I wonder if she does this with all of her patients.

"I'm not sure," I say, snugging the receiver between my chin and
shoulder to dry my hands. "He seems to be throwing up a lot."

She's quiet for a moment. "How much is a lot?"

"A couple, few times a day? I'm not really sure. Isn't it normal to be
sick from chemo?"

"Not with what he's on. The point is to help him not feel sick." She
sounds worried.

"Who is it?" Benny calls from the living room. He can't hear over
the TV.

"It's Ruthann," I call back. "Just a sec, I'll bring you the phone." To

Ruthann I say, "You talk to him. He always acts like everything's okay with me."

"He's protecting you," she says, and I swallow.

Benny calls from the other room, "Are you two gonna talk about me behind my back, or do I get to say something?"

"I'm coming, I'm coming," I say, walking across Yolanda's prized beige carpet to hand him the cordless. "You don't have to get your Jockeys in a twist."

He snorts an appreciative laugh at that and takes the phone, but doesn't raise it to his ear until I turn to walk away. Only when I turn the water back on do I hear the low murmur of his voice.

At dinner, I have one bite of mashed potatoes to make sure they taste good, and I can tell they do, in an academic way. Creamy but still a few lumps, just the right mix of butter and salt. "What did you tell Ruthann about being sick?" I ask.

"That I've been sick." He scoops a mound of potatoes onto his fork, then dredges them through the peppercorn sauce I've made for the roast. "This here is one hell of a meal, Ellie. I don't believe I've ever had so much good food in my life." He picks up a long, thin green bean and eats it like a french fry, twirling it in the sauce before popping it into his mouth. It's amazing that he can still eat. I wonder if any of this food stays in him long enough to provide nourishment. I wonder if it's the food that's making him ill.

"You told her how sick? How often?" I take a tiny bite of meat, roll it in my mouth. The protein is necessary, I know, but I have trouble swallowing it. I'll save the rest for Buddy.

"Yes, ma'am. Don't you worry. It's taken care of."

"She's going to do something about it? Talk to Krall about your chemo?"

He gives me a look and plunks a huge wedge of roast beef in his mouth so that he can't talk. He smiles a goofy smile, his mouth struggling to stay closed around the meat.

I laugh and try to relax, take a sip of the locally brewed ale I picked up at Freddy's. Theoretically, Benny's not supposed to have any, but Ruthann shrugged when I asked, like, *what's it going to hurt?* When I asked about rich or heavy foods, she did the same thing. "Does he enjoy it?" she asked. I nodded, and she said, "There you go."

Her blend of medical expertise and common sense make me appreciate this whole hospice thing. Benny need never step foot in another hospital if he doesn't want to. I asked Ruthann if there was anything I was supposed to be looking out for (thinking, of course, that he might die on me overnight when I could have done something to prevent it, like . . . what? Call an ambulance? Give him CPR? It's not easy to reconcile that the point is not to try to save him).

She said, "I can tell you all the nitty-gritty now, or we can take this one step at a time. For some reason, you strike me as a one-step-at-a-time person." I had to agree I was, and I was thrilled to hear that Yolanda is handling all of Benny's legal and financial matters. You'd think I'd have heard them talking on the phone, which they apparently do, but I haven't. How he manages to keep so many secrets in such a small house is a mystery.

When Benny's wiped his plate clean with a piece of white bread spread frosting thick with butter, I push my plate aside, lean my elbows onto the table.

"So, Uncle Benny. Tell me this."

He rolls his eyes with a pained *what now?* expression.

"I was just going to ask, if you could have anything in the whole world to eat for dinner tomorrow night, what would it be?"

He looks off into the distance, thinking. "Fried pork chops and pan gravy, the way my mother used to make it."

"Did she have a special recipe or something? A secret ingredient?"

"Same as all country women," he says. His eyes have a wicked glint. "Good old-fashioned pork drippings."

"You mean bacon grease?"

"Fat rendered from the hog. Mother'd cook it down and separate the lard from the cracklings. She'd use the good, pure fat for baking, but the stuff with the cracklings? That's some of the best eating anywhere. You fry up your eggs, your meat, your potatoes in it, or you just sop it up with some good homemade bread. Mm, mm." He's on cloud nine just thinking about it.

"Can do," I say, and stand to clear the table.

The next day, I've called every butcher in a fifty-mile radius, and not a one carries pork cracklings. The closest approximation of Benny's prized drippings will probably be a combination of lard and bacon fat, supplies easily procured from Fred's. I'm not entirely surprised to find that the Fred Meyer store closest to Benny's, however, has no lard in stock. "Try Roseway, maybe, or Concordia—someplace in Northeast," says Britney, the prepubescent assistant manager, referring to poorer neighborhoods, immigrant neighborhoods. Just another reminder that I am now ensconced in the Southwest, the most vanilla of Portland's four distinctive quadrants.

I drive up the highway, across the Marquam Bridge to the east side of the Willamette, the working-class side, the funky-in-a-not-quite-comfortable-way side, not nearly as innocuous as the more gentrified west that I've always lived in. Somehow, the Northeast's inner neighborhoods retain their blue-collar or hippie or ethnic roots even with the addition of coffeehouses and cafés, gift shops and bookstores. And the old bungalows and English cottages are seriously cute. If I ever bought a house, it would probably have to be over here, though many of these neighborhoods are getting almost as pricey as the west side.

At the exit for Hollywood, I turn off the highway. Britney didn't mention the Hollywood Freddy's, but it's worth a try. I turn up Broadway, past Ethiopian restaurants and tattoo shops, naturopathic doctors and heating-oil contractors. At the light I swing into the parking lot, park near the requisite companion Starbucks, and head into the spacious fluorescent glow, the store layout as familiar as my own apartment. A Fred's is a Fred's is a Fred's. Just like McDonald's or Home Depot or Holiday Inn: Once you know one, you know 'em all—an unadventurous consumer's dream, and one that is slowly putting every mom-and-pop out of business.

I head for the back, thinking the dairy section would be a good place to find lard, it being a multitudinous collection of animal fats. Weaving through slow-motion elderly shoppers and stock clerks with boxes spilling at their feet, my mind goes into work mode. While I'm here, I should pick up supplies for my latest *American Family* article: "Beyond Con Carne: 7 Bold New Chili Recipes."

At the wide rear aisle that runs the length of the store, I glide past milk, yogurt, and cottage cheese to butter and butterlike products. I don't remember the last time I saw a package of lard, but I remember waxy translucent paper with blue writing wrapped around a large rectangular white chunk. "Lard, lard," I mumble, scanning all the way to cheese, then back. Would Crisco work? I just want to get this right. Maybe I should ask the butcher while I check out the pork chops.

At the meat section, I head instinctively toward the premium case. Beautiful butterflied chops lie next to thick tenderloins and mounds of pork-apple sausage. Benny's mother would have butchered the pig herself, I suppose, or his dad would have. They'd have cut meager portions by today's standards, thin triangular slabs to make Porky's sacrifice last longer.

"Can I help you?" says a squat Latino man with a drooping mustache. His white coat, like a doctor's, is smeared with blood.

"I need some pork chops, but I need them less . . . I don't know. Just not quite so thick and wonderful looking."

"Thin sliced?"

"Like when we were kids, you know?"

He nods. "I can cut some of these down for you, but maybe you should try my uncle's *carniceria* on Belmont. They do all that thin-sliced meat, all fresh, good stuff."

"Oh, my God," I say, "I think I used to go there with my aunt, years ago. What was it called, Chuy's?"

"Chucho's." He winks. "Not that I don't like to give Uncle Fred the business, but Uncle Chucho has just what you're looking for."

"Hey, do you think he has lard?"

"You bet. The real stuff, too. Not that processed crap."

"Pork cracklings?" It would be too much to ask for.

"*Chicharrones?* Of course." He waves a thick hand in the air and walks toward a young mom eyeing the fresh bay shrimp. "*Chicharrones,* lard, pork chops. The dude has it all."

"Thanks," I call after him, and turn to go.

"Eleanor Samuels." The voice behind me is pleasantly familiar, yet I'm so stuck in my pork-fat reverie I'm not quick enough to realize it is Henry's until I've turned to stare him square in the face.

"Oh!" is all I can manage to say.

"Indeed," he says, smiling.

Somehow, Henry suckers me into having coffee at Starbucks. Well, he invites me and I say yes, feeling like a home wrecker.

We squeeze into chairs tucked around a small table in back. Behind Henry a triptych of framed child art hangs on the wall. Crudely lettered on the top of one drawing are the words I AM KARA. I AM HAPPY.

Determined to keep the conversation to small talk, I ask how the restaurant's doing. Henry says fine, fine. He tried to call; I say I know, I just got busy. The article turned out great. Nods all around.

When the green-haired barista calls out "Tall mocha, double breve," Henry jumps up to retrieve our drinks, then places mine to the right of where a plate would be if this were a meal, along with a napkin, sugar, and stir stick all precisely squared to the table.

"So," I say, "what are you doing across the river? This is not the first place I would have imagined bumping into you." I try to smile, feeling like I'm stretching a hide over bones, and take a searing sip of my mocha.

"I live a few blocks from here," he says. "Fifteenth and Siskiyou."

"Really? I thought you lived in the Pearl."

"I work in the Pearl. I can't afford to live there."

"I just thought . . . you know. I didn't know."

"How would you?" he says, raising his eyebrows, taking a delicate sip of his espresso and steamed half-and-half. Why didn't I order one of those? His face is pinker than usual, his hair even rowdier. My feelings for him haven't budged an inch.

"And how's your wife?" I say, then clamp my mouth shut. I don't ask these kinds of questions. I don't dig for dirt. I'm too apt to find it where I don't want to.

He raises his eyebrows. "I imagine she's fine. I don't really know. She lives with her parents."

I get it. Separated. Not divorced. Tenuous filaments still stretching between them like Benny and Yolanda. I nod, bite my tongue. I'm not saying another thing.

"I'd like to explain the situation," Henry says, and his face turns serious, bottom lip jutting, fingers tapping the paper coffee cup. "It's not what you think."

"You know, it's none of my business. Don't worry about it." I take a gulp of my drink, feel the long, sliding burn from tongue to gullet, and stand. "Thanks for the coffee. I've got to get going."

"Wait, Eleanor. Please. Let's talk."

"Why?" I'm fumbling through my purse for keys. All I wanted was some lard, for crying out loud. The last thing I need in my life is someone else with secrets.

"Because . . . you know. I thought we had some kind of . . . God, you know what I mean, don't you?"

I look back at him, trying not to notice the sincerity in his eyes. "I don't have the slightest idea what you're talking about." I wince, wondering if he saw it. "You're married."

"But I don't love her. If you'd just let me expla—"

"No," I interrupt. How typical. How shameless. "I don't care. You're married."

"I'm helping Namhla and her family stay in the U.S.," he blurts, and I squint at him. I look at him, in fact, for the longest moment I've ever looked at someone without speaking or moving in for something more amorous.

"She's from Tibet?"

He nods. I almost fall for it, but then it hits me: I wonder how Namhla feels about it.

"You know what?" I say. "The bottom line is you're married, for whatever reason."

He purses his lips, nods, then stands and offers his hand to shake. "You're right, Eleanor. You're an honorable and moral woman, and you are absolutely right."

I take his hand, feel it close over mine, let it linger there too long.

"Well, then," I say, finally pulling away. "Be sure to look in next Tuesday's paper. It's a pretty good piece."

"Good-bye, Eleanor Samuels," Henry says. He sits back down, glum.

As I turn to go, I glance at his left hand.

No ring, and no white strip.

Benny cuts a bite-size piece of pork, turns the fork this way and that in his hand, examining the crispy fried exterior while checking for my reaction in glances he thinks are sneaky.

"Oh, for God's sake," I say to appease him. "Eat the damn thing."

He sops up some extra gravy and gently slides the fork in and out of his mouth. As he chews, his face loses the playful grin. He swallows and looks down at the table.

"What? Is it too chewy?" I saw at my own chop, the smallest of the bunch, to taste it. "Too much salt or something? Too overdone?"

Benny looks up and his eyes are soft and liquid. "No, honey. It's perfect." Tentatively, he cuts another piece, chews it slowly, then another. By the end of the meal, he's eaten his entire pork chop and fried potatoes and sopped up the extra drippings with a thick slice of homemade bread, made with, of course, lard. When I offer him apple crisp for dessert, he finally puts his hands in the air.

"Gawd, I couldn't eat another bite. Maybe after my stomach settles some," he says, and I get this weird vision of Benny as bulimic, throwing up so he can power down more food. The way I've successfully cut and scooted my food around on my plate, though, is a clear indicator of who has the real food issues in this house. At some point I know I have to start eating again or I'll end up like Karen Carpenter.

After the ritual of TV, dessert, more TV, and Benny trundling off to bed, I walk over to the bookshelves, take down as many photo albums as I can carry back to the couch. It's time I got to know Benny better. Maybe he'd like to talk about his life, his old friends and family.

I open the book on top of the pile, a rectangular brown and gilt pressboard cover with black pages. Square black-and-white photos of people I don't know have tiny dates imprinted along one curlicued edge: Oct.

1959, Apr. 1960. Five years before I was born, before Mom and Dad were even married.

Young men in suits and skinny ties, girlish women in skirts and sweaters. They look like friends, hanging out in someone's sparse Danish-modern living room holding highballs, cans of beer. Smoking, always smoking. Looking far more sophisticated than my generation did at that age.

I wonder if these are from Benny's bachelor days in Missouri, or his first marriage, his social circle before she died. I look closer to see if I can pick out Benny as a young guy with hair, turning the pages to scan the different people. Which young woman would be his wife? The one with freckles and pearls, or the buxom one who's vamping in every photo? Then my heart jumps. A close-up shot of my mother stares back at me, her curly raven hair coiffed short and neat, lips dark, eyes bright as she laughs and points at the camera, cigarette in one hand. She is so young and fresh-faced I want to tell her to be careful.

How did Benny get ahold of Mom's pictures from her single days? I've never seen them before; maybe she doesn't even know he stole them. I can't imagine Benny doing anything so underhanded and creepy.

I turn the pages quickly now, looking for more shots of Mom, impatient at all the other people laughing and clowning in the photos. Then I see it and stop dead, the book vibrating now in my tight grasp.

It's a picture of a man and woman standing in a kitchen doorway, their profiles as they lean against opposite doorjambs, unaware of the camera. They hold hands across the space between them. The woman is pregnant.

I slam the book shut. Adrenaline pumps full force through my body. I have to talk to someone, but who? I have to do something, but first I have to know:

What were my pregnant mother and Benny doing together in 1960, two years before she married Dad and three years before she had her oldest daughter?

chapter thirteen

All of the best secrets used to be stored in Mom's underwear drawer. Anne was the one who'd sneak into my parents' bedroom in the middle of the day, when Mom was having coffee next door with Mrs. Brainard, or in the kitchen on the phone with her sister. Anne, stealthy and courageous, would pilfer rare, exotic finds and bring them to our room under her shirt, dramatically dropping to her knees in the middle of the fluffy white carpet and producing the booty.

One time it was a blue diary, like a child's, with a lock but no key. We tried bowing open the cover to peek inside at the pages, and creased the cheap cardboard. Mortified, Anne sneaked it back into Mom's drawer posthaste. We thought for sure we'd be in trouble, but we never heard a peep about it.

Other times it might be a letter from Mom's sister, filled with cusswords and gems like, "You have no idea how lucky you are, married to a hardworking man with those gorgeous little girls. If I have to listen to one more goddamn man lie about his job, his income, or his marital status, I think I'll have to shoot myself." We didn't understand what all the drama was about, but the mystery of it was delicious.

Once it was a pair of lacy black underpants with just a thin strip of crotch, not the kind of underpants our mother wore. Hers were full-size, a rayon-cotton blend in pastel shades only. We knew she had mint green and butter yellow, pink, blue, beige, and lilac—not to mention a few pairs of white—but we had never seen these dark see-through things before. My stomach churned at the sight of them, but Anne said maybe our aunt had given them to her as a present. Anne decided to keep the underpants, stuffing them deep between her mattress and box spring, for what purpose I had no idea. It was another mystery about our mother's life, to be sure, but this one didn't feel quite so thrilling.

The phone is in my hand. Benny is asleep in his room. I have lain awake listening to Buddy purr wetly in my ear all night, trying to sort a spiraling conflagration of thoughts into some useful plan. What do I do about this? Who do I tell? Who dare I ask? I keep wondering who that person turned out to be, that lump beneath Mom's maternity blouse with the Peter Pan collar. My half sister? Half brother? Where is she now? What's his name? Did my father know?

This isn't something to talk about on the phone, I decide, and dress in the semidarkness of predawn. I leave Benny a note on the kitchen table:

Early appointment. Take the green pill and two pink and white pills after you have some breakfast, then another green one and a yellow one at 10:30. I should be back before lunch. Call my cell if you need to.

I drive west through suburbs and shopping centers, turn south on the Pacific Highway, and drink in the sudden green of forest punctuated by occasional small towns, orchards, Christmas tree farms. It's nearly seven thirty when I arrive in the elegant orderliness of vineyards and wine country. At the tiny berg of Dundee, I take a right, head up a steep hill, winding through fields of Pinot Gris, Chardonnay, and Riesling, and then fields of preternatural minimansions. I find Mom and John's—a stucco French-country monolith—and park in front. She's lived here nearly a year, yet I've only been inside once. She must feel like a princess in a fortress, like she finally won the lottery.

Someone moves through the house, turning a light on, then another. It could only be John. When my mother finally got to stop getting little girls ready for school, she became an avid late-morning sleeper. Left to her own devices, she probably wouldn't get up before ten.

I'm not feeling that patient.

Armed with the photo album, I walk up the winding slate path, neatly bordered by trim green grass, not a blade out of place. At the ornate iron door, I push the doorbell and hear chimes inside, like in a church.

I yawn from sleep deprivation and nervousness and realize I haven't brushed my teeth. If my surprise attack doesn't kill her, my breath surely will. Do I have mints in my purse, gum? I hug the book to my chest and decide not to care.

A curious head appears in the entryway window and then the door swings open. John stands holding a dainty toile-pattern coffee cup, wearing jeans and a Mariners sweatshirt, his silver hair neatly combed. His feet are bare upon the hard wood of the entryway, toenails yellow and far too long. I quickly look away.

"Why, Eleanor," he says, "what a pleasant surprise. Come in." As if it isn't bizarre that I'm standing at his doorway early on a Thursday morning with no forewarning or precedent for a visit.

"I need to talk to my mother," I say, stepping inside. "I don't imagine she's up yet."

"No." He chuckles pleasantly—I'm almost sure of it—and says, "How about some coffee? Bebe brought home one of those French press pots, and I can't get enough of the stuff. Have you tried it?" He leads me through the formal dining room, which looks as if it seats twenty, into their granite-and-cherrywood kitchen that I secretly covet. If I told Mom I liked it, though, the corners of her mouth would curl into that smug smile, the one most people think is cute because it shows her dimples. I have learned to avoid doing anything that elicits that smile.

Motioning for me to take a seat at the granite breakfast bar, John pulls another toile cup from the cupboard and pours from the press pot. "Cream, sugar?"

"Listen, I didn't come here to be a pain, but I really need to talk to Mom."

He nods, setting the coffee in front of me, along with a matching sugar bowl and creamer. "Certainly, Eleanor," he says. "But I think your mother might be more responsive if we don't interrupt her beauty sleep."

Even though I'm starting to like the guy, I say, "If you don't go wake her up now, I will, and she probably won't like the way I do it." I pull my lips into a grimace of a fake smile and take a sip of coffee. "You're right about the coffee, though. It's fabulous."

He nods, sets his cup on the counter. "Okeydoke," he says, and strolls gracefully from the room. He's unflappable, probably a good quality in a salesman.

After a few moments, he returns, smiles, and takes a seat at the other end of the counter to drink his coffee.

"She's coming?"

"Of course," he says. "It will be just a moment. I'm sure you understand."

I swallow, take a deep breath through my nose, the way Suzanne taught me, blow it out my mouth. Why did I never go back to see her? She would have talked me out of this, had I given her the chance. Had I thought about it in the sensible light of day, not under the crazy-making cover of darkness.

After I've finished my coffee, I stand and walk my cup to the sink. "This is nuts," I say to John. "I'm going up there."

"I understand," he says, and I see it in his eyes. He does understand. He's the one who lives with her now. Surely he's felt the sting of her mercurial love by now.

I climb the wool-carpeted steps and arrive on a wide landing, tall windows in front of me glowing orange with early-morning sun. Several doors surround me.

"Mom?" I call out. The photo album is damp on the side I hold against myself. I wish I'd eaten something.

"In here, honey," she says, voice coming from a double doorway on my left. "Just putting on my face."

I close my eyes, not moving. She will never change.

"Honey?"

I open my eyes, and she is standing in the doorway, mascara wand in hand, head wrapped in toilet paper to preserve her coiffure, white satin gown snug against drooping breasts and a football-shaped mound of old-lady stomach. *When did that happen,* I wonder? Her lily perfume wafts toward me.

"Are you all right?" She looks at me with concern, genuine and maternal, and I bite my lip, feel my nostrils flare, the back of my throat fill.

"Not really," I say, and begin to bawl, the way I always have since I was a kid. "Crybaby!" I can hear Anne say.

"Come here, Ellie," Mom says, holding out her free hand, but she makes no move toward me. "What's the matter? What's all this?"

For just a moment I am tempted to go to her, to feel her wrap her arms around me, which I think she would do if I let her. Maybe she would lead me into her room, sit with me on her bed, and we'd have a long talk about everything that's ever gone wrong between us, and she'd prove to me that the dates on the photos were wrong, that Dad was indeed in one of the pictures, that Anne was lolling in her stomach, biding her time until her birthday arrived.

I can't live her fairy tale lies any longer.

"You tell me," I say, shoving the photo album at her. She looks at it as if she's not sure she wants to touch it, but then she sighs and comes over to take it from me. When I've let go, I reach up to wipe my face dry. That's the last damn time I'll cry in front of her.

"What is this?" she asks.

"Open it."

She pulls the cover open just long enough to scan the first page, then grimaces and closes the book.

"He gave these to you?"

"No. Of course not. I'm living there, Mother. What did you expect? It gets boring. I was looking through his old pictures."

"Why on earth he keeps these around . . ."

"Jesus, Mom." My voice is loud. "That's not the point."

"The point is that these are private, Eleanor, and you have no business—"

"Of course it's my business. You think nobody noticed you and Benny and your special little friendship? All those years and we all had to pretend it wasn't happening?"

The photo album and mascara wand drop to the floor, coal black brush skiffing a stain across the carpet. She covers her face with both hands, square-cut diamond on her ring finger winking in the now brilliant light from the window.

"You have to tell me," I say.

She shakes her head, like if she doesn't look at me, I'm not really here. I reach up and pull her hands from her face. They feel fragile and insubstantial in my grasp, and I realize that all that stuff about having big and small bones is true.

"You have to tell me," I say again, and she opens her eyes but doesn't look at me.

"I'd rather not."

"I know," I say, and let go of her. "But you have to."

The baby wasn't Benny's, Mom says. She'd made a foolish mistake in her junior year at Northwestern and slept with the man she thought she'd marry. She looks down at her hands clenched around the photo album, and I look, too. Veins bulge through tissue-paper skin, and faded age spots persist even though I know she bleaches them. We are sitting on her bed, as I'd imagined, but this is not the talk I longed for.

"What about the baby?" I ask.

"I don't know. I gave her up for adoption."

Her. I have another sister.

"What were you doing with Benny? What . . . Jesus, Mom. You were with Benny. What the hell have you been hiding all your life?"

"It's too much for me, Eleanor, all this . . . all this questioning. This is very upsetting for me." She sits up straight and folds her arms across her chest, looks me in the eye for the first time. Her face is smeared and tear streaked. The toilet paper hangs raggedly from the left side of her head. And still she has this poise, this regal I'm-in-charge posture she always manages to find, even in her depths. If I wasn't so angry, I'd leave her alone.

"Just two simple questions, then."

She sighs, shakes her head.

"Appease me, Mother. I'm upset, too."

She considers this, then shrugs. "But you're to tell no one."

"That's not fair. Anne and Christine should know. John should know."

"John knows. And I'll tell your sisters in my own way, and in my own time."

"Fine. Did Dad know?" My heartbeat quickens, as if I'm about to jump off a cliff. Why should this question scare me more than any of the others?

Mom draws a deep breath, exhales. "I didn't want him to. It was all before I'd met him, but I think he figured it out."

"You think? You never talked about it? You never explained or dealt with it?" No wonder I'm single, with this as a role model.

"We alluded to it, but no, we never directly spoke of it."

I make an exasperated sound, and her eyes flame.

"It was your father's choice as much as it was mine, Eleanor. You can't possibly understand."

"Fine." My eyes sting, but I continue. "What's the deal with Benny? You knew him before and you pretended not to."

"Oh, Ellie, so what? So what if we were friends before?"

"Friends?" I grab the photo album from her hands, flip through the pages until I come to the picture of the two of them in the doorway, holding hands, turn it toward her. "This is just friends?"

She lets her eyes flicker over the photo, takes a deep breath, and sighs before speaking. "You don't want to hear this story, Ellie. Trust me."

"Tell me."

"I've always tried to protect you because I know how much Benny means to you, and you to him. You're his favorite."

I snort, feel myself color. "Christine's his favorite. And why should you have to protect me?"

"Honey." She takes my hand, holds it against the 450-thread-count sheet. "Your uncle Benny isn't quite the angel you think he is."

"Jesus, Mom. I know you two"—I almost say "cheated," then remember how much trouble that word got me into all those years ago—"were together."

She shakes her head. "Benny Sloan has pursued me since the day I met him on campus."

"He went to Northwestern?" I've never heard anything about Benny going to college.

"For a time, but he dropped out. His family couldn't afford it, and he wasn't bright enough for a scholarship."

Bullshit, I want to say, but I'd rather hear the rest. "Okay, so—"

"I was going steady with this other fellow and never gave Benny the time of day. I was young and stupid and didn't realize that his befriending me, taking a special interest in me when I was having my troubles . . ." She sniffs and looks away.

"What?"

"That's always been his way, Eleanor, to work his way into my life, first then, and later, when I'd married your father and had you girls. And after your father died."

"You're telling me he put the moves on you after Dad died?" I know Benny, I know him in a way that is unspoken and concrete, and I know he wouldn't have done this.

"Not sexually, for God's sake, Eleanor. The man has more class than that." She rubs the soft sheet between her fingers, then reaches up to tidy the unraveling toilet paper hanging from her head. "He said he would leave Yolanda if I wanted him to, that he would take care of me." Her eyes fill and she turns away, animal sounds escaping her throat, embarrassing sobs she can't stifle.

"Mom," I say, touching her shoulder.

She pulls away, shakes her head, hand shielding her eyes.

"Did you want to be with him then?"

Again, she shakes her head, wipes her face on her palm, turns back to me. "Absolutely not," she says, then stands and walks back to her vanity table. She sits on the brocade stool, extracts a tissue from a floral box, and dabs at her eyes. "I hope I have sufficiently answered your questions. You can see it's a very painful topic for me, and I don't want to discuss it again, do you hear me?" She turns to look at me, and I see that, indeed, there is deep grief in her eyes, more than I've ever witnessed, even at Dad's funeral. Still, I know she's lying.

"Yes," I say, feeling nine years old and reprimanded, once again, for daring to ask about the truth.

As I'm leaving, Mom turns from the mirror, her face recomposed. "By the way, honey, you look wonderful. You've lost so much weight! What diet are you on?"

I stop in the doorway, breathe in through my nose, out through my mouth. "I am caring for a dying man, Mother. A dying man you haven't asked me about once since I stepped foot in here, or even called to say hello. Somehow, I've lost my appetite."

And then I leave her bedroom, her house, her world, and fly back home to mine.

chapter fourteen

It's nearly nine a.m. when I get home, and Benny is still in bed. Benny, Mr. Five o'Clock Riser, rain or shine, daylight savings or no. But lately he's been sleeping longer, napping more. Disappearing a little at a time.

"Ben?" I poke my head into his dark room, see the lump of blankets shift. "You okay?"

"Mmm," he mumbles. "Mm hmm."

"Want some breakfast? You need to take your pills."

He murmurs another assent, and I gently pull the door closed, go put the photo album back in its place on the shelf. When the time is right, I'll ask Benny about it. Surely he'll tell me the truth, which scares me almost enough not to ask him a thing. I sigh and head for the kitchen.

"You in the mood for Belgian waffles?" I call out, clanging a bowl from the cupboard. "With chocolate chips and whipped cream?" Benny's losing weight, even with all the intake, and I keep trying to think of things that will fatten him up.

He can't hear me, but I know he loves waffles, so I lug the ancient waffle iron from the pantry, plug in the cloth-covered cord, pull out the old tin canister of flour, the baking powder, a battered half-open box of powdered sugar, which puffs a sweet cloud of white when it slips from my grip to the counter.

From the fridge I extract butter, heavy cream, and eggs, then bump the door closed with my hip, feeling impact more on bone than on flesh.

It's an odd sensation, and not an altogether pleasant one. How it is that I can still get a kick out of preparing food when I don't want to actually consume it? I appreciate the aromas, the textures, the idea of the final product itself and its presentation. I just don't want to put it in my mouth. The thought of it makes my jaw tighten, my stomach threaten to heave. I don't know if I've changed forever in this regard, or if it's a temporary condition, like sympathetic morning sickness, but it leaves me with an uneasy feeling. I've always wanted to be thinner, but I can't help thinking that this might be worse than overeating. I used to get some kind of nurturing at least, some kind of solace. Now I don't know what's sustaining me.

When I've mixed the batter, I throw a drop onto the griddle; it sizzles and sets. I turn the temperature down a notch and pour the first waffle. Another bowl from the cupboard, a dash of vanilla and a pinch of powdered sugar, and I whip cream into silky smooth fluff, set it aside without so much as tasting it.

With two waffles warming in the oven, I wipe my hands on a dish towel, set the table, then pad down the hall to Benny's room. "You doing okay in there?" No answer. I knock. "Benny?"

I open the door, head starting to buzz, and say again, "Benny?"

The blankets heave and fall back. "Goddamn it," he says in a thin, wavery voice as he struggles to sit upright.

A wave of heat burns through my stomach, my chest, up into my face. *This is hell*, I think, right here, right now, and I hurry to his bedside.

Benny is snarled in sheets and pajamas, hair wild against the pillow. The fusty funk of the unbathed rises from the linens. "I don't know what's wrong with me," he moans. "I'm all glued together."

Detangling the sheets, I lean into him, place my arm under and beneath his bony shoulder blades and lift. He clings to my arm, grip tentative. His hands fall away, so I have to rebalance myself, one knee against the mattress, the other foot planted firmly on the floor, and pull him into a sitting position, jam pillows behind him.

"There," I say. Out of breath, lightheaded. "Are you okay?" I ask, but all I can think is *turn for the worse, turn for the worse*. Why didn't I read ahead in Ruthann's little plan?

"Yeah, I'm fine," he says, leaning back into the pillows, eyes jittery. "Just got stuck, I guess."

"You were pretty tangled up," I say, offering him a bone.

He takes it, nodding. After a moment, his breathing slows back to normal, and the sugar-cookie smell of waffle drifts into the room.

"Do you want me to help you to the kitchen?" I pick up his robe from the chair by the bed and hold it out to him. He lays it across his lap and strokes it with bent fingers.

"You know, I don't believe I've ever had breakfast in bed," he says, looking at me from beneath heavy lids. "Not my whole life. What do you think about that?"

I swallow and paste a smile on my face. "I think today is your lucky day, mister. Sit tight. I'll be right back."

He nods, attempts a smile. As I'm leaving his room, I look back and he's closed his eyes, let his face go slack, and folded his hands together in his lap, index fingers pointing skyward: *This is the church, this is the steeple. . . .*

In the next room, Buddy lies asleep on my desk chair. I pick up her warm, heavy body and push her through Benny's door. Good kitty that she is, she trots to his bed and hops up. He doesn't open his eyes, but his hand finds her soft fur, strokes her until she has settled in a rounded lump against his side.

"Ruthann," I whisper into the phone in the kitchen. "It's me. Something's wrong. He can't get out of bed."

"I can be there by eleven."

"Thanks. There'll be a waffle with your name on it."

"In that case, I'll try to make it earlier," she says, and I manage a laugh as I hang up. What would we do without her?

Benny eats just over a third of his waffle, but he finishes the whipped cream, licking even the stem of his fork to make sure he gets it all, shooing Buddy away when she discovers just what it is he's consuming.

"Aren't you eating?" he asks me as I reach for his plate.

"I did earlier," I say.

"Ellie." Benny keeps a hold on the edge of his plate and we play tug-of-war.

"Benny," I say. "I did."

He sighs and lets go of the plate, lying back against the pillows. He looks exhausted. "You know what I've always liked about you, Miss Roosevelt?"

"What's that?" I stand, leaning my thigh into the mattress, Buddy pawing her way up my torso to try to reach the vestiges of cream on Benny's plate.

"Take those waffles, for instance. You don't just make waffles. You make goddamn chocolate chip waffles with whipped cream. You don't just eat something, you really taste it, you enjoy it. You always have." He winks and reaches over to scratch Buddy's head. "Used to have trouble hanging on to my desserts, as I recall. You were a little bit like this one here."

I flush, embarrassed. Benny's the one person who's never made me feel bad about my weight, about my eating. But here he is—

"It's a wonderful thing, Ellie, to be so alive. That's what it is. You've always been so full of life and the enjoyment of it." His eyes glisten, and he wrinkles his nose, shrugs. "Guess I'm just turning into a sentimental old sap."

I try to think of something funny, something light to deflect his direct appreciation of me, of how I am—or used to be—but I can't.

I load his plate on the tray and hand him one of the eggcups we use to sort his doses: yellow cup for first thing in the morning, pink floral for midmorning. Blue is lunchtime, green-striped is afternoon, blue floral for dinner, and white is bedtime. "We almost forgot. Pill time."

"I'd better let my stomach settle some first," he says, placing the cup on his bedside table. "I'll take 'em in a while."

"Do you need help with the . . ." I nod toward the bathroom.

"Don't know." He's as reluctant as I am to think about it. "I'm okay for now."

"If you're sure," I say, picking up his tray. "Call me if you need me." I escape down the hall and into the kitchen, lean against the counter, and close my eyes.

• • •

Later in the week, when I've finished my piece on chili for *American Family*, I call Christine, just to hear someone else's voice. I tell her how Benny couldn't get out of bed, how Ruthann brought him a walker, showing him how to pull himself up in the morning, how to stabilize and balance before taking each step. "Use it or lose it," she barked like a drill sergeant, but Benny seemed relieved to hear that he wasn't yet bedridden. She asked me to walk her to her car as she was leaving, and said, "You may want to start thinking about a home health-care provider."

"God," Christine says, tears in her voice, "this must be so hard for you. How do you do it, El? It's got to be killing you."

"What's the alternative?" I snap, not meaning to, not really. But I don't feel all that bad when she says, "I know. I just feel guilty that you're doing it all. Why isn't Aunt Yolanda helping out?"

"I don't know," I say, but it's the one thing that now makes more sense than it did before my little chat with my mother. This is the thing I really want to talk to Christine about, but I know I won't.

"Do you want me to come up there?" Christine sounds unsure, as if she'd like me to let her off the hook.

"Maybe," I say, "but you have so much going on, and you're so far away. I'm the one who's here, that's all."

"Yeah, if only you'd escaped, like Anne and I did."

"You escaped?"

"As soon as I could," she says with a *well, duh* tone in her voice.

"Why didn't I?"

"Because you didn't need to. You were happy."

"I was? When?"

"I don't know. You've always seemed content."

"Maybe I was just lazy."

"I don't think so. It's only since what's-his-name that you've turned all morose."

I try to think back to my pre-PR job days. I was definitely happy while I was with Daniel, right up until he screwed his assistant. But what if I'd moved to one of the big food cities right out of school, like San

Francisco, New York? God, Paris? Why have I stayed here so long? I shake my head, sigh. Spilled milk, that's all it is.

There is one thing that makes me happy, lately, I realize, and that's Benny's face whenever I feed him something he loves. And there was another thing, but he's married, and he has too many secrets that I don't want to know about.

In the glow of the computer screen, I read:

> Dear Ms. Samuels,
> Not to be insensitive to your needs at this difficult time, but I see that you are, indeed, writing for other publications (I do keep my eye on the competition, you know) and I'm wondering if you will ever write for me again. If I get down on my knees and beg? If I send you bouquet after bouquet of roses, yellow, pink, or that fabulous orange color you see so much these days? If I said I knew I'd been a horse's ass but that I was merely fighting the urge to play Prince Charming and come to your rescue because I knew I should be more professional than that, but that I seem to have a soft spot for one Ms. Samuels?
> Oh, do reply, please, or my heart may break.
> S.

My jaw unhinges, my eyes blink hard, then stretch wide. Quickly, I scan back to the top of the e-mail and see that, yes, it came from Stefan's address. It's not a joke, and I'm not just imagining it.

Stefan likes me.

He's thinking about me. Okay, mostly about work, but still. He wanted to *rescue* me.

I type:

> Dear Stefan,
> Yes, I've been working. It helps to think about something other than vomit and laundry and how long we have left.

I stop typing and read, then erase.

> Dear Stefan,
> Yes, I'm working again. How kind of you to notice my little
> old byline. Please feel free to contact me about assign-
> ments—

I stop, thinking, thinking.

> —or just to converse. I've always had a soft spot for you,
> too, as I'm sure you know. You're the best editor a girl could
> have.
> E.
> P.S. Regarding methods of bribery, flowers are never a bad
> idea, but I kind of like the thought of you on your knees.

Alluring but inscrutable. I hit SEND.

From the moment I found the photos of Benny and my pregnant
mother, I've worried over when to bring it up with him. I've been waiting for the perfect moment, a time when nothing else is more important. So far, it hasn't come. Maybe it doesn't matter what his version of
the story is. I think I know the truth. They loved each other. They had
a baby out of wedlock and gave it up for adoption. That kind of pain
would have to tear anyone apart, but it must have killed Benny when
Mom married Dad. When he lost his wife, his first thought must have
been to move closer to Mom. I'm not excusing their behavior, their dal-
liances, but what would our lives have been like if we'd never met
Benny?

Later that night, when the snoring from Benny's room takes on a
deep-sleep rumble, I call Christine back. Reid answers, which surprises
me for some reason. I never think of him as actually existing, not on the
physical plane. He never comes with Christine to Portland, and he
never answers the phone. Hearing his flat, nasal drone makes me wish
he hadn't answered now. All I can think of are mucus-covered towels.

"Reid, what a surprise!"

"Not really," he says. "I do live here." Then, "Chris!"

I grimace at his "Chris." She's so not a Chris, but then this is a man so intent on being economical that he hasn't purchased shoes since his mother's funeral. In 1989.

"Hi!" Christine says, out of breath. "What's up?"

"What are you doing? I haven't interrupted anything randy, have I?" I shudder to think about it.

"God, no. I was just up in Reid's office. We're making it into a nursery." She sounds happy, but I bet he's not. "I'm painting it pale blue and celadon, with peach accents in case it's a girl." Just like Mom.

"You aren't supposed to be painting, are you? Aren't you like five months now?" I remember some magazine article or wives' tale from years ago. "Is he helping you?"

"It's latex. It's fine."

"So he's not helping."

"No." Clipped and neat, which means he's in the room.

"Want me to put the fear of God in him?"

"No," she says again, this time cheerier. "Everything's great. Reid's finally finished editing the eco-terrorism piece—"

"Is he pro or con?" I interject, but she continues as if I hadn't spoken.

"—so he's teaching summer sessions this year."

"He'd better," I say, although this is good news, and maybe even a sign that people can change.

"How's Benny?" she says.

"Asleep. I don't know. I think he's probably okay, just getting weak."

"God."

We're both quiet.

"I called you about something else," I say. "I found out something I wish I hadn't."

"What?"

"I don't know if you want to know."

"Ellie! You can't do that, not after you say something like that."

I take deep breath. "Mom had a baby before . . . before Anne. Before us."

"Really? Did they lose it?" She sounds frantic. "Do we have some horrible gene or—"

"No. God, no! No, it didn't die. It was a girl. She gave her up for adoption."

"Wow." She pauses. "But why?"

"It wasn't with Dad, Christine. It was before. She was still in college."

"Oh, my God. Mom? Our mom?"

"And I'm not supposed to tell you."

"How'd you find out?" she asks, and suddenly I panic. I'm not sure if I'm ready to share the part about Benny and Mom just yet. After years of not speaking of it, I don't know if I even can.

"I found some old pictures," I say, hoping she won't press it. "She was pregnant. It was 1960. So I asked her about it."

"Wow. Can you imagine keeping that secret for so many years?"

I'm silent, suddenly woozy with a clammy nausea that is becoming more frequent now that I don't eat. I try to focus on something, on the thought of Christine standing in her dark 1970s-era kitchen that Reid won't let her redo, wearing a Kmart maternity sweatshirt, no doubt, and caressing her abdomen, trying to fathom how someone who's gone through what she's going through can give up her baby to strangers.

I fill her in on the sketchy details I have, sans Benny, expecting her to react much more strongly than she does. I've always thought of her as the delicate flower in our weed patch of a family, but she takes it in stride. "I guess everyone has their secrets," she says, then asks, "Did Mom name her?"

"I don't know, I didn't ask," I say, and suddenly I want to know more than anything what this girl—this woman's—name is. "Anyway, I just didn't want to be the only one who knew."

Christine sighs, then says, "So, Anne's court date has been postponed. She's not testifying for another five months. Now she's thinking of resigning."

"Thinking of! Why doesn't she just get out of there?"

"It's not that easy," Christine says, defensive. "It's her whole life, that job. What else does she have?"

My family is a mess. Each of us is broken in some way, missing something vital. I can't say this to Christine, and certainly not to Anne. They're trying so hard in their lives, but their situations are so bleak. Christine in a horrible marriage with a self-absorbed, controlling man on the fringe of normalcy. About to bring a child into it. Anne on the brink of a ruined career, and nothing else to shore her up. And Mom. God, it's pathetic. So many secrets, so many false fronts.

And me. Maybe I'm the worst of all.

As we're about to say good-bye, Christine whispers, "I'm going to come help you, El, as soon as I can figure out how to talk Reid into it."

I sit on the couch for a long time, dead phone in hand, staring at the row of photo albums on the shelf. What other secrets do they hold? Do I really want to know?

In the same funk that used to send me to the refrigerator, I head for my computer, click open my e-mail, and search hungrily for new messages from Stefan, of which, of course, there are none.

The routine of life with Benny takes on a rhythm that feels alternately devastating and full of purpose. I think I understand now what it is to be a mother, to have the complete well-being of another as your sole purpose. I fit in my work (three, count 'em, *three* new stories from Stefan) around Benny's needs and ever changing schedule. For now, our days start late in the morning. He sleeps in the afternoons and wakes again for evening, falling asleep on the couch in the dark between time of late night and not-quite-morning. We keep blankets and pillows in the living room now, rather than try to get him to bed, which suits both of us fine. Ruthann keeps hinting that it will soon be time to rent a hospital bed, so Benny can be more comfortable, but he resists. He's a frail old fart, but still, his independence is more important to him than ever. He hates taking the medication, but so far I think I've done pretty well at figuring out how to get all those pills down Benny's gullet every day. Not that he'll take them in my presence, but I also never see them in the trash, never hear the toilet flush after I've given them to him. I guess his independent streak just includes pill taking. I'd gag if I had to take so many.

We don't tell Ruthann things that would get us into trouble, like we've bagged the stretching exercises that bring tears to Benny's eyes. Sometimes Benny stays in bed or on the couch all day. And I still haven't gotten the nerve to give him a sponge bath, even though he's taken on a permanently musty smell that I sometimes find myself holding my breath against. He does the best he can, but I doubt his hair has been washed in weeks.

There's something satisfying in our defiance of the pamphlets and Pollyanna instructions we're supposed to follow. We are rebel fighters, Benny and I, and we are fighting in the only way we know how.

As the signs of summer dawn on Portland—the return of the farmers' markets, the Rose Festival parade, five consecutive days without a raindrop—Benny seems to brighten with the extra daylight, the shafts of sun from the window lighting his craggy face. He pulls himself up on the bars of his walker and step-plunk-steps to the sliding glass door, where Buddy is mewing her high-pitched trill at a robin pecking seeds beneath the feeder.

"Whatcha got there, pussycat?" Benny says. "A little lunch? What say we just let you out and see what you're made of?"

"I don't think Buddy's a very good hunter," I say. "She's all talk."

"I don't know, she looks pretty interested to me." He flicks the lock on the aluminum frame.

"No, really, Benny. I don't think we should let her out."

"Don't you worry, Miss Roosevelt. I'll keep an eye on her."

Like he can run as fast as a cat freed for the first time in months. Like he can run.

"Ben." I try not to sound like I'm speaking to a small child. "Come on."

His crooked fingers wrap around the handle, try to push. "A cat needs fresh air," he says, but the door's not budging. "Everybody needs fresh air every once in a while. It's not natural being stuck inside all the time." He strains against the door. "Damn thing needs some WD-40." Veins bulge on the backs of his hands, in his neck.

"Geez, you're determined," I say, standing, scooping Buddy into my arms. She's chunked up considerably, and squirms like a sleek seal in my grasp. Reaching around Benny's walker, I push the door open. "Wow, it's nice out here."

"What'd you go and do that for?" Benny says. "I almost had it."

"You loosened it up for me. Come on, let's go out. It'll do us all some good." I step onto the patio, concrete cool beneath my socks, but the air is balmy with the scent of jasmine. With soft paws Buddy pulls her top half up onto my shoulder to get a better look around.

"It's supposed to get up to eighty-two degrees today," I tell him. "Isn't that great?" I've become a confirmed devotee of StormCenter 5, which seems to call itself StormCenter 5 even when there is no storm. "Maybe we should have a barbecue tonight." Benny loves barbecues more than anything. I turn to look at him still standing inside the doorway. "What's wrong?"

His eyes are soft, wounded the way they were right after Yolanda left. "How am I supposed to keep my strength up if you do everything for me all the time?"

"Your . . . ? God, I'm sorry, Benny." His strength? Since when did he care? "I just wasn't thinking. Really, Ben, I'm sorry."

Buddy is now fixated on a squirrel on the back fence, her haunches tensed and twitching, and I tighten my grip on her. "No, kitty. You can't get down."

"Let her down. Let her do what she's supposed to do. She's a cat, for Christ's sake."

I'm stung at being admonished two times in rapid succession by someone who in our previous lives never had a problem with anything I did. "But I don't want to lose her. She might run away." A tickle develops in my sinuses, a prelude to crying.

Benny sets his walker on the patio, then steps down to join it. "She's not going anywhere. She knows who feeds her."

The tickle starts to burn and my nose fills, then my eyes. I turn away, hugging Buddy harder. She lets out a low growl. "How do you know? She might not come back." Against my will my shoulders shake, and I stifle the sob that tries to erupt.

A hand is on my back, a metal object against the outside of my calf. "She loves you too much to go too far, Ellie. Don't worry so much."

"I have to worry," I say, voice quivering and nasal, like a child.

"No, honey, you don't."

"Yes, I do!" My voice is near shouting. "Nobody else does. Nobody else is even here. What am I supposed to do?" I grip Buddy so tightly she yowls and claws free, leaving scratches across my forearms as she bounds to the concrete and twitches her tail, then leaps through the grass toward the squirrel.

"Goddamn it, Benny," I say, and turn from him. I consider chasing Buddy, but she's long gone. "Great."

We both stand silently, watching the space where Buddy disappeared, birds chirruping and a soft breeze stirring the tree limbs. Somewhere, someone is practicing piano; a plane drones lazily overhead. After a long moment, Benny says, "Well, like it or not, I'm still here," and turns his walker toward the door.

chapter fifteen

So why shouldn't you be pissed off at your uncle?" asks Suzanne Long from her chintz-covered chair, and I wonder why I thought this might be a good idea.

"Well, first of all, he was right. The cat came back at supper time."

She waits for the real answer.

"Because he's dying," I say. Then, softer, "Because I love him."

"Those sound like pretty damn good reasons to be mad to me," she says, leaning forward, clasping her hands on her bare knees. "Have you thought about extra home health care? Respite care?"

"It's not that bad," I say, finding it hard to look at her. She's so perfectly pretty in a floral skirt and loose blouse, summery and fresh, while I'm still wrapped inside my winter sweats, although a smaller version than what I must have worn here a few months ago.

As if reading my mind, she says, "You've lost weight."

"Mm hmm." I nod and force a smile. "A little."

"On purpose?" She looks at me too deeply, and I nod again, look out the window. In the next yard, a bank of rosebushes explodes in romance colors: pinks, whites, bloodred. Next to them, green spires of naked foxglove have lost their blossoms.

"Eleanor?"

I look back at her and sigh. What am I doing here?

"I can't eat anymore. And I try. But it repulses me. Sometimes I put something in my mouth, even something good, and I can't swallow it."

"What would it mean if you could swallow? What would it mean if you could eat?"

God. This is too simplistic. I didn't make out a check for fifty bucks for this kind of drivel. "That . . . that everything was normal," I say, rolling my lips inside my teeth.

"And it's not," she says. "It's all really fucked up."

I am getting so sick of crying. Suzanne places a box of tissues in front of me.

"Has anyone ever mentioned you have the mouth of a longshoreman?" I ask, grabbing a handful of Kleenex.

She smiles and wrinkles her nose, which I now notice is hookish and not at all perfect. "Sometimes that's the only way people will listen to me," she says.

I blow my nose loudly, a gaggle of geese, then say, "I hate this. Besides, how can you possibly understand? You're beautiful, you have this great job, you . . . I don't know. You have poise, perfect control. Good clothes."

She laughs, then reaches for my hand. "I know this is hard, Eleanor. What you're doing is really brave."

I snort and turn away, and she squeezes my hand.

"It is, trust me. I don't know if I could do it."

"Of course you could. You're a therapist."

"I see clients for one hour at a time. I don't know if I'd have the inner strength to take care of someone round the clock."

"But you're still thin. And there's still the clothes."

She smiles, ducks her head. "Thin doesn't necessarily equate to healthy. What's more important is that we find a way to live our lives authentically and for ourselves, you know?" She looks back into my eyes, and I see it. Her life hasn't been any easier than anyone else's.

"Can I ask you one more question?" she says.

"If you must."

"Who benefits from all these rules of yours about food and eating?"

I open my mouth to answer, then close it, bite my lips. I shake my head at her. How did I never know this before? All this time I thought I ate in defiance of my mother and her desire for me to be thin, but no matter how much sugar I ingested, nothing could take that bitterness away.

It only made it more palatable.

Outside on the sidewalk, I stop and close my eyes, breathe deeply, inhale the urban neighborhood smell of mown grass and faint exhaust, revel in the sounds of internal combustion engines and life, trains in the distance, a river of white noise. I miss my neighborhood, especially at this time of year when the small yards are bursting in color, old houses and buildings nearly obscured by foliage and leafy tree branches, streets dappled with occasional spots of sun that break through the shade. On a whim, I decide to walk along Trendy-third Avenue, window-shop. Maybe I'll stop in at Frozen Moo, have my first guilt-free ice cream since I was ten.

Rounding the corner onto Twenty-third, my heart fills at the sight of the old-house storefronts, people hurrying, talking on cell phones, fathers with children with backpacks, dreadlocked hippies in earnest conversation at a picnic table outside of Coffee People. A revoltingly pierced girl who couldn't be more than fifteen sits on the sidewalk with a mongrel puppy in her lap and a cardboard sign that reads: "Spare change for puppy chow." I pull several bills from my purse and stuff them into her pale, dirty hand. She'll probably buy drugs, but today I don't care.

The bell tinkles as I open the door to Frozen Moo. I look at the bulletin board, but Suzanne has never replaced the business card I took.

Inside, the place is packed with barely dressed teenagers and moms with kids, outdoorsy types in hiking shoes or cycling shorts, and a few older couples out for a midday stroll. Instinctively, I look to see if there's anyone fatter than I am, but then I remember I'm not the same size I was. I have no idea what I look like anymore.

At the counter, two teenage boys man the scoops, high schoolers on summer break. They're clearly not as efficient as the usual help, taking far too long to build a decent double scoop, staring at the cash register keys as if they were written in Swahili. It will take forever to get a cone at this rate.

Do I really even want one? I work to imagine the cold, creamy sensation, the sweetness, and I don't feel repulsed. Heartened, I study the list of flavors overhead, even though I know them as if they were my children's names. The only flavor that sounds not too cloying is vanilla, and a waffle cone sounds delicious. This is going to be the most normal thing I've done in months.

Finally, at the front of the line, I place my order with the taller of the two boys. His long, skinny arm snakes into the case, fumbles for a while in the vanilla bucket, then produces a sloppy ball of ice cream at the end of his scoop. He shoves it so hard onto the cone that it cracks. I consider asking him to redo it, but I'm not sure he'd do any better, so I dig money out of my purse and wait for him to ring up the sale on the register.

As his eyes search the keys for the correct button, my attention shifts to one of the older couples at a table in front of the window. I hadn't noticed at first glance that the woman has only a few cotton-candy wisps of hair beneath a blue kerchief. She is frail and her face is sunken like a dried apple. Her husband spoons ice cream into her mouth, which she seems to enjoy in a distracted kind of way, never looking at him directly. The man, however, never takes his eyes from the woman's face, his wife, I decide. His face holds such concentrated tenderness that I look away quickly, feeling as if I've intruded somehow.

"Dollar ninety-five," says the boy, and I hand him two dollars, turn, and leave the store as quickly as I can and pace up the sidewalk to the girl with the mongrel puppy.

"Would you like an ice cream?" I say, stooping to hand it to her. "I haven't touched it."

"I don't eat dairy," she says, staring at me flatly.

"Well, you should." I thrust the cone at her. "You look like you could use some protein, some calcium, for God's sake." The puppy scrambles for a lick. "At least let him have it," I say, rising, turning to go, but when I glance back, she's sharing the cone with the dog, tongues touching in a way that makes me shudder.

• • •

I drive through the retail district and head downhill toward home, my eyes misting at the sight of old apartment buildings and painted ladies, dilapidated storefronts. They all look beautiful to me today, especially once I'm on my block. Why haven't I come home in so long? I park at the curb, and yet another whim sends me across the street instead of going inside my building. I press the buzzer for Irina Ivanova's apartment. Suddenly, I want to see the white sheen of Tati's hair more than anything, watch her walk on wobbly legs to her mother.

"Yes?" An older woman's voice.

"Oh, is Irina there? Irina Ivanova?"

"No."

"Is this still Irina's apartment?"

"No."

"Oh. Well, do you know where she went?"

"No," she says, sticking with curt monosyllables.

"Well, then, sorry to bother you."

No answer. It's as if I were never even here, like I'm James Stewart in *It's a Wonderful Life*, only with no Clarence to guide me.

Inside my building, the hallway has a new-paint smell, and indeed, it's been painted a fresh coat of institutional beige. I climb the steps to the second floor, remembering each squeak and moan of the ancient floorboards. Past the Nguyens' beautiful red door, the door to my apartment looks ugly and plain, and I resolve to paint it when I move back, a cheerful lime green, maybe, or plum.

Inside, I remember why I chose this place. It wasn't the dishwasher at all. It was the way the afternoon light filled the room with a peach glow, the high walls curving into the ceiling, and the sheer sensation that this was a place more me than anywhere I'd ever lived before. I don't want to be at Benny's anymore. It's strangling my soul, sucking me dry. I drop my purse in its old place by the phone on the table and notice the message light blinking. I quit checking home messages after a few weeks at Benny's. Everyone I know has my cell number.

I hit the button. Three messages. The first one is from weeks ago.

"Hi, it's Anne. Call me."

Have I talked to her since then? I can't remember.

The next message is Anne again, from last week.

"It's Anne. I guess I should call Benny's, huh? I don't know. I just don't know what I'd do if he answered. I've been so awful about keeping in touch with him, and now . . . well. You know. Now it would seem like I was only calling because he's . . . you know. God. This all sucks. My life sucks. Your life sucks. Christ. What else can happen?"

And the next is from just four days ago.

"Eleanor? Where are you? This is your cell, right? Well, it's the only number I can find. Listen, I was thinking about it, and maybe you're right. Maybe I should come home, for a while, anyway. I'm starting to hate this fucking place."

I should call her, but I can't do one more thing. I'll do it tomorrow. I walk to my bedroom, to my bed, rumpled and unmade as if I'd just woken up in it this morning. I slide off my shoes, crawl onto the mattress, fall to my side in a heap, wishing Buddy were here. I love my pillows, I love my fuzz-worn sheets, the thick down comforter that presses down on me, weights me so that I cannot move. I breathe in the quiet, out the hot, sorrowful air trapped in my lungs, in the stillness, out the weight of caring, until my breath is as cool and serene and empty as the space around me.

I wake, and the light inside the apartment has gone deep gray. "Oh, for God's sake," I say, scrambling up, finding my shoes. I teeter as I stick my feet into them, still groggy and disoriented as if I've been in a coma, nauseated with not eating. What time is it? What day is it, for that matter?

I rush to the phone, punch in Benny's number.

He answers on the first ring.

"Benny, I'm so sorry. I fell asleep. I'm on my way right now."

I fumble for the switch on the lamp by the phone, look at my watch. It's ten after eight.

"Ellie? Where are you? Are you all right?"

"I'm just at my apartment. I fell asleep."

"Well, thank God. I didn't know what'd happened to you. I was wondering if I should call the police."

"Are you okay? Have you eaten? Have you taken your pills?"

He chuckles. "I'm fine, I'm fine. There's so damn much food in that refrigerator there's no way I could starve. Don't worry. I'm watching *Matlock*."

"But I was going to go shopping, make you something special."

"Honey," he says. "You don't always have to do that." He laughs. "We could eat Burgerville, for all I care. Relax. You're going to be no use to me if you put yourself in the hospital."

"I'm fine."

"Well."

"I am."

"Then let me ask you this, Miss Roosevelt: Have *you* eaten?"

"I was asleep."

"I mean, today?"

"Oh, Ben," I say, rubbing my forehead. "Let's just worry about you, okay?"

"I'm sick of worrying about me," he says. "You're the one who needs worrying over."

I sigh. "Why are we having this conversation?"

"Search me," he says. "I just answered the phone."

Give Thanks for These Healthy Holiday Recipes!

BY ELEANOR SAMUELS

Just because it's Thanksgiving doesn't mean you have to overindulge in fat, calories, and carbohydrates. Our holiday experts have developed these six light and easy alternatives to heavy, traditional Turkey Day fare, and no one will suspect they're not the real thing!

I stare out the sewing room window at the surprisingly sultry afternoon, stunned to realize June's nearly over. Sunlight washes the color from the grass, the trees, and I wish I could go to the coast where it's cool, or to my favorite old spot along the Clackamas River where there's a strip of beach beneath tall poplars and slow-moving currents just perfect for kicking around in an inner tube.

Do nearly forty-year-old women do that? It's been so long, I can't remember if there were only kids in the water or not. How old was my mother when we went swimming there? Thirty? Thirty-five? She wore a black-and-white polka-dot bathing suit, and her hair in a white swim cap with pom-poms. I haven't been game to wear a bathing suit in a couple of decades, but I'm starting to think maybe it wouldn't be so bad. My girth is diminishing, although my flabbiness is just getting worse. Maybe I should be one of those people who go to the gym.

Benny shuffles behind me in the hall, holding the walls and door-frames instead of his walker.

"If you fall, Ruthann will kill me," I call.

"Better you than me," he says, and I smile. Benny's feeling better. No more vomiting, although I suspect he's having problems at the other end. He uses inordinate amounts of air freshener and has taken to hand washing his underwear in the bathroom sink. I take the don't ask, don't tell approach when it comes to anything in that department, which I'm certain is entirely inappropriate for a primary caretaker, but I know Benny is happier this way, too. His color is better, and I heard him in the shower the other day. He shaved this morning, humming tunelessly as he scraped white foam from his cheeks and neck. If I didn't know his prognosis, I'd say maybe he was on the upswing. Who knows? You hear about cancer miracles all the time. Or maybe he finally adjusted to all that medication.

"Hey, Benny," I say, and turn to see him standing in the doorway, a couple of books in hand. So that's why he's not using the walker—maybe we could tie a basket to the front, like on our old bikes. "What would you think about me going away for the weekend, just tomorrow and Sunday? Ruthann says it would be okay if we had a home health person come in. She said your insurance would pay for it."

"Well, sure, Ellie. You go on and have some fun."

"I'd be back in time for dinner Sunday."

"Take your time. I'll give Ruthann a call and drum up somebody to come by."

"Actually, I think I know someone," I say, glad I never threw her phone number away. "And I'll go get your prescriptions refilled today. You're almost out."

"No, honey, Ruthann said she'd run by the pharmacy. You just go on."

"Well, okay," I say, unsure of how happy I should appear in front of him. "If you're sure."

He waves me off and turns to continue his shuffle to his bedroom, where I hear him plop heavily onto the mattress. It's the only place he reads, in bed. Until three months ago, I never knew this about him. I never knew he preferred red grapes over green, green apples over red, or that he used VO5 to keep his hair slicked in place. I like knowing these things. I even like being here, most of the time. I just need some time to myself. Going home, even briefly, has become all I can think about.

Later, I dial the number on the scrap of paper, and Alice answers in her frighteningly cheerful way: "Helloooo, this is Alice."

"Hi, Alice, I'm not sure if you remember me, but this is Eleanor Samuels and—"

"Of course I remember you! Oh, I am so glad you called! You never did give me your phone number. I've been worried to death about that cat. I stopped by your place a few times, but did you move or something?"

"The cat's fine. I still have her, and we're great friends. It all worked out fine."

"Oh, thank God. I've worried so much since that day. You just don't know."

I think I do. Which is why she's perfect. "Listen, I was calling for another reason. What are you doing this weekend?"

After we hang up, I go to Benny's room, rap lightly on the door frame. "Hey, we're all set."

"Oh?" He looks up from his book, Steinbeck's *Travels with Charley*, glasses perched at the tip of his nose. The other is one of his photo albums, a slim white binder.

"Remember me telling you about the woman who hit Buddy? How she was some kind of health worker? Turns out she's a fully licensed RN, she specializes in home care, and she's coming over tomorrow. She's free to help you all weekend, whatever you need. Even if you want her to sleep over, she can stay in my room."

"Is she cute?" he asks, winking, then pushes his glasses back to the bridge of his nose, his eyes growing as big as half dollars behind them. "We'll just see if she spends the night or not."

"You're terrible, Uncle Benny," I say, shaking my head, smiling. I don't know whether to be glad Alice brought Buddy into my life, or the other way around.

"Hey, how do you feel about Burgerville for dinner?" I ask, and Benny grins. Oregonians love their Burgerville.

"I never say no to french fries," he says.

I can't sleep. It's ridiculous, but now that I know I will soon be in my own bed, if only for a night or two, I just can't relax enough to fall asleep on what I've come to call the monkey bars. I feel like I should be climbing this stupid thing, not trying to rest on it. It could also be the double Tillamook cheeseburger, marionberry shake, and fries I consumed for dinner—more food in one sitting than I've had in months, and perhaps not the best choice for my touchy stomach.

I get up and pull on my robe, wander into the living room. Benny's sleeping on the couch tonight, TV flickering silently, Buddy curled in the blanket between his feet. I pick up the remote from the floor beneath his lank hand and click off the set. The room goes dark. Benny's breathing is even and strong. There will be a time when it isn't, I know, but I still can't imagine it.

I mosey to the bookshelves to find something to read. Maybe *Little Women* or *A Tree Grows in Brooklyn*—something happy from my childhood. The titles are faint, gray on gray in the dark, but I skim them with my fingers like I'm reading braille. On the second-to-top shelf I find *Val-*

ley of the Dolls and snort. It must have been Yolanda's. I pull it down, then stand looking at Benny's photo albums.

I take the slimmest volume, the white binder, slide it under Jacqueline Susann, and tiptoe back to my room. I sit on the bed and pull the album into my lap, flip open the cover to the first page. From behind yellowing acetate, a young girl's face looks back at me, twisted and distorted so that the lower half looks separate from the upper. Her teeth are too big for her mouth and stick out in a cartoonish way, and her eyes look like mine. Like my mother's.

Gut tensing, I turn the page, and the girl is tiny in a monstrous wheelchair, her body contorted, her hands clawing at air. The wheelchair is on a sidewalk in front of a blond brick building, and she sits surrounded by smiling women, kind women who love her, I can tell. They are wearing what nurses wore in the sixties, white dresses, some with caps, and the girl's wheelchair is festooned with crepe paper streamers. In another picture from that day, a young, thin Benny kneels beside her chair, holding a floppy-eared stuffed dog. He smiles, but it is only a false smile for the camera. His eyes are sad.

The rest of the book holds similar photos from different years, the girl growing slightly, the nurses changing, Benny aging, until they abruptly stop only midway into the book. Then a yellowed newspaper clipping, a death notice from Bybee Funeral Home: Rosemary Elsa Sloan, born April 11, 1960, died March 4, 1971. Survived by her father, Benjamin H. Sloan. A small private service at the funeral home.

With unsteady hands, I close the book, slide out of bed to sneak it back into its place. My entire body is tingling, stomach roiling, my head another person's, floating down the hall into the living room. There, Benny is sitting up on the couch, blanket tucked around his legs, Buddy curled peacefully in his lap.

"I was wondering where that went," he says, looking at the photo album in my hands. He clears his throat. "I suppose you're curious about the girl."

I nod, devoid of words, and hand him the book. He treats it gently, as if fragile. His eyes glisten.

"Her name was Rosemary, for her mother's mother, but we called her

Rosie. Well, me and the nurses at Moreland Home. Her mother, well . . ." His voice fades and he swallows. He looks at his feet, then at the ceiling. Then at me, head listing in defeat. "Her mother, my first wife, she . . . she had a hard time of it, and the baby was so sick, and they couldn't do anything to help either one of them."

I nod, dumbstruck. His first wife. My mother? But my grandmother's name was Katherine.

He sighs, stroking Buddy now, and she settles deeper into sleep, one paw hanging off his leg, opening, closing, kneading nothing but air.

Finally, I ask: "What happened, to your . . . wife?"

He squeezes his eyes in a grimace, the corners of his mouth trembling against the answer.

"I lost her in childbirth," he whispers, and hangs his head to cry.

It doesn't matter what he says. I know the truth, from a place so old and familiar I could double over with it: Nobody adopted my sister. Because she was not perfect, my mother gave her away.

When I've helped Benny to bed, pulled his door closed against the hall light, I go to the bathroom and kneel next to the toilet. My stomach convulses, and in one fluid motion the contents of my stomach surge up and out like a shot, breaking free of my body, of the corporeal plane, leaving me empty and huddled on the floor, shaking and sobbing a strange sound over and over. The timbre of it is eerie; I'm horrified to realize it's the word "Mom."

I remember this from some hazy, off-kilter dream I used to have, the stench of vomit, the sense of everything being horribly skewed in a way that was irreparable. I remember calling for my mother. And as I lie here on the floor, I remember that it is not a dream.

After I'd thrown up all over myself and the couch that day, I called for my mother in my fever delirium. Crying, trying to escape the smell, I pulled myself up and walked unsteadily to the front door, leaning on the knob as I opened it. I blinked in the stark, hot sunlight, everything, even the grass, stripped of color. Mom's station wagon was still in the driveway, so I called for her again. I walked outside, afraid the neighbors would see me covered in bile, feeling my pajama bottoms stick to my legs. "Mom!" I called, standing in the front yard, then wandered unsteadily to the street, hot sidewalk burning my bare feet.

Up a half block or so I saw Benny's old sky blue Valiant, the car he had before he met Yolanda and bought a decent one. I walked toward it, not wanting to. As I drew closer, I saw them, wound so tightly together that they didn't see me until I was beside them.

Benny saw me first and pulled his arms away from Mom as if he'd suddenly realized he was touching poison. Mom didn't seem to understand until Benny nodded in my direction, just outside the passenger's-side window. He wouldn't make eye contact with me. He looked down and pinched the bridge of his nose with his fingers.

"Honey," Mom said, voice thick and strange, "what are you doing?"

"I got sick," I said as she quickly extracted herself from the car.

"Oh, no, Ellie, what have you done?" She looked me over, then leaned back into the car and grabbed a bag.

"Look what Uncle Benny brought you," she said, pulling out a green bottle. "Ginger ale! Wasn't that sweet of him? Now let's get you back in that house and cleaned up. Say good-bye to Uncle Benny."

Benny's car sputtered away. My mother didn't touch me as we walked back to the house, even though I weaved drunkenly on my feet, feeling as though I might faint. I was too much of a mess. She just kept saying how nice it was that Benny had come by to help me, how she'd given him a big hug to thank him for me. She stopped just outside the front door and turned to me, her eyes hard, her expression stern. "If you ever tell anyone about this, Eleanor, it will just kill your father. You're a big enough girl now for me to tell you this. Dad's not like us. He wouldn't understand." She looked at me another moment more, then asked, "Okay?"

I nodded, swallowing her secrets, her lies, vowing never to throw up again.

She was especially nice to me the rest of the day, helping me clean up, finding me fresh pajamas, soothing my head with a cool washcloth. When my sisters got home from school, and later, when Dad arrived from work, she told them, "Ellie's had such a bad time of it today. Her fever got so high she was imagining things. Weren't you, honey?"

I may have nodded, grunted in acquiescence. I don't remember.

"But on the plus side," Mom continued, smiling prettily, "she's probably lost at least three pounds. She hasn't eaten anything in days."

chapter sixteen

The doorbell rings as I'm brushing my teeth the next morning, and I look at my watch. It's seven thirty. Alice Desmay is half an hour early. Benny's probably still asleep, and I haven't straightened up the house yet. I feel like a rag that has been rung out.

I rinse and spit as quickly as I can, wipe my mouth on the towel, but as I'm pulling the bathroom door open, voices waft down the hall. Benny's answered the door.

"Hi," I say, meeting them in the entryway, trying to smile. "What time did I tell you?" I look at my watch.

"Oh, I know, I know, I'm early," she says. "Bad habit of mine. But I saw this one here"—she nods toward Benny—"picking up the paper, so I knew someone was up. You know, you're pretty good with that walker, Mr. Sloan."

Her hair is blonder than it was, frizzier, but her style is the same: fluffy, floral summer dress. "Where's dat poor li'l kitty?" she asks in a baby voice, looking around, as if she might find a half-starved and neglected Buddy at her feet, begging to be rescued.

I start to protest, to say something to remind her why she's here, but Benny beats me to the punch. "First things first," he says. "Whatcha got in that bag?"

"Doughnuts!" She opens it for him to see inside.

They're going to get along fine. I just need to trust that she truly knows what to do in an emergency besides worry.

Later, Benny thwarts my attempts to give Alice the lowdown on his health care, saying, "I can show her the ropes, Ellie. And she is a nurse, you know."

Funny that we're acting as if last night never happened, which I suppose is the pleasant side benefit of having a stranger in the house first thing in the morning. "Fine," I say, looking at Alice, "but make sure he takes his pills. He hates it; he's like a little kid." I turn to him. "If you need help remembering what you take when, the chart's on the—"

"Fridge. I know, honey, I know." Sugar glaze crusts his top lip. He's having fun; he likes having someone new to regale with his old stories. Fresh meat, we'd say, if she wasn't standing right here.

"Okay," I say. "It just feels weird to . . . you know."

"I know." He cocks his head at me, pressing his lips together in a sad little smile, his eyes aqua in the bright morning sun, red rimmed from last night.

Tears come to my eyes, surprising both of us. "I don't want to go."

"Sure you do, honey. You just won't know it till you're outside the door."

"Promise?" I turn my head, embarrassed in front of Alice, but she's wandered to the patio door, discreetly giving us more space. "Promise you'll be okay?"

"Cross my heart," he says, not finishing the phrase, for my sake, I'm sure.

He's right, of course. Just two blocks away, and I'm flooded with relief and giddy excitement to be free and out in the already warm summer sun; I can't decide whether to cry or laugh. I'm not even going to think about the girl in the pictures. My sister, or half sister, I suppose. I feel a kinship to her that is inexplicable, an old sadness that I've carried all along, but could never name until now. Rosemary. The missing link in our family.

• • •

My first stop in my neighborhood is Nob Hill Grocers. Funny, but all of a sudden I want to eat. Not crap food, certainly not cheeseburgers, but real food. Good food that doesn't come in a box or can or wrapper.

The store smells of roasted chicken and freshly ground coffee, raw meat and ripening stone fruit, the lemon detergent they use to scrub the old sheet-linoleum floors. I inhale and feel the smile form on my face. It's been so long since I've been inside any market other than Fred Meyer, which smells of plastic and the thousands of people who pass through every day.

By instinct, I head for the produce section. There, the close quarters of slim Ichiban eggplant, baby bok choy, brilliant red chard, chartreuse-and-purple asparagus, sends me into paroxysms of delight. I'm glad the store is nearly empty; I'm *ooh*ing and *aah*ing with produce lust at the colors, the smooth, shiny textures set against frilly leaves.

I fondle the palm-size plums, the soft fuzz of the peaches. And the berries! It's berry season, and seven varieties spill from green cardboard containers: the ubiquitous Oregon marionberry, red raspberry, and blackberry, of course, but next to them are blueberries, loganberries, and gorgeous golden raspberries. I pluck one from a container, fat and slightly past firm, and pop it into my mouth. The sweet explosion of flavor is so familiar, but like something too long forgotten. I load two pints into my basket.

The asparagus has me intrigued. Maybe I could roast it with olive oil and fresh herbs, like the sprigs of rosemary and oregano poking out of the salad display, and some good sea salt. And salad. Baby greens tossed with lemon-infused olive oil and a sprinkle of vinegar. Why haven't I eaten a salad in so long? I'll choose a soft, mild French cheese from the deli case, have it for an hors d'oeuvre with a beautiful glass of sparkling Prosecco, say, then roast a tiny chunk of spring lamb that I'm sure the nice sister will cut for me, and complement it with a crusty baguette and roasted asparagus, followed by the salad. Followed by more cheese and berries for dessert. And a fruity Willamette Valley Pinot Noir to wash it all down. My idea of eating heaven, a French-influenced feast that reminds me of the way I always thought my life would be. Why shouldn't

I cook this way for myself? Why does it always have to be about someone else?

Maybe that's been my whole problem. I've been so busy trying to figure out what Benny wants that I've forgotten what I want. I head for the meat section with a renewed sense of hope.

After putting away the groceries, I dig through my left-behind pots and pans in the lower cupboard. At the back, I find a roasting pan for the lamb, a portion somewhat larger than I asked for, but I can take the leftovers back to Benny's. Funny that I'm craving lamb on a hot summer day. I haven't had it in years.

I slice fresh garlic, rub it into the meat with olive oil, then insert the thin wafers into tiny slits I cut along the grain. After rinsing my hands, I hold them to my face, inhale the garlic perfume still on my skin. I could easily wipe it away on the faucet, a spoon, any piece of stainless steel, but I've never understood why people find it offensive. It's the smell of anticipation, the promise of a wonderful meal in the offing.

Opening the spice cabinet, I breathe in the fragrance of all those jars I left behind: saffron threads, cardamom pods, star anise, Tahitian vanilla. I almost weep at the sight of my Fleur de Sel. No one ever gets my obsession with sea salt, especially expensive sea salt. They don't understand that it brightens the flavor of food, wakes it up, like a condiment. Regular table salt just makes food salty. If only someone understood that and appreciated it with me.

And then it hits me. Henry would. Yes, Henry with the wife, with the secrets. No one else seems to care about such things. Why should I?

I pop open my bottle of Prosecco, pour a fluteful even though it's not quite lunchtime. The sweet effervescence goes to my head, seeing as I have so little food in my system, and I quickly drain the glass, for bravery. Then I cover the pan to let the meat marinate in the refrigerator for the day, and walk to the phone on the table by the window, the window that looks out over the world and traffic streaming by, car windows down, celebratory arms and hands and fingers extending into the warm summer sun, undulating up and over and through the wind with the slow beautiful movements of exotic dancers.

• • •

No one answers at PanAsia. There's just the recording for reservations, and a suggestion that I call back after four p.m. to speak personally with someone. I need to speak personally with someone now, so I find Henry's home number and address in the phone book. I don't know whether I should call him or try to bump into him in his neighborhood again. Seeing as I'd rather not run into him *and* his wife, I decide to call.

I'm not surprised to get his machine, but I am disappointed. What if I can't convince him to call me back?

"Hi, Henry. It's Eleanor. Listen, I feel bad about the way we parted the last time I saw you, and I was wondering if you were free for lunch or coffee or a drink anytime this weekend? My life has been in upheaval since I met you, and I never explained. If you're not too busy, I'd love to talk to you again."

I leave both my numbers in case he threw them away after I so righteously bounced him out of my life at Starbucks. What was I thinking? That men who like me just pop into my life every day? Since Daniel, Henry is the first man who has looked at me fully, at the whole of me, and seemed to like what he saw. My heart starts to pound, and I realize I cannot just stay in this apartment on this beautiful day waiting for a man to call me.

I go to my bedroom, throw open the closet door. The smell inside from being closed so long is stale and mildewed. When I get home for good, I'll clean out my closet and dresser. I'll wash all my clothes, give away those that don't fit or that are just plain awful, which is the majority of them. I'll restock with new clothes in brighter colors, tighter sizes. I'll begin anew.

For now, however, I have to contend with a palette of gray, black, navy, and forest green, a somber and frumpy selection that doesn't feel like me anymore. I scavenge toward the back where older clothes reside, from my working days, and find a short-sleeved pink blouse. My summer khakis are back there, too, and I pull both out, peel off my sweats, and head for the shower. With eyes closed, I stand and let the water flood over me, cascading over my face, down my front and back, streaming from the tips of my fingers. Then I shave three months' growth from my legs, exfoliate every square inch of skin, and put extra conditioner in my hair.

Benny doesn't own a full-length mirror, so when I step out of the shower and see myself in the silver-backed mirror on the door, I gasp. First I notice only that my breasts have gone flatter and smaller, but then I see the inward curve of my waist, the slight gap between my lower thighs even when I stand with my legs together. I'm not thin by any stretch of the imagination, but I am not fat, either. The thought of a man seeing me like this sends warm blood into places it hasn't sought in way too long. I touch my stomach, my sides, sliding my hands over damp skin.

I turn to check out my butt and moan. Not a pretty sight, still, with its trapezoidal, lumpy shape descending into dimpled thighs. I sigh and head for the bedroom, pull a pair of underwear from the back-of-the-drawer batch that didn't make the trip to Benny's—those I reserve for times I haven't gotten around to doing laundry. As I step into them and pull them up, something doesn't feel right. The silky beige fabric hangs in the back like droopy diapers. The elastic must have lost its hold. I dig through the drawer looking for a better pair, but after trying on two more, I finally get it. My butt may not be perfect, but it no longer fits in my old jumbo underpants. On one hand I'm thrilled, but they're all I have to wear today, of all days. I find the least offensive pair, pull my baggy khakis over them, and resolve not to remove anything until well after dark.

I comb out my hair, brush on peach blusher long retired behind a sticky cough syrup bottle, then swipe at my eyelashes with mascara. Something is bubbling up inside me, whether it's the wine, the zing of reawakened hormones, or simply the pleasure of being alone and the possibilities that holds.

And here I thought all I'd want to do this weekend was sleep.

Once outside, it feels completely normal to be slipping into my car, planning a route that will take me first by the restaurant, then around the corner to Kafé Kizmet, then across the Burnside Bridge into the northeast and Henry's neighborhood. The air smells of roses and honeysuckle, dry earth and lunchtime traffic. Where might Henry eat lunch? Where would I eat lunch if I were a chef who cooked Asian food every day? Italian? Mexican? Or would I make a grilled cheese at home?

I picture him, tall and robust, heavy, probably, by medical charts, but undeniably appealing. A man like Henry eats meat. As I pass PanAsia, I already know where to look for him.

I skim over the river on the Broadway Bridge instead of the Burnside, water below shiny indigo and dotted with boaters enjoying the warm Saturday. A water-skier slices through the wake of a barge pushing pulp downriver to the Columbia.

On the east side, I cruise down Weidler, the eastbound one-way twin to Broadway's westbound. At Thirteenth Avenue, I turn and head back down Broadway toward Bridgetown Deli midblock, long famous for its imported cheeses and meats, its turquoise Naugahyde booths and refusal to install an espresso machine. A meat eater's heaven, and it's close to Henry's house.

Sandwiched between an expensive shoe store and a Vietnamese hair salon, the deli is packed to overflowing with people seated at outdoor café tables and waiting in bunches by the door. I slow to look for Henry, then his car, then a place to park, but at this time of day I'll never find anything.

I decide on a new tack. I'll drive by his house and see if his Jeep is there or not. If not, I will have a beacon, something to search for. Not many people drive rusty Jeeps. As I'm rounding the corner onto his block, though, panic overtakes me. What if he sees me—*again*—looking for him?

I almost change my mind and pull over, but then I realize: This mission is all about letting Henry know I'm looking for him. I don't think it's only for sex, but so what if it is? It's a new and freeing thought, and I breathe deeply and motor slowly toward his house, past bungalows and English cottages, until finally at the far end of the block I see it—not my dream Portland foursquare, but a hefty Colonial with a wide front porch and eyebrow windows on its second story. It looks like Henry: friendly, big of body and soul, open to the world.

And a rusty Jeep in the driveway, right next to a small white car, blue-and-yellow Free Tibet bumper sticker prominently displayed on its rear end.

Like a bad puppy with its tail between its legs, I slink toward home, down Broadway, over the bridge, back into my own neighborhood, wondering how on earth I thought I was going to seduce anyone, let alone this very married man.

I pace the length of my apartment, trying to shake it off. It's okay, I tell myself. There's nothing new in this situation. You just got your hopes up a little is all, but the point is, you're still alive. You've still got a spark, a fire that can be rekindled.

The phone rings and I consider ignoring it, but it could be Benny. "Hello?" I answer, hating how tentative my voice sounds.

"Well, well, Eleanor Samuels."

"I can expla—"

"Was I ever surprised to hear your voice on my machine. I hope I haven't missed out on lunch. I got caught up with Namhla's attorney, working through some details. Paperwork and stuff about my, ah, situation. Funny that you should call. I mean, now."

"Now?"

"Now that I'm practically a divorced man."

"You're—"

"And a damn hungry one at that. How about that lunch?"

I take a deep breath. "Why don't you come over to my place. I'll cook for you."

"No one cooks for me. They're too intimidated."

"Oh, I'm intimidated," I say. "But I have all this food. Lamb, salad, wine—"

"Lamb? Why didn't you say so? I'm on my way."

After giving him directions and hanging up, I scurry around the kitchen, throwing the roasting pan into the oven without preheating, drizzling supple asparagus with oil, scattering herbs. Laying out the cheese and a few crackers, finding another champagne flute.

If Henry gets here quickly, we'll have three hours before he has to leave for work. The meal will take thirty or so minutes to prepare, during which we'll chitchat and grow less awkward around each other. We'll linger over the food for an hour or so. That leaves plenty of time for anything else that might occur. I run to the bathroom to freshen up my blush.

At Henry's arrival seventeen minutes later, I am struck first by how large he is, then by how young he looks, just as I was the first time I saw him. Eager, loud, happy, and so male. He is all ruddy skin and blond-red hair, freckles, and soft T-shirt fabric. I want to place my hand where it pulls across his chest. I want to laugh at his stories, I want to sit with him at the table, and I want his eyes to follow me as I rise every so often to check the lamb and vegetables or toss the salad.

Instead, I say, "Hi," and give an awkward little wave of my hand. Where is the steaming seductress?

"Look at you," he says, eyes softening. His head tilts, and a look I cannot read traverses his face. "You okay?"

"Great!" I say too enthusiastically, then, "Don't I look okay?"

"Yeah, oh, God. Yeah." He looks embarrassed. "I'm an idiot. Let me start again. Hello, Eleanor. You look lovely today."

I laugh, and he shakes his head, then grins again, looks around. "I am inside Eleanor Samuels's apartment."

"This is it," I say, backing up, gesturing like a flight attendant. What is it with the goofy hand motions? I quickly pull my arms together and fold them in front of my chest, then realize that's bad body language and drop them to my sides, fingers humming with the want of touching him. "I hope you're not too hungry. It'll be another thirty minutes or so before everything's ready. Oh! I have some Chaource and crackers, and Prosecco."

"If you're trying to seduce me, you had me at hi," he says, winking. A line from a movie I can't remember.

"Right." I force a laugh, which turns into a snort.

He doesn't seem to notice, just walks into the living room and looks at the books on my shelves, and the empty spaces where an inordinate amount of dust has gathered. A red rhinestone from Stefan's picture frame winks in the sunlight from the window.

"I guess this place is kind of barren. That day you saw me, with all my stuff?" I walk toward the kitchen to get the drinks. "I was moving in with my uncle, down in Lake Grove. We'd just found out about his cancer. I'm taking care of him." Settling the bottle and glasses on the table, I turn to go back for the cheese plate, but Henry has moved across the room quickly, deftly for his size. He takes my wrist in his hand, broad thumb on my pulse, and looks at me with such intensity I can't look away.

"Wha . . . ? Is that, is that what you've . . . oh, Eleanor." He shakes his head, tucks his bottom lip so that his chin juts forward. "Why didn't you tell me? I had no idea what you were going through."

"Yeah, well. You know. Life." I shrug, swallowing back the emotional swell that churns up whenever someone is kind about my situation.

"It has to be so tough. Is there anything I could do? I mean, for you?"

My nostrils flare, and I swallow again. Has anyone ever asked me this question before? If so, I cannot remember. I breathe in two three, out two three, and he waits. Finally, I say, "You know what I really want?"

"What?" He reaches for my other hand so he is holding both. My jaw relaxes, my shoulders slump.

"It's embarrassing. I just . . ." I stop, unsure how—or if—to proceed. "It's stupid, but I'd just like someone to lie down with me. Just . . . you know. Just the company of that."

He flinches, not against me or my request, but with a look that tells me he understands. He nods, then says, "Would you like to do that now?"

"How about until the timer goes off?" I say, and he smiles. I lead him to my bedroom, slide off my shoes, and Henry unsticks the Velcro of his sandals. Without looking at him, I climb fully clothed on top of the sheets and blankets. He lies beside me. I roll so that my back is to him, and he pulls himself toward me, spooning me, arm loosely draped around my middle. His body is warm, solid, and substantial. A long, slow sigh escapes from me, and that is the last thing I remember until later, when he is whispering to me, "Don't wake up, don't wake up. I'm just going to go to work for a while. I'll be back." And then I return to the deep, dark cocoon where nothing matters and nobody needs me and I am safe.

chapter seventeen

When I finally wake at nine thirty-seven, according to my bedside clock—p.m., I'm guessing from the darkness in the room—I am dazed, thick with sleep, and half of my face is covered with dry saliva. I call, just to hear the sound of it, "Henry?"

I know he isn't here, but I don't remember him moving, climbing out of bed, or the sound of the door opening and closing. Nothing smells burned.

I pull myself from the bed, blouse twisted sideways on my torso, and stagger into the kitchen. The food has all been put away and there's a note from Henry on the table by the phone:

Sorry I had to leave. I'll be back after I close (10:30? ish?) to enjoy the meal with you if that's okay. The Chaource is delicious, by the way.

Henry

P.S. Did you know that you make little whistling sounds in your sleep? And just an occasional snore, but not too bad, really. Considering how hard you were sleeping. I feel honored to know this about you and will never use it to make fun of you. Well, I'll try not to.

P.P.S. For the record, I now know more about you than I do about Namhla.

I smile and put my hand on my cheek and feel the crusty remains of drool. God, I have to get cleaned up. Maybe I can find something a little slinkier to wear. I'm about to head for the bathroom when I notice the phone lying faceup on the table, clicked to ON and silent. Henry thought he was doing me a favor by taking it off the hook. I quickly replace it in its cradle, resisting the impulse to check on Benny. He or Alice would have called my cell if they really needed me.

In the mirror, my face is mascara smudged, drool encrusted, and grinning. Henry. Oh, Henry. Isn't that a candy bar? How fitting, considering I want to taste his mouth and fingers and things I can't even let myself think about yet.

I pull my hair into a loose ponytail and wash my face. Then I wander to the closet, unbuttoning the blouse, sliding off my pants, unhinging my bra. Down to the baggy underwear, I wrap myself in the pretty but wholly impractical silk robe my mother bought me two Christmases ago. It's not my color, and the way it clings to my body has always been uncomfortable, but tonight the silk feels daring against my skin. On a whim, I reach under the robe and push my underwear down my thighs, letting them drop around my feet before I step out of them and kick them into the laundry pile.

I feel indecent as I walk into the kitchen, and I like it. I pull open the fridge door, take out the lamb. It is perfectly done. I have no recollection of the timer going off, let alone Henry getting up to deal with it and the rest of the food.

It's really too warm to have hot food. We'll eat it all cold, I decide, pouring myself a fresh glass of Prosecco, opening the Pinot to breathe. We'll have a picnic on the floor, or on the bed. We will be impetuous and wild, the way I used to be. I think I still know how to do it.

At quarter to eleven, the doorbell rings. I smooth my hands over my hips, down my hair, which, without winter's humidity, is soft and compliant. I've finished the Prosecco, and the blood in my veins is thrumming with anticipation.

I glide to the door, feeling hips sway, silk on skin, the glow of heat gathering, and unlock and swing the door open. The bright hall light makes me squint, but even so, I can see clearly that my visitor is not the one I expected, even though she's nearly as tall as Henry.

"Do you ever answer your phone?" my sister Anne asks in a tone I've heard most of my life. She has a double-wide briefcase in one hand and a wheeled suitcase in the other. "Did I wake you? Were you in bed already?"

All I can think to say is, "Anne."

"This wouldn't be such a surprise if you ever answered the phone," she says, one leg twitching with annoyance. "Are you going to let me in?"

I stand aside, and she rolls her bag past me into the living room, setting her briefcase beside the couch. Her casual gray suit is formal by Portland standards, and her short hair spiked more with salt these days than pepper.

"God, what a day!" she says. "I've been stuck in one airport after another, and then I let the taxi go at Benny's. Why didn't you tell me you weren't living there anymore? I had to wait outside in the dark half an hour for another one. You'd think a place that calls itself a city would have better taxi service and some damn streetlights."

"Are you staying here?" I ask, not wanting to let go of my fantasy night. Not just yet.

"Great. I can't get ahold of anyone, and when I finally do, my own sister doesn't want me to . . . wait a minute." She looks around, seeing the wine on the counter, the two glasses beside it, the candlelight flickering from the bedroom. "Is there a *man* here?" Saying the word man like she means "elephant," or "Martian."

"Not yet," I say, glancing at the clock.

"Oh, that's too perfect." She flops dramatically onto the couch. "No one gets my message I'm coming, no one picks me up at the airport, no one's home at Benny's—"

"What?" I interrupt. "Yes, there is. He was probably just asleep. And there's a nurse there with him."

"No, Eleanor. No one. The house was dark, and I rang the bell, called his number, and banged on the door for a good ten minutes. I'm pretty sure the neighbors were about to call the police."

She's wrong. She doesn't know how hard he sleeps. Maybe he told Alice to go home. That would be just like him. I grab the phone. As I pick it up, my heart sinks. When I put it back in its cradle earlier, it didn't hang up properly; it's been off the hook this whole time. I dig through my purse, pull out my cell phone. The screen is dark; it's out of juice.

"Oh, for God's sake," I say. "Goddamn it." I dial Benny's number and listen to the repetitive electronic trill. Trying not to count rings, I look at Anne. "What are you doing here, anyway?"

"Nice, Eleanor."

I give her a look.

"I got a call yesterday that Dynoco settled, then another one that said I was being allowed to resign. They may as well have slit my throat over an altar. I'm their fucking sacrifice, even though I didn't do a damn thing but what they told me to do. I mean, talk about your good news–bad news bullshit. I tried to call you on your cell, but you never *ever* answer."

"I hate to break it to you," I say, deciding to hang up after eleven rings and dial Alice's number. "You've been calling my home number for weeks."

"Well, at least I've been trying to stay in touch," Anne says, stretching her arms overhead. "Anyway, I decided to take your advice, so here I am."

"Indeed," I say, hearing Henry's vocabulary in my voice, and as if summoned, there is another knock at the door.

I answer with the phone still ringing endlessly in my ear. Henry's sexy smile evaporates as I gesture toward Anne on the couch. She gives the same little wave I did hours ago.

"Hi," she says. "Unfortunately for you, I'm one of those pesky relations, come to stay."

He looks at me, and I roll my eyes and nod. "Henry, this is my sister Anne. Anne, Henry." He's walking over to shake her hand when I get Alice Desmay's machine.

"Hellooo," the recording says, "you've reached Caring Home Care and this is Alice, your personal home-care provider. I must be out caring for another client. If you'd care to leave a message . . ."

"Jesus," I mutter, then, at the beep, "Alice? Are you there?" I wait in case she's screening. "If you're not there, then where are you? Where's Benny? Call me." I start to hang up, then remember: "Call me on the home number. The cell's dead."

"So, Henry," Anne's saying, "I didn't know my sister was seeing anyone. You see, she hasn't called me in something like four weeks, even though I've called her many, many times."

"Can it, Anne," I say, and dial Ruthann's number. "Something's really wrong."

This shuts her up, and Henry asks, "What's the matter? Is it your uncle?"

"Do you have a phone with you?"

He nods and digs his cell phone out of his shorts pocket, drawing Anne's gaze to his muscular, pink-skinned thigh. "What do you need?"

"Start calling hospitals, Meridian Park first. See if Benny Sloan's been admitted. You, too, Anne. I know you have your cell on you, Miss Queen of Communication."

Then Ruthann says hello in my ear, and I want to drop to my knees in gratitude. "Ruthann, it's me. Do you know where Benny is?"

"Ellie, no. What's wrong?"

"He's not at home, and no one's answering the phone there. I left him with a respite nurse. He hasn't called you?"

"No," she says. "Has anyone checked inside the house? Does a neighbor have a key?"

"I don't know," I say. God, why didn't I think he might still be in there? "I'll run down there now."

"I'll make some calls," she says. "Where can I reach you?"

"Somebody give me their cell number," I say to Anne and Henry, both looking dazed from my last set of instructions. Then Anne quickly rattles hers off, and I repeat it to Ruthann.

After we hang up, I look at Henry. "I have to go to Benny's."

He nods. "Get dressed. I'll drive."

"I'm coming, too," Anne says. To which Henry replies, "Of course you are."

• • •

Warm air blows loudly through the open Jeep as we speed south on I-5. The night is moonless and dark, the stars pinpricks in the purple-black sky. My hair is blowing around my head like seaweed in a strong current, and I try to hold it back with one hand as I search for a hair tie in my purse. I look back at Anne in the rear seat, certain she's hating this rustic ride, but she looks absolutely serene, head back, eyes closed, letting the wind wash over her. She's taken off her suit jacket and wears a white sleeveless top. Her arms are sinewy and long, like Dad's.

I look at Henry, and his profile is serious, determined. "Thank you," I call over the wind, snapping ponytail into place, and he turns and nods, smiles a grim smile.

"I'm sorry," he says, and I nod and shrug. Then we turn our attention to the road ahead.

At Benny's house, dark and empty-looking, just as Anne said, I dig out my house key and open the door, and before I can stop her, Buddy shoots through my legs, across the yard, and out into the night where I can no longer see her. In a matter of seconds, I know why. A foul odor rolls from inside, one I can't place but that smells worse than the worst smells imaginable, like rotting meat, vomit, feces, and a chemical spill all rolled together. "Benny?" I call, stepping in and holding my hand over my face.

Anne walks through the door behind me and turns on the light. "Jesus," she says, pinching her nose. "What is that?"

I walk quickly through the living room into the dining room and kitchen, down the dark hall toward Benny's bedroom, the smell growing worse. Nausea grips my gut, twists my intestines, my esophagus, and I choke out another "Benny?" I don't want to find what I'm afraid I will.

At the doorway to his bedroom I stop, steel myself, and turn on the light switch. "Oh, oh, God . . ." I hear myself wail, and then the sound of Anne and Henry behind me.

"Ellie, what—"

"Ah, geez, what happened?" Henry says, stepping around me into the room. "Benny!" he calls, but Benny is not here, Benny is not dead on the floor as I thought he would be. Something horrible has happened, though. The foul substance emitting the odor is everywhere: on his sheets, on the floor, and we have all walked through it.

"I'm going to barf," Anne says, and runs to the bathroom. "Oh, shit, it's worse in here," she cries, and hurries outside.

"Come on," Henry says. "This is going to make us all sick."

"I should clean it up," I say, feeling dazed and sweaty, and then Henry is guiding me down the hall and through the living room and out into the open air.

"Give me your shoes, and go sit on the curb," he says gently, and then he is talking quietly to Anne, who is retching near the lilac bushes, and then he has found the garden hose and is cleaning all of our shoes.

When Anne stops throwing up, she comes to sit with me. In the dark she looks pale and ethereal. "Ellie, what's happening? Is this how sick he's been? Have you . . ." I shake my head and she swallows, lying back on the grass. "God. I wish the phone would ring. Should we call someone?"

"I should have been here," I say, staring at the sparkling asphalt of the street, illuminated by the lone streetlight at the end of the block. The night is still; there is no sound except the steady swish of water from the hose, and then even that stops as Henry twists off the spigot.

Soon I hear him tapping numbers into his phone as he walks across the lawn. He hands me the phone. "Thought you might want to check your messages."

"Oh," I say, taking the phone. "Right." Why am I so thickheaded? I didn't even think to do this. I have a message.

"Eleanor, it's Alice. We did try to call you, but we couldn't get through. Benny had a pretty bad day today, and we couldn't get control of his diarrhea, so I took him to the ER for some meds, and now we're over at River—"

I hear Benny in the background.

"Your uncle wants to talk to you." Then, "There you go, just sit up a little."

"Ellie?"

Then Alice's voice from afar: "No, it's her machine. Go ahead and leave a message."

"Oh, uh, Ellie, I've decided to come stay awhile at the hospice. I had a little problem today that they say is probably not going to go away anytime soon, and I didn't want to, you know. It's better for now, I think, if I stay here. It's really a pretty good place. Got my own room, and a TV, and I can bring anything I want down here—"

"What's wrong?" Anne's saying, and it's only then I realize I'm crying.

"Ellie, honey, don't go back to the house. Stay at your apartment. Alice is going to get the place cleaned up, so don't worry about anything. It's all being taken care of."

And then it's Alice on the phone again, giving me the address, details that I don't hear, and Anne's phone is ringing, and she's introducing herself to Ruthann, who is apparently telling her the same news because she's nodding and saying, "Mm hmm, mm hmm," and Henry is looking helplessly at us both, but trying, I can tell, not to intrude.

I was right to love him. I know that in this moment, but I also know that it will be some time before we will be able to even think about wild reckless abandon, or long, sensual meals together, or just going out to a movie or for a drink or anything that resembles normal life. What I don't know is if he'll want to wait.

"My uncle's gone to the hospice," I tell him, "because he didn't want me to have to deal with anything like that." I nod toward the house, and Henry sighs, folds his big hands together, and I could swear he prays for a moment before he looks back up at me.

"Will you help me find my cat?" I ask.

"You have a cat?" Anne says, in much the same way she reacted to my having a date earlier, and the three of us set off into the dark, calling Buddy's name over and over, until finally we return to Benny's house to find her curled up on his front step.

Part 3

Out with the Old, In with the New! 9 New Dessert Traditions for a Healthier New Year

BY ELEANOR SAMUELS

It is three a.m., and in spite of tonight's events, anxiety over this stupid article pushes everything else from my mind. Stefan assigned it two weeks ago, and I have only one week left to complete it. How will I do that now? I worry that I've yet to even think about ideas for this piece, let alone try to make them. I worry about my bakeware, my KitchenAid, trapped inside Benny's house. God, my computer. I worry that the last thing I'll have time for now is baking, never my strong suit, anyway.

And I worry that these are the things I'm worrying about.

I make myself think about Benny lying in a strange bed. Is he sleeping? Is he frightened? Does he let himself think about dying?

Why haven't I ever talked to him about dying? Maybe he needed someone to talk to and I ignored the whole topic, fixating on getting as many pills and as much food as possible down his throat every day. We haven't talked again about Rosemary, about my mother. Maybe he needs to deal with the loose ends of his life.

I decide to go back to thinking about healthy holiday desserts. Just until dawn.

chapter eighteen

By the next morning, Christine is on her way home to Portland.

"I knew I should have come earlier," she says. "Besides, if Anne can be there, so can I." I don't argue with her kindergarten logic. Reid the Frugal must have convinced her to drive rather than fly, so she won't be here until tomorrow. I try not to let myself think about what could happen to a six-months-pregnant woman on the road alone in a 1972 Honda.

Anne and I are still drinking coffee in our pajamas. Neither one of us seems to want to officially begin the day. I've hardly slept, and Anne's been awake for hours, having slept on my couch, which is almost certainly worse than Benny's. We should be getting dressed, making phone calls, making plans, driving to the hospice. I should contact Alice about helping to clean up Benny's house. I don't want to do any of these things, so I pour each of us another cup of coffee.

"So," Anne says. "Henry."

"Yeah." I sigh. Henry. "Cute name, isn't it?"

She nods. "Kind of Old World."

"Or New World. All those movie stars name their kids things like that: Jack, Henry, Aloysius. It's like they're trying to convince everyone they're really not vapid and superficial."

"Methinks you're changing the subject," she says, raising her eyebrows and giving me a wry smile. She turned forty last year, yet she has no lines on her face. She's always been the plainest sister, her features angular while Christine's and mine were rounded, but with age she is becoming striking-looking while I'm just sagging into a puddle of skin.

"So?" she presses. "Would he have spent the night if I hadn't arrived on your doorstep?"

"I don't know," I say. "That was pretty much our first date."

She winces. "Really? Shit."

"Yeah, well, you were the least of the interruptions."

She nods, looks down at the table. I watch the leafy tree branches outside the window wave lazily against the blue sky.

"God, I love Portland in the summer," I say. "Is it great living where it doesn't rain nine months a year?" I can't even imagine it.

"It rains in Boston," she says, then sighs. "I need to tell you something."

For some reason I think she's about to tell me she's gay—I've suspected it at times—so I do my best to put on my sisterly, I'm-here-for-you face and say, "Go ahead."

"I've wondered for a long time if Benny might be your father." Her gray eyes burn into mine. "Yours or Christine's. Maybe both."

"What?" It hits me in the solar plexus, pushes the air from my lungs so quickly I think I might not catch my breath. What does she know that I don't?

She twiddles her thumbs on the table. "I've been trying to talk to you about this for years. You either shut me down or I chicken out."

"You've never—"

"Eleanor," she interrupts. "Why do you think Mom and Benny had such a connection? It's not just a stupid photography class."

"I know, but—"

"I overheard them one night when we were kids, out on the patio when they thought no one was listening. You and Christine and I were playing cards on the picnic table, and Dad was someplace else. It was so serious, the way they were talking—not like they usually were. Benny said something like, 'We did what was best for her, Bebe,' and Mom was crying, kind of, and saying, 'I don't deserve to be a mother.'"

She stops, looks down, then back up, eyes damp. "I know it isn't me.

Look at me. I'm all Dad. Besides, Benny never paid half as much attention to me as he did to you two."

"Benny loved you as much as he loved us."

She shakes her head and turns away. "I don't think so," she says into the palm of her hand. Her voice is shaky.

"They did have a daughter together," I tell her, reaching to grab her wrist, to pull her back toward me. "Two years before you were born. She had a birth defect or something, and she lived in a home. They named her Rosemary, and she died when she was eleven."

Her face screws up in hurt or anger, I can't tell, and she says, "How long have you known this? Why didn't you tell me?" She begins to cry and pulls away, embarrassed.

"I just found out," I say. "I was going to tell you, I was going to call, I swear."

"Did you tell Christine?"

I nod, say quietly, "Yes. But not that it was Benny's. You can't tell her that. It would break her heart."

"Damn you, Eleanor," Anne says. She pushes out of her chair and stalks into the bathroom, slamming the door behind her. There is the shudder of the shower faucet, and then the white noise of water hitting tile.

Last night, when Henry dropped us off at my place, Anne said her good-byes quickly and walked to the door, leaving us alone in the Jeep.

I thought about asking him to come in, but I couldn't. I smiled at him and said, "Well."

"Yes," he said, smiling back. "Well."

"Thank you for being so wonderful about all this. What a weird day." I shook my head and opened the door.

"Eleanor," he said. "Come here."

I moved toward his outstretched hand and he brought it to my face, cupped my cheek.

"You take care," he said, and kissed me on the opposite cheek. His hair and skin smelled of cooking oil and onions. "Call me if you want to."

"I don't know what's going to happen, or when, or—"

"Don't worry," he said. "Just do what you need to do. I have the patience of Buddha."

I smiled and climbed out of the Jeep, then walked toward the building. At the door I turned to wave, and saw him watching me. In spite of everything that had happened, what I wanted most was to sleep with him, to sink into that heavy fog where I was safe and small and protected. It seemed like the most selfish and indulgent thing I'd ever desired, though, so I smiled and waved, then stepped inside and closed the door.

With Anne safe in the shower, I dial Alice's number.

"Hellooo," she says. "Caring Home Care."

"Alice," I say. "It's Eleanor."

"Good. You're up. I've been waiting to call you."

"I just wanted you to know I'm going to clean up the house. You don't have to do it." *I'm his real caretaker*, I want to say.

"Absolutely not," she says. "I get paid to do it, and I have a crackerjack team of cleaners. You don't want that to be one of your last memories of your uncle."

"What?" I say, and it sounds shrill, frightened. "Is he dying?"

"Ellie."

"No, I mean, now. Is he dying right now?"

She sighs. "His blood pressure is low, and last night wasn't good. These could be signs that he's entering what we call the active phase—"

"I know what it's called," I interrupt. The words from Ruthann's pamphlets. "But he was getting better. You saw him. He was more energetic than he'd been in weeks."

She sighs again. "It's not unusual for someone to rally before this phase."

"Maybe it's just all the heavy food I've been giving him. Maybe if I just—"

"It's not the food," she says.

"Well, then, couldn't it be the medication? It made him sick before. Maybe he should just stop taking it." *Quality of life*, I remind myself. *It's about quality, not quantity.*

"No, the steroid wouldn't make him sick like that."

"I mean the chemo. It made him puke for weeks, and now this."

"The only medication your uncle's on is dexamethasone, a steroid to keep the brain tumors reduced enough that he can be coherent and conscious." She pauses, then adds, "Temporarily," as if I don't know anything.

"No," I argue. "He takes all that other stuff, too. I give it to him, five times a day, every day."

"He doesn't take it. I'm sorry, but you should know. He hasn't in weeks. He was afraid to tell you."

Goddamn that man and his secrets.

"Fine," I say, stomach flipping. "If that's the way he wants it."

"It is," she says, her tone gentle now, and I suppose meant to be soothing. "There's nothing you can do but respect his wishes."

"Well, then, I guess I won't clean up his house, since that's the way he wants it, too," I say, knowing I sound worse than a kindergartener. "I won't help him anymore if he doesn't want my help."

"I know this is hard—"

"Thank you for your assistance," I interrupt. "We probably won't be needing you anymore, either." I'm trying to hang up before she hears that I'm crying, but I pause too long.

"It's absolutely normal to be angry," she says in that too-caring voice.

"Go worry about somebody else," I say, and click off the phone.

The shower goes silent, and I know I only have a couple of minutes before I have to deal with Anne again. I want to wallow in this feeling, this anger, this righteous indignation, even though I know it's pissy and mean. I punch the numbers into the phone.

"Hello?" my mother answers, sounding happy and normal and far removed from all that is falling apart around me.

"He's dying," I say. "Soon. He's sick and shitting himself, and your daughters are the only people he can count on." I click the phone back off and sit hard in my chair, hands trembling, heart hammering, breath almost impossible to catch.

The drive south on the highway is nothing like last night's emergency mission. Anne and I are silent, and the windows are closed tight against the heat outside, air-conditioning sputtering and smelling of mildew. I switch on the radio to allay the discomfort between us. Traffic is heavy, coming to a crawl before we even get to the Ross Island Bridge.

"What is it with this traffic?" I say, sounding as irritated as I feel. "What day is it?"

"Sunday," Anne says, looking out her window at the tree-covered embankment that rises into the West Hills. Hot pink sweet peas climb out of the brush, pushing toward the light.

"There is no way it's only Sunday," I say. Could it be? It feels like a week's passed since yesterday.

Anne shrugs.

"I'm sorry I didn't tell you about Rosemary. I should have." I tap my right turn signal and the driver in that lane eases up, lets me slip in front of her. I nod in the rearview, wave.

"You know that wouldn't happen in any other city," Anne says.

"What?" I turn to look at her.

"People don't just let other people cut in front of them in traffic. And it's not only Boston, or L.A. or New York. It's Denver, Seattle, for God's sake. Portland is the only city I've ever been where people slow down to let you in. It's freakish."

"It's normal," I say, relieved to be arguing about this. "It's human nature. We look out for each other."

She snorts. "Right. You keep living in Wonderland here and you'll always be able to think that."

"Fine by me. Wouldn't you rather live in Wonderland than where people don't care about you?"

She turns to me, fervent and animated. "You think these people care about you, Eleanor? You think they're being kind to you personally?" She clucks in her throat, expelling a hard sigh. "They're just trained monkeys. This place is so provincial, they don't even know there's any other way to do it."

"Thank God for that," I say, pull over one more lane, wave at the next driver behind me, and exit onto Highway 43.

• • •

From the address Alice gave me, I'd thought the hospice was going to be in some sprawling medical office park south of Lake Oswego, surrounded by pricey neighborhoods and rolling green hills. I pictured it looking like one of those newly ubiquitous retirement centers that I always mistake for chain hotels. Instead, we find ourselves in a run-down enclave of poorly built split-level ranches from one of Portland's building booms in the 1970s, tucked off Highway 43, but not far enough that you can't hear every car that zooms by.

"This can't be right," I say, turning at the correct address into the driveway of what appears to be just another house, although better kept than the others. Farther down the long drive, though, and a long addition at the back becomes apparent, and a small parking lot with a sign: RIVERVIEW CARE FACILITY, VISITOR PARKING.

"God, how depressing," Anne says. "Wouldn't you think with a name like Riverview, there might actually be something nice to look at?"

"Maybe it's better inside." I park by a tall hedge with a gate and get out of the car. "What do you suppose is back here?" I ask, walking toward the gate.

"Ellie, come on."

I bite my lip and swallow. She said Ellie. She's not mad at me.

"Just a quick look." I peek over the top of the old wooden gate. "Oh, my God! You have to see this, Anne. It'll only take a second."

She rolls her eyes and scuffs her loafers through the pea gravel toward me.

"Look," I say. She has to stand close to me to see through the narrow space.

"Wow," she says, and I can tell that she is seeing what I see: the ebullient greens and depth of color that only an old, well-tended garden has. Rosebushes flank a stately hydrangea; wisteria drips from the fence. Raised beds flaunt the pinks and yellows and purples of a profusion of cutting flowers, and a small patch of perfect lawn abuts a stone patio with wrought iron tables and chairs.

"It looks like Yolanda's garden," Anne says.

"*Here's* your Wonderland," I tell her.

She nods, and we go inside.

"I kind of thought it would be more medical," I whisper after we've checked in with the receptionist. We're standing in a normal living room, albeit a large one with unmatched couches and chairs arranged in a semicircle around a TV cabinet. An open doorway leads to a room with rows of long folding tables and chairs, and three hallways radiate from the opposite side of the room.

"I kind of thought it would be more sanitary," Anne says in a normal voice, indicating a stain on the carpet. "What do you suppose that was?"

"Well, hello," a male voice says behind us, and we suck in our breath like guilty children. I try not to snicker as Anne turns and tries to make nice.

"What a lovely place you have here." She offers her hand to a balding black man with a clipboard. "I'm Anne Samuels-Richardson, here to see Benny Sloan, and this is my sister Eleanor Samuels."

I nod and place my hand in his. He squeezes it without shaking and smiles at me with kind eyes.

"Nice to meet you both," he says. "Benny was telling me all about you this morning. I'm Archie, Archie Patterson. No Jughead jokes, now. I've heard them all."

"Dr. Patterson?" Anne asks, and he chuckles.

"Nope. I'm the hospice director, handyman, and gardener. Now," he says, checking his clipboard, "you have another sister, right? Or am I thinking of Mrs. Bloomquist's grandchildren?"

"Christine," Anne says, still scanning the place for imperfections.

"She's on her way from California," I say. "She should be here tomorrow."

He marks a sheet on his clipboard and continues. "And you've been the primary caretaker, right, Eleanor?"

I look away. "Not a very good one."

He *tsks* and says, "Well, you must have done something right, because that's one grateful old guy in there."

I nod, but I can't look at him. For some reason all I can think about is the day Buddy ran away, the barbecue we never had.

I dig for a tissue in my purse. Anne's leg starts to twitch.

He studies us for a moment—me sniveling, Anne now tapping her foot on the floor—then says, "Let me show you to Benny's room. We can talk more later."

Anne doesn't move at first, and I realize she's scared to see him. For some reason, even though I've seen Benny every day for the past four months, so am I.

chapter nineteen

It's no mystery why so many Portlanders worship summer. For three-quarters of every year, we are cold and sodden, starved for sunshine, bound with rickets or scurvy or whatever it is you get from lack of natural light. We are slowed by the fog of seasonal affective disorder, SAD in a major way.

And now that it's the golden time, the time of long days, peeling off clothes and wallowing in soft, warm light, now that the trees are filled with leaves and birdsong, and people sit on their porches and have barbecues and go hiking without a rain shell, now that one could possibly take in an outdoor concert at the zoo or the public rose garden, sit on a blanket with a bottle of wine and a companionable—no, downright sexy—man, well. Now.

Anne and I enter Benny's room cautiously, quietly, my elder sister lagging behind to let me lead the way. "Chicken," I would call her if the situation weren't so solemn.

"There you are," Benny says from a hospital bed in what otherwise could be an ordinary bedroom, although with plenty of seating for visitors. "And Miss Annabelle! Ruthann told me you'd come to town." He struggles to sit upright; he's been napping. An IV stand is the only other piece of medical equipment, and when Benny sees me looking at it, he says, "It's just some fluids to get me back on my feet. I've been pretty crook."

"Well, you look great," I say, going over to give him a peck on his grizzled cheek, and he almost does. "Don't you think?" I turn to Anne. Her face has soured like milk.

"I'm sorry," she says. "I have to sit down for a moment." She finds her way to a chair.

"I know, honey," Benny says. "I look like death warmed over, don't I?"

"Benny!" I say, then look at Anne. "He looks great."

She nods and fake smiles. "I guess I'm just a little overwhelmed and exhausted. Life has been so—" She stops, embarrassed, fiddling with a button on her blouse. "Well, it's nothing compared to . . . oh, Jesus."

"Don't worry, honey," Benny says, patting the bed beside him. "We're not having a contest. Come sit here. It's been so long since I've seen my little Belle."

And what am I, chopped liver? I'm thinking, until I see Anne's face soften and fall in upon itself.

This is what she came home for.

"I'll be right back," I say. "I'm going to find the restroom."

"Come here," Benny says again to Anne, and she walks to his bed and sits next to him, letting him fold her in his skinny pajama-ed arms as she hunches awkwardly against him and cries.

I wander back down the short hallway into the living room, where several wheelchairs are now parked in front of the TV, elderly occupants engrossed in the opening credits of *Days of our Lives*. Were it not Sunday, this might not seem so strange, but then I notice the whir of the VCR.

In the dining room, Archie sits with a cup of coffee, and a few feet away, a wheelchair-bound woman obese beyond morbidity fusses over a pale and listless teenage boy with shoe polish–black hair.

"Care to join me?" Archie says, smiling. "Coffee, tea, soda? It's all self-serve, over by the window." I nod and walk toward the drinks, passing the woman and the boy, trying to determine which of them is the patient.

"Hi there," the woman says as I squeeze past. I try not to gasp. She has no legs. "I'm Doris Knox, and this here's my son, Billy."

"Bill," he says in a lackluster baritone, and I smile at him.

"Eleanor," I say, "but my mother calls me Ellie."

He nods, feigning a smile.

"My uncle came in last night," I say to his mother. Her makeup has been painstakingly applied: eyebrows drawn, lips lined, powder clinging to the fine hairs of her face.

"Well, then, maybe we'll get to know each other. Lord knows I'm always here."

I smile and move toward the coffeepot, but I don't think we'll be bonding with all these sick and dying people and their families. There's no reason Benny can't go back home now that the emergency is over. We can put a hospital bed in the living room. I can learn to handle bed-pans and oxygen tanks, whatever I need to. I can be stronger than I've been, I know that. Benny should be home.

After dispensing a squirt of watery coffee, I decide on tea, then make my way back to Archie's table.

"Sorry about my sister," I say, taking a seat across from him. "She's a little . . . I don't know. Abrasive at times."

He smiles and shakes his head, hands cupped around his coffee. He wears a wedding band on one hand, a class ring on the other.

"No need to apologize," he says. "This all takes some getting used to, and you're probably just more up to speed than she is, I'm guessing."

"I suppose." I dunk my tea bag up down, up down in the steaming water. "Benny seems to be doing pretty well."

He nods. "He was in trouble when he got here, but he's stabilizing now. We'll continue to make him as comfortable and pain-free as possible. He's on an antidiarrheal, but the fluids are temporary, just to replace what he's lost. We've also started him on pain medication, which might make him groggy."

"So he could go home soon?"

Archie takes a sip of his coffee, then sets it on the table and looks into it, like he's trying to read his coffee grounds. The top of his head has the symmetrical shape of a violin or a guitar, a male-pattern-baldness piece of art that fades into his forehead.

"When Benny came to us last night," he says, "we asked if this would be a respite-care visit." He looks up. "He said no, that he wanted to stay here with us."

I take a deep breath. "He just thinks I can't do it, or that I don't want to. We've been avoiding things that felt too embarrassing, or too . . . I don't know. Personal."

He nods. "It's difficult."

"But I can do it. I know I can. I want to. I'll do better now." Like if I can convince him, it might be true.

"You know, I'm sure you can, but I don't think that's the issue here." He looks at me for a long moment, then says, "If Benny stays here with us, he'll have round-the-clock medical attention. He'll have plenty of company—"

"But he has company!" I say, cheeks flushing. I was only gone one night.

"I mean people in the same stage of life, people who work with the dying every day and know their issues. I'm sure you're a wonderful care-taker, Eleanor, but there are other things to consider." He pauses. "Have you asked Benny what he wants?"

"Well, no," I say, sitting back in my chair. The straight wood backrest digs into my spine. "I'm pretty sure he wants to be at home, though. I mean, why else . . ." I break off and shake my head, feeling like a peeved child. Why else would I have given up everything else?

"You need time with Benny and your family to talk it through. I'm sure you'll come to the best decision." He drains his coffee cup and stands. "Well, coffee break's over. When you and your sister have a sec-ond, come find me and I'll give you the ten-cent tour, okay?"

I don't think so, I'd say if I were more like Anne. He assumes Benny's staying.

"That is, if you'll be staying," he says, smiling, and walks away. I take a sip of tea and scald half the taste buds off my tongue.

Billy wheels Doris past, and she reaches out to touch my shoulder. "Come visit sometime. Room 6A, on the other side of the building. Back by Archie's garden. It's a shame there weren't any rooms left back there for your uncle."

"He's only here for respite care," I say. "We'll be going home soon." I know she's trying to be nice, but I don't want Benny to be part of this club.

"Oh, I didn't realize," Doris murmurs, and she and Billy push away.

Anne meets me coming down the hall from Benny's room.

"He's having a problem," she says, grimacing. "The nurse is in there with him. We're supposed to wait out here."

"What kind of problem?"

"He doubled over in pain, asked me to find his nurse, and that's as much as I want to know, okay? Let the professionals deal with it."

"But—"

"Eleanor! Give it a rest. Why didn't you tell me he looked so . . ." She slumps into the couch, and her jaw quivers for a moment before she regains control. "You could have at least warned me. He could tell I was shocked. That has to make him feel great, me practically fainting at the way he looks."

"But he actually looks pretty good," I say. "Really."

"No, actually, he doesn't. You're just used to it."

I consider this for a moment, and we're both quiet.

An anguished voice comes from the TV: "*Oh, Marlena, what have I done?*"

"Can we get out of here for a while?" Anne asks. "Go get some coffee or something?"

I dig the keys from my purse, hand them to her. "Go ahead. I'm staying here."

"Fine," she says, rising. "Want anything?"

"Nope," I say.

"Oh, come on. What's wrong? He's not going to mind if we go out for a while."

I shake my head.

"Fine," she says again, walking away.

"I didn't even get to see him yet," I say as she reaches the door.

She turns and says, "Oh," tone softer now. "The nurse will come out to tell you when you can go back in. All right?"

I nod and close my eyes, try to breathe deeply. What I have to talk about with Benny should be between just the two of us, anyway.

"Ellie?" a female voice says, and I open my eyes.

The light in the room has shifted to late-afternoon intensity, and I'm damp with sweat wherever my body meets the couch. Earnest voices debate far too loudly on the TV now, some stupid talk show for voyeuristic losers. Nobody's watching it.

"Hi, I'm your uncle's nurse," says the woman standing over me. She's tall, taller than I am, even, sporting a boy's haircut and purple scrubs.

"Oh, hi," I say, struggling to my feet. "Guess I fell asleep."

"I came out earlier to get you, but you looked so peaceful," she says, extending her hand. "I'm Grace." She shakes my hand with the strongest grip I've ever felt from a woman. Stronger even than Ruthann's. What is it with these supernurses? I resist rubbing my knuckles where she squeezed them together.

"Can I go in now?"

"Sure," she says. "He's sleeping, but you can sit with him if you'd like. We've got lots of books and magazines, crossword puzzles, stuff like that. To pass the time."

"Oh." There go my plans for the big talk.

"He's having a tough time, no matter what he tries to tell you." She smiles, and I know that Benny must like her. Her face is open and friendly, tanned from time outdoors and freckled across her cheeks and forehead.

"Do you have a few minutes?" I ask.

She checks the watch face on the inside of her wrist. "As a matter of fact, I do."

"Can we go somewhere more . . . private?"

"Sure," she says. "Have you seen Archie's garden?"

We settle into chairs next to the wisteria, a few heavy clumps of which are still in fragrant bloom, even in this heat. I breathe in, sigh out, pick up my hair from my neck to cool off.

"I'm just wondering," I say, "from a medical standpoint, if Benny needs to be here. I mean, what if he really wants to be at home? I don't want him to have to be here because I couldn't take good enough care of him."

"Well, no," she says, "it's not medically necessary. Do you want my opinion?"

I nod, holding my breath.

"No matter how able you are as a caretaker, it seems to me Benny's the kind of guy who might make it a tough job," she says. "He doesn't let on when he's not feeling well. He doesn't want to be a burden, or maybe he's too embarrassed about certain things to have you help him."

I nod. To say the least.

"Well, maybe if we take care of him, he can relax more and do what he needs to do before dying. We're not his family; we're *supposed* to do the yucky stuff. Maybe you could help him with other things, like talking about what his life has meant, writing his memories down. Or maybe he needs help wrapping up something that feels unfinished."

Tears spring to my eyes and I nod, but I can't answer. If I could get Mom to come here, push them together in his room and close the door, maybe they'd realize that some things are more important than hurt feelings and events from so long ago it doesn't matter anymore.

Grace says, "That might mean more to both of you than emptying bedpans and cooking and cleaning for him."

"Oh, I'm still going to cook for him," I say, blowing my nose, and she smiles. I look around the yard, still marveling at the volume and variety of flowers, at the surfeit of color. "Would it be okay to pick a few of these to put in his room?"

"That's what they're here for," she says, standing and glancing at her watch. "There should be some cutters lying around here somewhere, and the vases are in the kitchen, in the cabinet over the sink. Help yourself."

When she's gone, I wander through the garden, letting my mind still to just the task of finding the most beautiful specimens, even though I feel half guilty at plucking them in their prime.

• • •

Ernie and Ofelia Sandoval have been married for thirty-seven years, a fact they tell me within two minutes of meeting me. They could be brother and sister, each built like a small brick structure on sturdy legs, graying hair short and practical. Ofelia wears a flowered apron, though, where Ernie sticks to the simple white half-apron of restaurant folk. They owned a café in Corvallis, they tell me, until three years ago when they sold it to start working at Riverview.

"What brought you here?" I ask, filling a carafe-shaped vase with water.

Ofelia pats Ernie's broad chest. "This is where Mother Sandoval passed," she says, and a look passes between them that brings tears to my eyes. Why have I never noticed how much pain there is in the world? I've never really understood that no one is safe. Grief and pain are everywhere, and somehow, even though my own father died, I've missed it.

Ofelia turns to me. "You have someone here?"

"My uncle, Benny Sloan. He's kind of gotten used to my cooking. I was wondering if I might be able to use your kitchen sometimes?"

"Sure, sure," they both say, nodding in unison. Ernie says, "Help yourself whenever you want. Sometimes people make special things for birthdays, or bake cookies. It's an open kitchen. Just clean up." He smiles. "You like to cook?"

"Yeah," I say. "It's pretty much all I do."

"Hey, don't be telling him that or he'll have you in here helping out," Ofelia says, turning to boxes of groceries on the counter. She heaves an industrial-size can of tomato sauce and balances it on her hip like a grandbaby. "He's always looking for his next victim."

I look around at the basic equipment, the meager supplies. I could bring in a few things, donate an appliance or two, and it occurs to me that I might have found a place where I could do what I do best, and do some good.

"Hi, sleepyhead," I say when Benny gradually rustles awake. "How are you feeling?"

He looks at me dully.

"Look, I picked you some flowers." I carry the vase over, set it on the tray beside his bed. "What do you think? As good as the ones in your yard?"

He nods slowly and fumbles with the side of the bed.

"What do you need? Can I help?" He's trying to push the button to raise the head of the bed. "Here you go," I say, putting his fingers on the button. He still can't press it hard enough, so I press it with him, watch the slow-motion progression of his head and torso as they rise into sitting position.

"How long have I been asleep?" he asks, wiping at his mouth with curled fingers.

I pour a cup from the plastic pitcher on the tray and hand it to him. "A couple hours. But I gather you didn't sleep much last night."

"No, not really," he says, and drinks. When he's finished, I take the cup.

"Better?"

He nods. "Thank you, honey."

"Benny," I say. "Tell me the truth, okay?"

"About what?"

"Is this where you want to be? We could get more help at home, you know. They'll give us all the help we need if you want to go back. We can get more medical visits, get you a cute little aide to come bathe you and do all that private stuff."

His lips press tight and his nostrils quaver. He's quiet for a moment before he answers. "Honey, if it's all the same to you, I think I'd like to stay here."

"Of course," I say, turning to tug his blanket across his knees. I don't want him to see my face. "I just wanted to make sure."

"You take good care of me, Miss Roosevelt," he says in an unsteady voice. "If my daughter had lived, if she hadn't been in such bad shape, I would have wanted her to be just like you. You're a fine girl. Always have been." He finds my hand on the bed and holds my fingers.

I nod slowly, close my eyes, and we stay that way for such a long moment that I start to feel lightheaded. I want to talk to him about Rosemary before it's too late, about his life with my mother, but how do I start? Do I pretend I don't know anything? Do I tell him Mom's version of the story? Or do I accept his silence as a dying wish?

Finally, I open my eyes and smile, extract my hand and pat his. "Anything I can get for you?"

He shakes his head, staring at the blankets in front of him.

"What's wrong?"

"They got me in diapers."

"Oh!" I say, then, quickly, to soften it, "Well, not really *diaper-*diapers, are they?"

"As good as," he says. "But they think they can get my stomach to settle down."

"Good," I say, "that's good." It's barely five, but the Sandovals have started cooking. "Are you hungry?"

"No, not just yet," he says. "Maybe later."

I wander back to my chair, pick up the booklet I've been reading, "A Family's Guide to Hospice." "Check it out, Uncle Benny. I've been studying."

There's no answer. His eyes have closed, and guessing from the rhythm of his breathing, he's fallen back to sleep.

chapter twenty

Where are you?" I whisper into my cell phone. "You said you were going out for coffee." Anne's been gone more than two hours.

Over static, she says, "I'm almost there. It took me longer than I thought, but I've got a surprise for you."

"Yeah? Well, it'd better be a triple iced mocha."

"Even better," she says.

"I hate to break it to you, but a quadruple's just overkill," I say, walking into the living room, where a large family sits with the tiniest old woman I've ever seen.

"You'll see. Now hang up. I'm pulling into the parking lot."

I click off, sit on the arm of a chair close to the door. Try as I might, it's impossible not to eavesdrop on the family's conversation.

"Jeremy's going to band camp next week even though he doesn't want to," the mother is saying, "and Amber is still working at Burgerville." Fake laugh. "She spends all her money on clothes, and all her free time at the mall, don't you, honey? But I guess that's what girls do these days. I've tried to get her to look at colleges, but I know, I know. It's her life."

This is what we talk to dying people about? Our own personal burdens? The old woman hasn't uttered a word. I'd look to see if she's even listening, but I already feel like an intruder.

I stand to walk outside, but Anne beats me through the door. She turns to look behind her, and I gasp at her surprise.

"Oh, Ellie," Yolanda says, holding out her arms, and I am in them before I know it, and we're both crying and I'm saying, "I'm sorry, I'm sorry."

"Honey, for what?"

"I couldn't do it. I let him down."

"Shh," she whispers into my hair, and we stand entwined, swaying. "I should never have left you to do my job," she says, then pulls away, silver bangles chiming as she wipes the mascara from beneath her eyes. "What would we do without you girls? Thank goodness you were there with him."

If only I had been. "But I—"

"Eleanor," Anne interrupts, giving me a look, "has been a trooper. I wish I'd come home sooner."

"Honey, how could you know?" Yolanda says, absolving us, forgiving us, as she always has whether she knew how bad we'd been or not. "Now, where's the ladies' room? I'll let you girls in on a secret no one mentions until it's too late: When you get to be my age, all you do is pee."

"Down that hall, second door on your right," I say, pointing. Then to Anne, "I broke down and took the tour."

Anne looks the happiest she has since she arrived in Portland. I'm ashamed at the jealousy I feel. The things I've done for Benny are nothing compared to bringing his wife back to him.

When Yolanda's out of earshot, I say, "How on earth did you get her here?"

"That's why I was gone so long. She wasn't going to come. She thought Mom would be here."

"Right," I snort.

"I just don't get how all this turned into such a soap opera, so many years after the fact," Anne says. "What the hell happened?"

Like I know. The bathroom door opens, and we fall silent at the jangle of bracelets.

• • •

Benny and Yolanda's reunion takes place behind his closed door. Anne and I wait in the living room. She's in a La-Z-Boy by the window reading a *Christian Science Monitor*; I'm across the room on the couch, eyes closed against friendly intruders. What secrets are being told in Benny's room, I wonder, what wounds being exposed? Has Benny told Yolanda the truth over the years? Is he telling her the truth now? I try not to think about it. Maybe some secrets were meant to be kept. I certainly don't feel better for discovering Mom and Benny's indiscretions, and I'm not sure I feel better knowing about Rosemary. I breathe in, two three, out, two three, and open my eyes. All that matters now is now, and whether or not these two people can find some peace before it's too late.

Benny's door opens, and Yolanda wheels him out. They are puffy-eyed but laughing at something he's said, a corny joke, maybe, or a private one between them.

"Chow time," Benny says to Anne and me, and we join them. Wrapped in a robe the hospice must have provided, he looks gnarled and shrunken in the wheelchair.

How did I not see it before?

"I've got to bring you some clothes," I tell him, "and your other stuff. We need to make a list after dinner."

"Yes, ma'am," he says.

"I'm sorry," I say, embarrassed. "I was just—"

"No, honey," Yolanda says. "It's good to see someone else boss this old goat around."

We walk into the dining room, where the Sandovals are serving Sunday dinner family style: chicken and dumplings, fresh creamed spinach, puffy white bread rolls with slabs of butter. Jell-O—yes, Jell-O—salad, with grated carrots and apples and mayonnaise. Jugs of iced tea and Hawaiian Punch sit on every table, and more than a few adults—especially those who look like residents—choose the vibrant red pitcher.

I place tentative spoonfuls of each dish on my plate, dip the tines of my fork into the spinach, taste. I close my eyes at the sweet, creamy sauce laced with just the right amount of nutmeg and something else. White pepper. The chicken is tender, the dumplings soft and light. Before I know it, my plate is clean, and Yolanda looks at me and smiles. Benny is deep in conversation with another wheelchaired old man, sitting across from him and to the left. I think they're talking about car engines. The words "horsepower" and "revs" drift my way.

We could be sitting at a church social or a community fund-raiser like the ones we used to attend in Lake Grove, growing up. The mood is light, considering the number of gaunt faces amid family members, and laughter erupts every so often around the room. Benny's eating only his Jell-O, but his eyes are bright. Anne is exclaiming that she's eaten too much, and Yolanda asks for seconds on the creamed spinach. Ernie and Ofelia, when they aren't hustling to refill bread baskets or clear plates, survey the crowd with a look of tired satisfaction that I completely understand.

The next morning, Anne is still asleep when I get up to put on coffee. I've been wakened by Buddy's insistent kneading of my stomach. She hasn't done that in months; she misses Benny, or maybe Pauncho. Sometimes I think maybe I miss Pauncho, too. My body, though thinner, feels unfamiliar, uncomfortable, too many sharp edges where there used to be rounded corners.

Buddy trots across the floor and jumps onto the arm of the sofa where Anne is buried beneath a cotton blanket.

"Buddy," I whisper. "Don't you dare."

She lifts a paw, tentatively pats the blanket over Anne's head, then looks at me, like, *What are you going to do about it?*

Anne rolls over, and Buddy delicately steps into a space she's left between her arm and her head, turns three-quarters of the way around, and settles in to sleep.

As the coffee begins to drip, I grab the phone and head for my bedroom, closing the door to call Alice.

"First of all, I want to apologize," I say when she answers.

"I know you're going through a tough time," she says. "It isn't easy, and sometimes we just snap."

"Well, that's very kind of you." She has been more than kind. As much as I hate to say it, she has been, well . . . caring.

"Benny's house is all cleaned up, spic-and-span," she says.

"Thank you, and thank you for taking care of Benny the other night. It's so weird that it happened when I was gone, of all times."

"Not really," she says. "I see it all the time with home hospice patients. They wait until the wife or the sister or whoever is gone, and then, bang."

"What, they explode?" I knew the woman was odd.

"They let go. They break down. They die, sometimes, even. Strangest thing."

I close my eyes, imagining Benny letting go of the edge of a swimming pool, floating off until he's just a speck on the turquoise horizon.

Back in the living room, Anne stirs. Buddy hops to the floor and trots back into my bedroom to nap for the day. I pour a cup of coffee, my breakfast of late, but realize it won't do me today. Either I've reconditioned myself back to the routine of meal eating by last night's supper, or I'm just plain hungry. Rummaging through the fridge, I sigh at the neatly wrapped lamb—the only sign that Henry was ever here—then pull out eggs, cream, the rest of the Chaource, and fresh herbs.

"Morning," Anne croaks from beneath her blanket.

"Breakfast?"

"Mm," she says. "Mm hmm."

I crack eggs into a bowl, pour in cream, and mince herbs into tiny green specks. Anne stumbles into the kitchen in men's cotton pajamas, pours a cup of coffee, and leans against the counter.

"I've never understood why people like to cook," she says, taking a long, thoughtful drink. "Where do you suppose you got it from? Certainly not from Mom."

"I guess I'm just a rebel." I say nothing about Yolanda. Anne never went on our shopping trips, never stood in their kitchen, mincing herbs or juicing lemons. She was never invited. "How'd you sleep?" I ask.

"Lousy."

"You know, there's more room over at Benny's, and it's all cleaned up."

"You're kicking me out?"

"No! I ju—"

"Kidding! I'm kidding, Eleanor. You're right. I'll move over there."

"Only if you want to," I say, and we fall silent as I whisk everything together.

"So, El."

"Yeah?" I pour the yellow-green mixture into an omelet pan bubbling with butter.

"Don't get me wrong. I mean, I know I've probably teased you too much about your weight, but . . . are you okay?"

I turn to look at her, crossing an arm over my middle. "Yeah, fine. I've lost a little weight. Stress. You know."

She nods, takes another sip of coffee. "But you haven't gone all anorexic or anything, right?"

"No, of course not." I laugh. "I'm fixing breakfast, aren't I? Did you see all the food in the fridge?"

"Okay," she says. "Just checking."

"Anyway, you should talk. You've always been a stick."

"Yeah, but I'm wired that way. You're not."

I smile—that's the understatement of the century—and say, "I'm okay."

And the thing is, I might be. Where the smell of melting butter would have made me queasy at Benny's, it's now that lovely harbinger of something delicious that it always used to be. This familiar sensation of hunger isn't a dull annoyance to be quelled with a cracker; it's a yammering so insistent that I can't ignore it. And I don't want to. I want to taste real food again. Instead of the emptiness I've been living with, I want to feel sated.

Somehow, I am speeding back into life as Benny is speeding out. Is it the simple relief of no longer being responsible for his physical well-being? Is it being away from the smells and sights and sounds of illness? Or do the dying release their energy to those they love, a parting gift?

"Before we go today," I say, "I need to make a cake."

She snorts. "Just like that? And I suppose without a mix?"

I fold the omelet, then cut it in half and slide each portion onto a small white plate garnished with more herbs. "It's just as easy without a mix, and it will only take as long as it takes you to get ready." I hand her a plate, grab forks from the drawer. "Besides, I owe Benny a spice cake," I say, salivating at the warm slick of French cheese oozing from between perfectly cooked folds of egg.

Later, Anne is standing in the bathroom with the door open and Buddy is perched on the toilet tank, watching her brush her teeth.

"So, why the cat?" she calls through a mouthful of toothpaste, then spits into the sink and rinses.

"She's a pet, Anne. People have pets." I take a sip of coffee, tap my pen on the to-do list I'm making for today. *Pack Benny's stuff, check e-mail, bring Benny's bills for Yolanda.* The smell of baking cinnamon and cloves and allspice drifts from the kitchen. *Call Henry?* I could tell him Benny's doing okay. I could tell him . . . what? That I like him? That I miss him after just one day? How needy is that?

"Hi," Anne says to the cat, then reaches out to pet the top of her head. Buddy arches against her hand, knowing she will elicit a full-body stroke or at least a scratch behind the ears.

"Hey, she likes me," Anne says.

"That's her job." I tap the pen, tap tap. What else? "Oh, Christine called while you were in the shower. She's in Salem. We're going to meet her at Benny's; then we can all drive over together."

"I can't imagine her pregnant, can you? She's so tiny."

"She'll look like Mom did, I guess."

Silence, then Anne comes to sit at the table. "Did you call her?"

"Mom? She's not speaking to me." Anne looks worried. I say, "Maybe if you called her, worked your charms on her. Look what you did with Yolanda."

"No," she says. "If she doesn't listen to you, she's not going to listen to me." She stares at her hands, long fingers splayed across the edge of the table.

"Well, she might," I say, but would she? Do they get along any better than Mom and I do? "Are you going to see her?"

Anne shrugs, nods. "Sure, sometime. Not today." She stands. "I'm going to get dressed. Is that really what you're wearing?"

I look down at my T-shirt and khakis. "What's wrong with this?"

"Nothing, I suppose, for Portland," she says. "But you might consider ironing your shirt."

"T-shirts were invented so we didn't have to iron," I say, but I stand, pull it over my head, and walk to the long-neglected ironing board she's set up in the bedroom.

Benny's house smells of industrial-strength cleanser, but otherwise looks normal. His bed has been made with fresh sheets, and the carpet in his room is damp from shampooing. If I were a religious person, I'd say "God bless Alice Desmay."

Christine hasn't arrived yet. Anne has parked her luggage and brief-case in the hallway while she wanders through the house, exclaiming, "I remember this!" and "I can't believe he still has that."

I gather fresh pajamas for Benny, his robe, slippers, toiletries, and a few books, then pack them into a small brown valise from the closet that looks as if it's never been used. After pondering what else he'd want, I grab the white photo album and slip it in, snap the stiff latches, and set the case by the front door.

Next I pack my things to clear the sewing room for Anne, wondering when I'll have time to return for the kitchen equipment and computer, sitting dark and silent on the sewing table. I turn it on and wait for it to boot up while I survey my work area: ruffled tablets filled with illegible scribbling, research files, signed contracts for Stefan's piece, two new articles for *American Family,* and one for *Healthy Fit.* I check my incoming e-mail, but there's nothing beyond Metabolife and penis-enlargement ads. I hit COMPOSE NEW MESSAGE and type:

Dear Stefan,
I hate to do this to you, but my uncle's condition has worsened, and I'm afraid I won't be able to complete the dessert article. I'm not sure that a deadline extension would help.

Benny's now in the hospice, my family is arriving, and the situation, for now, is tenuous. Please accept my apologies, but I hope you will understand.

Yours,

E.

I send similar messages to *American Family* and *Healthy Fit*. There go my best clients; there goes my spotless track record. It's not like there aren't hundreds of hungry freelancers out there just waiting to fill my shoes, but I feel such relief that I could skip through the house.

Half an hour later, Anne and I are sitting at the backyard picnic table, sweating in the heat, fanning ourselves with the junk mail we're sorting, when we hear the chug and sputter of Christine's car pulling into the driveway.

We look at each other and shake our heads, then go to greet her.

Out front, Christine is trying to wriggle free of the small car.

"God," Anne mutters. "What if she'd had an accident?"

"Hi!" Christine calls, waving. Her hair has grown long and her cheeks are fuller, flushed as she arches her back and smoothes her hands over what looks like the butt end of a watermelon protruding from her midsection. She wears a form-fitting aqua tank top with BUDDHA-FUL emblazoned in red script, and drawstring pants tied beneath her belly. And here I thought she'd be wearing Kmart. I should have known better.

"Look at you!" I rush over to hug her, leaning over her tummy. "You look great!"

"How is he?" she asks.

"A little better." I can't bring myself to tell her anything too real. Not yet. "How are you?"

Anne comes in for her usual sideways one-arm hug and says, "Geez, Christine. You could have died in that thing."

"Good to see you, too." Christine elbows her the way she always has. "Congratulations on the settlement."

"And the resignation," I say.

"Really?" Christine hugs Anne again. "Good for you!"

Anne looks pleasantly embarrassed, and doesn't mention the nature of her departure. "So, are you staying at Mom's?"

Christine shakes her head. "Too far away. Plus, I don't think she's up for it. She's pretty upset about Benny." She sighs. "God. Isn't this just like when Dad died?" Her eyes well.

Anne and I look at each other, but rather than saying anything cynical, we open the hatch of Christine's car to retrieve her luggage.

"Jesus, how long do you plan on staying?" Anne says. The back of the car is filled with two hard suitcases, three duffels, and more than a few cardboard boxes.

"Christine?" I say, when she doesn't answer.

"I don't know," she says, and her face turns bright red. "I might not go back." And then she is crying into her hands, head bowed and shoulders shaking. "He wasn't even going to let me come!"

I take her in my arms and look at Anne. She shakes her head and narrows her eyes, and I nod back, shrug, and sigh. When Christine is cried out, Anne and I each take a suitcase from the back of the car, and the three of us walk toward Benny's house together, something we haven't done in twenty years or more.

At his first sight of Christine, Benny purses his lips and shuts his eyes.

She must look so much like Mom.

He recovers quickly, drawing a shaky breath. "I see somebody's been up to some hanky-panky," he says. "Get over here, you."

She laughs and goes to hug him, then pats her stomach.

"Touch it," she says.

"Well, I . . ." Benny falters, his eyes blink. He shuffles his hands in his lap.

"Go on, Ben," I say, setting his valise on the floor and walking over. I put the spice cake on his bedside table and lay my hand on the firm rise of Christine's belly, just above her new outie navel. "It's not as hard as I thought," I say. "It's kind of pliant, but not squishy."

"Amniotic fluid," Benny says, crooked fingers rising to cup the curve of the baby floating inside. "Sweet little girl," he croons.

"Girl?" Christine says. "Uncle Benny, what do you know that I don't?"

His eyes widen and he pulls his hand back.

"He was talking about you, Christine," I say quickly. "Weren't you, Ben?"

He nods slowly, and Christine chatters, and I pull Anne by the elbow.

"Anne and I will be back in a few minutes."

"We will?" Anne says.

"We're going to get a cup of tea."

"I'd rather have coffee," Anne grumbles.

"I don't think so," I say, pulling Benny's door closed behind us.

We find Archie inside a cluttered office. He looks up from his computer screen. "Well, hey there. Can I help?"

"She's giving me the tour," Anne says.

"Also," I say, "I wanted to ask you something."

He raises his eyebrows; the wrinkles of his forehead stop just short of his former hairline.

"Would it be possible to have a barbecue outside in the garden? Just a family get-together kind of thing?"

He nods. "Of course. We have a grill in the shed, more lawn chairs. Help yourselves."

"How about next weekend?"

He smiles that patient smile he did with me yesterday. "You might want to do it sooner rather than later."

Is it going to be this way every day? Every time I think I have a handle on the situation, something or someone comes along and says, "Oh, no you don't." I thought Benny might be here for weeks, maybe months. Even creepy Dr. Krall said one of his patients had lived a year, but then Benny's been off his protocol for who knows how long.

"Of course," I say, forcing a light tone. "You're right. Why wait? Do you think Wednesday would be good?" *Please,* I'm thinking, *please say yes. It's only two days from now.*

"Great," Archie says.

"Great!" I repeat with too much enthusiasm, then excuse myself and walk quickly to the bathroom. I lock the door, switch on the fan, turn the faucet to full blast. The mirror is too close, so I back away into the middle of the small room, knowing how I must look. Every muscle in my face contracts, all pulling together tightly, clenched so hard I know my face will ache tomorrow. A sensation rises from my chest through my throat, so thick and hot and powerful I think I might be about to vomit, but then I open my mouth and scream with no sound, no words, just hot air and steam and blood squeezing through constricted veins. I cannot breathe for expelling this thing, over and over, and it's only when Anne knocks on the door that I let myself draw a deep breath.

"Are you okay?" she says through the door. "Can I come in?"

I fumble to release the lock on the door, and then Anne is beside me, face ragged with crying.

"What did he mean?" she says.

I shake my head, and she grabs me in a tight hug, sobbing. I can count on one hand the number of times my sister has allowed me to touch her with any affection, but I clutch at her bony form, so much like Dad's, so awkward but tender in surprising moments. I remember that Dad held me once, just like this, when I found out my third-grade teacher had been killed in a car accident. He'd come into my room early, before I woke for school, and stood over my bed, saying softly, "Ellie." He'd read it in the paper, and he wanted to tell me before I heard about it from anyone else.

I let go of Anne and pull streams of toilet paper from the spindle to blow my nose, but end up pressing them into my face at a new wave of crying, barely able to breathe, senses obliterated by the surprise of this grief, so much deeper than I knew.

chapter twenty-one

Mmm, is this spice cake?" Yolanda says, dipping her pinkie finger in the icing to put in her mouth. "Oh, Benito, your favorite."

I haven't heard her call him that in years.

She's arrived in time for lunch, making everyone feel better, swinging her lime green skirt through Benny's bedroom door and packing a Styrofoam cooler full of soft, warm tamales from Chucho's. As I peel back the cornhusk, aromas escape that I haven't thought of in years: masa, lime, red chile. I remember a Christmas Eve party Benny and Yolanda threw one year, with her whole family there—siblings, cousins, grandparents. Their dining room table laden with plates of tamales, pans of enchiladas, and bowls of posole and menudo. The marionettes they bought all the kids that year. Mine was a French chef with requisite big hat and curly mustache; Anne's was an old woman with a hook nose, like the witch from Hansel and Gretel. Christine's was a princess. We've been typecast our whole lives.

After we've finished our tamales, Yolanda cuts large pieces of cake, loading them onto flimsy paper plates I found in the kitchen. Benny takes a plastic fork in hand, dodging and weaving it toward his plate on the tray. "Morphine," Yolanda whispered earlier as I watched him try to negotiate his tamale to his mouth. His fork finds his lips and he slides the cake into his mouth, closing his eyes, face crumpling in the way that means it's good.

Christine sits in an armchair with her feet propped up on the rails of Benny's bed, cake plate balanced on top of her stomach. Anne stands by the window, having said no to cake, thumbing through back copies of *Newsweek* (I don't ask if she's looking for pictures of herself). Yolanda leans a hip against the bed, close enough to help should Benny need it, far enough away so that he doesn't realize her intentions.

I take a bite of cake to make sure it tastes okay, surprised at the depth of flavor, the moist texture, and creamy frosting. You'd think I hadn't eaten a piece of spice cake in years, when in fact I ate an entire pan full just four months ago, the day I found out Benny was dying. And then I understand; I didn't taste it then.

Benny lays down his fork and says, "That's about the best spice cake I ever had, Miss Roosevelt. Thank you ever so much."

"But you've only had a bite, Uncle Benny," Christine says, already halfway through hers.

"One perfect bite," he says. "I don't believe I'll need to taste spice cake again."

Anne looks up suddenly from her magazine. Christine draws a quick breath, and Yolanda *tsks* Benny, giving him a look.

"Well, okay then, Ben," I say, and everyone looks at me now. "Why don't we make a list of things you'd like to have at least one more time?"

"Now you're talking," he says, and lies back to consider his list. "Let's see," he says, before slowly ticking off items: "Banana-nut bread would be good. Burgerville french fries, of course. Maybe a hot dog with mustard and onions." He pauses, squinting, then smiles. "And pineapple upside-down cake."

"That's it?" Anne asks. "Out of everything in the whole world, that's all you want?"

"Yup," Benny says, closing his eyes as if exhausted. His fingers lace across his sternum. "I'm a man of simple needs."

By two o'clock, Yolanda has gone back to work, Anne has borrowed my car to run errands, and Christine has disappeared. They're not used to this yet. They have no stamina.

Benny's sleeping, so I carry the cake pan and paper plates into the dining room, offering pieces to a group of three women playing cards and an older couple drinking coffee. The tiny old woman from the horrible family sits in a wheelchair by the window, gazing out at the street.

"Is your family coming to visit today?"

She stares at me blankly, then back out the window.

"Would you like some spice cake? It's homemade."

"She doesn't talk," says a teenage girl sitting nearby, and I recognize her as the granddaughter. She's reading a book.

"Oh. How about you? Cake?"

She nods. "Gram would probably eat some, too."

I cut two pieces, trying to remember the vilified Burgerville-working daughter's name. "It's . . . Amanda, isn't it?"

"Amber," she says, setting down her book. She has stringy strawberry blond hair and eyes so light they almost disappear into her pallid face. "How'd you know?"

"It's a small place." I smile, sliding a plate toward her. "What are you reading?"

She lifts the library-issue paperback to show me the cover: *Love in the Time of Cholera.* How old was I when I read it—twenty-four, twenty-five? Older maybe. This girl isn't the gum-snapping bimbo her mother makes her out to be.

"Have you read *One Hundred Years of Solitude?*" I ask.

She nods, shrugs. "I like this one better."

"Me, too," I say. "What's your grandmother's name?"

"Hazel," she says. "Gunderson."

"Nice to meet you, Mrs. Gunderson," I say to the old woman, putting a piece of cake in front of her on the table. She turns to me, looks at the plate, and picks up the fork.

"See?" Amber says. "She loves sweets."

"Who doesn't?" I say. "I'm Eleanor. You can usually find me in Room 4B with my uncle Benny."

"Cool," she says, picking at her cake with her fingers despite the fork I've given her. Mrs. Gunderson blinks hard at her piece, then digs in.

● ● ●

I don't see Doris anywhere, so I head down the long hallway of rooms, toward the back, finding Room 6A at the end of the corridor. The door is ajar. I tap lightly on it, hearing a TV at low volume.

"Hello? Doris?"

The TV mutes.

"Come on in," she says.

She's sitting on a double bed, filling most of it with her girth, wearing thick glasses to knit what looks like a complicated orange-and-yellow garment. A can of diet ginger ale sits on her bedside tray, along with a box of tissues and a stuffed toy poodle. She doesn't appear to be dying anytime soon.

"Hi," I say. "I thought you might like some cake."

"Oh, honey, thank you," she says, clacking her knitting needles, "but I can't have it." She smiles and nods toward a chair. "Sit and visit awhile?"

"Oh," I say. "I wouldn't want to keep you from your TV show."

"I just have it on for company." She picks up the remote and snaps it off. "Did you see my view?" She twists slightly toward the window. I move to see better, and there's Christine in the garden, sitting cross-legged on the grass with her back to us.

"Sit a minute, honey," Doris says again, looking over the tops of her glasses.

"Well, okay, for a little bit." I perch at the edge of a green vinyl chair, cake pan across my lap. "Where's your son today?"

"School," she says. "First person in our family to go to college. Smart kid. He got his GED last year when he was just seventeen." She nods in time with her knitting, then looks at me.

"How's your uncle, honey?"

"Better. He's on some medication now, so he's a little . . . better."

"Going home soon, then?"

"Actually, he decided to stay." I press my lips into a tight smile.

"Well, God bless him. And you, too."

"Thank you."

We sit quietly, then I ask, "So are you . . . I mean, how are you?"

"Well, I'm not about to die, if that's what you're asking." The knitting needles click, two three, then stop. "Not to be indelicate," she says, looking up and winking at me. "Some of us are just regular nursing home patients."

"Oh. Of course. Right."

I tap the edge of the cake pan with my fingers in time to her knitting. "But isn't it hard to . . . you know. Be around it so much?"

"Not really, no," she says. "Actually, I like it here. I feel useful." She shrugs. "I'm easy to talk to. People here don't seem to mind the way I look."

"You look fine!" I say too quickly.

She chortles, leans over to take swig of ginger ale. "I know how I look, honey. It's all right."

"No, I mean, really. I know what it's like to feel . . ." I stop, then start again. "The way I look disgusts my mother."

"Lord. Why on earth? I'd give anything to look like you."

I wince, shake my head. "No, don't say that. You're—you're lovely. I noticed the first time I saw you how much care you take in your appearance, how much you love your son. It makes you kind of, I don't know. Shine."

"My goodness," Doris says, eyes widening. "I don't know what to say."

"I'm sorry; I'm babbling. It's just that everything's . . . I'm so . . ." I wipe my eyes, laugh. "Emotional. About everything. God."

"You come visit any time you want, honey. You're a good person, I can tell. Your mother must be a damn psycho or something." She revs up her knitting needles again, clacking and maneuvering them through the yarn with ease. "Not that my mother was any better."

I step from the door leading to the garden and walk across the patio, onto the lawn.

Christine turns and looks at me, eyes swollen, nose red. "You should take your shoes off. This grass is so soft." She sweeps her hand across it, petting it like a pony.

I slide out of my sandals, dig into the lawn with my toes. "Nice," I say. "Benny would kill for this lawn."

"How do you do it?" she asks, pinching a blade of grass and pulling it out at the root. We used to love eating the white tip, a delicacy from our childhoods like honeysuckle nectar pods and marigold petals. "How do you act so normal? So, I don't know. Not devastated?"

"I am devastated." I hear the defensive tone, try to soften it. "I've been with him every day. You start to get used to it."

She leans back on one arm, using the other to cradle her belly. "I just mean that you have this way of still being normal with him. You can say things about his—his condition or whatever, and it seems so easy. I can't even imagine talking to him about it."

"Spend more time with him. It'll get easier."

"But what if I'm too late?" Her eyes fill. "He seems so tired, so sick." Her thirty-six-year-old face is still cherubic, more so with the roundness of pregnancy. She looks so much like the six-year-old version of herself. "I still wish I could have talked to Dad, just . . . you know." She sighs heavily. "One more time."

"Benny's still here."

"I know," she says, then her chin begins to tremble. "He's going to die, though, isn't he? I mean, pretty soon."

"I think so."

She begins to cry in earnest, lying back on the grass and covering her face with her hands. I lie on my side next to her in the grass, smooth a long strand of hair from her forehead.

"My baby won't know him or Dad. I won't have a father or a grandfather for my child. God, I don't think I can stand this!"

I move closer to wrap my arms around her. I can't say it doesn't occur to me how odd we look—two grown women lying in the grass, embracing—but this place is full of the terminally sad. Surely, we don't look that strange.

Later in the day, Anne is back from her mysterious errand, carrying a small but insanely expensive stereo system and CDs for Benny: Hoyt Axton, Glenn Miller, Sarah Vaughan, Vivaldi.

"How do you know what music he likes?" I ask, holding the front door open for her.

"You're not the only one who ever spent time with Benny," she says. And I see that, when she sets up the system next to his bed and pops in a CD, and Sarah Vaughan's voice fills the room, singing "Lover Man." Benny closes his eyes, shakes his head. "You have outdone yourself, Miss Annabelle. Is this the 1955 version?"

Anne nods. "Of course. Only the best." She sits in the chair by the window, laces her fingers together behind her head, and closes her eyes, nodding in time to the song.

"John Weinert." His tone never changes; he always sounds pleasantly assured. How is that possible?

"John, hello. It's Eleanor. How are you?"

"Fine, fine, thank you. And you?"

"Well . . . fine. Listen, is my mom around?"

"Yes, let me—"

"No, I wanted to talk to you, actually."

"Oh," he says. "Well, then."

"I know I'm not on the best terms with my mother."

"No," he agrees.

"But I think it's really important for her to see Benny, or talk to him on the phone. At least acknowledge him in some way. He's in the hospice now. We don't know how long he has left."

"I see."

"We're going to have a barbecue here at the hospice on Wednesday evening. Do you think you could talk her into coming?"

"Oh, well, I don't think—"

"If you could just try."

"Well . . ."

"Great. I appreciate it so much."

"I didn't—"

"I know, but you'll try. That's all you can do, I know."

He's silent, then says, "You know your mother loves you girls very much."

"I know." I sigh. The worst part is that I do.

• • •

Yolanda is going to make potato salad. Anne's springing for steaks, and hot dogs at Benny's request. Christine, being a vegetarian, is making a green salad and getting her own tofu burgers to grill. As for me, here's my list:

> Banana-nut bread
> Burgerville french fries
> Mustard and onions for the hot dogs

And, of course,

> Pineapple upside-down cake.

chapter twenty-two

Tuesday blends in where Monday left off, Yolanda, Anne, Christine, and I coming and going from Benny's room, watching mindless TV in the hospice living room, talking with other families, catching quick naps on the couch. There is nothing to do, and yet we can do nothing else. We are waiting for something that we don't speak of, other than to report every snippet of news we each pick up from various sources: his nurse, Grace, Ruthann, Archie.

Benny's vitals are continuing their slow downward spiral, Grace says, but so far, nothing drastic. We like her reports; they're always couched in such optimistic terms. Ruthann spends a lot of time talking with Benny. I wonder if she's become his confessor. Archie spends time with us, helping us understand the physical process of dying, the emotional process, for both the person who is leaving and those who aren't. He's so patient and kind that I hope he's somebody's father.

This morning, Christine witnessed a brief conversation Benny had with his dead mother upon waking from a nap. She asked if he could see her but he didn't answer, just looked befuddled at her question and rubbed his arms. The morphine is taking its toll, leaving him itchy and uncomfortable.

He's not hungry for anything and eats only a bite or two at meals. He makes a sucking noise if you hold the straw in his water glass to his mouth, but I think it's just to fool us into lowering it. He no longer asks questions about the outside world, his house, not even our lives. We've winnowed down the world to just this space, just these moments when he's not asleep, just the holding of hands, the rubbing of shoulders, the combing of hair. Bed up or down? Room dark or light? Music or quiet, talking or silence. Everything has been reduced to only these small matters, and they take on an infinite importance.

"He wanted the Vivaldi," Anne reports after lunch, eyebrows lifting to convey the significance.

"Grace brought him a Popsicle," Yolanda says in the midafternoon. She's taken leave from work. "Orange, his favorite. And he ate half."

We are so egalitarian in how much time we each spend alone at his side and we do it without any formal agreement, just nods and body language and noticing the expressions on each other's faces, the puffiness of eyes, the number of tissues wadded into tightly clenched hands. My sisters and I have abandoned any snide comments we might have made to each other even yesterday, put aside our lifelong squabbles and petty differences.

It's during one of my alone moments with Benny, just as the sun is dropping lower in the sky, sending hot streams of light through the window against which I shut the blinds, that I decide to talk to him about matters more weighty.

"So, Ben," I say, taking a seat in the easy chair we've positioned next to his bed. He moves his head on the pillow in my direction, but his face is in shadow, a few stripes of sunlight from the window crossing his chest.

"So," he says, voice tired. "Ellie."

I've been rehearsing the next line, which makes it no easier to say: "Is there anything left that you want to do or say that I could help you with? A letter to anyone, a phone call, or . . ." I falter, feel warmth spreading from my chest to my neck.

"Yes," he says, voice quieter still. I wait, knowing how hard this must be. The blanket over his chest rises and falls, rises and falls, stripes of sun moving hypnotically in an optical illusion until my eyes grow heavy in the half-light. Benny snorts and I jerk awake, pinpricks of adrenaline in my scalp, and it's then I realize that Benny has fallen back to sleep.

• • •

On Wednesday morning, I wake suddenly and panic—where is everyone? Where's Benny?—until I realize I'm in my own bed and everyone else is safe in theirs.

When my sisters and I said good-bye to Benny last night, actually waking him at nine o'clock to let him know we were going, I felt inadequate and without the right words. I didn't want to leave without saying something important, whatever that big thing is that must be said before it's too late, but instead I said, "Do you need anything else before we go, Ben? Are you okay?"

Sleepily, he shook his head. "I'm fine."

Even though he'd eaten nothing for dinner, I asked, "If you could have anything in the whole world to eat tomorrow, what would it be?"

He looked at me with watery gray eyes and shrugged. It wasn't even really a shrug, just a small, tired movement. I wondered what he really needed, if it had something to do with my mother, and it panicked me.

"Can't decide?" I said, absurdly jovial. "How about oatmeal cookies? With nuts, no raisins?"

He nodded slowly, a comma of a smile resting on his lips. I could have said "yak"; I could have said "snowberries." He was just being kind.

"Okay, Uncle Benny," Christine said, fussing with his blankets. "You get some sleep. We'll be back tomorrow."

Anne waved from the foot of the bed, echoing, "See you tomorrow."

"Bye-bye," Benny said, but still, Christine hadn't moved. She now had the blankets balled in her hands and had started to cry.

"Bye-bye," she said, then went to hug him. "We love you."

Anne and I fumbled our way over to do what Christine made look so easy, to kiss our uncle good-bye. I whispered, "We'll talk tomorrow, okay?"

Yolanda stayed parked in the easy chair. We'd already kissed her good-bye. She made damn sure of it.

It wasn't until I was nearly home that I remembered we were going to have a barbecue the next night, which is now tonight. I can't imagine Benny sitting in a lawn chair anymore, can't picture him holding a can of Blitz, eating a hot dog, even cracking a joke. That part of him is already gone.

He is safe, I think now as I lie in my bed, the pulse in my neck thudding the pillow. He has the best care possible. He is not in pain. Is today the day, or will I just wake up with this feeling every day until that day?

I get out of bed, feed Buddy, who seems a little despondent herself, then pull ingredients from the cupboards: flour, sugar, butter, oats, nuts. And no raisins. When the first batch is in the oven, I call my mother.

Ruthann is in Benny's room when I arrive, standing by his bed, holding his hand. They are talking seriously, it seems, or she is, anyway. She sees the Tupperware in my hands and her eyes light up.

I hand her the container. "Oatmeal cookies," I say. "They're too crispy."

"I love crispy," she says.

"You love anything." I pause, look at Benny. He looks different. His gaze is distracted. "Everything okay?"

"Actually, Ellie," she says softly, evenly, and my skin prickles, "Benny's doing great, but it's all happening."

I want to run. I want to sit down. I want to throw up. I want to do something other than what I am doing, which I realize now is gripping Benny's arm as if I can hold him here forever.

"Yolanda's been with him all night; she just went to rest for a while. He asked her for some juice at about midnight, I guess, and when she came back from the kitchen, he was no longer able to speak comprehensibly. Probably the brain mets. So we've stopped the dexamethasone."

"But that means . . ." I can't say it.

"Yeah, kiddo, you got it. It'll be hours, maybe days. But he's not in pain, he's not distressed. His breathing sounds labored, but he seems comfortable. He's just feeling a little sleepy, aren't you, Benny?" She smiles at him, puts a hand on his forehead. "He's not very responsive, but you should talk with him about anything you want to, or just sit with him. Touch is good. Hold his hands, rub his feet. Let him know you're here." She cocks her head at me. "Okay, Ellie? It's an amazing time in our lives, especially when the people we love are with us."

I nod, loosening my grip on his arm so that I am merely laying my hands on him. "Will you stay, too?"

"Of course. You just tell me when you want private time."

"I think I might," I say. "I mean, now, before everyone else . . ."

She comes around and hugs me for the first time since I've met her. She is so short I have to bend down, but her embrace is as strong as her handshake.

And then I am alone with Benny. Uncle Benny. The man I have loved most in my life.

"So," I say. "Ben." Silence. Touching his arm, sliding down to his hand, entwining my fingers in his, feeling the wedding band on his finger. I smile at that, the bittersweet perfection of that. He squeezes my hand lightly, I think, but his eyes don't focus on mine. They look behind me, at something I can't see. He breathes in as if he's coming up for air between swim strokes, deep and just slightly desperate. It's hard to believe he's not afraid.

"Are you really okay?" I whisper, trying to sound like I'm not crying. "Or are you just trying to impress Ruthann? It's me, now, Ben. Ellie. You can be scared, because I sure am."

I pause, leave a silence for him to fill. It grows unbearably long. "So, Mom called this morning, and she wanted me to tell you hi," I lie. She wouldn't come to the phone. "She said to tell you she's thinking about you, Uncle Benny. She really is, even if she doesn't act like it. I know she loves you, no matter what happened."

His gaze doesn't change.

"You know, we were supposed to talk about what you still wanted to do, what you still wanted to tell me. Is there something I didn't do, or we didn't do, that we should have? Did we wait too long?"

My nose is running too much to continue, and I have to stop and snatch tissues from his bedside table, blow my nose like a trumpet, that gaggle of honking geese. I laugh at the sound, which is ridiculous, I know, when someone is dying right in front of you, but it is funny, that noise, and Benny's expression shifts: a slight squint of the eyes, a curl at the lip.

"Nice, Ben," I say. "Kick a girl when she's down."

And then I go to his valise in the corner, pull out the white photo album, and sit next to him on the bed.

"I thought you might like to see these," I say, opening to the first photo of Rosemary. I hold it open in front of him. "How old was she in this picture? Five, maybe? Six?" I turn the page. "And look at you, Mr. Full Head of Hair. Nice tie."

His breath catches for a moment, startling me, and then he coughs and seems all right again.

I turn the page slowly, and again, through the years until we are at Rosemary's obituary. I read it aloud to him, then reach down and squeeze his hand, once hard and dry with calluses and now softening, starting to curl and turn in upon itself like an embryo. I remember what Ruthann said, and I keep squeezing, massaging, so he'll know I'm here.

"How did you do it, all those years?" I ask, and again I'm crying. "How could you stand to watch her marry someone else, have someone else's children? How did it not kill you?"

I wipe my eyes with my forearm. "I wish she'd stayed with you. I don't understand her. She loves you. I know it."

I start to close the album against my knees, and a corner of a photo slips from between two pages taped together at the back. A hiding place, and one that wasn't there when I last looked at this book. I tug at the photo, pull it free, and a handful of dog-eared pictures tumble into my lap.

I pick them up like playing cards, square them into a pile against the photo album, front side down.

"So," I say. "Did you want me to see these, Ben?"

His fingers move inside mine.

"Okay, then. Let's take a look." My heart is pounding as I flip the pile over to the top photo, a studio portrait proof of a dark-eyed young woman, circa 1970-something. She has full plum lips and an easiness in her expression. I relax. "Yolanda," I say, marveling, as I always do, at her simple beauty.

The next is a scalloped-edge black-and-white that is old and creased—a spotted, one-eared dog sitting on porch steps. "King?" I say. "I bet it is."

Another from the same era of a shiny, big-fendered car with huge chrome bumpers. A square color photo of Anne, Christine, and me clowning in our backyard, doing the twist, I'm pretty sure, on a hot summer night. Another old black-and-white of a serious young man in a uniform, standing stiffly beside a stern man and plump woman in good Sunday clothes. "Your brother," I say, "and your mom and dad."

And then I am looking into the faces of my mother, my toddler sister Anne at her feet, and myself as a baby straddling Mom's hip. The photo is dated 1965, and we are standing next to Rosemary's wheelchair, in front of Moreland Home. Anne is crying, and I have half of my hand in my mouth, but Mom is smiling for the camera, free hand resting on Rosemary's head. She looks happy.

She looks like a good mother.

I stare at the photo for a long time, unable to process the information I'm being shown, just looking into the past, holding in my hands everything Benny has ever loved.

Finally, I clear my throat. "They're wonderful pictures," I say. "Let's look at them one more time." I hold each photo in front of him, approximating where his gaze is falling, letting him take a last long look. I imagine that he is saying good-bye. At the last photo, I stop, as stunned to be seeing it for the second time as I was the first. I stare at it until it is no longer unfamiliar, until I have memorized its composition, its light and shadow. In 1965, Rosemary would have been five years old. She had six years left to live. And then it hits me that the year Rosemary died would have been 1971. The year Benny came into our lives.

"Are you the sad man?" I remember Christine asking, and I wish we'd been less shy around him that night. I wish we'd hugged and kissed him, seen him for who he would become in our lives. The ache of wanting it is too much, though, too unbearable to let myself feel, so I scoop the pictures together and return them to their hiding spot, then hug the book to my chest, stretch my legs alongside Benny's.

Beside me, he has closed his eyes. He breathes in, *hahrrr*, out, *hahrrr*, and I wish we could just sit and watch *Andy Griffith* on the damn TV.

"You know, Ben," I say, laying my head back against the pillow, "Thelma Lou was sweet, but I would've figured you for a Miss Crump man."

chapter twenty-three

His dying was a miraculous thing, a wonder. Like birth in reverse.

Late in the evening on Wednesday, we'd all migrated to Benny's room, no one wanting to leave. Somehow, we'd tuned into his rhythm over the long hours and days we'd been there; it had become the rhythm we all moved to. When his breathing changed, we changed. We drew closer, or we backed away if it eased. He'd been laboring at this new intensity for almost a full day, and we'd clung to his breathing as if it were proof that he needed us still, when it was really proof that we needed him, and he knew it.

His vitals were slipping, his breathing growing even harsher, louder. His eyes were closed most of the time, and the fluttering moments they were open we couldn't tell if he saw anything or not. We told him we were there. We massaged his hands, his arms and shoulders. Yolanda smoothed lotion on his feet, laid cool washcloths on his forehead. Ruthann swabbed his mouth with moist cherry-flavored sponges on sticks, like lollipops for the dying. For a while, Christine sat at the edge of a chair, leaning over the bed so that her head was resting next to Benny's on the pillow, whispering into his ear. Anne sat next to the window, staring intently at Benny and chewing her lips until I thought they would bleed. I couldn't let go of his hand, but whatever movement there'd been had stopped.

At nearly eleven p.m., Yolanda rose from her chair at his side, stood over his nearly translucent form, and said, "Benito, sweetheart, you've had enough now." She leaned down to kiss his cheek, and whispered something against the side of his face, smoothing her hand across his forehead. Then she stood and we all pulled in closer, each of our thighs or hips or bellies bumping the mattress. We wrapped our arms around each other, or touched his arms, his legs. For once, none of us were crying.

"It's okay, Uncle Benny," Christine said, and I cringed at what might come out of her mouth next; I hoped she wouldn't say anything about going into the light. But that was all she said, "It's okay," over and over, and pretty soon we were all murmuring softly.

"You can let go," Anne said.

"Go with God, my love," said Yolanda. "I'll see you in heaven."

"We love you," said Christine.

And I said, so quietly that it really wasn't even speaking, "I won't tell anyone, you old fart."

And then I said, "Forgive her."

Amid our murmuring, Benny's breathing became more erratic, his chest rising and falling farther at each inhalation and exhalation. It slowed then, and I found myself counting seconds between breaths. Finally, no more breaths came, and I stopped counting. He was as peaceful as a baby sleeping in his mother's arms. Labor and delivery.

chapter twenty-four

The church is empty and quiet when Anne, Christine, and I arrive forty-five minutes before the service is to begin. There is no coffin, no body. Benny's ashes are in Yolanda's safekeeping. She's thinking of fertilizing the flower gardens at the house this fall with her new, improved mix, she said, winking, and I don't doubt she will.

The small sanctuary of light wood and colored glass bursts with flowers, some from florist shops, some from people's gardens: marigolds, daisies, zinnias—flowers that thrive in the heat of summer. "Benny had so many friends," Christine says as we all stop midaisle to take it in.

To the right of the pulpit sits a glossy red tray holding a pyramid of oranges, a glass of tea, a stick of incense, unlit. I suck in my breath, cover my mouth with my hand. I never called him.

"What do you think that is?" Christine asks.

"It looks like some kind of offering," Anne says.

I kneel to take a small white envelope from beneath the glass. Inside, a plain white card reads:

With profound respect and sadness for your family,

Henry Bouche

"Who's that?" Christine asks, reading over my shoulder.

"Ellie's got herself a man," Anne says, and pulls Christine away to tell her the juicy details.

I turn the card over, but the other side is blank. Disappointed that there isn't a more personal message, a familiar sense of doom rushes in— will he really wait? Is he really trustworthy? Or is he just like everybody else? I read the message again, gaze upon the perfectly stacked oranges, the care taken in each item's placement, and I know he came all the way down here to do this himself. I remember his loose embrace as I slept, so familiar even though we barely knew each other. And he never lied to me—I just never let him tell the truth. I tuck the card back into its envelope, place it back on the tray for later, when we're poring over cards and notes and good wishes, writing thank-you notes, and imagine Anne and Christine and Yolanda teasing me about my new boyfriend.

The church begins to fill, first with Yolanda's profusion of family members. After Yolanda, they seek out Anne, Christine, and me, the older women hugging us like we're long-lost daughters, the men shaking our hands and casting sympathetic eyes to the floor. And then the mechanics and their wives come, and Benny's neighbors. One of the photography-class couples even shows up, just minutes before the service starts, and then it's time to sit down.

The church minister walks out, followed by Yolanda's priest, who says a blessing in Spanish. Yolanda has returned to the faith of her girlhood, and her parting gift to Benny is one more lottery ticket for heaven, she hopes.

The service begins in earnest, and I float away somewhere, not listening, wondering what Benny would think of all this. He'd be tickled at the truckload of flowers, at the impressive attendance. I have no idea if he believed in heaven, and I realize for the millionth time that I knew so little about Benny even though I sometimes felt I knew him best.

As a kid, I hoped heaven would be a 3-D version of our Candyland board game—unlimited consumption of candy being the ultimate reward. I've never been one to believe in fluffy white clouds and angels playing harps, but it's hard to believe there's absolutely nothing. Did Benny's soul die along with his body, or did he travel down that beam of light toward his mother and father, his brother? Rosemary? Is there a heaven that we can't even imagine, or is it simply here on earth? Maybe Benny's heaven was when he was a child and didn't know what life had in store for him, or when Yolanda married him. Maybe it was back when we were all a family, passing the potato salad, blowing out birthday candles, leaning back in lawn chairs as the cricket-chorus night descended upon us. Maybe heaven came and went, and we never knew it.

The priest and the minister bow their heads. I lower my head with the others. "Dear whatever-you-are," I pray. "Please just let him be at peace."

From the hushed quiet, "Lover Man" begins to play on the stereo Anne bought for Benny. A young man, Yolanda's nephew thrice removed, has been employed by my sister as DJ, and seems to relish his job sitting at the front of the church. A murmur moves through the crowd, a small laugh of surprise, and then everyone settles in to listen and dream their own thoughts to Sarah Vaughan's smoke-and-pepper voice. I close my eyes and picture the Fremont Bridge, Benny dancing along it, arms open as if he's holding a partner, eyes closed, face smiling and peaceful as he steps into the low-hanging clouds and disappears.

When the song ends, the minister asks if anyone would like to speak, and Christine rises, new polka-dot maternity dress rustling against me. She walks to the front and smiles at the audience, then breaks down, arms rising against her face, body stooping in a pregnant crescent.

"Oh, shit," Anne whispers, then stands and strides to Christine, puts an arm around her to try to lead her back to her seat.

"No," Christine wails, standing her ground, and sobs harder.

Anne's face colors, but she stands with Christine while she cries, in front of everyone, protective arm around her shoulder. After blowing her nose and wiping her face, Christine motions for Anne to sit down, and says, "God, I didn't think I'd do that!"

Everyone laughs, whether from relief or empathy, who knows. As she begins to speak, I turn around to look at these kind people behind me, to smile a thank you to those I know. What I'd thought was a good-size crowd of fifty or so has grown to include a large standing-room crowd at the back of the church, doors open and spilling people outside onto the sunny sidewalk. The looks on their faces remind me of the guests at my father's funeral, only I didn't get it then. I didn't feel the solidarity of sitting together to mourn the end of a human life, didn't understand the importance of this one last ritual: paying respect, praying for that better life we all wish so desperately for when someone we love is floating off into the distance. Tears come to my eyes for the first time today, not just for Benny, but for Dad and for all the things we never were to each other.

And then I see her, deep in the shadow of the back right corner—a small, older woman in a form-fitting black dress, hair perfectly coiffed under a loosely draped scarf, and movie star–size sunglasses on her face.

My mother has always been the most dramatic person I've known.

I turn back around, smiling, which is a fairly inappropriate response to Christine's earnest speech. I press a crumpled tissue against my lips and try to focus on the rest of the service, until the opening notes of Vivaldi's *Four Seasons*, and we all rise and turn to go.

My mother has beaten a hasty retreat. She's nowhere in sight.

At Benny's house, the small rooms are jammed to overflowing with people. In the past five minutes alone, I've met his insurance agent, his barber, the guy who sharpened his lawn mower blade. People fill the back patio, the front step, the yards front and back.

"We're going to run out of everything," I grumble to Christine as we throw more hot dogs, steaks, and burgers on Benny's old barbecue grill outside. Yolanda's sisters and cousins arrived early to set out the salads and appetizers and side dishes, but it's all going fast.

"They're not here for the food," Christine says, ripping open another package of hot dogs. "They just want to be as close to him as possible."

An old man in a bolo tie and suspenders approaches us. I vaguely remember that he is one of Yolanda's uncles. "You girls, you shouldn't be doing that," he says, waving an arthritic hand much like Benny's at us. "Go, go. I'll see to this. This is man's work." He beats a fist against his chest, taking a macho stance.

"No, really, it's okay," I say, smiling through gritted teeth. "We want to."

"Well, I don't," Christine says. "Come on, just let him, Ellie."

"No," I say, too strongly, too stubbornly. "If I'm not doing this, I won't know what else to do." I pause and she looks at me, not comprehending. "This is what I do. I cook. I feed. Food is what I do for . . . I don't know. For everyone."

"Let someone else do it for a while," she says, taking my arm, smiling at the old man, and pulling me away. "Maybe it's time you learned how to do something else."

I weave in and out of the crowd, stopping to chat with the photography-class couple, who remember my name even though I don't remember theirs. "Johnson," the man says. "Virginia and Lou. We've kept up with your mother over the years, mostly at Christmas. We always enjoyed our time with your family so much."

And then it's this neighbor and that dear old friend, all of whom saw me seated at the front of the church and who want to tell me how sorry they are and what a wonderful guy Benny was.

All I can say to any of them is "I know."

I'm looking for my mother. It may be stubborn and childish thinking on my part, but if she made an appearance at the church, she may come here. I cover the entire backyard with no sightings. She's not in the living or dining room, not in the kitchen. I doubt she'd be in either of the bedrooms; still, I peek into Benny's bedroom and the sewing room, both empty.

I cut back through the thicket of people in the living room and step through the front door, into the sweltering afternoon. It figures that the weather would be sunny for Benny's big going-away party. My mother's Saab is parked a half block away, wedged at an angle between two other cars, and she's sitting in the driver's seat.

I walk quickly toward her, hoping she won't drive away when she sees me. "Mom," I call when I get close. "Why don't you come in?"

She shakes her head and holds her hand up against me, palm out. Stop. She is crying beneath the Sophia Loren sunglasses; she is a wreck, but so am I. So is everyone. Why should she suffer any more profoundly than the rest of us?

I lean down, hand on the hot roof of the car, looking at her through the open window.

"Mom. Seriously. Just come in."

"Eleanor, you of all people should know that I can't. I just can't." She shields her face with the hand that tried to stop me, and turns away.

I straighten, stand in the middle of the street. The afternoon is still, not a breeze or cloud in sight, and filled with summer-afternoon sounds: lawn mowers, kids shouting in someone's backyard, sprinklers ratcheting and hissing, ratcheting and hissing. I take a deep breath, hold it for a moment, then close my eyes. I want to pound on the top of her car with my fists, grab her by the throat and drag her out of the stupid car. I want to scream at her until she gets a clue that she is not the only one on this earth who ever lost someone she loved.

I sigh, shake my head, look back at the house. Benny always took such pride in its appearance, sticking to his first color scheme of white with salmon-colored shutters, painting it himself every five years. The lawn is perfectly edged against the sidewalks, the trees in their deepest leafy green.

I look back at Mom, her head now tilted back against the headrest.

I walk to the passenger's side, open the door, and get in.

"Let's get out of here," I say. "We need to talk."

chapter twenty-five

Mom drives us through Benny's neighborhood, skirting the tall forest that pervades these parts, scraped clean only where developers found the need to build. She takes twisty back roads that I've never known existed, heading deeper into the trees, and pulls off onto the shoulder at a small clearing above the banks of what must be the Tualatin River. Giant firs tower over us, surround us in all directions, and it looks familiar, though I could swear I've never been here before.

"Where are we?" I ask. "Is this a park?"

She nods distractedly, waves her hand. "Brown's Ferry or River Run. I can never keep them straight."

"Did you used to bring us here?" I crane my head to look around outside. Closer to the river there are a few picnic tables, a horseshoe pit.

"Oh, probably. I must have." She sighs, slumping into her seat, staring straight in front of her. "I suppose he told you everything."

"And which topic are you referring to?"

"Eleanor," she says. "Don't be smart."

"I just want to know why you lied to me about Benny being Rosemary's father."

"Oh, for God's sake. Did he tell you that?"

"He didn't have to. He's named as her father in the obituary."

She flinches, and I wish I'd used a softer word, but what would it be? Death notice?

"Honey, believe me. I would know. Karl Milgrew was the father. Not that he ever took any responsibility."

"Well, then, what didn't you tell me the truth about?" *Aha*, I think. *Snared in her own trap.*

"I didn't mean it that way. Don't put words in my mouth."

I sigh, exasperated. "Mother. You just said, 'I suppose he told you everything.' You're going to have to tell me what 'everything' means, or we're never going to get anywhere."

"Fine," she says, sitting up in her seat and removing her sunglasses. She pulls the visor down to fix her smeared eye makeup in the mirror, then slaps it shut and puts her sunglasses back on. "But I mean it, Eleanor, when I say this is for your ears only."

"Fine," I say.

Mom repeats her story about falling in love with the now identified Karl Milgrew in college. She got pregnant. Karl decided to ignore the problem, moving on to the next pretty girl with mischievous eyes and a sassy walk. "He dumped me," she says. "Benny was such a dear friend, one of the few good young men. He stood by me the whole time." She stops, looks down at her hands in her lap. "I never told my mother, you know. She would have hated me. My sister knew, but I wouldn't let her come."

When she went into labor, she called Benny. He drove her to the hospital, and they told the admissions nurse that Benny was the father. They were clearly unmarried. She didn't blink an eye, Mom said. Must have happened all the time.

The labor was troubled from the start, contractions boring through Mom's body like cyclone after cyclone. The doctor gave her gas for the pain, but after eight hours, ten, twelve, the baby still wasn't budging.

"The gas wore off," Mom says. "I have never been so ill in all my life." She writhed and retched for hours more, sweating, screaming, vomiting bile, and peeing the bed. She called for Benny, and the nurses let him come into the labor room.

Benny stayed with her, calming her, talking her out of her ill-conceived attempts to get up and leave, telling her the baby would be there soon, they just had to be patient. The nurses all said he was the only father they'd ever seen who stayed for more than just a perfunctory visit. Most men returned to their seats in the waiting room and read the newspaper, or left and waited for a phone call. Most of them couldn't stomach such a thing.

"They knew something was wrong, but they wouldn't tell me," she says. Her nostrils flare, and I see that it still saddens her to this day. "That baby never had a chance."

Sometime in the eighteenth hour of labor, Mom's doctor decided to deliver the baby by Caesarian section. "I was petrified; I didn't want them to cut me," she says. "I was so young. You should have seen my figure." She shakes her head. And now I know why my mother never wore a two-piece, never wore sexy underwear. We all must have been delivered this way.

The baby was born with cerebral palsy and a long list of defects and conditions that neither Mom nor Benny could comprehend. The doctor didn't think she'd live more than a few days. Benny sat with Mom through the first night in her hospital room, the second, the third. While she slept like the dead, he sat in the chair next to her, napping, watching her sleep.

She woke in the predawn hours of the fourth day to see him sitting with the baby bundled in his arms. "You have to name her, Bebe," he said. "She needs to be somebody."

"I can't," she said, weeping. "I just can't." So Benny named her.

"Why Rosemary?" I interrupt.

"For my mother," she says. "Katherine Rosemary."

Benny wanted to marry Mom, to give the baby a father, to give her a husband. "I was tired, I was confused, and I was in so much pain. I should have said no."

"You? You're the first wife? You always said he was a widower!"

"Widowed, divorced. There's not that much difference when you've lost someone you love." The corners of her mouth pull down, and she drops her forehead into her hand. She's been lying her whole life, and she's lying now.

"Are you trying to tell me you didn't love him back?"

Her shoulders heave; she wails a thin high sob. "Of course I loved him. Don't you see?" She screeches the words like some jungle bird in danger of predation. "That's the whole problem. I did love him, god-damn it!"

And then she is sobbing words in a rush, the history of our family fly-ing apart in a tangled, ugly mess.

"I left him because I was depressed. I didn't know about postpartum, I didn't know it wasn't him. I married your father because I thought he'd make everything better. He was so different from Benny and me, so solid and practical. You don't realize this, but your father was a catch; he was smart and handsome. He was all set to start a good job out here, and he wanted me to come with him. It was so far away; it was perfect."

She sniffs, then shakes her head. "But I couldn't stand being without Benny. He wouldn't move here, not at first, but I begged him to. I wore him down. He'd already left college to go to work to support Rosemary, but he never complained, even though the only job he could find was fixing cars. And he always spent every penny on her, always finding her the best home, the best doctors."

"And Dad didn't know any of this?" I sound angry, childish, and I'm not even sure why I care so much about Dad, except that I remember the anguished, wounded sound in his voice that night, so many years ago, in our kitchen.

"He knew I'd had a child out of wedlock and married hastily. I told him she'd died. The rest he guessed." She turns to look at me, and my face is reflected in each lens of her sunglasses; I look away. "Not many men would have married me with my, let's just say *history*, Eleanor. I'm not sure I deserved him in the first place. Why on earth would I tell him anything more?"

It's all too much. My mother is too much. I fold my arms over my chest, lean my head against the seat to look out the window. The trees, the way they're spaced, the background brush. I know this place.

"This is the place where you took that photo of Benny," I say, sitting upright. "The one you gave him when he married Yolanda."

"Yes," she says, looking out the window. She sighs, then says, "I took that on the day I told him I'd decided to leave your father. I wanted to capture the look on his face when he realized we could finally be together, but . . ." She trails off, shrugs her shoulders.

"Oh, my God. You did?" I turn to her. What would our lives have been like? Broken by divorce, or blessed by a loving father? "He said no?"

"He's a . . . he *was* . . . a very moral man. He wouldn't break up our family."

"But that time I was sick, and you two were in the car—"

"I said he was moral, not saintly. After that he married Yolanda, of course, and it was over between us."

I nod. I can still see his look of revulsion at my catching them together that day.

"Did you want to get together after Dad died?"

"He wouldn't."

"Then why'd Yolanda leave him?"

She closes her eyes. "Because I finally decided to tell her everything about Benny and me, all the parts he'd never have told her. He protected her so much from . . . all of that. He told her about Rosemary but not me. He stuck to that same old 'girl back in Missouri' story he always told. I knew she'd hate him for lying to her all those years."

"God, that's . . . that's so horrible. They were so happy."

She turns to me again, takes off her sunglasses. Her eyes are dark hollows, her skin red and blotchy. "You think I don't know that?" she sobs, then starts the car. "It only made him hate me more."

We drive in silence back to Benny's house. Before I get out, I say, "There's just one more thing I have to know."

She looks at me wearily.

"Who's my father?"

"Oh, Eleanor," she says. "Just be happy you were born whole and healthy, okay? The rest of it doesn't matter."

"You don't know, do you?"

"Not a word to your sisters," she says, patting her hair, shaking her head as though she can shake off her past. "You promised."

"Actually, I didn't," I say, and get out of the car. "And for the record, Benny didn't tell me anything. He protected you, just like he always did."

The crowd has thinned. The bowls and platters on the dining room table are bare, and I'm starving. Aunt Yolanda is in the kitchen with her back to me, washing dishes, bracelets jangling. She turns her head when I come in.

"Honey?" she says. "You missed all the food. I saved you a plate—it's in the fridge." Her brow furrows in concern. "Is everything okay?"

I walk over to her, put my arms around her shoulders from behind, and lay my head against hers. She smells like cloves and soap. She smells like garlic and onions and chocolate chip cookies and watermelon and barbecue smoke on a hot summer night.

"Yes," I say, not wanting to let go, and she turns and wraps her arms around me, not asking any more questions, just letting me sink into the soft, full sweetness of her.

"Yes," I say again.

chapter twenty-six

I've always thought of summer as my favorite time of year, but now I prefer autumn, which arrives at the end of the month, along with Christine's baby, if all goes according to plan. The scorch of summer is starting to dissipate, and all I can think of are deliciously cool cloudy mornings giving way to crisp sunny afternoons. Maples and oaks and ginkgoes and redbuds in every warm hue of the color spectrum, tenacious leaves clinging to branches, waiting for the big eastern wind that will bring them down, and the return of the rain. The warm, sweet-smelling presence of a baby that will help us forget what's missing. The ever lengthening span of time since the day Benny died late in June, spooling out across the seasons, and then, mercifully, the years.

I moved my food processor, my KitchenAid, my pots and pans and spices back home the week after Benny died. I cleaned out my closet and cupboards, mopped the floors, scrubbed every surface until I couldn't clean anymore. Buddy watched me from the windowsill. She'd never seen me that way before, and she appeared concerned for my sanity, but eventually she got used to it and found a stripe of sunlight to sleep in.

When I felt completely cleaned out, resettled, and ready, I called Henry.

"Hi," I said when he picked up.

"Hi," he said. Like we'd been talking to each other every day.

"Wanna come over for dinner Monday? I'm making my famous meat loaf."

I laughed. "Famous, huh? Who else is coming?"

"Just you," he said.

As I pulled up to the curb in front of his house the following Monday, the daylight was already in its descending shimmer, and I sat in the car without moving, watching the rosy light seep through a big-leaf maple in his yard, moving so quickly I could almost see the shadows lengthening. The eerie quiet spooked me, and I was relieved when I heard the front door open, saw Henry step out, barefooted in jeans and a white button-down shirt.

I got out of the car, embarrassed. "I was just about to come in."

"Whenever you're ready," he said. He looked good. Really good.

I grabbed the bottle of Australian shiraz I'd brought, swung the door closed, and walked up the drive, past alternating shrub-size lavender and rosemary, touching them, rubbing their scent into my fingertips, and then along the stone footpath toward him, brushing my hand over a stand of lemon balm. I brought my hand to my face to smell the heady combination of scents, breathed them in deeply, and Henry smiled.

It felt like we'd been doing this forever, like I'd been coming to his house, embracing him at the door, setting my purse and wine on the old oak table in the entry. Inhaling the savory incense of home-cooked food and embracing him again, rubbing my face against the soft fabric on his chest, feeling his broad back beneath my hands. I knew we'd walk past the comfortably wide couch in the living room, over the worn Oriental rug. I knew the table in the dining room would be set with flowers and candles and cloth napkins, and that it would always be this way, whether for meat loaf Mondays or Thanksgiving.

And I knew dinner would be late.

We walked silently past the table, holding hands, Henry leading, and I peeked into the kitchen as we headed for the small staircase at the back of the house.

"Will anything burn?" I asked, knowing already that he'd laugh, thinking I'd made some clever double entendre, and that when we kissed, I'd whisper, "I'm burning."

• • •

And so it goes. Henry loves to cook for me. I've discovered that I love to be cooked for. My sharp edges have rounded again, and I can't say I'm not relieved. Thin may be in, but it's not me. I'm most comfortable with a little padding to absorb the bumps and knocks of life, to fill in and round the architecture so that a cat can nap comfortably in my lap and a man can always find something soft to hold on to.

So far, eating is just eating. I haven't binged, and while I'd like to say I haven't worried about it, I have. When it happens again—and Suzanne said it most likely will—I'll try not to sink into that hole I could never name before.

"It's called shame," Suzanne said. "Just close your eyes and watch yourself climb out, shake the dirt and muck off, and move on."

"Maybe I should fill it in," I said. "So no one else falls in."

She laughed and shook her head. I knew what she was thinking: Will I ever stop taking care of everyone else?

Call me eternally neurotic, but I hope not.

Yolanda invited my sisters to stay at the house as long as they'd like, and I know Christine would like to stay there permanently. For now, until the baby comes, she's working at Powell's, the biggest bookstore on the planet, as far as Portlanders are concerned. When we were cleaning out Benny's things, we had her take most of Benny's books there to resell, but I kept my favorites: *Little Women*, *To Kill a Mockingbird*, *Adventures of Huckleberry Finn*, *The Old Man and the Sea*, *Travels with Charley*.

I left my computer at Benny's. It gives me a good excuse to drop by, and it's not like I have that many articles to work on these days. I still get the occasional assignment from a smattering of smaller magazines, but *Cooking for Life*, *American Family*, and *Healthy Fit* were my bread and butter. I haven't tried to replace them.

Even though Anne has a nifty little laptop, she uses my big rig to troll the Web for jobs. She's already flown to interviews in Memphis and Dallas, but she thinks they only agreed to see her to avoid trouble. She doesn't believe she'll be hired by anyone. She's put her Boston apartment on the market and is looking at the far less expensive condos on Portland's waterfront. "Even if I don't end up living here, it would be an investment," she says, but I know what she's really doing. The sewing room was always intended as a nursery.

Christine's been feeding Anne and me ideas about small businesses we could start together with our modest inheritances from Benny: coffeehouses, bookstores, gift shops, the usual things women who are dissatisfied with their lives dream of. Anne tolerates this with only a slight roll of her eyes, and I try to remind Christine that the biggest project of her life is about to arrive—how on earth could she handle a business, too?

Today, though, as we sit at Benny's kitchen table drinking coffee, putting off taking the last of his clothes to Goodwill, Christine draws a deep breath that scares the hell out of Anne and me, seeing as babies don't always agree with doctors about their due dates. She says: "I've got it! Shecret Shauce! We can bottle it and sell it at farmers' markets or on the Internet!"

We both laugh at her, but then Anne's face grows thoughtful. "It was pretty good stuff," she says. "Hey, Eleanor, what would happen if we blended it, so no one knew it was fruit cocktail? Then we wouldn't even have to give away the shecret."

I get up and walk to Benny's cupboard, pull out ingredients: vegetable oil, soy sauce, garlic powder, salt, pepper, and one can of fruit cocktail. The only thing I can blend it in is Benny's old Osterizer, which actually works better than any appliance I've got. The finished product is a beautiful peach color, silky in texture, and tastes almost perfect.

"All it needs is a bit of sweet chili sauce to perk it up," I say. "Here, taste."

Who knows? A family dynasty might have been born from the ashes of our fathers.

I leave Anne and Christine to talk sauce, and retreat to the sewing room, now being kept neat as a pin by Anne. I've been ignoring a particular e-mail for months, the reply from Stefan when I told him I couldn't do the article. I sit down and turn on the computer.

I've read it only once before:

> Dear Ms. Samuels,
> I certainly understand that this a difficult time in your life. That said, I'm beginning to doubt your commitment to *Cooking for Life* and to your career. I believe I've been most patient and supportive, but I don't recall using my mother's illness and death as an excuse to not perform my job.
>
> We will try to find another writer at this late date for the healthy holiday desserts piece. We may have to kill the piece entirely, in which case I will have to scramble for content. I feel it is your responsibility to this magazine to provide us with a replacement piece as soon as you are able. After that, I'm afraid, we will no longer require your services.
> Cordially,
> Stefan

I've been thinking about my answer for weeks, writing and rewriting it in my head. I hit REPLY and type:

> Dear Stefan,
> I know you're mad at me, and I'm sorry I let you down, but I made a choice I could live with. The thing is, I just can't stand to write that kind of crap anymore. Do you ever stop and think about the things we do to women in the name of magazine sales? I mean, *healthy* holiday desserts? Can't we ever just enjoy something?
>
> I'm not sure what I want to write about next, but it's coming to me slowly and I'm just waiting until it gets here. Until then, I'm spending my free time cooking for the folks at Riverview Hospice, a place more cheerful than it might sound. I get to use butter and cream, fat-marbled beef,

bacon. Oh, God, and cheese! You wouldn't believe how much fun I'm having.

Attached please find my replacement article. I know it's not what you're expecting, but it's all I've got.

Respectfully,

Eleanor Samuels

Then I attach the following article, and hit SEND.

How to Eat

BY ELEANOR SAMUELS

Why do most women in our country have an obsession with food, the eating as well as the not eating of it? We gladly feed others, yet we struggle with our own hunger. Is food a panacea to fill our empty souls? Have we lost touch with something vital—say, self-fulfillment, or even just self-acceptance—and all we can do is medicate ourselves with the pleasure of fat and calories (or heaven forbid, carbohydrates)? On the other hand, if we don't eat and lose weight, might someone love us more? If we're hungry and our stomachs growl, are we more virtuous than if we're full and satisfied?

I'm just one woman, with my own variations on the female love-hate relationship with food, but I say, let's start a revolution. Let's make food simply food again, sustenance and nourishment, and fun when the occasion calls for it. From here on out, I will try my best to live by these seven secrets of the sane and happily well fed:

1. Eat when you're hungry, and don't when you're not.
2. Eat food that tastes good. Period. No exceptions.
3. Eat food that leaves you sated instead of waiting for the next allotment.

4. Eat food that nourishes your soul as well as your body. Consider it a spiritual quest.
5. Savor every bite. Enjoy every meal. If you're not fully aware and appreciative of what you're eating, you're just wasting it.
6. Eat with friends, with people you love, or with your own good company—anyone who appreciates food, drink, and good conversation as much as you do. (This would not include a TV set.)
7. If you start worrying about eating, stop it. Be happy you can eat.

Jennie Shortridge loves to cook and loves to eat, and has been called a "good eater" by one, if not both, grandmothers. During her varied career, she has worked as a plumber, sung in rock and roll bands, cooked in the occasional café, developed recipes for Mountain High Yoghurt, and written for women's magazines. *Eating Heaven* is Jennie's second novel, and she is currently at work on her third. She makes her home in Portland, Oregon, with her husband and two eccentric but charming cats. Visit her Web site at www.jennieshortridge.com.

eating
heaven

JENNIE SHORTRIDGE

This Conversation Guide is intended to enrich the individual reading experience, as well as encourage us to explore these topics together—because books, and life, are meant for sharing.

A CONVERSATION WITH
JENNIE SHORTRIDGE

Q. Eating Heaven *is your second novel. How was the experience different from writing* Riding with the Queen?

A. *Eating Heaven* is actually a rewritten version of the first novel I attempted, then stuck in a drawer when I realized it wasn't very good. Like *Riding with the Queen*, it's a story that's straight from my heart, inspired by the time I spent with my dad and stepmother, Jeanne, as she was battling pancreatic cancer. After publishing *Riding with the Queen*, I decided to take another crack at it and began from scratch, using the same basic story and characters as before, but setting it in Portland, a natural for a story involving food. I fell in love with the characters all over again, and when I finished, I had this great sense of satisfaction that their story would finally see daylight.

Q. *In* Eating Heaven *the main character, Eleanor Samuels, becomes the primary caretaker for Uncle Benny, who has a virulent form of cancer. You mention that you were inspired by your own family's situation. How so?*

A. During the five months my stepmother, Jeanne, was ill, our family pulled together in the way families do at such times. I think because her condition was terminal, we all felt helpless and didn't know what to do. For a good deal of that time, though, she still really liked to eat, so I'd ask her what she felt like having, and then I'd make it for her. At one point she wanted pineapple upside-down cake. I made one and took it to her, and as she ate it, she really seemed to be savoring it. After she finished, she said, "That was so good. I believe that's the last time I'll need to eat pineapple upside-down cake." It struck me as such an acceptance of her situation, even though we never talked about her dying, and I was inspired to write about it first in an essay (published in *Mademoiselle* in July 1997. To read, visit www.jennieshortridge.com). In the book, Eleanor and Benny have this same experience, and many others that were inspired by real life.

After Jeanne died, I grew closer to my dad, who was on his own for the first time in a long time. I made casseroles and took them to him and we talked on the phone nearly every day. I was inspired to write the relationship between a grown woman and a fatherlike figure because of that time together. It was quiet and simple, but tremendously powerful. Tremendously real.

Q. In the conversation guide for your last novel, Riding with the Queen, *you said that you were interested in expressing "themes of tolerance and acceptance." How did you go about writing toward this in* Eating Heaven?

A. Big people are one of the last groups our society thinks it's okay to discriminate against, stereotype, and make fun of. Ironic when Americans are getting fatter every year, yet fat jokes on TV and in movies are not considered offensive, for some reason. I have plenty of friends who are big, happily or unhappily so, and they're dealing with the same stuff we all are in our lives. We all have coping mechanisms. The difference with people who eat as a coping mechanism is that you can see the result. I wanted to show readers who Eleanor is and how she battles with eating and weight, body image and self worth—as so many of us do.

At the same time, I also wanted to open up the issue of compulsive and binge eating disorders, which are disorders you don't hear a lot about. The more I researched and talked with women dealing with them, the more I realized how prevalent they are and how dangerous they can be, not only to emotional health but to life itself. These disorders often lead to obesity, which causes something like 300,000 deaths per year in our country. And those who suffer from eating disorders feel horrible about themselves way too much of the time. So again, I wanted to put a human face on what our society thinks of as an unattractive issue.

Q. *Eleanor's sisters are very important to her and to the story. Do you see yourself and your own sisters in them? Do your relationships with your sisters reflect Eleanor's relationships with Christine and Anne?*

A. As with the sisters in *Riding with the Queen*, not so much—not literally, anyway. However, my relationship with them is why I like to write about sisters. I love how the intricacies of common experience and interconnectedness bond sisters together sometimes and tear them apart at others. I have the kind of sisters who stand up for one another no matter what, and who are there in a heartbeat if one of us is in trouble. Sure, our relationships are complicated and not always on the best footing, but our loyalty and love for one another surpass all other circumstances. And those are the kinds of sisters I try to write. For me, family has always been my foundation, even when we drive one another crazy.

Q. *Portland comes so alive in* Eating Heaven—*the markets, the weather, "Trendy-third Avenue." How long have you lived in Portland? Will you set future novels there?*

A. I've now lived in Portland for more than three years. I began to write *Eating Heaven* in my first year here, when I was in the romance phase of my relationship with my new hometown, and I think that comes through in the story. Coming from the high and dry desert of Colorado, I found that the Oregon landscape is all about life and growth and renewal, abundance in the form of green everywhere, and water, and a wonderfully creative and bohemian spirit in its people. I love it, and yes, my next novel takes place both in Portland and on the gorgeous Oregon coast.

Q. Eleanor's struggles with food will feel familiar, on some level, to many readers. Why do you think the issue of food is so fraught in our society?

A. I think media has become like a drug—a poison, actually— because we let it influence us to do things that are unhealthy or just plain stupid, like not eat, or eat things that don't taste good and aren't doing our bodies any good. We buy in to what they're showing us rather than take a look around at the real world and realize that most people will never look like models, nor should they. Why are we more desirable and lovable if we look like the current "perfect person" prototype? It changes with every generation, anyway. Why not just be a good, healthy you? I'm not saying I don't struggle with it. I do. Although I've always been on the solid side of average weight, I've always felt too big. I'm currently obsessed with the fact that my face has decided to migrate toward my chest and there ain't no diet or gym for that, honey! I'm trying to accept myself as I am and, better yet, to value myself as I am.

Q. The family situation is so charged in this novel, yet it's easy to sympathize with almost every character, even when we disagree with how he or she is acting. Who was your most difficult character to write?

A. I guess it's whom you might expect: Bebe, the mother. She's narcissistic and self-centered, yet she loves her family even as she inflicts damage upon them. People do that to one another and never realize it, or they justify it away. Her pain is revealed bit by bit in the story but her behavior is never entirely exonerated. She's a tough character, and she challenged me in a good way. I liked her a lot more by the end than I did in the beginning.

Q. What are you working on now?

A. My third novel is about a woman who has settled comfortably into midlife—the quintessential good girl living in a small Oregon coast town. She has the perfect husband, the perfect family, the perfect house and job until the rug is pulled out from under her. To deal with it, she becomes very, very bad. It's a lot of fun to write!

Q. Eating Heaven *is full of mouthwatering descriptions of food, and you've graciously included a few recipes here. Have you been a food writer, like Eleanor? Who cooks at your house?*

A. I do most of the cooking at my house, but to be fair, Matt, my husband, makes breakfast every day and cooks a mean tuna casserole. While I haven't written for food magazines, I have always loved to cook and have spent time cooking in small cafés at various times in my life. I've also developed recipes for Mountain High Yoghurt, including their most popular recipe, Easy No-Bake Cheesecake. (It's fun to know so many people are eating my creation!) Like Eleanor, my love of cooking stems, of course, from my great love of eating, but also from that deep, primal place somewhere between the brain and the soul from which creativity springs. I kind of go into a trance when I cook, as when I write, and ideas come to me. Where it's a chore for some people, cooking is fun and invigorating for me.

As I did with the music in *Riding with the Queen*, I wanted the food in *Eating Heaven* to be representative of feelings, moods, even eras, which is why I used a lot of comfort foods and old-time family-favorite kinds of dishes, like the following:

Ellie's Boeuf Bourguignon Lite

This is the recipe from Eleanor's "Lighten Up Your French Favorites" article, which she thinks of as "Lighten Up Your French Favorites Until They Taste like Cardboard." Tested on my own friends at dinner, though, this light version takes advantage of good wine and fresh herbs so you don't even miss the bacon or butter.

Servings: 4–6

1 cup Burgundy or Pinot Noir*
3 large cloves garlic, minced
2 pounds beef (loin, sirloin, or top round),
    cut into 2-inch chunks
1 tablespoon olive oil
1 small onion, chopped
1 cup baby carrots, chopped or whole
1 cup celery, chopped
2 tablespoons flour
1 cup low- or nonfat beef stock

---

* These are actually the same grape. For an authentic-to-the-book experience, try an Oregon Pinot Noir.

1 cup mushrooms, sliced
2 tablespoons fresh rosemary, minced
1 tablespoon fresh thyme, minced
1 teaspoon allspice
Salt and pepper to taste
Flat-leaf parsley for garnish, coarsely chopped

Mix wine and garlic in a glass or stainless steel dish; then add meat and marinate for at least one hour. At high heat, sear beef chunks on all sides in an olive oil–coated Dutch oven, reserving wine and garlic. Reduce heat to medium and stir in chopped onion, celery, and carrots. Cook until onion begins to soften. Using a sieve or sifter, sprinkle meat mixture with flour. Stir while cooking until a crust forms on the beef. Pour in wine and beef stock, scraping the pan to deglaze it. Add mushrooms and fresh herbs and seasonings. Bring to a boil, then reduce heat and simmer for at least 1 hour, and up to 3–4 hours.

Garnish with parsley and serve with boiled new potatoes, mashed potatoes, or Eleanor's favorite: buttered noodles.

Benny's Favorite Spice Cake

There's something about spice cake that seems old-fashioned and out-of-date, yet make one and people's eyes light up. As a metaphor for the relationship between Benny and Eleanor, I think spice cake is just about the perfect food.

2⅓ cups flour
1 teaspoon baking powder

1 teaspoon baking soda
1 teaspoon salt
1 teaspoon cinnamon
1 teaspoon nutmeg
½ teaspoon ground cloves
½ teaspoon black pepper
1 cup butter
1 cup sugar
3 eggs
2 tablespoons fresh or bottled minced ginger
1 cup vanilla yogurt

Preheat oven to 350° F. Coat a 13 inch × 9 inch cake pan with oil, butter, or cooking spray. In a large bowl, mix together the first eight dry ingredients (flour through pepper) and set aside. With an electric mixer, cream together butter and sugar until smooth. Beat in eggs and mix well, then stir in ginger. Add dry ingredients one cup at a time, mixing until smooth. Fold in yogurt by hand or using the mixer's lowest speed so that the yogurt doesn't "break," or lose its consistency. When the mixture is well blended, pour batter into the prepared pan and bake for 30 minutes or until an inserted toothpick comes out clean. Let cool and then frost with Cream Cheese Frosting (see below).

Cream Cheese Frosting

1 8-ounce package cream cheese
4 tablespoons (½ stick) butter, room temperature
1 teaspoon vanilla

2 teaspoons triple sec (optional)
2 cups powdered sugar

Using an electric mixer or food processor at low-medium speed, mix cream cheese and butter together; then add vanilla and triple sec. Slowly mix in powdered sugar one cup at a time. Do not overbeat or the cream cheese may become grainy. Frost cake and enjoy the leftovers on cinnamon-raisin bagels!

Dad's Shecret Shauce

This recipe is from my own childhood and straight from my dad's mouth. It sounds horrifying to some, but it's fantastic on beef. Really. I've quantified the ingredient amounts because, like Eleanor's father, Richard, Dad's recipe goes like this: "You take a can of fruit cocktail, some vegetable oil, stir in a little soy sauce . . ."

Servings: about 2½ cups, enough to marinate 2–3 pounds of meat

1 15-ounce can fruit cocktail in heavy syrup
¼ cup canola oil
2 tablespoons soy sauce
2 tablespoons white or apple cider vinegar
½ teaspoon garlic powder
½ teaspoon of "whatever spices you've got," according to Dad—
    meaning thyme, basil, oregano, marjoram, or whatever sounds
    good (I prefer thyme)
2 tablespoons Asian sweet chili sauce (optional)

CONVERSATION GUIDE

Mix all ingredients together in a glass or stainless steel baking dish and use to marinate beef, pork, lamb, or chicken from 12 to 24 hours in the refrigerator. Pour off marinade (safely washing away the bits of fruit so no one knows your secret) and grill or broil meat as usual.

Find even more recipes from Eating Heaven *at www.jennieshortridge.com.*

QUESTIONS
FOR DISCUSSION

1. The characters in this novel are struggling to learn how to properly care for one another on many different levels. In what ways do they succeed or fail to be nurturing?

2. How does Eleanor's attitude toward food change throughout the book? What does her inability to vomit signify in her life? Her decrease in appetite?

3. The author does not reveal Eleanor's actual size. Why do you think she made this decision, and how do you feel about it? What do you imagine Eleanor's size to be, and how does it differ from or match your group members' perceptions?

4. Food is described so intimately and beautifully in *Eating Heaven*, it is almost a character. How does the author use food to tell the story? Find passages where food reveals emotions, desires, connections, or conflicts.

5. What spurs Eleanor to see Suzanne Long, the food therapist? Why does she stop seeing her? What does Eleanor learn from Suzanne, and what does she learn on her own?

6. Why does Bebe refuse to see Benny, even when he is dying?

7. What is Bebe referring to when she tells Eleanor on page 153, "Benny isn't quite the angel you think he is"? How did your perceptions of Bebe and of her relationship with Benny change over the course of the story?

8. What would you do if you found out that your family had a secret they had kept from you all your life?

9. Eleanor eats when she is stressed or upset. How do Anne and Christine cope with their life-changing problems?

10. What, for Benny, is the most difficult part of his illness?

11. Think about the men in Eleanor's life—Benny, Stefan, Henry, and her father. How are these relationships similar or different? What issues, if any, does Eleanor resolve with these men by the end of the book, and how?